D1330222

COSTA DEL SOL

By Des Wilson

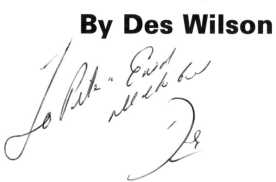

A SANTANA BOOK

Updated and re-published July 2005

First published in hardback in the UK
in 1990 by Macdonald and Co (Publishers) Ltd,
London and Sydney

Re-published in hardback 1990

Published in paperback in 1990
by Sphere Books Ltd

Costa del Sol
is published by Ediciones Santana S.L.
Apartado 41, 29650 Mijas Pueblo (Málaga), Spain
Tel: (0034) 952 485 838. Fax: (0034) 952 485 367
info@santanabooks.com
www.santanabooks.com

Printed in Spain by Gráficas San Pancracio S.L.

Depósito Legal: MA-1.061/2005
ISBN 84 89954-45-3

ACKNOWLEDGEMENTS

All the poetry in this book is by Federico Garcia Lorca, translations by Carlos Bauer (Poem of the Deep Song and Ode to Walt Whitman & other poems, City Lights Books, 1987 and 1988).

In addition to my own travels in Andalucia I owe a particular debt to David Baird's "Inside Andalusia" (Mirador Publications), John Hooper's "The Spaniards" (Penguin), Julian A. Pitt-River's "The People of the Sierra" (University of Chicago Press), and Jan Morris's "Spain" (Penguin).

I owe a debt to my wife Jane for limitless encouragement; to friends who kindly read and commented upon the manuscript... Perrott Phillips, Marcel Berlins and Geoffrey Wansell; to Paul Wilson who helped out in an emergency; to Barbara Boote, who published the first edition; and to my friend James Ross of Bookworld España for his encouragement.

Des Wilson was born in New Zealand in 1941, left school at 15 to become a journalist, travelled to London in 1960, and eventually became well-known in the UK as a politician and campaigner on social issues (he was founder-director of the housing campaign SHELTER and the Campaign for Freedom of Information).

He has been a columnist on The Guardian and The Observer and a contributor to The Times, The Spectator and The New Statesman. He contributed major features to The Illustrated London News for 10 years and was deputy editor for two. He has also appeared frequently on radio and television.

He has written a number of campaigning and political books, and another novel, Campaign.

He lives in Cornwall in the UK.

Through the high passes
two gentlemen are strolling

(New
sky.
Blue
sky!)

...two gentlemen are strolling
who before were hunters

(Old sky.
Gold sky!)

...two gentlemen are strolling
who before were...

(Night.)

PROLOGUE

His was an old man's face. A peasant's face. Andalucia itself, especially this mountainous region, the *Serrania de Ronda*, was etched upon it. Its relentless summer heat in the colour. Its poverty and injustice in ravine-like lines across the coarse skin. Its dignity and secrets in the calm, enigmatic eyes. Occasionally there was a grimace as the mule stumbled on the rocky ground and jarred his barely-protected bones, but for much of the slow journey from the high walls of Ronda across the *finca*-covered plain and over the hills towards his lonely *cortijo* many kilometres away, it was a face as unmoving as it was rough, a mirror-image of the land itself.

Until now.

Now, as he tugged on the rope around the mule's scrawny neck, drawing it to a halt, his eyes widened with surprise, then narrowed in a mixture of suspicion and contempt.

The stranger, the *Americano* he knew as Canning, standing on the narrow track, blocking his path, was in his mid-thirties, tall, slim, with hair so sun-bleached that it was almost white. He was dressed immaculately in an expensive lightweight grey suit, a burgundy-red shirt, and a grey tie that accentuated cold grey eyes. On the streets of Malaga or Seville he would have been one of many, just another banker or lawyer, but, standing on this stony mountain path so rarely used that it was almost indistinguishable from the surrounding terrain, he looked singularly out of place, his appearance in total contrast to that of the man he faced.

It was less an encounter between generations, between affluence and poverty, between urban and rural man, than it was a confrontation between centuries and cultures.

"*Hola*, old man."

There was no answer. The mule and his once-more expressionless rider were now so still that, in silhouette on the hilltop, they looked as if they had been sculpted out of the landscape.

As in a way they had been, for both animal and man had been conceived and born in the *sierras*; they had for years together survived the hot summer days and the bitterly cold winter nights because of their ability to blend into and live off these hills and valleys. This was why, according to local legend, the man had avoided capture. Some said for being a *guerrillero* in the civil war. Others said for being a smuggler, a *contrabandista*. Still others, for being a *bandido*. It was even said that at various times he had been all three. To these stories the old man would slowly shake his head, perhaps with the hint of a twinkle in those tranquil brown eyes. If he had not been captured, he would say, it was because he had not been hunted. He was, he would claim, just a peasant... at times a charcoal burner, a whitewash maker, a breeder of pigs, a shepherd, and now a hunter of rabbits to sell in the restaurants of Ronda.

Whatever the truth of the legend, this last was a fact. The few who had seen him hunt said he knew a rabbit was there before he could see it, that his senses were so tuned to these sierras that he could creep close enough to his targets to almost catch them by the ears. This, they said, accounted for his high strike rate, the few wasted pellets, and the regular score of 100 or more rabbits that would be hung in straw baskets on either side of the mule as he travelled once a week to Ronda where within hours they appeared on the menu, usually cooked in garlic - *conejo al ajillo*. This, too, was why he was known as *El Conejero* - the Rabbit Man.

If he now wondered how Canning could appear from nowhere looking so clean and cool when he must have had to climb and hike for several hours from the road to this isolated place, he showed no sign of it.

But then hadn't his one old friend, Miguel, on whose stone floor he had slept only last night after they had been gently and good-naturedly evicted from their customary corner of the bar in Ronda... hadn't Miguel challenged him many times: "*Señor Conejo*... Mr Rabbit... when do you show what you think in that peasant head of your's? When do you ever smile? When do you show anger? Or surprise? When does your face change... when does it show you're alive...?" Always the old man's only answer had been to call for another bottle of red wine, his face as impassive as it was at this meeting on the mountain path.

"I came to see whether you've changed your mind," the man called Canning now said in crude but comprehensible Spanish.

The rider slowly, almost imperceptibly, shook his head.

"Oh, come on, old man." The American was pleading, but with ill-disguised exasperation. "Why must you live like this? Look at you - you're decrepit, you've damn-near had it. Soon you won't be able to climb on that mule. Soon you won't be able to see the rabbits, won't be able to hit them with that old gun of yours. Then what? Where will you get the money to buy your food, your *vino*? Take the money, old man - you can forget all this, live your last days well, make your *cortijo* warm in the winter, or live in Ronda, or even on the coast. Make sense, old man."

The rider's only response was to tug at the rope, and then to use it to flick the mule around the neck. It remained rooted to the spot. Even when he gave it a gentle kick he was mutinously ignored. But these were old adversaries, rider and mule, and the second kick was less gentle, the third a painful warning that the familiar ritual had gone far enough. The mule mournfully inched forward towards the younger man, who was forced to step aside.

"This is your last chance, old man, Rabbit Man. Don't be a fool. Take the money. Live your last days well."

As he passed, the rider looked briefly down into the American's face. At last he spoke.

"*Adios*," he said.

With that, the mule and his master picked their way between the rocks, down into a gully, then up to the brow of another hill. There they paused while the old rider looked down into a magnificent, barely-accessible valley, his eyes ranging across the cork and cypress trees to its green meadows and its dramatic-looking ravine, then on to a small cluster of orange and lemon trees surrounding a lonely white stone farmhouse, *el cortijo*. His gaze took in the little crops of yellow sunflowers, a golden pasture of bloom, the herbs growing wild on the hillside, lavender, sage and thyme, and then the bare red and brown hills rising, one after another, beyond the valley itself.

If his friend Miguel had been there then, at this moment on top of this hill, he would have seen for the second time that day an uncharacteristic change of expression in the old man's eyes. But this was not a hardening into suspicion - this was a softening. He was nearly home, both reassured by the familiar and peaceful scene below and relieved that he would soon be able to drag his leathery bottom from the esparto and straw saddle on the mule's bony back and exercise his stiff and aching legs.

Eager to be there, he nudged the mule onwards and downwards. There was no resistance now. The animal was also responding to the draw of the valley. Resentful and stubborn it could be, but, contrary to the rider's many slanders upon its name, the mule was not stupid; the sooner it got to *el cortijo* the sooner it would be relieved of its human burden.

Instead of taking the obvious detour to the right at the foot of the hill to avoid the ravine, they cut across the grass-covered floor of the valley to where this fissure in its floor was bridged by a few logs and planks tied together with thick rope. Men as brave as matadors would have blanched at the thought of crossing the ravine this way, but the old man and his mule approached it without fear. This was their own bridge. Their short-cut to home, food and sleep. They could have traversed it blindfolded.

The ravine was only five metres wide. They were halfway over the makeshift bridge before the old man was conscious of being followed. There was a sound, and then stunning pain as a sharp rock hit the back of his head. The shock of the blow caused him to jerk the rope round the mule's neck and it stumbled to the left, its front legs beginning to crumple under it. Desperately he tried to drag it back to its feet and to the right. For a few seconds it appeared as if the animal was regaining its balance but then, fatally, its rider concentrated all of his strength on one last pull. It had the opposite effect. The mule's legs slid from under it and, together, animal and rider toppled sideways and tumbled into the crevasse.

The mule fell with an awful, panic-stricken, honking wail, a sound so full of terror that rabbits in their grassy hiding places froze in fear.

The man fell without a sound. Possibly panic had stilled his ancient heart. More likely he was just as stoic in the face of death as he had been in life.

For a few moments all was silent and unmoving. It was as if even the mountains themselves were shocked by the drama that had been played out within their hidden valley. Then the blonde American stepped from the shade of a tree above the ravine and descended carefully to its edge.

On reaching it he lit a cigarette and, it being his last match, carelessly tossed the empty book into the chasm at his feet.

For several minutes he looked down, trying to discern any movement. Then he untied the rope around the logs and planks and one by one hurled them onto the bodies far below.

The nearby *cortijo* looked as if it had been abandoned for years. The stranger guessed it probably had been before the old man moved in, confident of being undisturbed by an absentee landlord. Beside the stone hut was a crudely-made wooden lean-to, a shady resting place for the mule, shared with a few tired-looking hens. Part of the *cortijo* wall was blackened; clearly the old man had for most of the year heated water for his contraband coffee or cooked his rabbit stew over an open fire. There was no door, but a heavy, hand-woven woollen curtain kept out the light and the heat of the sun. The focal point of the one room was another fireplace, a big grey-stone one, ashes still in the grate. It was surrounded by sticks and logs and in front of it was an old rocking chair. To the left of the fireplace there were a table and two chairs, a number of pots and pans and some cutlery on a wooden bench, and two old rifles propped up in a corner. To the right, but near to the fireplace for warmth, there was a pile of bedding on the clay floor. Rabbit skins hung from the beams in the ceiling.

The smell of the skins, no doubt redolent of home and good hunting to the old man, caused the stranger to recoil in shock, but, grimacing in disgust, he began thoroughly to search the meagre furniture and possessions.

Onto the table he put every piece of paper he could find. There weren't many. He studied each carefully but whatever he was seeking was not there.

Frustrated, he tossed the last item onto the pile and went over every inch of the hut a second time. His only fresh discovery was a dirty, torn envelope containing some photographs, most of them years old and badly faded, but one or two more recent, and one a striking colour picture of a beautiful, dark-haired girl, aged about 12, in traditional Andalucian costume, taken, judging by the background, at a *feria*.

Finally, satisfied that the object of his search wasn't to be found, he left, too intent on removing his tie and gasping for clean air to immediately feel the impact of the mid-afternoon sun.

After a few minutes he took the path back to the top of the hill from where, sweating now, he looked down on the same peaceful and desolate scene the old man had surveyed less than an hour earlier.

Just as he was about to turn away, a movement caught his eye.

He stared intently into the valley. There it was again, near to where the bridge had been. Definitely a movement.

Was there a witness to the old man's death?

He waited for a few tense minutes and then, at last, he saw what it was.

A rabbit.

He smiled, grimly.

"No-one's going to kill you," he thought. "There's no Rabbit Man now... there'll be no *conejo* on the menu in Ronda for a while."

He turned away and began to walk west towards the road he had left some four hours back, the road that would return him to Ronda, to San Pedro de Alcantara... to the Costa del Sol.

And he left behind him... silence...

... a rolling silence,
a silence
in which valleys and echoes slip.

CHAPTER ONE

The plane began its descent above the hills surrounding Malaga, swept on over the shimmering Mediterranean, and then swung in a leisurely semi-circle across the sea to land on the bumpy single runway beside the Rock of Gibraltar some 130 kilometres further south.

At the front of the plane the Club Class steward sighed with relief. It had been a miserable journey. He flattered himself he was convivial company, but the only two passengers in his small section, both men, travelling separately and self-absorbed, had ignored his hospitality, each only toying with the smoked salmon and scarcely touching their champagne. He could have been catering for a funeral.

As the plane came to a stop a few yards from the small terminal building, one of the men, the distinguished-looking, expensively-dressed one, picked up a black leather briefcase and moved swiftly, impatiently to the exit.

The other, Bill Sheedy, the unshaven, untidy-looking one, hesitated before slowly unfastening his seat belt and gathering together his belongings.

Sheedy's problem was that he couldn't decide what to do about the red-haired girl sitting a few rows back in Economy.

For the whole of the flight he had been absorbed by the dilemma... or what he perceived as a dilemma, because for once Sheedy, calm, easy-going, imperturbable, rational Sheedy, was not thinking clearly, shaken by the sudden surfacing of half-forgotten desires and unfamiliar doubts... all caused by the girl with red hair.

There were, he had convinced himself, just two options. To consolidate their friendship as it was, close, good-humoured, trusting, but platonic. Or to risk jeopardising it by, in effect, raising the stakes and seeking to become her lover.

Now, as they walked across the tarmac, he felt her softly take his arm.

"Hey Sheedy," she said, "thanks for the bubbly."

Embarrassed that his office had booked him Business Class when she was flying Economy, he had asked the Chief Steward to take her some Laurent Perrier.

"That's OK," he said, "I wish you had let me change places. Then you could have had the slippers and hot towels too."

"Only old men like you wander round in public in slippers. I prefer to show off my toes." She lifted a shapely leg and wriggled a foot at him, her brightly-painted toenails glinting in the sun.

He laughed. Now he was back in her company her relaxed confidence in their friendship was already making his confusion and uncertainties seem foolish. He felt better. Maybe he could handle this thing - whichever way it went.

"Come on," he said to her, "let's get our bags and hit the road. Tonight you're going to have your first *gambas al pil pil* and *conejo al ajillo*. If the garlic doesn't knock you out, the Rioja will."

.

Already Sheedy's fellow passenger, Sir Brian Cruickshank, unencumbered by luggage, had waved his UK passport at immigration, passed by the one sleepy customs officer, and was climbing into the chauffeur-driven olive-green Rolls Royce that had been waiting outside the terminal, conspicuous alongside a score or more of tiny, weary-looking hire cars.

Cruickshank, too, had spent the journey tormented by unaccustomed doubts.

He, too, was now reminding himself to keep a sense of perspective, but with less success than Sheedy, probably because his problem loomed larger. His project - the Spanish project that would seal his business career, consolidate his wealth, change his whole way of life - appeared to be in jeopardy, and all because of the insane act of one man.

"Is Mr Canning waiting at the yacht," he asked the chauffeur.

"Yes, Sir Brian."

"Good."

But there was no pleasure in his voice, only controlled anger. He sat back and, as he had done on the plane, gloomily reviewed the options.

He, too, had concluded that there were only two courses of action, but in his case both were unpalatable.

Whatever he chose to do, the fun had gone out of the thing.

And for that the man he was travelling to see would not be forgiven.

How much more straight-forward life had been just four hours earlier. Her flight from New York had been delayed and Sheedy had settled himself at one end of a semi-circular bar in the departure lounge of Gatwick's South Terminal. Un-typically, he had ordered a gin and tonic. He didn't usually drink before noon but he was counting on the chilled gin to give him a bit of a lift after a sleepless night and, judging by the way the alcohol hit the spot, it had been a good move.

He didn't mind the delay. He liked the slightly manic atmosphere of airports and amused himself by inventing stories about the other travellers - who they were, where they were going and why.

A big fair-haired man, Sheedy was just over six feet tall and of what he liked to describe as 'comfortable build' (i.e. by no means disguising a love of food and drink). A 'variable' 47 (also his description), he could, when rested and relaxed, get away with being nearer 40, while after a bad night he looked much older. His face was his strength, full of warmth and humour, encouraging trust. People found it easy to talk to him, quickly took to him. As a reporter he got half his stories that way. His blue eyes were the outstanding feature; they were watchful and perceptive but - and this was the giveaway - they were kind. In his days as a managing editor he had been a hopeless disciplinarian of the younger staff members.

But he could also be tough and obstinate. Scores of victims of his investigative reporting could testify that he had been fearless and relentless in pursuit of stories they would have preferred unpublished. Employers and even colleagues and friends could also find him discomfortingly stubborn. Sheedy was not a 'yes man'. He was an uncompromising searcher for truth, a reporter of the old school, raised on a small local paper in Connecticut to believe journalism was about public service as well as private gain. He had come to New York with a reputation for getting his stories right and for striving to make the power of the media work for those who had most need of it, the disadvantaged and exploited.

After several years as a top City Desk reporter, his life was threatened by a crime syndicate he was investigating.

The newspaper took it seriously and, over-ruling his objections, it transferred him to the Foreign Desk to get him out of the country for a while. As he good-humouredly complained at the time, this gesture of concern would have been more convincing if they hadn't then sent him into the holocaust called Vietnam, from where he became famous for his distinctive coverage of the war. Refusing to get by on the hand-outs and the carefully-arranged front-line trips organised by the army's PR men, Sheedy was one of the first to reveal the unique horrors of that conflict, to tell of its dehumanising effect on the US servicemen as well as on the Vietnamese. This didn't make him popular in Washington or with the jingoistic brigade but his fellow journalists recognised the risks he was taking and the truth he was telling. To them he returned a hero in his own right.

But he also returned to a wife who had become sick and so, abandoning reporting, he elected to work on the subs desk of a Manhattan tabloid so that he could be within reach in an emergency. Soon he became the paper's news editor, then its managing editor.

Sheedy didn't talk much about the war. When the subject was raised he would become withdrawn, the shadow crossing his usually good-humoured face suggesting he had been permanently saddened by what he had seen. But, apart from that, he did like to gossip and reminisce and sort out the world's problems with other reporters over a few drinks. He was uncomfortable with the new breed of hungry young hustlers who were cutting each other's throats in the competitive world of modern American journalism with no apparent desire to make friends with colleagues.

After a few years working uneasily, albeit well paid, on the tabloid, he had, to his surprise, made it to the upper levels of the best-seller list and earned half a million dollars from a book on American involvement in South-east Asia. Its publication coincided with the death of his wife and was followed by a deep desire to leave New York, to change his life and surroundings. He travelled extensively and ended up in Spain where he invested his royalties in a villa on the Costa del Sol. From there he now produced and presented a weekly 30-minute investigative programme for a television company broadcasting from neighbouring Gibraltar.

As he publicised the high pressure tactics of time-share salesmen, exposed drug smuggling, and waged war on corrupt officials and greedy developers, he became to his relatively small Costa del Sol audience, mainly English expatriates, a bit of a celebrity. "Good old Bill - he'll show them". But to Sheedy it was no big deal. He was just doing the only thing he knew how, and the rest of the time he was engrossed in his love affair with Spain... devoting his plentiful spare time to exploring the ancient cities and white towns (the pueblos), enjoying the food and wine, and, in particular, researching a book he hoped to write on the Andalucia of Federico Garcia Lorca, the poet murdered in the civil war.

Sheedy attributed his fascination with Lorca to their shared love of Andalucia, but friends wondered whether Sheedy, who was so profoundly affected by the loss of his wife, was really identifying with Lorca's own obsession with death. Why else would he, late at night, when the wine had turned to whisky, endlessly recite the more plaintive of Lorca's laments to anyone who would listen?

Earth
ageless
of oil lamp
and pain.
Earth
of deep wells.
Earth
and arrows.

But now, on this morning in the departure lounge at Gatwick, while he was considering whether or not he should have a second gin and tonic, the primacy of his love for Andalucia and its martyred poet were being contested by another. One more challenging. One he had believed he had experienced for the last time.

The possibility had, of course, existed ever since he got Kate's letter.

"Hi, Sheedy," it had said. "Guess who's coming to Spain? How about a bed for a few days? The floor will do. I'm flying into Gatwick on the 18th of March and then directly on to Gibraltar. Can you drop me a line and tell me how to find you? Can't wait to see you, you old grouch, love, Kate."

He had replied that he would be in London that weekend and

would fly down with her. He had been looking forward to seeing her the way you look forward to fun, news of old friends, and the chance to share new discoveries.

But that was all.

Sheedy hadn't loved a woman, hadn't wanted to, since Jan died after suffering a devastating form of cancer. They had been childhood sweethearts in Connecticut, had attended the same college, and had married the weekend before he began work as a junior reporter on the local newspaper and she as a librarian at the local school. From then on nothing stood a chance of coming between them. Not even learning that they were fated to be childless. Not even his two-year absence in Vietnam (from where he wrote a letter every night, 15 or 20 sometimes arriving at the same time thanks to the vagaries of the post). Not even his once being deposited on their doorstep in a pool of his own blood after pressing his research into crime too far.

But no-one, he believed, who had spent night after night lying awake tormented by the tears of the woman he loved while she endured such pain that she ended her life pleading for death, no-one would want to expose himself to that kind of love a second time.

Or to the overpowering sense of impotence in the face of her suffering.

So he hadn't loved or wanted to love since.

Anyway, apart from occasional attacks of anguish when he was alone late at night, attacks repelled by bottles of Scotch imported weekly from Gibraltar, life had been good. He was answerable to no-one and there wasn't time to get lonely; he had, as always, accumulated good friends, and there was plenty to do. There had been nights of warmth from time to time, usually after a few drinks, usually more of an intimate cuddle than a passionate coupling, but they had been followed by crippling, albeit irrational feelings of guilt, and he was increasingly content to go home alone. No woman, he had decided, was going to turn up with enough desire and determination to clamber over all the barriers he had consciously and unconsciously erected to protect that part of him that was best closed off, forever Jan's.

Until that morning at Gatwick, when a woman's voice asked him whether he always sat in bars laughing to himself and he turned round to look into a face that caused such a crashing and crumbling of psychological blocks that you could almost hear them hitting the ground.

She was in her late twenties, with red hair, fresh face and freckles, and green eyes that challenged and laughed at Sheedy at the same time.

Reflecting on it later, he realised the possibility had always been there. She had been his special protegee on the paper, an exceptionally talented photographer, the one he could never get angry with, the one whose early career he had guided as if she were his daughter. He had always been... what's the word?... fond?... yes, fond of her, indulgent of her enthusiasm and her excesses, proud of her talent.

But now, maybe because there had been building up within him a stockpile of unacknowledged need, maybe because she had a head start in his affections over any other candidate, maybe because the girl internee had become a beautiful and vibrant young woman, maybe because of all of this and more, "fond", inadequate word at the best of times, no longer seemed enough.

He had been expecting an old friend with whom he was comfortable. That hadn't changed. Yet at the same time she had become also a stranger, one he found instantly desirable.

"Hi, Sheedy, you old tyrant," she said, "bit early for the booze isn't it?"

"For Christ's sake, Kate, I was giving up on you. You look terrific... I always said you would make a hell of a woman."

"I was a woman when you said it, Sheedy. You were too busy bullying reporters to notice."

"I was never a bully."

"OK, I know. Anyway, how are things?" For the first time the laughter left her eyes as she searched his face, ready to disbelieve what she heard.

But he told her he was in good shape and, compared with the sad, haunted figure he had been when she last saw him, at Jan's funeral, he looked it.

"I hear you're a big shot TV man down there."

"Hardly. Its a small station. My stuff's mainly aimed at the Costa del Sol, at the English living down there. Still, its fun and maybe useful. But what's really terrific is Spain. I love it. You'll love it. Anyway, its good to see you. What made you decide to come?"

"It was.... well, a last-minute decision." She went quiet.

He looked at her thoughtfully. "There's been a problem, hasn't there?"

"Damn it, you know me too well, Bill." Her face clouded over. I guess when I tell you what happened you'll say I'm just running away. Fact is, I've had a rough time. I had a big story that went badly wrong. I'll tell you all about it later, but what mattered was that either the picture editor or I had to take the blame, and there was no way he was going to let it be him."

"Creep."

"It's worse than that, Bill. You expect people to betray colleagues these days, well, some of them, you know how damn competitive it is in New York, but we were... well, we were lovers too. I just couldn't believe it when he set me up to take the blame for a mistake that was really his." She paused, biting her lip at the memory. "I guess I was ready to get out of the paper anyway, its got more and more gross recently, but after the way he behaved I simply couldn't bear to go to work and even see him at his desk. So I told him he was a double-crossing, heartless asshole... and then I walked out."

"Holy shit." Sheedy was angry and amused at the same time, but most of all he was relieved.

It was hardly a major disaster.

She would get over it.

It was mostly her pride that was hurt. And she was free and she was no-one's and that was a minor miracle that suddenly mattered to him a lot.

"But why Spain?"

"No particular reason." She evaded his eyes, then feeling his sceptical gaze, she laughed."Oh hell, I might as well say it... because you were there. I figured you could help me sort it out. I guess I needed old Sheedy's shoulder one more time."

For a moment they just looked at each other, affectionately. Then he said "I'm glad. I can't tell you how much", and he asked about her plans.

"I don't have any. I need a break. I figured I would get some sun and do some water-skiing, then maybe I'll research a few photo-features for a while."

"Terrific. That's all we hacks in Spain need. A competitor."

They laughed and then she suddenly slipped off the bar stool and came closer to hug him.

For a moment he buried his face in her soft hair. He couldn't believe what he was feeling, didn't trust himself to speak.

Fortunately he was saved by a flashing red light on the departure board. The plane was boarding.

If he were honest with himself, and he usually was, he was more than a little relieved they were not sitting together, so unsettling was her physical presence and so confused were his feelings.

"Christ," he thought as he absent-mindedly toyed with his drink, "I want her."

But why should she want him? She was at least 20 years younger. A few hours with her and, age apart, all sorts of differences and incompatibilities would surely emerge.

He remembered how she had looked, walking in front of him to the plane. She was about five feet nine, tall for a girl - (damn it, why did he keep thinking of her as a girl? He'd have to watch that). She was wearing a white track suit, comfortable for travelling, soft-looking and close-fitting, and she walked with the grace of an athlete. When she had turned to smile and tease him about travelling "with the nobs" while she had to slum it "with the peasants", and then laughed when he offered to swap and told him age must come before beauty, her face had looked so young and fresh that he suddenly felt absurdly silly in his middle age and embarrassed by his crumpled suit and unshaven appearance.

Really, the whole thing was ridiculous. She saw him as a father figure, not a possible lover. She had come to him for refuge, not excitement.

And even if she could come to love him, did he have the right? She should be building a life with a younger man, not with him.

On the other hand, some women preferred older men.

And he didn't feel that old. In fact, he didn't feel old at all. Maybe he needed to lose some weight, but, he lied to himself, that wasn't impossible.

Now, as he was leaving the plane, he came up with a kind of a plan. She had come for a shoulder to lean on, and his would be there. But he'd be damned if he'd be cast as an avuncular uncle, or father figure. He would try to be a friend as she would be a friend, care-free and full of fun.

And he would buy time by taking a few days off work, they would spend a few days driving in the mountains.

They would go to Granada, Cordoba, Ronda, maybe even Seville.

That way she wouldn't be meeting the lusty, suntanned young animals at the beach wearing the flimsy pouches that passed for swimming trunks these days... at least, not meeting them until things had become clearer. Sheedy felt in no shape for that kind of competition.

Back in Economy, Kate, weary of travelling after the all-night flight from New York, and made even more sleepy by the champagne, had dozed for an hour or so and day-dreamed about Spain for the remainder of the journey, untroubled by the questions worrying Sheedy. She was, of course, much more in tune with her feelings than he was. He had been right when he guessed she was more fed-up than heartbroken by the betrayal she had experienced in New York. She needed a change and a good time after seven tough years building a career, and of fighting to get what she knew were good pictures into a bad paper. A combination of Sheedy and Spain, she had decided, were just what she needed to get her act back together.

And she had known he would be pleased to see her. He may not have loved her as she had loved him, but he was a good and caring friend.

And she had loved him. From the first day she had come onto the paper as an internee, straight from journalism college in her home city of Boston, she had liked and respected him and, as she thrived on the attention he gave her, she had fallen hopelessly in love with him (hopeless, she realised, in every sense, because everyone knew how close he was to his wife). His opinion became all that mattered. When he praised one of her pictures she would walk 40 blocks home because she was on too much of a high to sit still; when he found fault, or when, under pressure, he used someone else's picture, or worse, an agency picture, without even a consoling word, she would cry all the way home in a taxi. When he called out at the end of the day "anyone for the bar ?" she would be the first to move; the happiest hours of her life had been spent sitting in smoke-filled bars with the small group of veteran reporters from their own paper and the rival New York Times who congregated around Sheedy to gossip about papers and New York and the Mets and the Jets and the world generally. If she was a good news photographer, and she was, she owed it as much to the encouragement and the hints she picked up from that group as she did from her experience on the paper.

She knew Sheedy hadn't known how she felt, had just been responding to her ambition and enthusiasm. She was sad when he was gone and working on the paper never seemed the same, but life had gone on. She had got a place on the Upper West Side and worked hard to build her now considerable reputation as a photographer. She had survived three or four affairs, at least two of them good while they lasted, before the latest disaster.

It had been a surprising reunion. Maybe she had expected to meet an emotional wreck, or a much older man. What she had not expected was a Sheedy who looked remarkably the same as he had before Jan became ill, as good-humoured and trustworthy as ever, but fitter and burnt brown by the sun.

She was surprised, too, how moved she was to be back in his company. She had come to believe over the years that her's had been a classic case of hero worship, that she had just been fortunate to have a decent boss who believed in encouraging youth. But now they were together once more, away from the paper and New York, each free of emotional entanglements and he no longer her boss and mentor, she felt a re-awakening of the old deeper feelings. It had, after all, been more than hero worship; this was a good man, and an attractive one too.

Just the same, there was for her none of the inner turmoil Sheedy was experiencing. On the contrary, any doubts she had entertained about landing herself on Sheedy had dissolved.

Kate was in a mood to take life and Sheedy as they came. Friends. Housemates for a while. Maybe colleagues if there was some work they could do together.

And, what the hell... if there was only one bed and he wanted to wrap her up in his arms and keep her warm, that would be ok with her too.

While Bill Sheedy and Kate Callaghan were climbing into his battered but still powerful late 70's sports car and setting off for the Costa del Sol, the green Rolls Royce was already leaving the dusty Spanish border town of La Linea and turning onto the crowded and hazardous main highway from Gibraltar to Malaga.

In the back Cruickshank, former permanent secretary at the Treasury, now chairman of a number of City companies, including the fast-rising Anglo-Spanish Investors Ltd, was recalling for the umpteenth time the telephone call that had ruined his weekend.

He had on Friday been in his penthouse office in one of the new skyscrapers towering over the City of London. It was the close of a busy day, a busy week, and he was enjoying a Scotch and a cigar and meditating as he looked out at the lights of the city and their reflection in the water of the Thames. It was a well-established routine. He called it his 'special hour'.

Cruickshank had been experiencing a difficult patch. The past year had been an awkward one for the Blair administration. The Iraq war had led to a breach of trust and a difficult General Election and there were signs that his Chancellor's grip on the economy was loosening. The City was jittery and as a result unreliable. A number of his subsidiary companies were in trouble. Only this morning he had chaired the Board meeting of one that would have to be sold at a considerable loss.

And now this precious moment at the end of the week, this hour of peace to review these difficulties, was being disturbed.

Expecting no calls of importance and assuming his secretary had temporarily taken leave of her senses, he answered with an asperity that made his displeasure only too clear.

His temper was not improved by the identity of the caller. Jason Canning, his young American project coordinator in Spain, was efficient; Cruickshank couldn't fault him there. The problem was his manner, and in particular his attitude to Cruickshank. For some reason the Englishman couldn't understand, he always felt as if Canning was amused by him... that he, Cruickshank, was the subject of some private joke. This he was not accustomed to and didn't like.

He spoke curtly. "Jason, I presume you're impatient to tell me our problem with the old man has been overcome?"

"In a manner of speaking, Sir Brian, but I'm afraid not the easy way." The casual, slightly-mocking drawl grated on Cruickshank's nerves. "He wouldn't even talk about it. It was hopeless. No matter what I offered him, he just didn't want to know."

"What do you mean, didn't want to know? Offer him more." If, as he suspected, Canning had a sneer on his face, Cruickshank's tone was calculated to wipe it off. "Are you really telling me you can't out-negotiate a peasant, Jason? Look, you're trying to beat him down a few pesetas while every day's delay is costing millions. Stop toying with the man and make him an offer he can't refuse. I don't care how much he wants, it can't be much compared with what's at stake."

"Sir Brian, that's not necessary or possible. The old man's no longer around to negotiate." The American paused for a few seconds, then added without emotion "He's dead."

Cruickshank sat forward in his chair, unable to repress feelings of relief. "Dead! What do you mean, dead? When? How?"

"He had an accident... well, a sort of accident. In any case, he's out of the way now... I'm already investigating the next steps we should take."

There was a lengthy silence while Cruickshank, relief giving way to apprehension, slowly reviewed every word Canning had said.

Then, anxious to be convinced he had misunderstood, for surely he had misunderstood, he carefully asked: "Jason, what do you mean by 'a sort of an accident'?"

"He fell down a ravine."

"Fell ?"

"Well, if he's ever found it'll look like a fall. No-one'll even bother to climb down and get him. He's just an old man who fell down a ravine. No-one's likely to think he was helped on his way, let alone trace it to you."

"Me!"

He couldn't believe what he was hearing.

"Trace it to me! For Christ's sake, why should they trace it to me? Its not any of my doing."

He couldn't remember standing, but he was on his feet. Lowering his voice, he said "Jason, if I understand you correctly, and I hope I do not, if you're responsible for this... this man's death... you must be mad."

The voice at the other end remained cool. "Look, he was old and worn out. He was going to die soon anyway. In the meantime, as you say, he was costing you a fortune every day he lived. Now you can get the project moving. It was the only way."

Carrying the phone, Cruickshank walked to the window and looked out, as if seeking reassurance in the familiarity and the solidity of the City, its lights glittering in the dusk.

He was only starting to believe what he had heard.

Canning must be a psychopath.

He had killed the old man.

The project and he, Cruickshank, could be linked to it.

He believed in being tough, yes, even ruthless when it came to business, it was the only way, its what he was paid for, but this... this was crazy. Disaster.

It was also incredible. He was a highly reputable City figure at the head of an equally respectable group of companies. How could he be involved in the sordid killing of a complete nonentity somewhere in Spain?

Surely the answer was that he couldn't. He must be reading more into Canning's words than was justified. Or maybe the American was up to some game of his own, trying to unsettle Cruickshank?

Distrusting the lack of privacy provided by the phone and needing to see the American's face as they talked, he curtailed the conversation. "Jason, I'm still hoping I misunderstand you. But I don't like what I hear. I'm coming down."

He quickly reviewed his weekend plans.

"On Sunday. I'll be down on Sunday."

"There's no need for panic, Sir Brian..."

"I'll decide that. You stay on the yacht until I get there. Don't move. Do you understand?"

There was a sullen acknowledgement and a click as the phone was put down.

Quickly he dialled the number of his outer office and, struggling to appear composed, summoned his secretary to re-organise his weekend. After looking at a series of clocks showing the time in the world's financial capitals, he added "And see if you can get Mr Jordan in New York before he goes for lunch."

As his secretary, accustomed to sudden changes of plan, calmly left the room, Cruickshank went to the desk to pick up the Scotch and cigar, but instead of returning to the window he walked to the far end of the room and stood before a huge model of the Spanish project.

Breath-taking in its originality and size, it was to be constructed in and around hills and valleys south and inland from Marbella, between San Pedro de Alcantara and Estepona, and was intended to be a recreational resort so expansive and exclusive that even Sotogrande, further south, would be over-shadowed by comparison.

Despite the fact that every penny he possessed, huge sums he was borrowing, a high percentage of his company's resources, and the money of a number of other investors was at stake, Cruickshank had complete confidence in "the Spanish project", and never failed to feel excited and proud when, before leaving in the evening, he had one last look at his model. It was to be the achievement of his business life. It would not only make a huge sum of money, it would allow him to live in Spain for much of the year in luxury and with considerable influence. (Cruickshank suffered occasionally from arthritis, so far not seriously, but he was advised by his doctor to avoid as much of the English winters as possible.) Also the project would remain after him as a monument to his daring and imagination and leadership. Just as the vision of Jose Banus would forever be commemorated by the Puerto Banus marina, so would he, Cruickshank, be forever remembered as the creator of his as yet unnamed village on the Costa del Sol.

Just a glance at the model usually made him feel better, no matter how bad the day had been.

But tonight it was not so.

His heart was pounding, his mind reeling.

How could it have happened? The peasant had been a damn nuisance but somehow the problem would have been overcome. Now the man had been killed, and, unless Canning had been exaggerating his part in it (and Cruickshank feared not) he had not died accidentally but been deliberately killed.

Murdered!!

Not by Cruickshank, not at his command, but in his name.

And no matter what he chose to do about it, whether it was cleared up or covered up, it would cast a shadow over the project... possibly over his whole life.

Cruickshank was in his early-fifties, tall and lean, his fair hair thinning. His half-moon spectacles made him look more like a senior academic than a businessman, but his rather severe appearance changed the moment he smiled; it was generally acknowledged that the humour that entered his face, the hint of mischief in the twinkle in his eyes, were genuine, the key to his charm. The possessor of a brilliant analytical mind, he had been a high-flier in the civil service from the start and after reaching the top at an exceptionally early age had found himself hankering for the chance to match his skills with others in a more competitive and less secure world. On reaching 50 he made an impressively easy transition from Whitehall mandarin to top financier, picking up directorships and then chairmanships almost at will. This had enabled him to develop a luxurious lifestyle that he shamelessly enjoyed and had shown no desire to share by re-marrying after a discreet divorce some years earlier. Employing his knighthood and diplomatic skills to the best possible advantage, he had been a particularly effective operator in the United States, attracting an unusually high percentage of American investors in a number of his companies, and especially in the Spanish project. It was Theodore Jordan, the biggest, the most financially committed of those investors, who now came on the line.

Cruickshank came straight to the point. Canning had been Jordan's nominee. Now he wanted to know more about him.

There was a pause and then, thought Cruickshank, a too-careful edge to the responding voice. "Of course. But what's the problem?"

"I'm afraid that must wait until we meet. It's not a matter we can discuss on the phone. When do you next plan to be in London?"

"Well, there are a number of things I could usefully do there. I could fly over on Concorde on Monday."

Again there was a careful edge to the voice that Cruickshank found disconcerting.

He suggested dinner on Monday night and, after completing the call, poured another Scotch, re-lit the neglected cigar, and went back to the rocking chair in the window.

There he sat for a very long time looking disconsolately out into the night.

CHAPTER TWO

Bill Sheedy's villa was one of a small Spanish-style cluster built round a swimming pool in a spacious garden of grass and sub-tropical flowers on a hill about three kilometres from the *costa* on the Ronda road. It offered spectacular views of the mountains further inland and, from the balconies at the front, of the bustling town of San Pedro and the sea beyond it.

It had taken just over an hour to drive from Gibraltar. Sheedy, who had produced a much-praised television programme on the suicidal driving and notoriously high accident rate on the N340, the main coastal road stretching the length of Andalucia, from Cadiz in the west to Almeria in the east, had been content to concentrate on the traffic, leaving Kate to chat about old friends in New York, and about her plans for swimming and sunbathing, water-skiing and wind-surfing. Now, as he accelerated up the hill to the villa, he suppressed a sudden, heart-thumping vision of her lying topless on the beach, and at last interrupted her happy monologue.

"Hold on a minute, Callaghan, just cool it. You're going to start by seeing the real Spain so that you get your priorities right. I'll give you one day by the pool and then we're heading for the hills."

As they drove into the villa grounds his spirits were further lifted as they always were on his return by the bright light, by the clarity of the definitions, by the colour and warmth of the place.

And, as she walked around the villa, exclaiming with delight at the roomy, two-level lounge with its big stone fireplace and uninterrupted view to the sea, and again as Sheedy took her into a bedroom suite with an equally spectacular view, he felt buoyed up by her pleasure. "I'm giving you my room," he said. "I can look at the view any time; you should have it while you're here."

She dropped her bag and, wrapping her arms round him, she

kissed him on the cheek and buried her face in his chest.

"Bill, what can I say... I 'm just so grateful... that you're you, and that you live in this place, and that I can be with you for a while."

Touched and suspecting she was near to tears, a condition he put down to exhaustion as much as emotion, he quickly lifted her off her feet, sat her on the bed, and walked out of the room, saying he was going to make some coffee.

"Once you've unpacked I suggest you have a *siesta*," he called back to her. "You must be whacked."

By the time he returned with the coffee she was already asleep, stretched out on top of the bed in her track suit, her face half-hidden by a swirl of red-gold curls. He reached out and gently moved the hair aside and stood for a few moments absorbed by her beauty.

Then he quietly drew the curtains and left her alone, retiring to the smaller suite where he showered and shaved and, after dressing in light-blue trousers and a dark-blue

sleeveless shirt, slipped out of the villa and drove to San Pedro to buy fish and other ingredients for a *paella*, all the time thinking about her and all that he would like them to do together.

Even the old men who sat and drink coffee and cognac outside La Antartida bar at the top of San Pedro's main shopping strip commented to each other *"El Señor Bill sonrie mucho hoy"*....

...*Señor* Bill smiles a lot today.

Puerto Banus is just a few kilometres up the *costa* from San Pedro, about halfway between San Pedro and Marbella's "golden mile" of Arab banks and palaces and the exclusive hideaways and playgrounds of the rich. Usually referred to by the cosmopolitan residents of this part of the Costa del Sol as "the port", Puerto Banus has grown since Bill Sheedy first travelled to Spain in the Sixties into one of the biggest marinas on any of the costas, with hundreds of yachts surrounded by scores of bars, boutiques, restaurants and nightclubs, and behind them, apartments and stores and a cinema. The most expensive restaurants are on the front, just a few feet from the water's edge - places like the Red Pepper, Los Bandidos, and Antonio. Above and behind them, white-washed buildings have risen higher and higher, like man-made cliffs over-hanging the harbour. Immediately off the front you find the packed Old Joy's Pub, Navy, and O'Grady's

Irish Pub. Then neon lights and arrows point the way down other alley-ways or up mysterious, enticing stairways to bars and night clubs tucked away at every level, out of sight of the casual passer-by... not least the busy Premier lap top bar above the even more popular Lineker's sports bar, the place run by the former England footballer's brother.

Puerto Banus is a mix of class and tack, of quality and rip-off, of the gracefully and the tastelessly rich, but the biggest group are those who just come to look and fantasise. These dreamers and the voyeurs of the wealthy pour in every day, the middle-aged to promenade up and down the rows of yachts, exclaiming at their size and opulence, and the younger set to sit in their best gear outside the Salduba Pub, Sinatra's Bar, or Café Banus and throw glances at each other... and dream of accidentally finding themselves next to a wealthy young yacht-owner who just happened to be lonely and single.

The more sophisticated or wealthy who frequent the port usually do so only because they own, rent, or are guests on a yacht too big to be moored anywhere else. The biggest of these are at the western end of the marina. Some are more like small ships, two or three storeys high, their impressive size matched by the luxury of their spacious bars and lounges, dining rooms and bedroom suites. These yachts are worth many millions, some of them literally hundreds of millions of dollars.

One of them this spring was La Gaviota, The Seagull, dark-blue, sleek, breath-takingly luxurious, with its interior rooms on two levels, and a swimming pool on its main sun deck. It had been purchased by Anglo-Spanish Investors Ltd. Apart from appearing as an increasingly valuable asset on its balance sheet, the yacht was used by the company for entertaining investors and useful contacts, and for both the leisure and the business headquarters in Spain of its directors, especially the chairman, Sir Brian Cruickshank. (He also owned a well-guarded and equally-luxurious villa on the beach near San Pedro, but this - and, some suspected, the yacht too - was mortgaged to the hilt to help finance the Spanish project.)

It was to this small ship that the Rolls Royce now glided from Gibraltar, its owner temporarily distracted from his problems, as he always was on this journey, by close inspection of the tidal wave of concrete sweeping up the *costa* all the way to Malaga. This was the downside of the Costa del Sol. Developers, unchecked by proper planning controls until it was too late, had turned a once wild and beautiful coastline into one almost uninterrupted line of buildings extending from San Roque, just north of Gibraltar, to Nerja, an hour's drive beyond Malaga. Some of them attractive in the Spanish style, many of them hideous blocks of flats and hotels. Fifty years back the English writer Laurie Lee had hiked up the coast and written of a "beautiful but exhausted shore, seemingly forgotten by the world." At that time, wrote Lee, "you could have bought the whole coast for a shilling." Now the strip of land between the sea and the main highway was so over-exploited and badly-developed that those who could afford the prices were buying land and building further inland.

Inspecting all this usually raised Cruickshank's spirits. He became more convinced every time that he had come up with the right idea and captured the right piece of land at the right time.

Thinking this now, he momentarily experienced the old excitement but, just before the car reached the Nueva Andalucia complex opposite Puerto Banus, they passed the turn-off to a small unpaved road. Emerging from it onto a dirt track skirting the main highway, oblivious to the heavy traffic, like a survivor of centuries-old Spain stubbornly resisting the passing of time, was an old man, bent almost double over the neck of his mule, obviously on the way home after working from dawn to dusk at one of the fincas nestling in the foothills. Cruickshank felt as if a cold hand had reached out to clutch his heart; this was probably how the other old man had looked, the one it appeared possible Canning had killed.

Back came the memory of the phone call and with it the anger.

Why, in God's name, had Canning done it?

How much was he, Cruickshank, responsible?

He desperately tried to recall his orders; had there been any words of his that Canning could have misinterpreted, taking them as a hint that he, Cruickshank, had wanted this to happen? He couldn't believe it was so. The idea of harming the peasant had never entered his head. No, there had been no misunderstanding. If Canning had done this thing, he had done it on his own initiative.

As the Rolls turned into Puerto Banus he decided what to do. He would record his interview with Canning, obtain a clear account of what happened, and, if it was as Cruickshank feared, he would take the tape to the police. The publicity would hurt him a little and it wouldn't help the project, but surely his open and honest handling of the affair would earn respect. He would not be an accomplice to murder, he would be the one who exposed it; he would not be part-killer of the old man, he would be his avenger.

Trying hard to look his usual commanding self, he walked quickly up the gangplank of the yacht, barely acknowledging the salutes of the crew members at the top. His butler Hobbs was waiting with Jason Canning on the deck. He nodded coldly to the latter and told him to report to the library in 30 minutes.

The library could have been in an English country house. It was book-lined, and furnished with thick dark-brown carpets, red leather armchairs and a beautiful antique desk. Cruickshank asked the butler for a Scotch on the rocks, told him to keep the Rolls standing by, and asked not to be disturbed for 30 minutes, when he would like Canning to join him. They, too, were not to be disturbed.

Left on his own, he took from his desk the small cassette recorder he sometimes used to record complicated negotiations, inserted a brand-new tape, tested that it was operating properly, and placed it under a magazine close to but out of reach of the armchair by the drinks cabinet.

Satisfied that all was ready he slowly reclined in his own chair, a replica of the rocking chair in his London office, and sipping the Scotch, carefully rehearsed the questions he would need to ask.

Thirty minutes later Canning entered, his cool demeanour and the customary hint of a mocking smile causing Cruickshank to clench his fists under the table to hide his anger.

He waved him to the chair near the hidden cassette recorder, but didn't offer him a drink. "Jason, I want you to tell me exactly what happened to the old man. Exactly."

The younger man slipped casually into the armchair and lit a cigarette.

"I found him in a bar just outside Ronda a couple of weeks back. I offered him three million pesetas. He just shook his head. So I offered five million, then seven and a half. As I told you on the phone, it was hopeless. He wouldn't discuss it. I don't think he knew what seven and a half million pesetas was or what he could do with it. So I spelt it out to him at some length, then, just in case he was cleverer than

I imagined, I went up to ten million and even hinted there could be more. I told him I would come back in a week. And I left."

"Who saw you together?"

"Only the barman and he took no notice. He'll never remember we were in there."

Cruickshank looked coldly sceptical. "Go on."

"Yesterday morning I went back, but this time I cut across the hills near to where he lives. There was no-one within miles. I swear no-one saw us. I tried to persuade him, but he wouldn't even talk. He was either incredibly stupid or bloody-mindedly contemptuous, I couldn't tell... he was kind of impassive. I tell you, we were going to get nowhere."

He paused, as if this was all that needed saying.

Once more Cruickshank felt the chill hand on his heart. Canning clearly believed that, in the circumstances he described, murdering the old man was an unexceptional measure, that it was the logical, inevitable outcome of his failed negotiations, so customary a way of dealing with business that it was hardly worth discussing.

Who the hell was this man?

How could Jordan have chosen him?

Controlling himself with difficulty, he demanded to hear the rest.

"Well, there's this ravine near his hut. He was crossing some kind of bridge, just a few bits of wood... if that was his way of going home it was only a matter of time before he fell off it... all I did was help a little."

"How?"

"I hit him on the back of the head with a stone. He and the mule fell off. And that's it. If he's found, if anyone actually goes down there, any mark on his head will just look like one of the bruises he got when he fell. No bullet hole, no knife wound. No-one could ever prove it wasn't an accident."

So there it was.

There was no longer any doubt.

Cruickshank's indignation swelled. His voice rising, he exclaimed "But it wasn't an accident, Jason. You killed him. Don't you understand that whether you covered up the crime or not is hardly the point? You, Jason, are a murderer. What on earth makes you think that I, the company, or anyone else involved in the project can countenance such criminal behaviour? Who or what do you think we are? The Mafia? You must be mad, Jason. I'm afraid we can't allow it in our name, we can't pretend it didn't happen, we can't protect you."

The younger man looked undisturbed.

"You don't *need* to protect me, Sir Brian. I told you, it will be written off as an accident."

"I don't think you understand, Jason. You will be exposed because I intend to do it. I may play hard but I am not abandoning the rules of the human race I belong to. I have my duty as a citizen and I intend to carry it out."

Canning smiled cynically, indifferent to the other's anger. "Isn't that a bit pompous in the circumstances. It could be argued that I was acting for you. You told me to do what was necessary to get a deal."

"Necessary within the usual confines, Canning," Cruickshank raged. "You have gone beyond them, far beyond them - for God's sake, man, are you so amoral that you really believe that an instruction to do what is necessary in business extends to killing anyone who gets in your way ?"

The young man rose to his feet. "This is getting us nowhere. I did what I had to do, what you needed done, what I believed to be implied in your orders. I should forget it if I were you, because if it comes out, and only you could make it known, I will simply say that I was acting on your explicit orders - to kill the man - and, as that won't be a legal defence for me, people will have no reason not to believe it."

Now the older man rose. "I'm afraid that's not so, Canning." He took the recorder from under the magazine, removed the cassette and waved it at the American. "I'm going to the police in Marbella with the recording of our conversation. I intend the Spanish authorities to see that I have as much respect for the law as they have.

"As for you," he added, feeling magnanimous in his mastery, "you will not in the meantime be detained on the yacht. What you do before they come looking for you is up to you."

To his surprise the younger man's only move was to casually sit down in the red leather chair and light another cigarette.

"Canning, do you understand what is happening?"

"Oh, I do, Sir Brian, I'm afraid it is you who do not."

For the third time that evening Cruickshank felt a warning chill. The man's confidence was unreal. There was something the American knew that Cruickshank didn't.

"Sir Brian, I most strongly advise you that before you go anywhere with that tape you speak to Mr Jordan."

Cruickshank's disquiet grew. He remembered the cautious edge to Jordan's voice when they had spoken the previous night.

Still he tried to remain calm, to keep control of the confrontation. "I hope you are not suggesting that Mr Jordan is the kind of man to condone murder, Canning, because I have more confidence in him than that."

"*Ring him,* Sir Brian." This time there was an authority, an insistence about the younger man's voice that added considerably to Cruickshank's fears.

"I assure you Canning that this will make no difference, but on the other hand it can only help to have Mr Jordan's endorsement of my action." He picked up the phone and placed the call. For some minutes they sat in near silence, Cruickshank quietly drumming his fingers on the desk, Canning smoking his cigarette. Then the phone rang.

"Mr Jordan? I'm sorry to disturb you once more and even more sorry to have to deal with this matter by phone. I assume your line is secure?"

Jordan, as he had always done, imitated the formality of the Englishman. "That cannot be guaranteed, Sir Brian, but in any case I strongly advise you to leave the matter until we meet in London. I am assuming, of course, that it concerns the task of tidying up we entrusted to Mr Canning and that I believe he has satisfactorily undertaken?"

"Tidying up?" There was the icy feeling around the heart again; this time Cruickshank thought it was going to freeze it altogether. "Am I to understand that you're aware of all the measures Canning has taken?"

"Mr Canning has our full confidence, Sir Brian, as I intended to convey when we meet on Monday."

Cruickshank could hardly believe his ears.

The Americans *knew* what Canning had done.

Condoned it.

Goddamn it, *they seemed pleased with it.*

"Mr Jordan, I am sorry to hear that," he said. " It would be a pity to lose your involvement." Then, choosing his words carefully, for God knows who could listen in, he said "I must tell you, however, that there are norms of behaviour I insist on adhering to."

"Sir Brian, I have authorised Canning to tell you a little more about our involvement in the project. You can be assured he speaks with my authority. I suspect that once you have heard him you will choose to reserve your options until we meet in London. Goodbye."

Cruickshank was left holding the now-dead receiver in his hand, his face taut and white, his mind struggling to grasp the fact that he was losing control of the situation, that perhaps he had never been in control.

Now it was Canning who rose from his chair, walked to the drinks cabinet and poured himself a Scotch, re-filling Cruickshank's glass at the same time.

"Sir Brian, I have no wish to fall out with you. I and my employers in the States are more than happy for you to remain the top man on the project. Your qualities are appreciated. But you need to know that you no longer own it. You'll recall that when you set up Anglo-Spanish Investors as the company to develop the project you put together 40 per cent of the money, Mr Jordan and his partners provided 35 per cent of it, and the other 25 per cent you spread around in such a way that it was unlikely anyone but you would ever be in charge. Well, its not been easy thanks to your caution and skill and its taken time, but we have purchased another 16 per cent. We own it. Naturally we had to pay a lot, both for the shares and the discretion of the previous owners. Hence an even greater sense of urgency than your's to get the project moving."

Cruickshank sank back into his rocking chair, his hand shaking too much to pick up the Scotch.

Greater urgency?

How could anyone have pushed the project harder and faster than he? Except by some sort of extreme behaviour. And what could be more extreme than murder?

Seemingly from a distance he heard a voice and realised Canning hadn't finished. "Now, of course you could pull out. But why? This remains your project, your idea, with your name the one everyone links to it. Are you really going to let the unfortunate affair of this one crazy, stubborn old man, who as I told you would have died soon anyway, cause you to lose all this, the yacht, the villa, the company, your good name?"

Cruickshank's mind was in turmoil, trying to grasp all the implications. Jordan and his company had come highly recommended by merchant banks of standing on both sides of the Atlantic, had been properly checked out, were investors in scores of highly-respectable businesses. He had personally conducted the meetings with them, both in New York and London. He had believed them to be a real find. And so far they had behaved impeccably.

Who really were they?

He had made a sarcastic remark about the Mafia earlier, but could that really be the answer? Were Jordan and company laundering money for organised crime? Even if they were, why did they need overall ownership? Surely their ends were satisfactorily served as investors without the notoriety and responsibility of running it.

Then there were the other investors. He had selected them carefully, spread the shares so that it would be almost impossible for anyone to reach them all without the company knowing. Yet that's what Canning was claiming.

Reminding himself of his own stature, his good standing in both the UK and with the Spanish authorities, he desperately tried to fight back: "Canning, I may lose some money and even the project altogether, but I will not be, I cannot be associated with this... this criminality. To cover up for you would make me an accessory to murder. I will not have it. I'm taking the cassette to the police. And," he said, his hopes rising as he saw a way out, "my guess is that once your behaviour is revealed the permission to develop will be withdrawn if you and your associates are in control. You'll end up begging to sell back to me."

Canning rose and walked across to the desk, leaning over so that his face was close to Cruickshank's.

"Sir Brian, I've tried to make this easy for you, but you're missing the point. Your cassette is worthless. You will never get it off the yacht. Almost the whole crew were chosen and employed by me, acting on behalf of my New York employers. They may be on the Anglo-Spanish Investors payroll but their loyalty is to us. Once we have the cassette – and you will give it to me in a moment - you will have no evidence that it was other than an accident and if you make such a charge it will be denied. It won't stick. You will be portrayed as a desperate man deprived of power and seeking to discredit those who stripped you of it. "You have only two choices, you can destroy yourself, at least as far as the project is concerned, or you can forget this thing and life can go on as it did before. The project will be built, you will preside over it, everyone'll be happy."

Cruickshank was hardly aware of the other taking the cassette from his hand and leaving. For a while he sat motionless until answering a discreet knock on the door. It was the butler. For a moment Cruickshank looked at him suspiciously, then relaxed. Hobbs, at least, was his man.

"The Rolls is blocking the walkway, sir, and we've been asked to move it. The chauffer wants to know your wishes."

For a moment he remained still, then, slowly, dejectedly, he looked up. "Tell Green I won't be needing it tonight. I'll sleep on the yacht."

As the door closed, he switched off all the lights save for a small one at the desk, poured himself another Scotch, lit a cigar, and allowed the rocking chair to tilt back. Sitting in the semi-darkness he made a tremendous effort to calm himself, to set his analytical skills to work, reviewing every detail, considering every facet of the problem. From the top drawer of the desk he took a piece of paper and, as he liked to do, listed the key points.

One, Jordan and his associates now controlled the project. Why they needed to was not clear, but hopefully it was just greed.

Two, the Americans were clearly happy to have him as front man and probably would continue to let him call the shots. However, for him to continue was to take advantage of, and thus share complicity for, the murder.

Three, he could expose the murder, but what would that achieve? While there was probably inadequate evidence to convict him, it would undoubtedly lead to the project being stopped. Thus he would gain nothing but lose everything.

Four, there was one thing he would achieve by going to the police - he would retain his self-respect. Also, people would believe him even if Canning could not be convicted, and his reputation for integrity would be seen to be justified, even enhanced.

Like others of his kind, Cruickshank was more than capable of rationalising his ruthless moments, of squaring his conscience with the inequities and injustices that were necessary if people, relatively few people, were to acquire and keep power and wealth. This was life, all part and parcel of the human condition. There were strong and there were weak, there were winners and there were losers, and the mark of intelligence and decency was not to naively combat that reality but to accept and enjoy its rewards while showing compassion and generosity to its victims. If there were any inconsistencies between his self-image and the effects of his activities and decisions he was oblivious to them; he genuinely believed himself to be a man of honour and genuinely cared about setting and maintaining what he believed to be high standards of behaviour.

But now a new thought struck him and once more he felt the cold hand on his heart... if he did appear to be ready to reveal all and thus cause damage Jordan and his associates and the project, what would they do to him? If they would kill a peasant because they couldn't be bothered to take the time to solve the problem another way, would they stop short of arranging another accident, this time for him?

He went to the port-hole and, drawing the curtain, looked out. Usually there was one crew member at the gang plank throughout the night. Tonight there were three.

Cruickshank shivered.

Who had tripled the guard?

And why?

For a moment it all seemed too unreal. His life in danger? No, this couldn't be happening. He was letting his imagination run away with him.

He picked up the phone, intending to ask the reason for the guard, but as it began to ring he put it down.

At least for the moment he felt better not knowing.

As he turned from the window his eye caught the small replica of the model on a table in the far corner of the study. He walked over and switched on the lamp beside it. Despite himself he experienced a moment of elation. It was magnificent in its conception, it would be one of the most pleasurable places to live anywhere in the world.

And on a hill overlooking it was to be his villa, from where, retired in a few years time, he had intended to reign, sovereign over all he surveyed, President of the Community, host, he had imagined, to some of the world's richest and most powerful, for who would be able to resist invitations to rest and relax in such surroundings and with such facilities? Yes, Cruickshank was a man of intelligence and integrity but he was not short of ego, or of appetite for the good things of life; he had intended to enjoy every minute of his last two or three decades.

So he came to the last of the questions on his sheet of paper: *Were his integrity and this ambition not reconcilable?*

Did he really have to abandon the dream?

Whatever he did, he couldn't bring the old man back. If he stayed with the project he could surely prevent any further excesses; he would be able to exact that guarantee as a reasonable price for his silence and continued involvement. This, he rationalised, would make him a protector of all involved, the remaining small investors, the workers, the local people, and ultimately the project's members and residents. It was not a dishonourable objective.

For nearly 10 minutes he stood looking at the model, then switching off the lamp, returned to his rocking chair and another Scotch. There he stayed until the early hours, slowly and wretchedly considering a question that 24 hours he would never have believed could possibly arise.

Was he capable of reconciling himself to murder?

It was dark now, and the Costa del Sol had become a glittering ribbon of lights. From his balcony on the hill Sheedy showed Kate the sparkling strip that was the golden mile and the bright cluster that was the ever-growing Puerto Banus.

They were drinking the French champagne she had bought duty-free at Kennedy Airport and were standing close together.

Behind them in the main room a log fire was crackling in the hearth, more for atmosphere than warmth, for they had decided to stay at the villa and dine on salad and the *paella* that Sheedy promised her was his speciality, the best, he said, in Andalucia.

Kate was wearing a gypsy-style red and white blouse and tight white jeans that exposed her figure to best advantage, and was effervescent in her enthusiasm for all things Spanish she had so far encountered - not least the villa, the view, and the warmth of the evening. Sheedy was both immensely happy in her company and at the same time tense, unsettled by an almost uncontrollable urge to take her in his arms, to run his fingers through her hair, down her back and over her shapely bottom, and yet afraid that even a fractional revelation of his desires and feelings could spoil the moment.

A sizzling from the open kitchen at one end of the room warned them that the *paella* was ready and they went in. Proudly he carried to the table the *paellera*, the two-handled steel pan piled high with rice and rabbit, prawns and mussels and *calamares*, all spiced with red peppers, garlic, and herbs.

She had watched him prepare it earlier, first cleaning the mussels and steaming them till they were open. Then peeling and cooking the prawns and cutting up the rabbit that he said he preferred to chicken. Then heating olive oil in the pan together with a couple of cloves of garlic and some bay leaf, and browning the rabbit in the same pan. She marvelled at the way he could chat while at the same time heating some ingredients, onion and peppers and rings of squid, and then removing them from the pan while sauteing others, feeding in saffron, peppercorn, paprika, and, of course, rice, then gradually bringing back each ingredient to add to the dish until the whole *paella* slowly cooked on a low heat.

Now, while it cooled for a few minutes, he tossed the salad and opened a bottle of Rioja and served her with a flourish of Spanish that she took to mean "eat well."

And she did. They both did, happy to reserve conversation until the first pangs of hunger were quelled. Then she asked him about his plans for the next few days.

"Well, I figure you'll be jet-lagged tomorrow so I propose you spend it by the pool while I clear up some work, and maybe we'll go up to Benahavis in the evening. I've got friends there and we can have dinner at one of the restaurantes, maybe Los Faroles."

"Where's Benahavis?"

"Not far. Three kilometres west of San Pedro, then seven kilometres up into the hills beyond Atalaya Park *campo de golf*. You'll be amazed. Its a small white village, yet it had about 20 restaurants at the last count. Maybe more now. There's a new one every time I go there. The whole village seems like one big restaurant."

"How did it get like that?"

"Well, when I first saw it back in the late Sixties there was, I think, only one, but gradually as first it, and then others, became popular and made money, the families opened more until virtually everyone in the village either works in a restaurant or in a business related to it.

"Anyway, in a day or two I reckon we should start with Granada and the Alhambra. From there we can go on a quick introductory trip to Cordoba, then across to Ronda. I know there's a *corrida* on Sunday, not one of the awful bullfights they turn on for the tourists on the *costa* but the real thing. I reckon we can spend two or three days in Ronda and thereabouts and then it'll be safe to let you onto the beaches of the *costa*."

"How kind," she responded with good-humoured irony. "Tell me about the *corrida*, how do you know we'll get in. Do you book tickets?"

"Ah ha, that's where Miguel comes in."

Then he told her how one time when he was in Ronda he ended up late at night in the corner of a bar with two ageing bullfight aficionados, a captain in the *Guardia Civil* and a hunter from the *Serrania de Ronda*, the mountainous country around the town. Sheedy had quizzed them on bullfighting and on life in the sierras until they were all too drunk to continue, and they had arranged to go to the following day's *corrida* together. Despite the improbability of them remembering, let alone all making it to the same place, it had worked out and since then they had met in the bar the night before each *corrida* and gone to the plaza de *toros* together the following day.

For reasons it was best not to enquire, the policeman, Miguel, appeared to have an endless supply of tickets, said Sheedy, so there would be no difficulty getting in.

"You'll love them. They're remarkable characters, complete opposites, Miguel fat and the Rabbit Man skinny, Miguel gregarious and jolly, the Rabbit Man more inclined to melancholy, Miguel opinionated, the Rabbit Man introverted. They look a bit like a Spanish Laurel and Hardy. But what they don't know about the sierras, no-one does."

"But why the rabbit man?"

"Ah, the rabbit man, *El Conejero*. I should warn you, he smells a bit. He spends all his time shooting and skinning and transporting rabbits on his mule, selling them to the restaurants in Ronda."

"What's his real name ?"

"I don't know. Even Miguel calls him *Señor Conejo*, Mr Rabbit."

She screwed up her nose in mock horror. "Holy cow... or should I say rabbit."

They laughed and drank more wine and he read her some Federico Garcia Lorca until the fire died out and, the jet-lag taking its toll, she became sleepy, eventually dozing off, her head coming to rest on his shoulder.

For nearly an hour he sat still, happy to feel her warmth and listen to her breathing, proud of her trust.

He remembered how Jan and he had often ended an evening like this, she falling asleep in front of the television, he content for a while to be her pillow. Miraculously, this time the memory was painless.

Finally he manouvered himself free and picked her up and carried her into her room. As he did so she woke. "Where are you taking me, Sheedy?" she asked sleepily.

"To bed."

"With you?"

With super-human restraint he softly replied "Not tonight."

"Oh... pity." Then, once more, she fell asleep.

His lay her down on the bed and pulled the covers over her. Then he kissed her on the top of her head and said "Thank's for saying that" and quickly left.

That night Sheedy dream't of Jan once more. She was on the roof garden of their flat in New York, her arms full of flowers she was planting in boxes. She was smiling, but he knew she was dying and he was sad. Then she was dropping the flowers, throwing her arms round him, telling him that it was alright, not to grieve.

He woke up with tears running down his face.

It was, of course, not the first time, but this time was different.

This time he felt no need for solace from a bottle.

This time he did not feel alone.

CHAPTER THREE

On the journey from the *costa* to Granada and Cordoba and then back south to Ronda, Kate came to understand why the writer Jan Morris had described Andalucia as *sol y sombra* - "sun on one side of the street, shadow on the other". She saw and photographed the contrasts. Widows, short, bent, broad-bummed, who still wore only black. The communal tap, in many *pueblos* still the sole source of water. Donkeys, still for many the only means of transport. But she saw also a people adjusting to the 21st century - to cars and motorbikes, to tv, satellite dishes stuck to the walls of century-old whitewashed walls, a noisy disco in places where only a few years back courtship took place via a grilled window of the *pueblo* home, the young *caballero* standing in the street, his *señorita* discreetly protected by thick white walls and watchful parents.

She photographed, too, the physical contrasts, the rugged scenery that changed from valley to valley, so that every bend on every mountain road produced its own surprise.

Sheedy talked to her of the Spaniard's fascination with death. Andalucia was, said Sheedy, at times a stoic place, yet it also staged events of great public emotion and excitability. It was a private, proud, secretive place, yet - still the contradictions - the families of small communities could by sheer physical circumstances have no secrets from one another, only from the outside world. It was a land of family, where the woman ruled the home but the man's superiority remained unchallenged on the streets.

She quickly developed a passion for the food - the cooking in garlic and olive oil, the big, firm tomatoes and crisp white onions, the fresh grilled fish of every size and shape, the roast meat chicken and lamb.

And she would always remember Sheedy, sitting on top of a hill, glass of wine in one hand, bread and *serrano* ham in the other, pointing out the tiny white towns sprinkled across the mountains like sparkling jewels in the sun, and reciting to her the words of his poet-hero Federico Garcia Lorca, executed in Granada during the civil war:

Dry land,
still land,
of immense nights.

(Wind in the olive grove.
wind in the sierra.)

Ancient
land
of oil lamp
and grief.
Land
of deep cisterns.
Land
of a death without eyes
and of arrows.

(Wind on the roads.
Breeze in the poplar groves.)

No wonder that as they arrived in Ronda Kate felt sated with spectacle. There had been the view of the Costa del Sol and the Mediterranean from Sheedy's villa, the view of the Alhambra across the valley from the Albaicin, Granada's old Moorish quarter, the view over the roofs of Cordoba from the Bell Tower by the Cathedral, the panoramic views of sunlit mountains and deep, shaded valleys on the San Pedro-Ronda road, the view from the bridge over *El Tajo*, the dramatic gorge that divides Ronda's old and new towns.

And now, in the late afternoon, she was looking at a magnificent view of the farms and the mountains to the south of Ronda from the balcony of their hotel, the Reina Victoria.

The hotel, built on the edge of a precipice, was plain but clean, the bed was soft, the water in the shower was hot, the view was intoxicating, and, after she had flung herself into its swimming pool to cool down, she had, with some difficulty, persuaded a waiter to deliver to her room a jug of ice-cold sangria.

She could not imagine anywhere in the world she would rather be or anyone she would rather be with.

As she stood on the balcony she cast her mind back over her first few days in Spain. She had woken late that first morning and found him standing beside her with a tray of fresh orange juice, coffee and croissants. He had spent most of the day in Marbella, leaving her to swim and read and doze beside the pool. That evening, as promised, they had driven to Benahavis for a feast of *gambas al pil pil, pollo al ajillo,* and a huge salad at Los Faroles with Sheedy's colleague, Manuel, and his wife, Juanita, who lived in a *pueblo*-style building above the village. She had contentedly listened as over several bottles of the restaurant's best red wine they had reminisced about their exposes of and encounters with some of the *costa*'s less savoury operators.

Kate had liked the Spanish couple. At first she felt envious of the shared experiences between Sheedy and his reporter, wishing it had been her who was a member of the team, but this was balanced at her pleasure at the way both Manuel and Juanita treated her as if she was Sheedy's girl, as if they were lovers. Kate didn't know whether Sheedy was aware of their assumption but she was surprised how good it made her feel.

Slim, dark-haired, and good-looking, Manuel told her how Sheedy had enticed him from a Malaga newspaper to work on the programme, how the older man had shared with him his experience and techniques, how they had become a team talked about far beyond the English expatriate community Sheedy claimed was his only audience. "I don't think he realises how famous he is becoming on the *costa, Señorita,* nor does he seem to care, one way or the other." She told him Sheedy had always been like that.

It was a good evening, so good that it was nearly noon by the time they woke the following day. So the trip to the *sierras* was postponed. Sheedy decided instead to go up the costa to Fuengirola to set up a story for three weeks hence. He suggested Kate accompanied him.

"Fuengirola is the best place south of Nerja for *tapas* bars."

Kate looked at him, uncomprehending.

"You don't know what *tapas* are?" asked Sheedy. "Ah ha, you're in for a treat Callaghan. Just because the Spanish don't have lunch till nearly two o'clock and dinner until nine in the evening, doesn't mean they don't get hungry. Especially if they're drinking. So they invented the *tapas* bar. *Tapas* are snacks. You can have a good meal just by strolling from bar to bar."

And so they went on a '*tapas* crawl' of Fuengirola. By the time they called at the nineth bar they had drunk enough *vino tinto* and eaten enough *calamares, gambas, boquerones, pulpo, busanos, coquinas, navajas, habas con jamon, albondigas,* and *patatas alli olli* to make lunch and dinner superfluous.

On Wednesday they had driven east to Malaga and turned inland for the climb to Granada where they went without their *siesta* and spent the afternoon in the splendour of the Alhambra and the evening climbing up the steps and wandering the tiny back streets of the Albaicin, the old quarter on the facing hill.

As they looked back across to the Moorish citadel, Sheedy told her how the last Sultan, departing the Alhambra for exile, had wept and said "here are the keys to paradise."His mother had been unsympathetic. "Do not weep like a woman," she snapped, "for what you could not defend as a man."

It was in Granada that Sheedy had his brainwave. He proposed that he and Kate collaborate on a coffee table book called "Lorca's Andalucia." Sheedy would select the poems and Kate would take the photographs. So enthusiastic did they become that they sat up half the night re-reading the poems and planning the journeys they would make. Kate had begun taking photographs the following day, in Cordoba.

Finally, this day, there had been the journey across to Ronda. All the way she had found herself falling back in love with the calm, easy-going, kind man who was her friend and guide. And sharing his enthusiasm for Andalucia, especially for Ronda. The town was all he had described and more, a dramatic fortress on a hill, welcoming yet secretive behind its walls, full of life and colour.

She had been stunned by the gorge, *El Tajo,* and had stood for nearly an hour on the *Puente Nuevo* (the new bridge, albiet 200 years old), looking down into the chasm with its waterfalls and ruins.

Sheedy told her of its extraordinary history, of how many of those who built the bridge or cut the steps into the wall of the gorge had fallen to their deaths, including the bridge's architect, of how until about 50 years ago horses killed in the bullring had been tossed from it onto the rocks below, later to be followed by men who had angered one side or another at the time of the Spanish civil war.

After lunch on the edge of the ravine he took her to the place he loved best, the oldest and most beautiful *plaza de toros* in Spain, built in the mid-18th century, the Plaza de la Real Maestranza de Caballeria. They sat in the shade while he shared with her what Miguel and the Rabbit Man had told him.

It was in this bullring that men had first abandoned their horses and fought bulls on foot, armed only with a sword and cape. The pioneer had been Francisco Romero, whose exploits were commemorated in a bullfighting museum under the circular stands, together with those of his grandson Pedro, a legendry artist of the *corrida*.

"It was Pedro who established the rules of the Ronda school of bullfighting.

"*The matador's honour lies in his never fleeing nor running before the bulls, provided he has sword and muleta in his hands.*

"*The matador must never jump over the fence after the bull has entered the ring.*

"*The matador must rely on his hands, not his feet, and faced with the bull should kill or die rather than save face or humble himself.*"

Kate was unimpressed. "Sounds like *macho* bullshit to me."

Sheedy laughed. "The English writer Kenneth Tynan said there was no point in preaching the virtues of bullfighting... the *aficionado* should never apologise, never explain. I don't intend to. You will just have to come and judge for yourself. If you don't like it, leave."

Kate looked at him, surprised. It had happened before: just when she was convincing herself Sheedy was a soft-hearted romantic, he would suddenly show his uncompromising side. Somehow it was reassuring.

Still she pressed him. "Ok, but even if you accept it for what it is, its still cruel. Isn't it ?"

He sighed, but good-humouredly. "I knew we were going to have to have this argument," he said. "That's a hard question to answer. Especially as the bulls can't answer it for themselves. If they could, its possible they would say they prefer dying with honour in the bullring to being butchered in their adolescence in order to become the steaks people eat while decrying bullfighting over the dinner table.

But I don't expect anyone to take my word for that.

"I acknowledge there could be a case for stopping the *novilladas* that sometimes take place on the *costa*, if only to protect the reputation of bullfighting. They often involve poor or inexperienced matadors and even poorer bulls. But I can only say that when I sit in this bullring as the sun sets over the mountains in the background and

watch the drama that takes place in the ring, the struggle between man and bull, then all of it, even the killing of the bull, becomes - at least to me - acceptable as part of the culture of this country in a way that I concede it probably wouldn't be in, say, Madison Square Garden. It is Spain, part of its character, its history, even its language."

"But they say its unfair," said Kate, "that the bull doesn't stand a chance."

"He doesn't. At least he doesn't stand a chance of living. Even if he wins, even if he injures or kills the *matador*, he dies, just as every animal bred to be butchered for the dinner table will die. What people forget is that the *matador* can die too. Or be badly injured. I saw some statistics in a magazine recently. In one year recently there were 814 bullfights and 49 matadors gored. That worked out at roughly one goring for every l6 bullfights. A good *matador* will fight between 30 and 35 times a season and stands to get a horn at least twice. Obviously a bad *matador* is more likely to get gored than a skilful one, but some of the greatest were killed in the ring. Manolete for instance. Its partly a matter of luck; Pedro Romero fought 5,500 bulls and was never hurt, whereas another star of the last century, *El Espartero*, was gored 82 times."

Sitting in the sun he recited Lorca on the fatal goring of a *matador*:

At five in the afternoon.
It was five sharp in the afternoon.
A young boy brought the white sheet,
at five in the afternoon.
A basket of already waiting lime,
at five in the afternoon.
The rest was death and only death,
at five in the afternoon...
... on the corners, groups of silence,
at five in the afternoon.

And the bull alone with a high heart!
at five in the afternoon...

...The wounds were burning him like suns,
at five in the afternoon,
and the throng was breaking the windows,
at five in the afternoon.
At five in the afternoon.
Oh, what a terrible five in the afternoon!
It was five on every one of the clocks!
It was five in the shade of the afternoon!

Soon after they had returned to the car and driven to the hotel.

Now she dragged herself away from the view from her balcony and banged on the door of the adjoining room. "Hey, Sheedy, come and have some *sangria*."

Like Kate, he was wearing a dressing gown, for after a day's driving in the hot sun they had both arrived at the Riena Victoria gasping for a cold drink and a shower. She poured him a glass of sangria and, taking his arm, led him onto the balcony. "Just look at that."

He laughed. "I know. I have the same view." He pointed to the balcony just beside her own.

"Oh, of course." She laughed too. "But isn't it marvellous. I love the little white farmhouses, what do they call them in Spain...? *El cortijo?*"

"Well, your Spanish is coming on. Not bad. Not bad at all."

He sank into one of the bamboo chairs on the balcony and put his feet up on the balcony rail. He looked across the plain at the foot of the steep drop, a plain set within a circle of hills, and imagined the Rabbit Man slowly making his way across the fields of corn and between the olive trees, past the *cortijos*, over the Rio Guadalevin, and then up to the ridge and beyond it into the mountains, observed on his lonely journey only by the occasional eagle or hawk. He wondered how long it took the Rabbit Man to make the part of the journey that was within sight of the hotel. He could imagine sitting there having breakfast, lunch and dinner, and still man and mule would be in sight.

"Yes, its one fantastic view."

"I'll say," she said, grinning as his dressing gown slipped away revealing sun-tanned legs almost up to his private parts. He hastily pulled it around him and blushed, causing her to chuckle mischievously. "I've seen legs before, Sheedy."

"Well, that's all you're going to see," he said. Normally his sense of humour would have more than met the challenge but the attention she was paying to his legs was causing a physical reaction the dressing gown was not designed to disguise. Holding his glass in both hands, he rested it on his lap, hoping it would cover the evidence.

She had moved to the railing, and was leaning over to look down to the foot of the precipice, pulling her dressing gown tight around her so that he could see she was naked under it, could clearly see the contours of her body. While her back was turned he quickly stood up and walked into the room and towards the door to his own. "I'm just going to finish unpacking," he called to her as he went.

"Bill..."

There was an appeal in her voice that stopped him in his tracks, his heart beating fast. He paused with his hand on the door knob, his back still to her.

Then he heard her come towards him and, turning, found her walking into his arms.

"Bill, I think we should have a *siesta*.

"Together."

Some time later, while he was showering, Kate poured a glass of *sangria*, and went once more to the balcony.

It was dark now and lights twinkled in the windows of the farmhouses.

She felt a great sense of peace and space, and also of pleasure that things had worked out, that she and Sheedy were now really together.

She thought of the men she had experienced in New York, younger, yes, maybe sexier-looking, but she thought too of her insecurities with them, of the demanding egos, of the competitive tensions, of the letdowns.

Sheedy she trusted.

Sheedy would never hurt her.

Sheedy had self-confidence, didn't need his ego boosting all the time.

And Sheedy was an attractive man in the fullest sense of the word.

"Hey, Sheedy," she called.

He appeared on the neighbouring balcony.

"I've been thinking about what you said after we made love – that you would understand if this was for me just a fling…

"And…?"

"Bullshit," she said.

And went to have her shower.

Back in the main square, the *Plaza de España*, the last of the tourist buses rolled away, back over the bridge, back to the *costa*. The ornate wooden doors to the bullring were slammed shut, leaving the golden sands of the arena to the ghosts of matadors past. The shutters came down over the souvenir shop windows in the Carrera de Vicente Espinel. And, with dusk, the church bells began to summons people to mass.

As it became dark and the night grew cooler, Ronda, the sunny mecca of tourists from the *costa* during the day, drew into itself, secure on its hill and behind its walls.

Cruickshank had done his best to surprise and disconcert the American.

Recognising the advantage of staging the confrontation on his home ground, he had arranged to meet Jordan in the bar of his Pall Mall club, and asked two of the members to join them for pre-dinner drinks, a member of the House of Lords and a senior civil servant. Jordan needed to be reminded who he was dealing with, and so far it was going according to plan. The American had clearly been impressed by the other guests and by Cruickshank himself, for, determined to give the impression he was unperturbed by the turn of events, that he was still in control, and looking particularly distinguished in formal dress, the Englishman had appeared relaxed and at home in these exclusive surroundings.

Not that Jordan appeared out of place himself. About 60, he was tall and walked with a limp, had a parchment-white but intelligent face, and was completely bald. Yet, in a dinner jacket, he too looked a man of substance, and, after his initial surprise at finding himself in such company, more than held his own in conversation, deploying all the charm and courtesy that had so beguiled Cruickshank in their previous dealings. And Cruickshank, vastly experienced in diplomacy, was not a man to be easily beguiled. As he watched the American he conceded that whoever the forces were behind Jordan, they had picked their front man well.

The Englishman, having agonised over the matter for 24 hours, had decided to negotiate a deal that would keep the project in being while strengthening his own hand and disciplining the Americans, especially Canning. He had planned the evening carefully. He was thankful that he had kept his cool during both his brief telephone conversations with Jordan. Canning may have seen him flustered, but Jordan had not, and, for all Canning's influence on site in Spain, Cruickshank guessed he was of no account at Jordan's level. With this man he could make a fresh start with the benefit of a weekend to recover from the shock and to prepare his ground.

He had decided, too, not to make an issue of the morality of the situation. Clearly, and he shuddered at the implications, this was not an argument likely to impress the American.

So, once in the dining room with its dark oak panels and oil paintings shining in the light from the chandeliers, the dinner and wine ordered, he built on the advantage he felt he had already established.

"Mr Jordan, I'm unhappy, to put it mildly, with the way your man Canning has dealt with our problem, but deal with it he has, and we are extremely fortunate that his... his behaviour... appears likely to go undetected. Whatever may be acceptable to you and your associates... and I dread to think... this is not, I repeat *not*, the way to do business in Spain, let alone anywhere else. If there is even a tiny hint of impropriety in connection with the project, all the necessary approvals will be withdrawn and we'll be out."

Convinced by Jordan's silence that he was re-establishing his authority, Cruickshank continued. He and his company may have lost the majority shareholding but they were still essential to the project. "I would go so far as to say that my involvement is vital if its full potential is to be achieved, if only because of the standing I have with the Spanish authorities. If you are in any doubt, ask yourself what the effect would be if I were to withdraw, especially if I was to explain exactly why."

Jordan looked at him expressionlessly. "And?"

"I'm prepared to stay involved on four conditions:

"I want to know exactly who you and your associates are.

"I want a legally-binding contract between the other shareholders and myself that establishes my chairmanship of the Company, my ownership of Villa No 1 and my Presidency of the Community for a term of no less than 10 years.

"I want your assurance that from now on the project will be developed in a legal and straight-forward manner... that what has happened will prove to be a once-only aberration.

"And I want Canning removed, not just from the project but from Spain."

The American looked at him thoughtfully. "Sir Brian, I'll give you English credit. You have style."

"Its not a question of style, Mr Jordan. I am, with many qualms, adopting a pragmatic approach to the position we find ourselves in. You should understand, however, that I have weighed carefully in the balance my duty as a citizen to have criminal behaviour dealt with by the law and, on the other hand, my duty to everybody who can benefit from the project, not just investors but the local workers. I have narrowly decided in favour of the second, but, of course, any further criminality would tip the scales overwhelmingly in favour of the first."

Jordan smiled. "You not only have the British civil servant's style, Sir Brian, but also his penchant for hypocrisy. However, I see no profit in discussing your motives. Suffice to say we respect your achievements and your remarkable abilities, and we value what you bring to the project..."

"Bring, Mr Jordan?" Cruickshank was provoked into indignation. "May I remind you who devised the project. It is you who bring, Mr Jordan, and you bring little that I am grateful for... just some additional finance accompanied apparently by the morality of the Mafia."

Now it was Jordan's turn to look pained. "Not the Mafia, Sir Brian."

"Well, who then?"

They were interrupted by the waiter. Once he had served their appetisers, Jordan leaned forward, his voice low but, to his listener, chilling: "You have been frank, let me be equally so. The fact is that you have decided to stay involved despite what has happened. Now, you may, if you feel the need, pretend to yourself that you're in some way superior to me and my associates, but don't expect me to think its so. In New York we have a saying about whores - they may be $500 a night whores operating from luxury East Side apartments or they may be $10 dollars back-alley whores soliciting on the street, but they're both whores. At this moment we are both planning to take advantage of Canning's impetuosity in equal measure and that, Sir Brian, puts us on the same level, whatever that level may be."

As the Englishman half rose in protest, Jordan, now in charge, waved him back to his chair.

"Let me reply to your four points.

"Yes to the conditions for your own involvement. We are, of course, content for you to remain the top man and be seen to be so. I will not insult your intelligence by denying the strength of the case you make. We would be at a disadvantage if you were to withdraw.

"Yes, of course, to your desire that the project is proceeded with on a legal basis. I should say, by the way, that for the sound reasons you have yourself spelt out, we do not entirely approve of Mr Canning's... shall we say... hasty action.

"That brings me to your other points. Despite the reservations I've mentioned, we would not be happy to withdraw Jason Canning. I think you will accept that until last week you found him suitable in every way. He can be given firm instructions about the standards of behaviour we both require. May I commend to you the old saying 'better the devil you know'?"

"Are you suggesting that his replacement could be worse, Mr Jordan?"

"I am suggesting that if you're able to reconcile yourself to the act, you should also reconcile yourself to the actor. Jason will be told to work with you on the old basis, with you clearly in charge. We would request that at least you try to make that arrangement work."

"Who is 'we'? Who are you? What exactly is it you want?"

"We are the same organisation you checked out from the beginning, Sir Brian. We invest on behalf of a portfolio of clients who wish their funds placed in a number of countries, including Spain. Our interest in the project is, in fact, a tribute to you. We believe it to be a brilliantly-conceived and potentially immensely profitable one. Our increased shareholding simply reflects the demand from our clients for opportunities to invest in it."

"You're *not* exactly the organisation I checked out, Mr Jordan. That organisation, as represented to me, did not engage in murder."

Jordan looked at him coldly. "I hoped that we had moved on from expressions of moral indignation. I do not deny that some of our investors have accumulated considerable funds in ways that may not generally be thought to be socially acceptable. But that need not concern you..."

Before he could continue, the waiter once more intervened.

Cruickshank thought rapidly.

They were willing to confirm his position and he would make damn sure the deal was water-tight.

They were giving him assurances about future conduct and, while these counted for little in themselves, Jordan did appear to understand that there was no need for criminal behaviour, that it could be counter-productive. Also, now he knew the kind of people he was dealing with, he was forewarned and could probably prevent other excesses.

As for Canning, well on that point Jordan was right. Given that he was dealing with criminals, albeit at a distance, better the devil he knew. And at least he had something to hold over Canning, even if he were not now equipped with the evidence.

As to who they were, Jordan had told him what he guessed. They were laundering money through the project. Money undoubtedly earned by crime.

But then who ever knew exactly where invested funds came from? Probably half the world's most respected businesses were partly financed by the profits of crime invested at one stage removed. Undoubtedly there was already a lot of illicitly-earned money being invested on the Costa del Sol.

The whole business was, of course, deeply disappointing. Despite his continued involvement in the project, and his desire to live on site in the winter months, it would have to be downgraded on his list of priorities. Instead of shedding many of his other business interests so that he could semi-retire into the Presidency of the community, he would need to maintain them so that, should any serious problems arise in Spain, he could brush them off as of little consequence compared with his wider concerns.

For a moment he felt despondent. Then, reminding himself that he still had the upper hand in this conversation, he began to deliberately fuss over his selection of vegetables and the tasting of the wine, showing no inclination to renew the conversation until he had tucked into his roast lamb. Jordan, shrewdly realising that his host was considering all that had been said, also made no attempt to force the issue.

Finally the Englishman spoke. "You've satisfied me as to who you are and I don't what I now know, even less Canning's continued involvement, but, on your assurance there will be no more criminality, and provided the contract I will give you at the end of this evening is signed, I will proceed.

"Second, I am placing a sealed envelope with my bank so that should I find it necessary, or should I suffer a so-called 'accident' myself, the full facts will be provided to the appropriate authorities in the United States, Britain and Spain. It may not represent evidence that would hold up in a criminal trial but it would be adequate to persuade the authorities to stop the project and cause investigations into you and your organisation that you would find more than embarrassing.

"If you are prepared to proceed on that basis, I suggest we cease discussion of the past and look at steps we need now to be taking to facilitate the enterprise."

It was Jordan's turn to take his time. "May I?" he asked, reaching for the wine.

"Of course."

"Its a splendid wine. A splendid dinner, Sir Brian. A splendid club. Perhaps if I spend more time in Britain you would consider nominating me for membership."

Cruickshank almost choked on his food. The audacity of the man. A criminal in his club. It was an unspeakable idea.

Jordan, who had been joking, but showed no sign of it, suppressed a laugh at the horror on the other's face and continued: "I think we understand each other. May we proceed to other matters?"

"Very well. Our first step must be to see how we can make the best of the fact that the old man..." Cruickshank faltered for a moment...

"Is no longer alive?"

"Quite." He stared at the American accusingly, affronted by Jordan's indifference to his own sense of moral outrage. "I'm afraid Canning's solution is not even as clear-cut as you seem to think. As the man is not yet officially dead, and hopefully will never be discovered, we need to persuade the authorities to presume him dead. Worse, if we can't do that, we may have to facilitate the finding of the body; that means testing Canning's claim that there is no evidence of foul play and that's a risk I, for one, would prefer to avoid."

Jordan concurred. "You're right, it would be better if he is not found. Personally I hope we can find a relative or heir of some sort, because a straight-forward deal is the easiest course and its unlikely anyone else would be as difficult as the old man. However, if no-one is forthcoming I have no doubt you can manage the authorities with the same skill you have shown in managing all the other arrangements."

The two men moved to the library for coffee, and it was there that Cruickshank raised the outstanding question in his mind. "I take it, Mr Jordan, that despite not having the majority shareholding I still have full power of decision as in the past? Otherwise, of course, it would be impossible for me to continue."

"We have no problem with that. Our increased stake is a show of confidence in your management, not a criticism."

"Very well. I will await your signature on this." He handed the other contract.

Jordan carefully read it. Then, without a word, he signed it.

Cruickshank was spared having to shake his hand by the intervention of a friend. Accepting an invitation to join him and others in the bar when their business was concluded, he coolly, almost abruptly, dismissed the American.

Jordan showed no sign of being offended, just as he had shown little sign of emotion throughout the evening. A dignified figure, he limped slowly to the stairs and disappeared into the night.

Cruickshank, trying hard to appear affable and at ease with his old colleagues, watched the American go. He had achieved his objective, yet he felt only a sense of loss.

As he looked at the other members, peers, MP's, civil servants, businessmen, all in dinner jackets, united in their bonhomie, a reassuring show of establishment strength, he thought once more of Jordan's hint that he should be nominated for the club and of his, Cruickshank's horrified reaction.

But what now made him any more worthy of membership than the American?

He looked up to a bronze plaque above the bar containing the club motto:

"Better to die 10,000 deaths than wound my honour."

And he wondered whether he would die those deaths, one by one, day by day for the rest of his life, for in one respect Jordan had surely been wrong.

Not all whores were the same.

Some, like Jordan, could come to terms with being a whore and some, like Cruickshank, never could.

It was a warm evening for March and the streets of Ronda were packed and humming with anticipation of the following day's *corrida*. In the bars and *bodegas* the men were talking loudly... talking, it appeared to Kate, at each other rather than with the give and take of conversation. Each appeared totally confident of his own judgment about the attributes of the matadors they would soon see.

They strolled down into El Mercadillo, the relatively modern part of town, up the popular traffic-less shopping street *Carrera de Vicente Espinel* and then left into the *Plaza del Socorro*. There the teenage *señoritas* were out in force, eyes flashing, dresses swirling as they walked in three's and four's round the colourful old square under the watchful eyes of some of the younger hombres, leaning on their motorbikes and trying to look *macho* with their Coca Colas, and the more world-weary eyes of the old men and women gossiping in its inner courtyard.

Sheedy led Kate through the crowds to a big three-storey building at the top of the *plaza*. "This is the Casino. Despite its name its not a gambling place. Casinos in Spain are gentlemen's clubs. Most *pueblos* have one, but this is bigger than most. Its where they held the court martials during the civil war. If you were found guilty you were taken straight to *El Tajo* and thrown into the depths below. It was an inexpensive form of execution. As you can see its a bit down at heel now. They've changed the name to the *Circulo de Artistas* and opened a bar that allows women, but to locals I guess it will always be known as the Casino."

Ignoring the sign *Privado* and nodding at the doorman who appeared to know him, Sheedy led her into a big covered courtyard, its roof made of glass, its fringes lined with old leather armchairs.

From the centre of the glass ceiling hung an impressive chandelier and on the wall was a giant clock.

He showed her the series of rooms adjoining, one with an immaculately-preserved snooker table, one for chess, the boards all set up and waiting for players, one for playing cards, its small square tables covered in green baize cloth, one a tiny library with newspapers and books and a notice saying *Silenco*.

Then he led her into a bar also full of men talking about bullfighting and betting with each other on the coming *corrida*, on which *matador* would win an ear, or two ears, or even the coveted honour of two ears and a tail.

In the far corner of the bar, smoking the biggest cigar Kate had ever seen, sat an enormous man in the green uniform of the *Guardia Civil*. He was not just rotund but tall, so that he towered over the low table and made the leather chair seem ridiculously small.

"Hey, *Señor* Bill," he cried, waving the cigar and pointing to two men sitting with him. "These two desperados will make space for you. I warned them they must." The two rose, nodded politely to Sheehy and Kate, and went to the bar.

"Miguel, this is *Señorita* Callaghan. Kate."

The giant Spaniard raised himself with some difficulty from the chair and bowed extravagantly, kissing her hand, and then calling for more wine.

Kate liked him immediately. His big round face was full of humour and mischief. There was about him an aura of good living and laughter. If the *Guardia Civil* had a tough, even sinister image, it had not been created by men like this one.

"And where is *El Conejero*?" Sheedy asked.

The policeman spread his hands in puzzlement.

"Who knows? I have not seen him. He has not come to town. It is strange. I have never known him miss a *corrida* before."

"Maybe he mistook the day."

"Impossible. He has no timepiece and no calendar but he can tell you the exact hour of any day. Don't ask me how, but he can. No, it is truly strange. But..." (and his face lit up at the thought)..."he may yet come. Lets hope so. He doesn't say much but I miss him. A good audience for my stories is hard to find." He roared with laughter. "And I miss my *conejo*, fresh from the valleys."

"And so," said Sheedy, settling himself into a chair and lifting his glass to the other, "do we have a good *corrida* ahead ?"

"I think so, Bill, I think so." He puffed on the cigar and almost disappeared in a cloud of smoke. "We have our own Ronda *matador* Pepe Luis Martin. He will want to be a success in front of his home crowd. I think it will be good. Pepe tells me he will be in his bar later. We will call in to toast his success."

The noise in the bar grew, and the smoke thickened, and eventually Sheedy persuaded Miguel to go with them to the Restaurante Pedro Romero opposite the bullring where he had booked a table. "For three, not four," he told the waiter.

The manager came running over. "*Señor* Miguel, where is *El Conejero*? We have no *conejo* left."

Miguel explained that he didn't know and, cheated of their rabbit, the three settled for a feast of *rabo de toro* preceded by *jamon serrano*, and accompanied by bottles of Rioja.

"This ham is good," Kate said, chewing with relish.

"I am told there is none better anywhere in the world," Miguel replied forking another slice for himself. "It comes from Huelva province to the south-west. It is the ham of the Iberian pig. You can always tell by watching the waiters slice it. If the ham has a black hoof and if the meat is dark pink it is probably an Iberian pig, not a factory pig but one that's been allowed to run wild for a year or two and been fed on acorns." He explained how the pigs were killed in winter and the hams were then packed in sea salt for at least two weeks to dry out the moisture. They were then cured for 18 months to two years. The cold winter caused the fat to break down and the meat to become firm. Then the hot summer played its part, causing the fat to melt into the meat so that the whole ham got its special taste. The curing process ended in a dry cellar or cave where the hams developed the mouldy coat they have when see hanging in the charcuterie."

"Well, I love it," said Kate.

"*Si, señorita*. It is good. But when you order ham ask if it is *pata negra* and if in doubt look for the black hoof."

Kate was enthralled by the conversation of the policeman who waved his hand at scores of bullfighting posters and pictures on the walls, for the restaurant was itself a virtual museum, and told stories of matadors and picadors and *corridas* and great Ronda occasions until full of food and wine they stumbled into the street at nearly midnight.

"Now we must go see Pepe Luis Martin," said Miguel, leading them out of the square and up a side-street to the Club Taurino, the bar owned by the *matador*. As they entered Kate noted the bulls heads on the wall, posters advertising Martin's 1988 appearances in Spain's great bullrings, Madrid in March, Cordoba in April, Seville in May, and Malaga in August. A notice board provided details of his recent results and on another piece of paper there were the signatures of *aficionados* who wanted to go in the club bus to see his fights.

Near the door was a big life-size colour picture of a good-looking, dark-haired young *matador* dressed in red and gold.

The bar was crowded but Miguel drove a path for them through the crowd towards a densely-packed corner. "Pepe?" he called loudly as he reached it.

"Hey, Miguel," Kate heard a voice call. "Make way *caballeros* for my friend Miguel."

The crowd parted and she saw a slim young man in red shirt and white jeans sitting in the corner surrounded by admirers. It was the *matador* in the picture.

"Pepe, this is my friend Bill Sheedy of whom I have talked. And this is *Señorita* Kate, his friend."

The young *matador* rose courteously and shook hands.

"We wish you well for tomorrow, *Señor* Martin," Sheedy said.

"*Gracias, Señor.*"

Kate looked keenly at the *matador*. What was it about his eyes that she found so disconcerting? Was it the lack of bravado? She had expected them to be bold, maybe even arrogant, but it was not so. Of all the men in the bar, Martin was the one entitled to an aura of *machismo*; yet of them all, he was the one who seemed to eschew it. Was it vulnerability she read there? She couldn't believe it was fear. No it wasn't exactly fear... more like caution. And loneliness. That was it. Surrounded as he was by fans, this man was lonely. Kate could guess why. Alone of the men in this crowded, noisy bar he would be in the arena tomorrow; alone he knew what it was like to face the bull. Not for him the unending debate about whether bullfighting was right or wrong, cruel or fair... only the knowledge that no matter how the dice were stacked in his favour, one mistake, one lapse of concentration, and he could be impaled on a horn propelled at him at speed by half a ton of fierce animal. She remembered the words Sheedy had recited in the bullring earlier:

> *Bones and flutes sound in his ears,*
> *at five in the afternoon.*
> *The bull now bellows near his brow,*
> *at five in the afternoon.*

How much exhilaration did the *matador* feel? How much apprehension?

The *matador* called for a bottle of wine for his guests, chatting for only a few minutes before excusing himself, saying he must get some sleep before the next day's fight. Miguel, Sheedy and Kate stayed on to finish the bottle and listen to the arguments all around them. When they left the streets were still full and Kate saw the two men were nowhere near to calling it a night. The journey, the love-making, the food and wine had, however, had its effect and she told the men to continue with their reveries while she would return to the hotel to sleep.

They walked round the backstreets to a smaller *plaza* dominated by an old church, Miguel stopping every few yards to speak to someone he knew, until they found the bar Los Zanos where they had made it their habit to end their evenings with the Rabbit Man before *corridas*. But he was not there. Over their fifth bottle of Rioja of the night, they talked on, joined frequently by other friends of Miguel's, until in the early hours Sheedy finalised arrangements for meeting the following day, said *buenas noches* and strolled a little unsteadily back to the hotel where he found the door between his room and Kate's left ajar.

She was asleep, her face picked out by the moonlight through the half-open window.

He quietly undressed in his own room and then, moving next door, slipped into bed beside her.

She half woke, turned and slipped into his arms. Her still unfamiliar touch was enough to cause him to harden. As she felt it she murmured something that sounded like "you´re a bull yourself Sheedy" and went back to sleep.

His heart full he, too, gratefully fell asleep beside her.

CHAPTER FOUR

Canning sounded the same as always when Cruickshank telephoned the following morning, cool, efficient, but slightly mocking.

Cruickshank was determined to demonstrate he was back in control, albeit a little discomforted by not knowing what Jordan had undoubtedly said to the younger American the previous night.

"Jason, I have no doubt Jordan has told you that he shares, or at least understands, my concern about the way matters have been handled recently, and that we have reached an accommodation that enables me to continue my involvement with the project."

"I'm pleased, Sir Brian."

There was no sarcasm in the voice but Cruickshank flushed with sudden fury at the other man's nerve.

Struggling to keep the anger from his voice, he said "I have a matter I wish you to deal with. The old man... I wish you to find him and if there is any difficulty recruit the assistance of the authorities. Do you understand what I am saying?"

There was a pause as Canning, appreciating Cruickshank's care over the telephone, read between the lines. Clearly they had to be seen to still be searching for the old man.

"Yes, Sir Brian. I will let it be known I am seeking him."

"I need hardly say that this matter must be handled with discretion."

"I understand. I share your concern."

I bet you do, Cruickshank thought to himself as he hung up without saying goodbye.

He summoned his secretary, one of a number of staff members called in to work this Saturday morning, and told her he intended to spend the weekend reviewing his full file of activities and delegating as much as possible. He then planned to spend three or four weeks in Spain in order to get the project moving. He asked her to arrange for him to have all the current files, fix a meeting for 12 noon with those departmental heads and project heads who were in the office, and call a board meeting for 9 a.m. on Monday. Also to arrange a flight to Gibraltar and arrange for the villa to be ready for his occupation. All communications equipment, fax, computers, telephones etc would need to be in good working order at both the yacht and the villa.

He watched her elegant figure leave the room and for a fleeting second felt an unfamiliar flicker of desire at the sight of long legs accentuated by a short, tight skirt. Then the phone rang and he became submerged in the business of the day.

They woke together and lay close for nearly an hour, hardly exchanging a word, each silently, happily adjusting to the fact that they were now lovers. And to confirm it they made love, this time slowly, warmly, almost lazily. Over coffee and rolls afterwards Sheedy outlined his plan for the day.

In the morning they would wander down to the foot of *El Tajo* and look up at the bridge and the gorge from below. Then they would stroll up to *La Ciudad*, the old town. Then, he suggested, they would have a relatively early lunch, rest ("likely story, Sheedy," she giggled) in the hotel for an hour or so, before meeting Miguel and hopefully the Rabbit Man for the *corrida*.

They spent the morning as planned in an increasingly crowded and excited Ronda, adding to their itinerary a market at the foot of the hill near the stone gates to the old town. There they strolled between baskets of tiny squeaking chickens, displays of colourful ceramics, piles of clothing, stalls of fruit and vegetables, racks of cheap electrical equipment, all part of a travelling "high street", Ronda today, some other town tomorrow.

They climbed back up the hill and stopped at a tapas bar for lunch. They were just tucking into some rabbit stew when an elderly man burst into the bar and cried *"Ha Tocado! Ha Tocado!"*

Immediately there was uproar. Others crowded round him, slapping his back. Drinks were ordered for everyone.

Kate was amazed. "What the hell is happening? What does *Ha Tocado* mean?"

"I have touched it," Sheedy replied. "Its their way of saying they've won some money on the lottery."

Almost shouting to be heard over the noise, he told her about the Spanish love of lotteries. The big one was the Christmas lottery. It was called *El Gordo*, the fat one. The tickets cost 25,000 pesetas each so most people purchased a share in one, usually a tenth, a decimo. But many people divided that into lots of smaller participaciones and sold them to friends. There was 50,000 milion pesetas in prize money with a fantastic top prize of 250 million pesetas. The draw took place on television over five hours and the whole of Spain tuned in. There had been some extraordinary wins, perhaps the most famous being in 1986 when the village of Herrera el Duque in poverty-stricken Extremadura won nearly 3,000,000,000 pesetas - about 25 million dollars. Nearly everyone in the village became a peseta millionaire after buying their share from the local bank manager. But there had been other remarkable wins. For instance, in 1977 the poor mountain hamlet of Criales hit the jackpot. Its ticket, purchased by a grocer and sold in shares, netted more than 450 million pesetas; that was four and a half million pesetas for every man, woman and child in the village.

Escaping the celebrations with some difficulty, they made their way back to the hotel for their *siesta* before, at just before five in the afternoon, they went down into the town and found Miguel surrounded by shouting aficionados outside the Plaza de Toros.

"Any sign of the Rabbit Man," called out Sheedy above the uproar.

"No, *Señor* Bill. He has not come. But you come, come now, we go inside. Ah, *señorita*, you have picked a good day for your first *corrida*."

The crowded old *plaza de toros* made a magnificent spectacle. Its carefully-swept sand was near-golden, the *barrera*, the fence round the arena, a newly-painted red and yellow. The colourful crowd were in tiers from ring level all the way up to the topmost cheaper seats were of every colour. Over the top of the brown tiled roof of the circular stand they could see the mountains to the east.

Into this arena to a fanfare from a small band came two gaily-dressed marshalls on horseback to receive the nod from
the President to allow the drama to begin. To a roar of applause the three matadors entered the ring side by side. Kate, finding the scene a photographer's dream, recognised Pepe Luis Martin as the one in the

middle. Behind them in a line came their aides. Miguel leaned over to explain. "Each *matador* has his *cuadrilla* of five. Those three walking behind Pepe are his *banderilleros*. You'll see them helping him in the ring, drawing the bull away if there's a problem, and eventually placing the *banderillas*. The two on horseback are the *picadores*. If the *matador* is the star and the *banderilleros* popular supporting actors, then the *picadores* are the villians of the piece. But you will see."

After doffing their hats to the President, the matadors retired to the narrow passageway behind the *barrera*. Then the first, Pepe Luis Martin, stepped into the ring, each of his three *banderilleros* positioned to help. The President waved his white handkerchief to a an old man who then leaned over from the front row and opened a heavy gate and waved his hat to attract the attention of the animal behind it.

For several seconds there was silence and then a gasp from the crowd as half a ton of bull came racing out at speed, its head down and its horns aimed straight at the slim figure of Martin, standing alone in the centre of the ring. Kate felt her throat go dry. But as the bull was almost upon the *matador* he made a pass with his cape, drawing the bull away from his body as if it were hypnotised, so that it ran harmlessly by.

The bull turned and charged, a huge, black, snorting tank of an animal hurling itself at the slim figure in front of him, but for a second time it was diverted by the leisurely swing of the cape.

Five times this was repeated and then Martin dramatically turned his back, leaving the bull seemingly rooted to the spot. The crowd roared appreciatively.

"Those passes are called *veronicas*," Miguel whispered. That last pass was a *media-veronica*. Its intended to force the bull to turn so suddenly that it stops it dead. Pepe has established his control of the bull."

Then after the sound of the bugles the gates opened and into the ring to hisses and boos came the *picadores*, big men (Kate thought ugly, but Miguel told her that all *picadores* looked ugly) on horseback carrying lances. "This is the *suerta de varas*," explained Miguel. "You may not like this." And Kate didn't. And neither did the crowd. Twice each *picador* jabbed the bull with his lance, drawing blood and weakening the animal. "Its a test of the bull's courage," said Miguel. "If it continues to attack it is a brave bull."

"Its cruel," said Kate. "Look how the crowd are booing. They think so too."

"Actually that's not so," said Sheedy. "They're booing because they think the picador is over-doing it and making it too easy for the *matador*."

The bugle sounded a second time and the *picadores* withdrew to a storm of hissing.

Then came the placing of the *banderillas*, with each of the *matador's* aides in turn standing on tip-toe and then running diagonally across the face of the bull to place the sticks with their sharp steel points in the muscle of the bull's neck. Each succeeded brilliantly and retired to cheers.

Finally, Martin faced the bull alone. Now he changed his colourful red and gold cape for a simple red one, the *muleta*, and, draping it across a sword, began a series of thrilling passes. One drew the crowd to its feet, as the *matador*, the *muleta* in his left hand, appeared to walk almost into the horns and then leaned away, confident he had so dominated the bull that it would follow the cape. "A *natural*," cried Miguel to Kate. "The classic pass."

Eventually it came time to kill and Martin, having won the approval of the President, and subdued the bull by what appeared to Kate to be a series of highly dangerous passes (in fact, Sheedy told her later, the bull was weary now and confused; the *matador* had him beaten), now stood directly in front of it and raising the sword to eye-level ran forward, leaned directly over the horns and plunged the sword in. For a moment the bull stood defiant. Then it toppled to the ground.

The crowd rose, cheering and waving white handkerchiefs, demanding the award of an ear, two ears, even a tail to the local hero. As the bull was dragged from the ring the President seemed unmoved but eventually he indicated the award of an ear. Now the *matador* with his *cuadrilla* walked slowly round the ring as people tossed in flowers, hats and cheered their local *matador* to the echo.

Kate sat back, exhausted by the experience. She had not liked the picadors, not liked the blood, not liked the killing. But it had been a magnificent, emotional spectacle and as the men around her removed their evil-smelling cheap cigars from their mouths and waved their cardboard sun-visors, their handkerchiefs, their arms at the President, and cheered the *matador* on his circuit of honour, she found herself abandoning her camera and standing and applauding him too.

The second fight was a bit of an anti-climax. The bull was pedestrian and the *matador* needed two attempts to kill it. The third went well for the *matador* except he chose to place his own *banderillas* and made a bit of a mess of it.

Martin came back to another roar. Kate felt sorry for the visiting matadors. They were clearly a supporting cast today. It was the local man the crowd was willing on. This time he confronted a big grey animal, more aggressive than the earlier one's and, thought Kate, Martin handled it with some care even after the *picadores* and *banderilleros* had done their work. The kill, too, was not as clean as the first and, despite the demands of the crowd, the President declined another ear. But it had been a good day for the local hero, two performances clearly to the liking of the crowd, the award of an ear, and he was alive and uninjured.

The day ended well, thanks to one of the visiting matadors who turned on a brilliant series of passes with the *muleta* and then killed cleanly.

The crowd poured from the arena, excited, talkative, satisfied, Kate amid them, emotionally drained by all she had seen.

"Well?" asked Sheedy.

"I don't know what I think. Except that I'm glad I saw it," she replied.

"And," she added, "I got some terrific pictures for the book."

It was about 8.30 and they went straight to a restaurant in the alley-way opposite the *plaza de toros* until Kate once more left Sheedy and Miguel sitting in the bar, not saying much now, exhausted, slightly drunk, but happy men. Miguel called for two glasses of Magno, the Spanish brandy. "Ah, Sheedy, our old friend missed a good one. But I tell you, I am worried. I have been a policeman many years, too long... I have, what do you call it, a... a..."

"Sixth sense ?"

"*Si.* A sixth sense. I think something is wrong."

"Well, maybe we can go and find out. I know roughly the part of the *serrania* he comes from, because he once told us, but do you know exactly where his *cortijo* is, and how to get there ?"

"I think so. I think we can get within two, maybe three hours walk

of it by taking a car to Atajate, but its a hard walk. Can you ride ?"
"Yes."
"Good. I have a friend who has a *finca* near Atajate. He could lend us horses. I tell you what Sheedy, we will go the day after tomorrow. I will come to your hotel at, say, eleven o'clock."
"You're on. Well, I"ll be getting to bed."
Miguel's eyes lit up. "Ah, *señor* Bill, if I had been you I would never have left it. The *señorita*. She is beautiful."
"Yes, Miguel, she's beautiful. And too young."
"No, *señor*. It is good for a man to have a young woman. Keeps him alive, keeps him full of... what do you call it?... vitality."
"But is it good for her, Miguel?"
"She may be young, but she is not a child, *señor*. Leave that for her to decide."
"Maybe you're right. See you in the morning." He gave the man a slap on the shoulder and left him calling for yet another Magno.

Cruickshank closed the door and, it now being late in the evening, went to his drinks cabinet. "A drink?"
"Thanks," said his guest. "Gin with ice."
"No tonic?"
"No thanks."
Cruickshank poured himself a whisky and walked across to the window. "Its been a long day. I've been clearing the decks for a month or so in Spain." He looked at the surrounding buildings, dimly lit on a Saturday night. " Have you seen my view?"
"Yes, once before. Its magnificent."
"Oh, yes, of course, I remember, at the time of the Middle East business."
Cruickshank had been involved in the financing of a complicated construction deal in the Middle East and, at a time when he was frequently travelling there, had been warned by the Foreign Office that he was on the kidnap list of an Arab terrorist group. He had turned Jim Miller to protect him.
"I gather from our brief telephone conversation that you're free?"
"Yes... or can be."
"I need someone. Loyal, discreet. You'll be with me or representing me down in Spain. It will pay well and you'll have no complaint

about the other conditions."

"Sounds good. What do you need?"

"A combination of fixer, bodyguard, and investigator."

"Bodyguard? In Spain?"

"I have a problem." He paused. "I need hardly say that this could not be more confidential."

"You know you can trust me."

"I do." He hesitated, then deciding that he had little choice, plunged on. "I've discovered that our biggest shareholder has been using the project to launder the profits of American crime. I don't know exactly who's involved but I suspect the worst. That need not in itself be a problem except that they seem particularly anxious to protect their money or get an early return on it. They've put a man in to watch their interests, ostensibly as an executive aide to me, but really he's their man. He's dangerous. In fact..."

Once more he hesitated. He had not wanted to share this secret with anyone.

"...in fact, he has already killed a man who got in the way."

Miller raised his eyebrows. "Not like you to get involved with people like that," he commented.

"Naturally it was my instinct to get out but its become too complicated and there's too much at stake for too many innocent people. I must try to save it if I can. But I need someone to watch my back, to watch this man Canning and to act as an early warning system for any further trouble."

His listener sat watching Cruickshank thoughtfully, turning his glass in his hands.

"How long would this be for ?"

"At least a year - maybe longer."

"The money?"

"£100,000. Plus keep."

Miler put down his glass." You're on."

"Good." Cruickshank handed him an envelope. "Here's some cash to help sort yourself our fast. Meet me at Gatwick on Monday morning; Miss Chambers can tell you the check-in time. In the meantime I want you to guard this envelope and on your way to the airport take it to my bank and hand it personally to the manager." He gave him another envelope containing the contract Jordan had signed.

Pleased and relieved the deal had been made, and noting the other man's glass was empty, Cruickshank suggested he help himself to another drink before he left.

Miller poured himself a second gin.

An enormous one.

Once more he drank it without tonic.

Cruickshank frowned. He hoped his newly-appointed 'minder' hadn't taken to drink since they were last together. He looked at him more closely. He did look thinner, pale, even a bit seedy. Should he have Miller himself checked out ?

But as quickly as the idea came to him he dismissed it.

It was late on a Saturday night and he was tired and in no mood to begin setting a watchdog on his own watchdog.

Anyway, the man was a professional... had always been reliable.

No, he had no cause to worry. He was in safe hands with Jim Miller.

Miguel had telephoned the Reina Victoria about 11 in the morning and suggested lunch in Sentenil, a town some 20 kilometres from Ronda. It proved a revelation. Unlike most *pueblos*, it was not built on the top of a hill or on a convenient mountain ledge, but in a ravine-like valley. Many of the homes were, in effect, caves, built into the sides of the valley so that only the white-washed facade and the door were visible.

They meandered down narrow streets sometimes completely over-shadowed by rock, Kate unable to resist peeping into the doorways and the darkness inside. She could see how cool these homes must be in mid-summer because already, in March, it was hot in the open but cool, even chilly in the shaded alleys and under the rock verandahs.

Over lunch she asked Miguel about the *Guardia Civil*.

There were, he said, four kinds of policemen in Spain. Generally speaking, all towns of more than 5,000 people, and some busy towns of less, employed their own *Policia Municipal* to enforce local laws.They were responsible for parking and traffic control and neighbourhood policing.

Larger towns, especially those of 20,000 or more, had been policed by representatives of two national forces, the uniformed *Policia Nacional* and the plain-clothes *Cuerpo Superior* but these were now combined into one.

For the majority of Spaniards, however, and especially in Andalucia, the *Guardia Civil* was the law. Recognisable by their green uniforms and ridiculous-looking black patent leather tricorns, the *Guardia Civil* had been established in the 1840's to control banditry. In those days they were usually the only enforcers of the law in rural areas and had special responsibility for guarding roads and frontiers.

In peacetime in the last century and the earlier part of this, they had devoted much of their energy to trying to control smuggling and to catch those who transported by mule, and even by dog, contraband whisky, cigarettes, coffee and even contraceptives, from the *costa* up into the *sierras*.

Because they traditionally sided with authority and were para-military in nature, being subject to military discipline, having military-type titles, and being entitled to military decorations, they came to be seen by many as more than just enforcers of the law, more a political force. Even in the late 19th century they were used to repress Anarchist uprisings and in the 20th, at least in Andalucia, tended to support the nationalist rebels in the Civil War whereas their own colleagues in the cities were more inclined to support the Republic.

In the past, and sometimes still, it had been a regular occurrence for *Guardia Civil* officers to mete out their own justice. Having caught a young thief they would beat him up in the cells and then send him off with a warning of much worse if he were to repeat the offence. Given what they heard about harsh treatment of those given prison sentences, local communities had at one time accepted this as a reasonable answer to the problem, but after the years of repression, and particularly when the policemen were no longer locals, it became less acceptable and their unpopularity meant they always travelled in pairs, were armed, and were never stationed in *pueblos* or towns where they were born or where their families lived.

These days, as memories of the past were dimmed and the *Guardia Civil* became more acceptable in their behaviour, they had in turn become more accepted. Some, like Miguel, no longer lived apart from communities, and even, as was the case with Miguel, became popular members of them... as Sheedy and Kate discovered that evening in Ronda as, in the company of the giant policeman, they meandered from bar to bar and drink to drink until they staggered to bed after midnight.

"I like him... I really like him," Kate said as they lay together in bed.

"Yes," said Sheedy. "One day I hope to get him to tell me more about his past. I have a feeling there's a terrific story there."

He chuckled to himself.

"What are you laughing about?" she asked.

"Well," he said, "I've not been able to draw him out after four bottles of *vino*. And that's my limit. My fear is that after about six bottles I'll finally get at the truth, but I'll be so drunk that the following morning I won't remember a word of it."

Jim Miller dreamt that his head had become a cement mixer. Far worse, he woke to discover that it had.

When he put his shaking hands to it, its surface was still. But with each turn of what felt like an inner cylinder there was an awful thump, the noise rebounding off the inside of his skull, as if an oozing mixture of sand, gravel, water and other muck that was once his brain was being thrown from side to side before sliding in a molten lump from the top of his head towards his throat.

Already a considerable quantity of liquid cement appeared to have run down into his mouth. There it had dried and hardened, turning his mouth into a dry, rough concrete cavity. His tongue had disappeared, presumably cemented into the roof.

Miller didn't know what was worse. The revolving ceiling he could see out of the funnel of his half-closed eyes, the painfully dry desert that was once his mouth and throat, or the terrible thumping of the mixer as it churned and turned within his head.

He rolled off the bed, falling painfully to his knees, and began to crawl, crab-like, towards the bathroom door. But it had gone. He turned round, still crawling, and began to move slowly in the opposite direction. There, to his relief, he saw the door. He must have previously been crawling towards the bare wall. Reaching his destination, still on hands and knees, he inched his way to the bath, turned on the cold tap, and put his head under it, turning it occasionally to pour cold water down his throat, hoping to be able to breath without the awful rasping pain.

After several minutes he progressed from firmly believing he was dying and headed for some kind of cement mixer's hell into feeling just plain bloody awful.

This he could handle.

This for Jim Miller had become the norm.

It hadn't, of course, always been so. A brilliant Special Branch officer who had moved into the more secret of the security services, he had met Cruickshank when he had been No 2 at the Northern Ireland office and Miller had been assigned to protect him.

The word in the 'business' was that Miller was destined for the top. In his mid-thirties at that time, Miller had a suitably unmemorable appearance for his self-effacing work - he was medium height, medium build, had medium-fair hair, and in even a small group of people he could, when he wished, go completely unnoticed. The wags in M15 used to say that his only party piece was an imitation of a piece of wallpaper. Within that medium-sized head there was, however, a considerable mind, a computer-like memory for detail, and remarkable powers of observation. Miller never forgot a fact or a face.

Few people knew what happened to Miller. Even those who did only knew the minimal details he would reveal. Or that his conscious mind would allow him to recall. Those details were that he had been sussed out by the IRA while on an undercover assignment in Belfast and captured. Only he, or his sub-conscious, knew what they did to him while they had him, but by the time he miraculously escaped his nerve was shot forever. Such courage and peace as he now found, he found in drink.

He was quickly and quietly pensioned out of the service and set himself up as a private security advisor, most of his clients also abandoning him because he had too much to drink at the crucial time.

He had taken to writing to those retired civil servants who had gone into industry. His letter had arrived on Cruickshank's desk just at the time of the Middle East affair. Cruickshank, who had felt safe with Miller in Belfast, had no reason to think the man had changed, nor did the Middle East experience give him any clue. In fact it proved one of Miller's few successes, partly because no-one actually made an attempt to kidnap or kill his employer, and partly because he couldn't get his hands on much drink in the Middle East and remained relatively sober.

Now, as he sat, his throbbing head in his hands, his elbows resting on the kitchen table, breathing in the steaming black coffee, he told himself he had to make a supreme attempt to conquer the problem. He reckoned he had hit the jackpot this time. The pay was at least £30,000 a year more than he would have asked for and, on this rainy March day in London, a year in Spain sounded like the answer to a prayer. He also doubted whether the work would be that exacting. He couldn't see why the Americans would want to make Cruickshank's life any more difficult. There was no profit in it. He could live well in the sun without facing any danger whatsoever. And without the danger, he believed, there would be no need for the drink.

Just the same he made a detour on his way to Gatwick to a small, basement shop in the backstreets of Camden Town. Its owner, who had taken what seemed an age to shuffle to the door, locked it behind them. Tiny, rotund and round-faced with big spectacles, and at least 70 years old, he peered bad-temperedly at his visitor. "Mr Miller, you know that I do not like to be disturbed so early in the day."

"I'm sorry, old friend. But I have a plane to catch."

The old man sniffed with irritation. "What is it you want?"

"A gun. But I want to pick it up in Spain. Do you have a contact there? Can you arrange it?"

"Spain... Spain..." The old man scratched his head. "What kind of gun?"

"Small. A small pistol. I want to be able to carry it in the inside pocket of a lightweight jacket."

"Wait a minute." The old man disappeared into a backroom. Miller looked anxiously at his watch. He was cutting it fine. The old man shuffled back. "Where can you be found in Spain?"

Miller handed him a card containing the phone number of the villa.

"I believe I can help. You will have to pay the supplier direct. I shall, of course, require a facility fee."

"I understand. I think you will find this adequate." He handed the man an envelope. "When can I expect a call?"

"It will take two or three days."

"Fair enough." And he was on his way.

In the City, Cruickshank had been chairing an edgy Board meeting. The news that Anglo Spanish Investors Ltd no longer owned the major shareholding in the Costa del Sol project had not been well-received by his fellow directors. They had, in any case, never shared Cruickshank's unqualified enthusiasm for the scheme, probably because it was he, not them, who stood to gain most personally. There could only be one Villa No 1 and one Presidency of the Community and they weren't candidates for either.

They wanted to know how, after investing so much of the company's own money in the scheme, Cruickshank could allow it to lose control. Cruickshank responded as positively as possible. The company had never had a majority shareholding, he reminded them - only the most shares. They had always known the opportunity was there for the Americans to seize control if they wanted to. The way he put it, it was almost as if he had planned the American buyout of the small shareholders. He stressed that he was still in charge and argued that if it were a success the Board's profits would be unaffected. "This is a vote of confidence in our idea. And if more money has to be invested it will fall to them to give a lead. What have we lost?"

Only one crusty, rather elderly non-executive director gave him real trouble. If Cruickshank didn't care, why had he gone to so much trouble to spread the ownership around? "I didn't say this is ideal," Cruickshank replied curtly. "I said it had its bright side and, as we have no option, its on the bright side we should look." He was tempted to add 'Look, if you think the shareholding's a problem, how do you feel about a landowner murdered in the company name and a syndicate hit man on its staff?'

Restraining himself, he instead began to report on a promising market survey about the project. Drawing on a reservoir of respect from the rest of the Board, he soon calmed the atmosphere. He had taken the precaution of putting the item on top of the agenda and adding several unrelated matters for decision, all of them to do with company ventures that were highly profitable. This both restricted the time for discussion of the Spanish project and ensured the meeting ended on a positive note.

From it he travelled by chauffeur-driven car to Victoria to catch a train to Gatwick where he met Miller as planned. The two flew to

Gibraltar and from there were driven to the yacht. Once there, he told the chauffeur to take his bags on to the villa and went directly to the study, calling for coffee and Canning.

This brief meeting was for Cruickshank a vital one. He was determined to show that the events of the past few days and in particular his unfortunate confrontation with Canning had not affected his confidence or his power. If Canning expected a cowed figure, he was in for a surprise.

He began by telling the American he wanted Green, the chauffeur, replaced and that he would himself do the choosing. "I appreciate that the crew and probably half our other employees are your handpicked men, Jason, but I cannot be bothered to remove them unless their specific behaviour warrants it. However, I will not be driven around by a man whose loyalty I cannot trust."

Canning nodded unenthusiastically.

Cruickshank then gestured towards Miller. "This is Mr Miller. He will be working directly to me as an aide and it should be understood by all the crew and the company staff that when he speaks he speaks for me."

Canning looked at the Englishman closely, his eyes narrowing. "Perhaps you could define more clearly Mr Miller's duties, Sir Brian."

Cruickshank had already decided to be open about Miller's role. Why pretend? And it would signal to both Jordan and Canning that he meant to call the shots from now on. "To counter balance you, Jason. I make no pretence of any other role. I have no doubt you are efficient but you are no friend of mine and you can hardly expect me to operate in an atmosphere of distrust."

"But I understood my role..."

"Your role will remain the same. I don't deny your competence. You will continue to handle business affairs and to report direct to me. But yours will be a company role. You will be my executive aide; Mr Miller's support will be personal."

Canning, unhappy, looked as if he were about to protest, but, noting the determination on Cruickshank's face, stopped himself and merely nodded compliance as the Englishman continued. "One final point Jason before we proceed to business. And, once made, we can get on without further reference to the past. I want you to understand that I am running this project and will brook no insubordination or countermanding of instructions. In particular I will tolerate no act of criminality of any sort... not even a parking ticket.. From now on this project will be developed impeccably. "

Canning, inwardly furious at being lectured in front of the new man Miller, had never-the-less got his feelings well under control. Cruickshank's reference to his instructions from Jordan was an unintentional reminder of what he had been told from New York; that the project needed Cruickshank and Canning was expected to keep him happy. So he lamely replied "Of course, Sir Brian. Mr Jordan has explained the arrangement and it is one that I am happy to be part of."

Cruickshank bit his lip, equally angered by what he interpreted as the other's damnable cool, and then said "Very well, lets get to business. What has happened over the past two days?"

"Not a lot. Its been a bullfight week in Ronda and I felt it was best to get that over before I went up there. In the meantime I've had to get our lawyers looking into the procedure if the old man can't be found. I hope there will be a report on your desk in the morning. We can then decide exactly and at what pace to proceed."

Cruickshank, refusing to use the chauffeur even once more, asked Miller to drive him to the villa.

The two Englishmen climbed into the Rolls and on reaching the main road turned west. Instead of turning off to the villa, however, Cruickshank asked Miller to continue. "I want to have a look at the site."

They drove past the turn-off to Benahavis and a few kilometres further, then, turning north, made their way up into the foothills on an increasingly rough road until Cruickshank indicated a dusty track between some olive trees. After 150 yards it came to an end and they parked the car and climbed between the trees until suddenly they were out in the open on the brow of a hill.

For a moment they stood in silence. Miller had turned down all offers of drink on the plane and damn-near drowned himself in black coffee. He was now desperately wishing he had sun glasses to counter the glare and dull the pounding in his ill-treated head, but he could still marvel at the view of the surrounding hills and valleys and of the coast.

Cruickshank was also feeling once more the thrill of pride he always got when he came to this place. "We own almost all that you see, Jim. There will be a series of small *pueblo* villages on the side of each of those three hills, a five star, membership-only hotel over there, a golf course in that valley to the east, and over there to the right, on the valley floor, a world class racecourse."

"A racecourse?"

Cruickshank explained. All the horses would come in from England, Ireland and France especially for the meetings. There would be three meetings a year, timed to help trainers to tune up their horses at appropriate times of the season. And the prize money would be such that it should attract the best. There would be special regulations to allow it and the company would split the take with the state, 50-50. The income would alone repay in only five years much of the money invested.

Sprinkled throughout the valleys there would be swimming pools built like small lakes, each with its own bars and restaurants, tennis courts, and a variety of other facilities.

It would be highly exclusive, literally out of bounds to anyone who needed to even look at the prices.

Miller was stunned. "How have you managed to pull all this off."

"Its taken some time, because we did much of the buying up of the land in small parcels before we even began to talk about our plans.

"As for the authorities, we've been more than generous in the arrangements we have made, both in terms of the public purse and guarantees of special memberships etc for those who matter."

"Incredible."

"Yes, I'm rather proud of it... Jim, would you mind waiting at the car for a few minutes."

Cruickshank watched the other descend and then made his way down a winding dirt path and up to the brow of another small hill nearby.

This was to be the site of Villa No 1, his villa, the home of the President of the Community.

For a short time he stood where it would be and as he did so, as he took in once more the beauty of the area, the views of the mountains and the sea, even of the Rock of Gibraltar in the distance, and as he was reminded of the size of the project, he felt the problems of the past few days begin to dwindle in proportion to the prize within his grasp.

This was too grand a project to be destroyed by the behaviour of Canning.

If there had been a way to rescue the old man he would, of course, have done so. But he couldn't. He couldn't save him and he couldn't bring him back.

What he could do was guarantee there was no repeat of this criminality.

He had been right to continue.

As had always been the case when he came to this place, he returned to his car in buoyant mood.

If he had been forced to tell the truth, he would have had to admit that his buoyancy, at least at this moment, was tinged with relief... relief that the problem of the old man had been solved.

Fortunately he was not forced to tell the truth, least of all to himself.

Sheedy had left Kate asleep in bed that morning and after a cup of coffee walked to meet Miguel who had commandeered a small green *Guardia Civil* car for the day. Sheedy hid a smile as the big man squeezed himself into the driver's seat, his gigantic thighs getting in the way of the gear lever. They drove over *El Tajo* and down into the old town and at the gate to Ronda turned onto the Gaucin road, the C341, heading west but mainly south until they reached the town of Atajate, a small white *pueblo* dominated by a big whitewashed church built on a hill above the main thoroughfare.

Miguel continued to the far end of the town and parked outside a bar-restaurante, roomy, modern, clean with a polished wooden bar. They ordered coffees and afterwards

Sheedy wandered up the main street and climbed the steps to the big wooden door of the church, but it was closed. He was watched with ill-disguised curiosity by three old men, one with a shepherds crook, sitting in the shade on the street corner opposite.

He returned to the car and they drove half a kilometre beyond Atajate before turning down a dirt track to an old, flower-covered *cortijo* surrounded by a field containing a number of grazing horses. There after the usual Miguel performance of hugs and slaps on the back and shouted greetings they picked up two horses and a string of directions from the owner who, Miguel explained, knew the Rabbit Man and had been to his *cortijo*.

"He says that he last saw *El Conejero* seven or eight days back, on his way into the hills. He has been expecting him. He usually comes at least this far once a week to sell some rabbits and pick up some supplies, and he always comes past on his way to the *corrida*."

They left the town and the road behind and rode east, initially shaded by trees until they climbed beyond them, negotiating barely discernable paths over the hills and down into small valleys, sometimes riding across hard rock, sometimes through shrub-land. Sheedy felt the sweat pouring in rivers down his neck and back, turning his shirt into a wet rag clinging to skin already irritated by insect bites. His jeans were sticking to him uncomfortably and his backside, not accustomed to the exercise, was beginning to feel raw. His throat was dry and his eyes aching were from the glare.

Just when he was about to suggest a rest to the well-padded Miguel, who despite his weight seemed unaffected by what was to Sheedy an ordeal, they came to the brow of the hill and he found himself looking down into a beautiful, wild valley, one that he would never have guessed was there. Running across its centre there was a ravine, a crude gash in the valley floor, as if a giant had taken a jagged knife and cut a slice out of the ground. On the other side was a white stone building, surrounded by what appeared to be orange and lemon trees.

"*Bueno,*" cried Miguel. "That's it, I'm sure that's it."

They encouraged their horses down the hill, round the end of the ravine, and across the grass and small flowers of the valley until they reached the *cortijo*. Dismounting, Miguel called out "*Hola...* are you there? *Señor Conejo?*"

There was no answer.

The policeman walked over and pulled aside the piece of heavy cloth across the door and he and Sheedy went inside. Miguel looked around with expert eyes. "*Si.* Its his place, *Señor* Bill. That's one of his guns. And look at the rabbit skins. But he's not been here for a few days, maybe for a couple of weeks. Look at the dust, and this bread..." he picked up a half-eaten loaf - "its hard as a rock." He shook his head. "It doesn't make sense. He left Ronda for this place nearly a week back."

"Could he have had an accident on the way?"

"Maybe, but I doubt it. I think we would have seen him or the

85

mule. We came the way my friend described, the way the old man always came."

Sheedy looked at a pile of papers on the table. "I wonder why he gathered all these together... what he was looking for."

"What are they?"

"Receipts. One or two brief notes. A couple of old newspaper pictures of bullfights. And some photographs. That's all."

The two went out into the fresh air and sat down under a lemon tree to drink from a leather *bota* of *vino* that Miguel had slung across his back before leaving the village.

"What do you really know about him, Miguel?"

The policeman sat silent, looking into the distance. Eventually he said "Not much. You know how little he said, *Señor* Bill."

"But you must have picked up a few things."

"He was a simple man. He killed rabbits and he cooked some for himself and he sold the rest, he drank *vino* until he fell asleep, and he loved the *corrida*, the *toros*."

"Did you never learn his real name ?"

"*Si*. It was Pepe... Pepe Rodriguez. That was it, Pepe Rodriguez."

"Who were his other friends ?"

"He was a loner. He knew many people, sold them his rabbits, bartered goods with them, slept on their floors, but who really knew him? I think, no-one."

"Did people talk about him, wonder who he really was?"

"There was talk, but I took no notice. I think he was a peasant of this hard land. He trusted his valleys and mountains and his mule more than he trusted people. People gave him nothing. The valleys and mountains gave him his living, the mule was his faithful servant."

Sheedy sat quietly for a minute. The perceptive American sensed that the Spaniard had chosen his words with unusual care. There was a story in this that Miguel was not telling. But he had no wish to press it. He had no doubt the policeman had his reasons for being discreet.

"You told me earlier he had a brother. Do you think he could have gone to see him - in Casares?"

"At the time of the Spring *corrida*? Miss the *corrida*? If there was passion in the man, *Señor*, it was a passion for this. He loved that *plaza de toros* and he loved the *corrida*. Loved it, he told me, from childhood. Go away at such a time? Impossible!"

"Unless he got a message that his brother was sick, or in some trouble."

Miguel touched his chin thoughtfully. "*Si*, Bill, that could be the answer."

For a while they sat quietly in the sun, Sheedy not in any hurry to climb back on the horse and begin the painful journey back. He looked across the valley and revelled in the peace of the place.

But the more he looked across it the more he felt that something was wrong, something was not as it should be.

He looked slowly from left to right, the whole length of the valley, but he could not see anything to justify the feeling.

And yet it persisted.

"Miguel, this is probably crazy, but the more I look out from here, the more I feel I'm seeing something that doesn't make sense, that's out of place. And yet I don't know what it is."

The policeman stood up and for a long time looked, as Sheedy had done, from left to right. "I can see nothing, Bill."

"Maybe not."

Eventually they climbed on the horses and began their journey back. At the top of the hill they stopped and looked down on the lonely *cortijo* and across the peaceful valley. Then they turned west and headed slowly back to the village, the car, and eventually, driving north and slightly east, to Ronda.

Cruickshank's villa was built a few feet above and beyond the narrow, stony beach. Surrounded by a security fence and guarded day and night, it enabled he and his guests to swim either in the sea at its front or in a swimming pool at the rear, the latter set in semi-tropical gardens.

The villa itself was built on two levels. The interior rooms were all large - Cruickshank liked space - and furnished in Spanish style and in the best of taste. His master bedroom suite was on the top, with its own balcony, and it was to this he went on arrival, to shower and change into a navy-blue silk dressing gown. Having done so he settled into a soft chair on the balcony with the usual cigar and Scotch.

Even in Spain he engaged in the ritual of his "special hour".

He was much happier than he had been at any time since Canning's call about the murder. That had been unfortunate but there wouldn't be a repeat. The Board meeting had gone well, and so had his meeting with Jordan. And he had enjoyed humiliating Canning that afternoon. If the young American had expected to be calling the shots he could forget it. Cruickshank was back in command and going to keep it that way.

Somewhere nearby someone was grilling sardines on the beach. It smelt delicious. Cruickshank began to look forward to dinner. He had just picked up a pair of powerful binoculars to watch a yacht pass by on its way to take shelter in Puerto Banus for the night when his attention was caught by a sound from the beach. He swivelled round, catching his breath as the binoculars focussed on a horse and rider picking their way along the narrow path between the villa and the beach.

She was sensationally beautiful, with the long, black hair of a classic Spanish *señorita*, and under her pink blouse firm-looking breasts bounced without the aid of a bra. Using his binoculars, Cruickshank, unusually but unashamedly a voyeur on the girl's solitary ride, could actually see her dark nipples protruding under the thin blouse.

Silhouetted against the silver sea and still-blue sky on a black horse, she looked like an oil painting.

His binoculars gripped so tightly that his knuckles turned white, he watched her until she was out of sight and then slumped back in his chair, Scotch in hand, stunned by the effect she had had on him.

Women had never played a big part in his life. His first experiences of sex had, in fact, been at boarding school, not with a girl but with a member of the school cricket eleven. Cruickshank had idolised him. Being allowed into his bed at night had been, as he saw it at the time, an honour. Unfortunately, they were discovered one night, Cruickshank a small naked bundle at the foot of the bed with his head between the other's legs. The older boy was expelled, the school losing a useful number 4 batsman, and Cruickshank was so savagely beaten that he had been sexually repressed ever since.

He had married a colleague in the civil service as much for convenience as love. He had been working closely with her for a couple of years and, while she was not a beautiful woman, he found her both attractive and companionable. And marriage made sense.

Their wedding took place at Caxton Hall one lunch-hour. As he rose in the civil service she got left behind and, instead of rejoicing in his success, became sour about it. When he was working late or out of the country she drank heavily. He was welcomed home with bitter remarks and a denial of any of the usual comforts. All this was reflected in a decline in her looks. He began to be embarrassed by her, then ashamed of her. To be fair he tried to talk it out, to persuade her to ride his success with him, not to resent it. He was not proud of it but told himself that in ending their marriage he was freeing her, too, from an intolerable prison for both of them.

Since then he had from time to time called on a woman in Maida Vale who discreetly and with considerable dexterity met his physical needs.

He was, however, a fit 53 year old, and, liberated from his London persona and enlivened by the free and easy atmosphere on the *costa*, had more than once been attracted by a young woman, without having the time or the nerve to act upon it. He had hoped, however, that he would one day meet a suitable woman to share with him his villa in the sun. Without consciously thinking about it, Cruickshank, this repressed romantic, was ready, for the first time in 35 years, the first time since school, to fall in love.

Of course he had not actually fallen in love with the girl on the horse. He didn't know her.

But he had been mightily attracted by her.

Attracted enough to slip on a pair of white trousers and a tee shirt and, taking the binoculars, walk quickly downstairs and out into the front garden to the beach. He was just in time to see her turning off up a track just beyond the last of the villas before the open stretch of sand and stones that led eventually to San Pedro beach. He realised she was going to the stables nearby, from where you could rent a pony, but he suspected her horse was too good for that, was probably looked after by the stable especially for her.

He began to make a mental note to make enquiries and then, thinking that he was acting like a teenager, chuckled to himself and, feeling suddenly light-headed, went back into the villa to dress for dinner.

Sheedy woke from his *siesta* and sat up so abruptly that he accidentally struck Kate with his arm.

"What's the matter, Bill?" she asked sleepily, rubbing her head.

"I've got it. How extraordinary - it came to me in my sleep. It was the track."

"Track? What track?"

"At the old man's *cortijo*. I knew there was something out of place and I couldn't figure what it was. It was the track... there was a track, probably made by the mule, running from the *cortijo* to the ravine."

"So ?"

"So there wasn't a bridge. Why would a track lead straight to a ravine and stop ?"

"I don't know. Why would it ?"

"I don't know either. Unless there was a bridge there. But there wasn't one when we were there."

"How old was the track ?"

"I don't know that either, but it didn't look that old. Look, maybe the old man had made some kind of bridge and it collapsed under the weight of him and the mule."

He sat for a moment, thinking. Then... "I'm going to go back."

Kate groaned. "Holy shit, Bill, aren't you making a bit much of this. The old man could be anywhere. He's probably killed all the rabbits where he lives and moved on."

He leaned over her, drawing back the sheet to uncover her breasts and gently running his fingers over them. "I know.

I'm sorry. But it won't take much time. You come too. We'll borrow the horses and you can have a ride. The scenery's terrific. Worth the trip for that alone."

She groaned. "Oh God, its the old obsessive Sheedy. Why did I ever get involved?"

"Because you like this," he said, running his fingers slowly down her front and between her legs and planting little kisses on her neck.

"Well... seeming as you're here," she giggled, drawing him down.

It was some time before they surfaced, their intimacy shining from their faces, but when they met Miguel at the Casino Club for what was intended to be their last night together, Sheedy was once more the hunter. "I just can't go back to the *costa* without looking down that ravine, Miguel."

The big policeman was for once silent, looking down into his glass. "It was careless of me not to look today, *Señor* Bill.

I will come with you." Then he added, "but if he is not there, and

I waste a day, you will pay for all the *vino* tomorrow night."

"Its a deal."

Cruickshank had asked his Spanish staff to arrange a small dinner party, just a local banker, a legal advisor, and the architect who would design the project's *pueblo* villages. They were to be accompanied by their wives and, in the case of the architect, also by a friend from Seville who was staying for the summer.

Rejoicing in the warmth of the evening, he told Hobbs he wished to dine al fresco, and awaited his guests in the garden.

The banker and lawyer and their wives came together and were drinking a vintage Jerez sherry when Cruickshank's other guests arrived. Julio, the architect, flamboyant as ever, greeted the Englishman with an extravagant embrace but Cruickshank, who would usually have reacted with distaste to the lack of reserve, hardly acknowledged either Julio or his wife Isabella, so astonished was he by their companion.

It was the girl on the horse, now wearing a short white dress. The architect introduced her as their family friend, Maria Garcia from Seville.

Cruickshank bowed with all the old-world courtesy he could muster considering that, uncharacteristically, he felt like abandoning all restraint, ordering the others to leave, and keeping only the girl for himself.

"*Señorita*, it is an honour," he said, looking deep into her dark-brown eyes.

"And for me, *Señor*," she replied, her voice as soft as the breeze in the palm trees swaying above their heads.

For what seemed an age he stood, captive to her eyes, while his other guests looked on. Had the butler Hobbs not come forward with a tray of drinks the evening could have stopped there, as if in a time warp. After the drinks were served, Cruickshank drew Hobbs aside. "The young lady - see she is sitting on my left. Change the table plan accordingly."

The girl had settled herself in a deck chair, her long legs crossed, her brief white dress halfway up her bronze thighs. If she was aware of Cruickshank's fascination with her, she gave no sign. With a huge effort, he pulled himself together and concentrated on his older guests, turning on the Cruickshank charm, deploying his gift for giving each in turn just enough of his full attention to make them feel they were particularly special to him that evening. But for him dinner could not come too soon, for then he had her beside him, and could for the first time talk to her directly.

"What do you do with yourself in Seville, *Señorita*?"

She answered him shyly. "I manage a boutique, *Señor*. It is owned by my guardian."

"Guardian?"

Julio, the architect, sitting on Cruickshank's right, joined in. "Not just an ordinary shop. Maria has had the good fortune to become a member of one of Saville's best-known families. For three generations they have been famous for raising fighting bulls and horses, and, contrastingly, for their trade in antiques, but the present head of the family has expanded into fashion, top quality clothes and jewellery. He was a close friend of mine at university. We have kept in touch."

"For how long are you visiting the Costa del Sol?" Cruickshank asked her.

"For some weeks, *Señor*."

"That is our good fortune." He smiled into her eyes and was rewarded by a shy lowering of the eyelids that made him want to laugh out loud with delight.

"Julio," he said. "You must bring Maria out on the yacht. I was planning to spend the weekend at sea. Will you come?"

The architect, for whom the project was an unprecedented opportunity and to whom Cruickshank was a client to be treasured, could not have been more pleased. "We would be delighted, Sir Brian, delighted." He beamed up the table at his wife, while Cruickshank smiled, idiotically he felt, at Maria. Then, afraid he was in danger of disconcerting the girl with excessive attention, he dragged his eyes from her and encouraged the conversation to become more general.

Later as he saw his guests to the gate he walked at her side once more. "Thank you for coming, Maria," he said. "You have made the evening a specially enchanting one. I look forward to seeing you at the weekend."

"It has been an honour, *Señor*," she said.

"An honour?" he replied, speaking quietly so that only she could hear. "I hope not. I hope you will come to feel that time spent in my company can be fun."

Suddenly she lifted her head, tossed back her hair, and looked straight into his eyes. He lost a breath and almost choked at her beauty in the moonlight. "I like men of honour, *Señor*," she said. And was gone.

That night he lay in his bed, the words "I like men of honour" going round in his head.

He fell into an uneasy sleep and in it saw an old peasant on a donkey falling, falling, down an endless pit.

Then the girl was there on her horse, falling too. They were both falling silently until she looked up and called to him... to him, standing at the top... "but I like men of honour."

Then she was naked and Canning was there and he was naked too and they were coupling even as they fell.

Canning was laughing, laughing at him, they were both laughing at him, and then there was only Jordan, limping towards him, Jordan standing looking down into the pit, Jordan telling him not to worry, that a whore, too, could have honour.

That night and with that nightmare he suffered the first of the many deaths he would suffer alone in his bed at night.

The first of the 10,000 deaths.

They looked down at him, all three of them, Sheedy, Kate and Miguel, standing in silence, side by side on the rim of the ravine.

Only his head was visible, his body covered partly by the dead mule and partly by the wooden slabs that were once a bridge.

Kate moved away first, distressed, but also sensitive to the deeper feelings of the two who had been his friend.

"Should we leave him, *Señor* Bill?"asked Miguel after a while. "Should we leave him in peace in his valley ?"

"I don't know." Sheedy turned away and, with the policeman following, walked slowly back to their horses to collect the leather *bota* of *vino*. Calling to Kate, they sat together on the grass, each thinking their own thoughts.

Sheedy looked sympathetically at the Spaniard, suddenly older and greyer, all the humour gone from his face. "I'm sorry, Miguel, I know you had a special friendship."

"*Si*, Bill. He didn't say much but I was used to his company. We drank a lot of *vino* together, saw a lot of *corridas* together... even argued over your hero Lorca together."

"I guess his bridge just fell apart."

"*Si*, ... his bridge and his world."

"I don't think we should leave him down there, Miguel. I think he should be buried. We'll have to get help and some ropes. If we go back to the village now we could arrange to collect him tomorrow."

Miguel nodded forlornly. "*Si*."

They stood up and Sheedy walked up to the big man. " Miguel, you and I will stay friends. We'll keep his memory alive. We'll remember him as we eat our *conejo* and when we meet for the *corridas*."

"*Si señor*."

Sheedy opened his arms and they hugged each other.

Kate, watching, marvelled at the friendships Sheedy struck up with the most unlikely people, and loved him for his compassion.

Urging their horses over the rough ground, they rode as fast as was possible back to the village and Miguel arranged for a local policeman and two or three farm workers to accompany them the following day. Then they drove back to Ronda from where, Miguel said, he would also find a doctor to go with them to the ravine.

Tired from the journey and aware they had to repeat it the following day, Sheedy and Kate went early to bed, lying awake in each other's arms for an hour or two, saying little, growing closer in their shared experience.

Miguel spent the evening in his customary corner of the Casino Club, drinking brandy and becoming increasingly morose.

The last to leave, courteously removed by the manager, he could be seen in the early hours, his uniform awry, standing in front of the *plaza de toros*, a half-drunk *botella* in his hand, tears rolling down his face.

Turning away he crossed the road to the pavement outside the Restaurante Pedro Romero.

On the window there was a small notice. "*No conejo today*."

He stood looking at it for several minutes, then said softly. "It will do for your gravestone, old friend...

"...it will say '*Pepe is dead - no conejo today*'."

Nobody knows you. No. But I will sing of you.
Sing of your profile and your grace for a later time.

CHAPTER FIVE

It was a classic Costa del Sol day, albeit more like July than March. The sun was blazing from a cloudless sky and all the way down the *costa*, from Torremolinos to Benalmadena to Fuengirola to Marbella to San Pedro to Estepona, the invading army descended upon undefended beaches. They came slowly plodding in ill-fitting flip-flops or hopping insanely in bare feet on hot sand... ungainly Englanders, olive-skinned French, fair-haired Germans, loners and lovers and families with squealing children, sun-bathers and swimmers, water-skiers and wind-surfers. They came with beach bags, beach balls, beach mats and beach umbrellas, with sun lotion and sun glasses, with paperbacks and Walkmans.

And on the beach near Puerto Banus they looked out to sea, envying Sir Brian Cruickshank's magnificent yacht, the sun causing its blue, green and white waves to sparkle as it sailed south from the port towards the African coast.

Reclining in a deckchair by the pool on the top deck, a glass of chilled champagne in his hand, Cruickshank had at last been able to forget the trials and tribulations of the past week and concentrate on the beauty of the young woman from Seville.

She was wearing a pink bikini. He remembered the pink blouse she wore when he first saw her. It was obviously her favourite colour. He asked Hobbs to collect any pink flowers he could find in the vases scattered about the lounges and bedrooms and make up a bouquet to put beside her bed.

He was surprised that, while shy in conversation, she was physically uninhibited. The bikini was revealing and she had joined in the pool games enthusiastically.

When sitting reading, her hair was pushed back and this, together with her dark sun glasses, made her look both sophisticated and older than what he had guessed were her 25 years.

Cruickshank himself was wearing white trousers and a blue sleeveless shirt, too sensitive about his pale skin and thin legs to sunbathe in her presence. This was in contrast to Julio, whose small red bathing costume enabled him to show off what Cruickshank disapprovingly, if irrationally, thought was an unnaturally muscular body for a middle-aged architect. Once he imagined he caught Maria secretly smiling at his own comparatively conservative appearance and he decided to engage in some private sunbathing at the villa at the earliest opportunity.

On the whole, though, it was going well. She was the only unaccompanied woman on the trip so it had been natural for Cruickshank to place her near him at lunch, and his attentive waiting on her needs and sensitive drawing out of her opinions had won, he dared to believe, at least one warm, grateful smile before they retired to their cabins for a *siesta* and shade from the full heat of the sun.

Now it was late afternoon but still hot, and he had come up on deck to find her alone in the pool. He sat watching until she swam to the edge, right by his chair, and looked up. "You are a fortunate man, *Señor*, to have such a beautiful yacht, to live such a good life."

"Yes," he said, feelingly unusually tongue-tied as he looked down into her face and struggled to keep his eyes from straying further.

"But you have no-one to share it with? No wife?"

"No."

"You have never been married?"

"I was once."

She rested her forehead on the side of the pool, her eyes closed, as if considering what he had said, so he took the chance to switch the focus to her.

"And, you, Maria, do you have plans to marry?"

"Of course."

"Oh." He must have sounded disappointed because she looked up and smiled at him, and then said, shyly, "but I have not yet found the man."

"Oh." He sounded happier this time. Then, aware of being alone with her for the first time, warmed by the sun, the champagne and her smiling face from the pool, he went a small way further than he had intended. "Maria, may I tell you that... that your company on the yacht makes me feel immensely happy."

Once more she dropped her forehead to the pool's edge, then she looked up, her brown eyes serious . "I am pleased that you are happy, *Señor*." With that she pushed herself backwards and, as she drifted away, called "It is always good to be happy."

The moment of intimacy was broken by the arrival of Julio, fresh from his *siesta*, full of energy for the pool, his pleasure at being a guest on the yacht making him even more flamboyant than usual. He took two or three steps and leapt in, landing beside Maria with a huge splash. She laughed with child-like abandon and, as he surfaced, put her hands on his head and pushed him back under until he came up spluttering and gasping for breath.

Cruickshank joined in their laughter, grateful for the diversion.

He needed time to think, to regroup after his untypical loss of restraint.

Was there hope in her reaction? Had she appreciated the passion, the yearning that lay behind his words? Or had she put it down to gentlemanly courtesy?

He didn't know, but he was not discontented with the encounter. No harm had been done, and just possibly a first careful step had been taken.

But just by him? Or had her questions, her share of the conversation been a small sign of her interest too?

Apart from the crew, there were nine people on the yacht, Cruickshank, Miller, Maria, Julio and his wife, and two English directors of the Anglo-Spanish Investors who were on a few days holiday with their wives. That evening they all had dinner in the superb oak-panelled dining room, the movable wall panels taken away so that they could look out to the sea and stars. Cruickshank was at his best, hospitable, witty, almost light-headed in his relief at recapturing his confidence after the near-disaster of the past week and in his delight at the presence of Maria, who looked dazzling in a long white dress with a dark brown pendant highlighting the colour of her eyes.

The Englishman had made a calculated decision to put Maria at the other end of the table.

If he had too recklessly exposed his feelings that afternoon, this would help her relax, allay her fears that he was coming on too strong too soon.

If, on the other hand, she had welcomed his words, then it would do no harm to show he was a man in control of himself, to assert his strength of character by his ability to relax with his other guests even while in her dazzling presence.

Also he was in no doubt that Julio and his wife had observed his inability to take his eyes of the girl; this would, at least for a few hours, calm their suspicions. Not that he was too worried about Julio's reactions. The architect was ambitious. If he thought that by introducing Cruickshank to Maria he would be held in higher esteem he would not get in the way of any friendship that developed. Isabella could, however, be a different matter. While the architect would not give their comparative ages a thought, his wife probably would. She clearly felt responsibility to their friends in Seville to watch over the girl and had, thought Cruickshank, been quick to join them when he and Maria had found themselves alone or at a small distance from the others. He went out of his way to be particularly charming to her over dinner and hoped that this, together with Julio's influence, would at least neutralise her.

After dinner the party adjourned to the yacht's small cinema to watch a new film specially flown in from America. Cruickshank waited until it had begun and slipped out, preferring to take a quiet walk on the deck and smoke a cigar.

The yacht, he thought, must be almost halfway between Morocco and the Costa del Sol, a few miles from Gibraltar, for he could clearly see the lights of both the African and Spanish coasts and, ahead, the concentration of lights at the foot of the giant shadow that was the Rock.

He hoped that at night he would be able to see the lights of Africa from his villa overlooking the project.

The project.

Why did they keep calling it that?

It was time to give it a name.

He was disturbed by a sound behind him. He turned to see Maria, stunningly beautiful in her white dress in the semi-darkness. She came over and they stood beside each other, looking out at the lights in the distance. Neither spoke, and the longer their silence, the more meaningful Cruickshank felt it becoming. And the harder to break.

In the end, with superhuman control, he chose to perpetuate the slight distance he had created over dinner and, resisting a nearly overwhelming desire to turn and try to take her into his arms, he said in a detached, conversational way "That must be Sotogrande over there? Have you been there?"

"No, but I have heard it is a big resort."

"Maria," he said, "it will not compare with the project we are building. Not be in the same class."

"What will your project be called, *Señor*."

"Brian."

"You will call it Brian?"

He laughed. "No. No, that is my name. I was asking you to call me Brian."

"But is it not Sir Brian."

He turned and looked at her and then, drawn in by her eyes, her watchful, cautious, beautiful eyes, he dropped his calculated manner and said softly. "I would be deeply hurt if you ever called me Sir, Maria. Please, just Brian."

Disconcerted by his change of mood, she turned away, looking back out to sea. "And your project *Señor* Brian, what will it be called?"

He was about to reply that it had no name when he had an idea. He knew now what he would call it. But, before he could tell her, they were interrupted. The film was over and the others were coming out on deck, glasses in hand.

Cruickshank called for Hobbs to bring another bottle of champagne and two glasses for Maria and himself and the group settled down in chairs and chatted until one by one the couples slipped away. As Julio and his wife rose, so did Maria. Cruickshank was disappointed but not too much so; age brought with it the benefit of patience and he knew there was no more he could have said or done that night without pushing it too far. But left on the deck alone, he poured himself one last glass of champagne and found himself analysing the position in his usual way, point by point.

He wanted her. He had never known such desire, such need. He wanted her urgently. But also forever. Just for himself.

Yes, just for himself. The very thought of anyone else having her, holding her, making love to her, sent a shockwave through his entire system.

They must marry.

They would marry.

He was surprisingly confident about that.

But, then, why shouldn't he be? He had made clear his feelings and she had not avoided him or backed away; on the contrary she had left the others and come looking for him. That did not necessarily mean she felt drawn to him but it probably did; perhaps his remoteness from her at dinner had worked and she felt a need to re-establish contact, be reassured about his interest.

Despite the age difference, he saw no reason why she shouldn't be physically attracted to him. Cruickshank possessed his share of vanity but this had its advantages; it ensured he kept in shape and cultivated his distinguished appearance, and it gave him the assurance now in coping with a much younger and beautiful woman.

She was, he knew, in every respect no ordinary woman. He suspected that she was more cautious than shy; he sensed intelligence and a powerful will behind the big brown eyes that, when turned towards him like searchlights, had the effect of paralysing his own brain so that he had to deliberately talk more slowly to avoid incoherence. No, this was no ordinary woman. Christ, he would be proud of her and devoted to her if she became his.

He went down to the library and turned the light on over the model.

It had been nearly 10 days since Canning had killed the old man and there was no sign that anyone missed him or cared.

He had cross-examined the American further and was satisfied that, if and when the body was found, it would be taken for granted that the old man was the victim of an accident.

He was confident the project was back on course and every day, helped by his developing obsession with Maria, he was finding it easier to forget the shadow that hung over it.

For some time he stood looking at the model, then removing the card beside it, the one saying "the project", he replaced it with a new one, with, in his handwriting, the name he had decided upon.

It would be called the Valle de Maria.

It had been a long day. Sheedy and Miguel had left Kate photographing Ronda and made their third journey in three days to the hills and valleys of the *serrania*, this time accompanied by three men from the village.

Sheedy, stiff, sore, and sun burnt from the earlier journeys, found it even tougher going and marvelled at the way Miguel, who must have been 20 years older and God knows how many stones heavier, appeared untroubled by the ride.

Once at the ravine, Miguel, calling upon the combined strength of all of them, had been the first to be lowered to the body, followed by the doctor, then Sheedy. The journalist found Miguel keeping the doctor at bay, standing over the body, looking puzzled.

"Its not right, Bill... somehow its not right. Look how the wood is piled on top of him. If the bridge must have fallen first, would it not be spread about, some of it under him?"

Sheedy's eyes narrowed. He carefully moved some of the planks and beckoned the doctor to examine the body. Several minutes passed before they received his opinion. "Fortunately the body has been sheltered from the sun by the walls of the ravine and by the wood from the bridge... I would guess he's been dead about 12 to 14 days. He's been killed by the fall. It appears he landed on his front as you find him now. The impact crushed his forehead."

Then, asking them to come closer, he said "There is one inconsistency. This cut and bruise on the back of his head. It could not have caused his death, and I don't believe it could have come from the fall."

"Could he have landed on his back and bounced onto his front?" asked Sheedy.

"Not possible, *Señor*. His back would have been broken and the back of his head would have been far more damaged."

Sheedy knelt down and looked at the cut. "Of course, it could have been caused by one of the falling planks. I guess his greater weight would have caused him to fall faster than the bridge, so that one or two bits of wood could have landed on him."

The doctor looked unconvinced. "It is a sharp cut, *Señor*. More likely to have been caused by a falling rock, perhaps dislodged when he fell."

Miguel began a careful search. "There is no log with blood on it. But there is this." He took off a bandana from around his neck and picked up a sharp-looking stone, big enough to fill his giant palm.

Part of it was discoloured with what appeared to be dried blood. He looked at it suspiciously, then wrapped it up and began a careful search of the ground and, with the aid of binoculars, the walls of the ravine.

Then beckoning to Sheedy to help, he wrapped the body in the threadbare blanket from the dead mule's back, tied it up in the rope, and waved to the men above to pull it up.

The doctor went next. While they waited Miguel looked at the mule. "Leave it to nature. We will uncover it so that the birds of prey can see it. They will dispose of it."

He suggested to Sheedy that he go up to the surface next. "It will need you all to pull me up."

Left alone he looked around once more, and then piled up the planks to one side of the dead animal. Just before he grabbed the rope to leave he noticed something spotlighted by a small circle of sunlight that had penetrated the depths and the gloom of the ravine. He walked over and picked it up. It was a match-book, empty, but on the front the name of a place he knew was in Puerto Banus – the "Premier - lap dance club."

While the doctor and Miguel's friend took the body back to the village, Sheedy and the policeman walked back to *el cortijo*.

The doctor said he would do the necessary paper work and arrange with the priest that there be a funeral.

"Let him be cremated," Miguel said, "so that his ashes can be spread in the valley."

He also told the doctor "Describe him as dying from wounds caused by the fall, *Señor*, but do not use the words accident or accidental death."

At *el cortijo* the two men made a careful search of the old man's belongings. Before they left Miguel picked up all the papers and photographs from the table and put them in his saddle bag.

Then for what Sheedy devoutly hoped was the last time they made the tortuous journey back to Ronda. A long hot bath later, in the case of Sheedy, and three or four brandies, in the case of Miguel, and they were dining with Kate at the Rocamar, a restaurant in the *Plaza del Socorro*, the two men tired and sombre.

No-one mentioned the old man until they had finished their main course, then Sheedy said "So, what do you think Miguel?"

"Most probably it was an accident, Bill. That is the most likely explanation. After all, who could have a motive for killing him. He had no enemies, harmed no-one..."

He paused, hesitated, then added..."at least not these 40 years."

Sheedy could see Kate picking up on the hesitation, preparing to ask a question. He gave her a warning glance and said "So you will leave it at that?"

Miguel went silent. "I have a..."

"Sixth sense?"

"*Si*, Bill. It is the sixth sense. It tells me that something is not right. The old man was a creature of the valley, a survivor. He would not let his bridge deteriorate until it fell apart like that.

"And I did not like the way the bits of wood lay on the ground, more as if they were thrown one by one.

"Then there was the stone with blood on it, the one that probably caused the gash in his head. It did not look the same colour as the stones in the walls of the ravine, but I did find stones like it on the surface nearby.

"Then there was this." He took from his pocket the match-book and gave it to Sheedy. "The old man didn't frequent the bars on the Costa del Sol, let alone lap dance clubs. Where would he get this ?"

"Where did you find it?"

"Near the body. And it could not have been in the ravine for many days, Bill. It is still crisp, nearly new."

Sheedy looked thoughtful. "You said it was probably an accident, Miguel. But you're talking as if it were not."

"Let me put it like this. If I had not known this man, if I had just been called to the scene, I would have written it off as an accident without a second thought. And, of course, that is still what it could have been. But because I knew him, because I could not visualise this happening to the man I knew, and because I cared enough to look more closely, I have seen other things. Maybe I am not objective and am seeing things that are not there. And yet..."

Sheedy responded decisively. "No, Miguel, you're not imagining things. The position of the logs, the stone with blood on it, the match-book that shouldn't have been there, each on its own means little.   But taken together they add up to grounds for suspicion." He put down his knife and fork. "On the other hand, as you say, it seems so motiveless."

Kate listened intently. "What will you do, Miguel?"

"I will make some enquiries. See if anyone knows anything that happened to him recently... if anyone knows anyone who would have cause to want him dead."

Sheedy said. "Maybe I can help. Why don't I do a three-minute segment on the next show, ask anyone who knows anything to come forward? The company won't mind; they'll think its a good human interest story - the death of the rabbit man of Ronda."

"Not many people in Ronda will see it, Bill."

"I know. But its worth a try." Sheedy stood up and hugged the big Spaniard. Kate, too, hugged him and kissed him on the cheek. He smiled expansively, the first real Miguel smile of the night. "Ah, *señorita* Kate, if I were a younger man, if I were not so full of *vino* and mutton stew" - he patted his stomach - "I would have to fight this man for your hand."

"*Gracias*, kind *señor*," she said. "But that is not necessary. Say the word and I will leave him for you immediately."

"Holy shit," said Sheedy, "and I was worried about those skinny young things down on the *costa*. Come on, let's go."

And pursued by a gale of laughter from Miguel they headed back to the hotel and bed where, if Sheedy had harboured any doubts, Kate dispelled them with a combination of affection and uninhibited agility that was to remain one of his heart-warming memories of Ronda forever more.

Cruickshank waited until Maria was below decks and then slipped into the pool. While he was there she came back and soon he found her splashing beside him, the proximity of her semi-naked body causing him to thank God he was wearing a loose-fitting swim suit. He moved a fraction closer. "Maria, would you have dinner with me during the week? Alone. It would give me great pleasure."

She looked away, then back at him. "*Gracias, Señor*. I would be honoured."

"Maria," he said firmly, "I beg you, do not be honoured. Just come."

"Then I will be happy to come."

"That's better. Friday ?"

She looked surprised. "But that is tomorrow night."

"I assure you the time will drag."

Cruickshank, ridiculously embarrassed by the contrast between her magnificent brown body and his paleness, did not want her to see him get out of the pool. He was, therefore, relieved to see her climbing out. "Maria," he called out, "would you be good enough to go to the top of the gangway and call Hobbs?"

She walked round the corner and he quickly climbed out and wrapped himself in a towel dressing gown.

Julio, glass in hand, strolled over and the two stood leaning back on the railings, while Cruickshank lit a cigar. "Maria is a beautiful girl, Sir Brian."

"Yes, beautiful."

"It was kind of you to ask her."

Suspecting the hint of a question in the other's voice, Cruickshank turned and looked at him coldly, but, remembering his need of Julio, forced a smile and said "She referred to a guardian the other evening?"

"Yes. I believe she is an orphan, or a least has no known family. The Garcia's of Seville - as I told you, an old and respected family - unfortunately could not have children and they adopted Maria and a boy... she calls him her brother... from an orphanage. My friend Juan Garcia told me that she had originally been found on the steps of the orphanage after an Easter *fiesta*. That suggests she was left by a gypsy family. She has been fortunate, Sir Brian, she has had the best education and been raised in a fine home by a family who love her as one of their own."

"What would normally happen to such a young woman?"

"How do you mean, Sir Brian?"

"What is the custom in Spain. Would a marriage be arranged?"

"No, not arranged. But her parents, or adoptive parents, will take care that she meets young men from the right kind of family. We are honoured that they trust her to us."

"But she must be a least 25. Surely she can take care of herself."

"Twenty-four, Sir Brian. But of course. She is not under lock and key. She is in charge of her own destiny. It is her upbringing that is the guarantee of a good marriage. And her loyalty to and her respect for her guardians. But who is to blame loving parents for wanting their daughter to be in the care of trustworthy friends?"

"Quite." Cruickshank thought for a moment, then suggested they stroll to the other end of the yacht from where, he said, they could now see the hills where the project would be. Once there, he turned to face the architect and said "Julio, I would appreciate a word in confidence."

The architect was flattered. "Of course, Sir Brian."

"Maria. I am attracted to her. Not," he added hastily as he saw the architect's face fall, "in a frivolous way. I would like her to be the woman I marry."

Julio looked stunned. "Marry, Sir Brian. But that... why that would be a splendid thing."

"Julio, I don't yet know and may not for some time whether Maria could feel the same, whether she would be content with an older man. But in the meantime I would welcome your advice on how I should establish myself with her adoptive parents."

"They are coming to Marbella for a weekend at the time Maria is due to return, Sir Brian. Why not have them as your guests on the yacht for a day. They will be left in no doubt about your suitability socially and materially, and I have no doubt that, when they come to know you, they will come to respect your other great qualities as I have."

Cruickshank, embarrassed now and wishing he had never begun the conversation, never-the-less plunged on. "I don't know whether I will be in a position to say anything then, whether Maria will have responded favourably to my... my... advances."

"It would be a mistake to raise the matter then, anyway Sir Brian. It would be better to go to Saville later and if all is well to raise the matter with my friend Juan then."

"Julio, I am grateful to you. I can trust your discretion?"

"Of course, Sir Brian."

"Good." He looked at the Spaniard's eager face and added

"I'm pleased that you'll be working with me on the project and... who knows?... other things."

The Spaniard flushed with pleasure. "You are too kind, Sir Brian."

He made a note to do all in is power to encourage Maria to respond to the Englishman's advances.

It would be as close as he could get to having his distinguished and powerful companion marry into the family.

Not that he was thinking in purely mercenary terms. Julio genuinely thought Cruickshank a great man. His friends the Garcias should be proud to have their daughter marry him.

"Holy shit, Sheedy, look at those boats."

"*Yachts*, for Christ's sake! Ships! But not *boats*. Their owners would spit if they heard you call them boats."

"Well, who cares?"

Sheedy had taken Kate to Puerto Banus. Settling her in a wicker tree underneath a palm tree at the Salduba Bar opposite the biggest of all the yachts he told her "This is really pseuds' corner, but its fun to sit and watch the world go by. Hang on while I go and book a table."

He left her and walked down to Los Bandidos restaurant. On his way back past Linekers a sign caught his eye. It was advertising the Premier lap dance club. He climbed the flight of stairs but the door was closed, He guessed it was too early.

He returned to the bar where Kate was being chatted up by a young Spaniard in sailing gear. She winked at him and he deliberately dawdled at the bar so as not to spoil the fun.

But then, noting the young man's slim physique and good looks, he had second thoughts. The two of them together reminded him that he was significantly older than Kate. He settled in the chair beside her and the Spaniard, looking disappointed, moved on - to another girl about two tables away. Sheedy chuckled. "Sorry, Callaghan, but my arrival doesn't seem to have broken his heart."

"That's ok," Kate said. "I told him my father was returning."

"Bitch."

She giggled. "Who's is that yacht, there. The dark blue one?" She pointed to a yacht towering over the others, La Gaviota.

"The Seagull? I don't know. Not bad, is it?"

They wandered down the rows of yachts and then into one or two of the boutiques, where Kate ignored Sheedy's warnings about the rip-off prices and bought a shirt.

Over dinner she asked him what was next on the programme.

"Well for me its just that - the programme. I have to start work tomorrow. Manuel has been researching a couple of stories for the first show and I have to put them together."

"Are you going to do an item on the old man?"

"Yes. But low key. After all, it could've been an accident. And I'm going to hold back the only clue we've got. The match-book. By the way, I thought I would take a look at the lap danced club after dinner. Get the feel of it."

"Get the *feel* of it.! I thought you weren't supposed to touch them."

He laughed, then later as they walked to the club he asked her what she would do while he was working. "Listen, since I arrived you've been rushing me all over Andalucia. This was supposed to be a holiday. I've had only one swim. I want at least a week reading and swimming and I can cope happily on my own, thank you."

"Ok, but if you're sunbathing at my pool wear a bikini top. The gardener has never been the same since the first day you were there."

"He's not the only one."

"You better wait at Linekers."

"Like hell. This is my one chance to see what happens in these places. I'm coming in."

Cruickshank had booked a table on the balcony of La Cote on the Ronda road, and Maria was enchanted by the view and the flowers and trees growing around the candle-lit tables. Dressed in a light-blue casual suit with even lighter blue shirt and a dark blue tie, with colour in his face from an afternoon working on his papers in the sun, the Englishman looked fit and handsome and more than appropriate company for the young woman, who had combed her hair back and chosen a sharply-tailored black dress with high collar that made her look older than her age.

Cruickshank was still trying hard to appear cool, to put her at her ease, although he himself was far from relaxed. His diplomatic and business career had taught him how to control feelings, to determine the pace of relationships, but even so these skills were stretched to the limits. The analytic mind, the nerves of steel that had served him well for more years than he liked to remember had, when in the young woman's company, all but proved inadequate. He had to struggle to control a child-like eagerness to please and impress, so afraid was he of making a mistake and alienating the object of his desire. If this was love, it wasn't easy to handle.

Trusting that Julio had not mentioned their conversation, he feigned ignorance of her background, wanting to hear it from her. "Tell me about yourself Maria. You mentioned a guardian. Are your parents not alive ?"

"No *Señor*. My mother died giving birth and my father died when I was three. "

"I'm sorry. It must have been a terrible start to your life."

"I was too young to really understand what was happening *Señor*."

"Brian."

"*Si. Señor* Brian." There was the darting glance from the corner of her eye, the shy smile again. He laughed resignedly.

"Anyway, where did you live then?"

She looked vague. "In the mountains."

"Did you not have other family?"

"*Si*. My father had two uncles. But they did not feel able to bring me up so I was placed with another family, a gypsy family. They were good to me but they had many children and they were poor. I think it became too much. When I was 12 they took me to Seville and I was put in an orphanage. Then *Señor* Garcia and his wife came to adopt me and I have been living with them since."

"And you have been happy with them?"

"Very happy. They have been like a real father and mother to me."

"That's good. And you work in the family business?"

"*Si*. I manage one of the boutiques."

"What do you do the rest of the time?"

"We have a busy social life. I ride. We have a small horse ranch, and also an interest in a cattle ranch. And I swim; we have a beautiful pool. I read and listen to music."

"What kind of music."

"The Garcias love opera and have helped me to learn to love it too."

"That is a a pleasure we share, Maria. In London my company has a box at the Royal Opera House. I have not missed an opera for some years. Where do you go to opera - not, I think, in Seville?"

"No, alas there is no opera house in Seville. *Señor* Garcia has many recordings and also we go for a few days to the seasons in Madrid and Barcelona."

"Is your home in the centre of Seville."

"No, it is a small hacienda on the outskirts."

"Sounds to me as if you have been very fortunate. But..." he could no longer resist the question..."why is it that the young men of Seville have not been fighting for your hand in marriage... such a remarkable young woman?"

She blushed at the compliment. "Some have, but I have been happy at home and felt no pressure to marry. I have not met a man I would wish to live with, a man who shares my pleasures and who is grown... not old... but..."

"Mature?"

"*Si, Señor*. I do not respond well to the *machismo* of many young Spanish men."

Cruickshank felt his hopes rising. He struggled to refrain from pressing the advantage but, deliberately or otherwise, Maria herself enabled him to keep their conversation where he wanted it to be: "And you, Brian? Why are you not married?"

"As I told you, I was once, Maria. Not happily. My wife and I decided we were making each other unhappy and parted."

Noticing a little frown, one that quickly came and went, he suddenly saw a problem. Was she a Catholic? Almost certainly. Would his divorce block the way? Panic. His self-discipline broke. He pressed. "It is a tragedy I deeply regret, Maria, for if I were to wish to marry a Catholic it could cause a real problem."

"I expect not if the woman wanted you enough, *Señor* Brian. It would be difficult, yes, but not insuperable."

He relaxed. Reclining back in his seat he looked straight at her. For a moment her eyes dropped, then she looked up and straight at him.

For a moment neither spoke.

Then he knew, as he had always known in negotiations over the years, that accord had been reached. Somehow, without a word being exchanged, they were both silently acknowledging that there was more to this dinner than the food, than gentlemanly hospitality.

He felt a great soaring of his spirits. Leaning forward, holding her eyes with the full force of his personality, he now spoke quietly, sincerely.

"Maria, I wish to say something to you. From the moment we met the other evening I have been captivated by you. I am not a teenager. I do not fall rashly in love with every woman I meet. Nor am I a philanderer. In fact women have not played a big part in my life. But I know now that whether I waited to say it for a week, a month, a year or 10 years, I would feel the same as I do now. I am deeply attracted to you. I want to share all that I have with you, have you in my life, have you as my wife. Is it possible... is there even the smallest chance...you could overlook the difference in our ages, that you could feel at least a little as I do, that it might be possible...?"

The girl looked down at the table, and then back up, straight into his eyes. "I have been aware of your interest, Brian." And I am honoured..." she waved her hand to stop him protesting..."yes, Brian, honoured by your interest. And I find you a kind and attractive man. But I cannot say to you now what I may come to feel. It is too soon for me. I would like to be your friend and I would like to spend time with you. Is it so urgent that I should respond ?"

"Of course not," he lied.

Cruickshank was fighting panic.

Had he had pushed it too quickly?

"Of course I understand. And I am honoured..." he smiled at her smile..."yes, I am honoured too that you would even consider me. How long are you here for...?"

"Three weeks yet."

"Then can we see a lot of each other?"

"I would like that."

"Good."

He reached out and took her hand. "Perhaps tomorrow you will allow me to show you the place where our project will be built. We could ride up into the hills."

She looked surprised. "You ride, Brian?"

"Of course." He was doubly pleased. That time the Brian had come naturally. And the riding lessons he had taken some time back and that had since appeared to have been a waste of time had paid off at last.

He signed their bill and they walked out into the warm night, strolling along to where the Rolls was waiting. "If you don't mind, my chauffeur will drop me off at the yacht on its way to taking you home, Maria. I have to take a call from the United States."

They sat silently in the back of the car, holding hands like teenagers. As they arrived at the port he said: "Tomorrow? Will it be convenient if my car picks you up at about ll o'clock."

"*Gracias*. I will look forward to it."

He reached out and gently drawing her to him kissed her on the cheek. "Until then."

He stood and watched the Rolls until it disappeared from sight and then walked back to the yacht to await its return to take him to the villa.

As he climbed up the gang plank he passed Canning leaving.

"Damn you, Canning," he thought. "If it weren't for you life would be as good as it could be."

CHAPTER SIX

Sheedy's office in Marbella consisted of one big room taking the whole of the floor above a bar. From there Manuel and he did their research, wrote their scripts and organised the programme. The film crews would come up from Gibraltar when required.

In one corner Sheedy sat in an old leather chair behind a desk stacked high with newspapers, letters, files, photographs, old scripts, an over-flowing ash tray and half-drunk coffee cups. Half buried in the chaos was a battered old typewriter. Manuel's desk could not have looked more different; it was neat, the few files carefully piled on top of each, and in the centre, his pride and joy, a brand-new computer. Between them sat their part-time secretary, Rosa, struggling to get their calls via a phone system that was somewhat short of what Sheedy had been accustomed to in New York. Altogether, there was an atmosphere of cheerful anarchy.

It was a programme day. Sheedy was just preparing to leave for Gibraltar when Miguel called from Ronda. Sheedy asked what was new.

"Not a lot. As we knew, *El Conejero* had no enemies in these parts. But there is one thing. I put the word about that I wanted to hear any out of the ordinary gossip about him. Yesterday a man who owns a bar just outside the town called out to me. He said that *El Conejero* had looked in to leave some of his catch and to have some wine and that he had been in conversation with a foreigner. He said it was either 'an *Ingles* or an *Americano.*' He said it was so unusual for *El Conejero* to talk to anyone, let alone a foreigner, that he remarked upon it to his wife that evening. "

"Did he hear what they said?"

"Only one thing. This is what is peculiar. He heard the stranger say 'you'll be hearing from me.'"

"Were they arguing?"

"The barman says not. But who could argue with *Señor Conejo*? It takes two to argue and he was always so non-commital. The only thing he argued about was bullfighting."

"What else did the barman say?"

"Nothing else. That was it. Apparently they spoke for about 10 minutes then the foreigner and *El Conejero* left at the same time."

"What did he say the foreigner looked like ?"

"Maybe 30, maybe a bit more, expensively dressed and white haired. I presume he meant fair-haired."

"H'mm. Any chance it was just a casual conversation, tourist wanting to chat to local character, that kind of thing?"

"*Si*. At first the barman thought that, especially as the young man did most of the talking. But what about the remark at the end?"

"Maybe he was arranging to get some rabbits, maybe he was a buyer for a restaurant, from the coast or somewhere?"

"That's possible, Bill... unusual, but possible."

"Ok. Well, let me know anything else you pick up. By the way, we're putting out a piece on the programme tonight. I guess you won't see it in Ronda. I'll keep a video for you to see when you're next down here."

"*Gracias*. Take care."

"You too."

Sheedy sat thinking. He knew that the first step to solving any mystery was to look for things people did that were uncharacteristic, for things that didn't fit the pattern.

The Rabbit Man just didn't get into conversations with strangers in bars. No way. It didn't fit.

If they were talking it was because they had business together.

But what kind of business?

Sheedy believed that the answer to that question would produce the missing motive... the reason why an apparently harmless old peasant had been singled out for murder.

The horse Maria had been riding when Cruickshank first saw her was owned by Julio and kept at a stable near the beach. From it he now hired a horse for himself and the two rode down the beach until they reached an under-pass that took them beneath the main highway and into the fields beyond. Soon they were climbing into the hills.

Cruickshank had risen early to pick up some suitable riding gear from a shop in Marbella and, with his sun tan coming on nicely, looked like a prosperous rancher. Maria was wearing a white tee shirt and jeans tucked into leather boots and was so desirable that just looking at her made Cruickshank ache.

When they reached the brow of the hill overlooking the valley at the heart of the project, they dismounted. Cruickshank opened a small saddlebag and took out a corked jug of *sangria*. Handing her a glass, he said "Well, there it is... the *Valle de Maria*."

She looked puzzled.

"That is what I have decided to call it."

For a moment she looked disconcerted, even concerned, and, quickly realising what she must be thinking, he said "Don't worry, my dear. If... and I hope it will not be so... but if you decide not to accept my proposal, I would still wish it to be so named. It will be a beautiful place and it should be named after a beautiful woman."

She blushed and looked down at her glass. "I am..."

"I know..." he interrupted, "You're honoured. You can't keep on being honoured, Maria. I just want you to be happy."

"But it is an honour, Brian."

He began pointing out the sites for the mini villages and the other features of the project and, finally, drawing her to her feet and leading her by the hand, he took her up the winding path until they reached the place where his villa would be.

"This is where my home will be, on this hill. It will be a beautiful home, and should you feel one day able to share my life with me, it would be your home too."

She turned and walked right up to him and took both his hands and looked into his eyes. "You are a kind, a generous man, Brian. I can understand why in your country they call you a Knight. You would have made a great Spanish nobleman."

She leaned forward and kissed him gently on the lips. He felt a great longing building up in him and was just going to reach out and pull her to him when she drew back and taking just one of his hands began to lead him back to the horses.

"But it is becoming hot," she said. "Its time to return."

He rode behind her, watching her shapely backside bouncing up and down on the horse in front of him, wishing for the chance to do things to it that he good-humouredly admitted to himself were anything but noble.

He wondered what his fellow directors in London would think if they could see him now, riding full of desire behind this beautiful *señorita*, his interest in balance sheets and board meetings waning by the minute.

They would think you had gone mad, Cruickshank, he thought good-humouredly, and maybe they would be right.

He laughed out loud.

At the sound, she turned in her saddle, and smiled at him.

And he knew then he didn't care. Didn't care what they would think.

If this was madness, so be it.

The programme always began with Sheedy talking to camera. Then the credits. Then would come the one or more items of the week, film reports, or studio interviews, or a combination of both.

Kate had travelled to Gibraltar with Sheedy to see it being made and sat now in the director's box as the show went on the air.

"Hi there, this is Bill Sheedy, tonight we look at how developers are trying to get round the new laws prohibiting building too close to the beaches of the Costa del Sol. We update you on plans for more flights into Gibraltar's airport. How will that affect the surrounding area? And we say farewell to the rabbit man of Ronda... and ask how did he die? Did he fall... or was he pushed?"

Up came the title: "Sheedy on the Costa del Sol". And the programme was under way.

With three minutes left, the second film report now ended, Sheedy appeared live on the screen.

"Now, a mystery.

"If you've been up to Ronda and perhaps had rabbit for lunch or dinner, *conejo* as its called in Spanish, the chances are it was hunted and killed by this man (an old picture of the peasant, taken by Sheedy at a bullfight, appeared on the screen)... Pepe Rodriguez... known as *El Conejero*, the rabbit man, or *Señor Conejo*, Mr Rabbit.

"For years he has come to that town from the mountains and valleys of the *Serrania de Ronda*, his mule laden with rabbits, all ready for the roasting pot.

"Pepe - the rabbit man - lived alone in a farmhouse in a mountain valley about three hours from the village of Atajate (Picture of the valley and *el cortijo* taken by Sheedy appeared on the screen.)

"He had no family we know of and few close friends, although he was a popular character in the area.

"Last week he was found dead. At the bottom of a ravine near his farmhouse. The bridge had apparently collapsed.

"Poor old Pepe. He died alone.

"Just one question: how did he fall?

"He was a careful man. Would he have let his bridge fall into such disrepair that it would crumble under him? It seems unlikely?

"But if he was pushed, who by and why? Who would want to kill this harmless old man?

"Probably no-one. Probably it was an accident.

"But if you know anything... anything at all... about the rabbit man that may clear up the mystery, and especially if you know anyone who could wish him harm, why not give me a ring?

"In the meantime, farewell Pepe, *adios* rabbit man. You'll be missed."

Cruickshank stood in front of the television set, his face white with shock. Miller had disturbed his 'special hour', running upstairs to alert him after he heard the opening headlines on the set in the downstairs bar. They had watched the final segment together.

Miller had never seen the normally imperturbable financier look so angry.

"Christ, Jim, that... that bastard Canning told me that everyone would assume it was an accident. Why is this man Sheedy suggesting otherwise? What has Canning overlooked?"

Agitatedly, he paced around the room. "Damn, damn, damn. I should never have let them convince me to let it pass. I should have known better."

He poured himself another Scotch and gestured to Miller to help himself. Miller, who had been making a superhuman effort to reduce his intake by pouring himself tiny gins and drowning them in huge glasses of ice and mineral water, called instead for a black coffee.

Cruickshank asked him "What do you think Jim?"

"Well, the presenter was pretty laid back. I didn't get the impression he had any evidence to suggest it was other than an accident. Remember, it was hardly a major item on the programme, more like what we in the trade call a fishing expedition. My advice would be not to over-react."

The financier walked onto the balcony and looked out to sea. "You know Jim, when I was a kid I was told by my father that one lie always led to another. I have a terrible feeling this one act, of which I'm innocent but which I've elected to ignore, is going to come back and hit me again and again.

"I still think this man Sheedy had nothing to go on," said Miller. "If anyone had seen it happen or they had any real reason to know it wasn't an accident, he wouldn't have been so tentative.

"Don't forget the only point he made was that it was unlike the old man to let the bridge fall into disrepair. Well, that's a bit weak."

Cruickshank cheered up. "And he did say it was probably an accident." He stood thinking for a moment, then, decisive once more, said "Jim, I want you to do two things. Get together with Canning and go over the whole thing again. Test his story. See if you can satisfy yourself that his account stands up. And find out a bit more about this man Sheedy, and why he's interested in this... this rabbit man."

The two men eyed each other without warmth. Canning, already resentful that the Englishman had taken his place as Cruickshank's confidant, was even more annoyed to find that Miller and not Cruickshank was questioning him now. Recalling Cruickshank's attempt to record their earlier conversation he insisted they discuss the matter while walking on the beach and only then after he had carefully checked Miller was not wired.

Canning was impressed, though, with the Englishman's professionalism. As he took Canning through his story, he kept tossing in little trip wires, checking detail after detail, so that the American was amazed at what the other man caused him to remember.

Miller took him back to the moment of the murder. "Ok, three things I want to check. First, what was the condition of the ground. Was it soft, muddy...?"

"Hell, no, it was hard as rock."

"Was it dusty?"

"No, more stony. I guess you're concerned about footprints. I'm confident there won't be any."

"Second point. Why for Christ's sake did you dismantle the bridge?"

"To make it look like it fell under him?"

"Why not make it look like he fell off it?"

"I guess I decided people would be more likely to wonder why he should fall than they would be surprised that a rickety bridge gave way."

"How did the logs and the planks fall? All over the place or in one pile?"

"I guess they fell in a pile around him and on top of him."

"On top? Doesn't that strike you as odd-looking? If the bridge fell first, he would be lying on top of the wood, not the other way round?"

"Not necessarily. He was heavy and the mule was heavy but the wood was light. It would make just as much sense for him to fall through the bridge and then for the wood to fall with him and after him."

"Ok, now what did you do afterwards?"

"I went to the farmhouse..."

"No, before then. Did you stand looking down?"

"I guess so. I just wanted to check he was lying still... he was dead."

"Did you do anything else but look ?"

"How do you mean?"

"Well, light a cigarette or anything."

"Yes, I guess so. Yes, I lit a cigarette."

"So there could be ash around the place where the bridge was?"

"No, because I only took one or two puffs and then walked off. There would be no ash there."

"And the match?"

Canning marvelled at the man's thoroughness. "Well, I... I... don't know... I... I guess I threw it down into the ravine."

Miller looked at him coldly. "Great. Bloody terrific. So there could be a dead match in the ravine?"

"For Christ's sake, that could have been dropped any time. By anyone. Even if its found it proves nothing."

Miller looked at him even more coldly.

"Now let's go to the farmhouse. You say you collected every bit of paper?" Canning described what he found, the receipts, cuttings, photographs."

"Why did you leave them there?"

"There was no reason to take them. Anyway, it would have looked strange if there was no paper in there at all."

"But you left it all on the table?"

"Yeah, I guess that was a bit careless, but it could simply mean the old man had been looking for something himself. I tell you, Miller, there's no problem. We just have to keep our heads."

Miller considered what Canning had said. His head was beginning to ache as it did whenever he went out into the sun, and his whole being was yearning for a gin, an ice-cold gin, a big gin.

He took his frustration and pain out on the American.

"Look, Canning, you have fucked up on this... fucked up properly. I tell you now that if a real professional was looking into the man's death, if I was, I would have rated it more than highly suspicious by now, especially as I would soon establish he was blocking action on the project. I would be calling on Sir Brian within about three days and on you not long after. Fortunately all we're dealing with here are the Spanish police who, I suspect, won't be taking it too seriously, and a tv reporter who has probably forgotten the story already. But don't come on all fucking cocksure with me. Because from me you get no points at all. Is that clear?"

The American flushed with anger. "Screw you, too, Miller." He stalked off, back to the villa and his car, and roaring the engine in his rage, drove out onto the main road.

He arrived back at the port just as Cruickshank and his lunch guests were climbing into the Rolls. Canning noticed that the architect Julio and his wife were accompanied by a young woman. He was struck by her beauty. Obviously Spanish, she was younger than the others, yet the way Cruickshank was helping her into the car he clearly fancied her and Canning couldn't blame him. He decided that if Cruickshank was getting involved, this was a good thing. A romance with a lovely Spanish girl would further tie him into the area, commit him to the project.

As the car went past the girl looked out of the window and just for a moment her eyes and Canning's were locked together.

The American was left with a feeling that he knew her, that he had seen her somewhere before.

He stood thinking for a moment, then shrugged. Maybe he had seen her at some other club on the *costa*? After all, the *costa* was really just a big village.

Anyway, he was bound to meet her with Cruickshank. He could ask her then.

Sheedy was woken by the phone ringing. As always after a programme, he and the others who had worked on it had wined and dined well and ll o'clock was too early, far too early to be taking calls. He groaned, clutched his head, crawled out of bed and reached the phone just in time. *"Hola."*

"*Señor* Sheedy... Bill Sheedy?"

"Yes."

"I am a regular viewer of your programme, *Señor*. I saw it last night. I have some information I believe you would find helpful. I wonder whether we could meet soon... maybe lunchtime today?"

This was the kind of call Sheedy had no choice but to take seriously. This was how half of his stories began. Of course it meant that occasionally he was exposed to a real nutter, but it was a risk he had to take. The worst that could happen is that he would spend lunch indulging someone's paranoia and that Rosa would then spend the next week keeping the caller off the phone.

Still this was a Sunday - couldn't it wait? The caller apologetically explained that it was difficult on weekdays. Sheedy reluctantly arranged a drink at one o'clock in San Pedro. The man suggested a *tapas* bar behind the Town Hall.

"How will I recognise you?"

"Its no matter, *Señor*. I will know you from the television."

"Then may I know your name?"

"Could it wait till we meet, *Señor*?"

"Of course. One o'clock then."

Sheedy looked at his watch. There was just over an hour and a half. He telephoned Miguel's office in Ronda and left a message for him to ring. Ten minutes later he did.

"Miguel, I think we need to review the matter of the rabbit man, whether I should do another item or let it drop. Why not come down to the *costa* tonight? We'll have dinner together at my villa and you can stay the night. Plenty of good food and wine and a council of war ."

Miguel having enthusiastically accepted, Sheedy rang Manuel and asked him to come too, and then drove to San Pedro.

It was a fairly new restaurant off the *plaza* at the top of the main street of San Pedro. Sheedy had hardly settled at a table, glass of wine in hand, when a short, dark-haired man in a navy-blue suit but open neck shirt came bustling in, looked around and then came over.

"*Señor* Sheedy, I am Ramon Aparicio."

Sheedy shook hands and ordered a bottle of white wine and some calamares, while Aparicio, looking around to assure himself there was no-one in the bar he knew, unfolded a map. Sheedy saw that it covered the *costa* from Marbella to Estapona and about 10 kilometres inland.

"*Señor*, I work for the authority that considers all applications by developers and others who wish to build in this area."

Sheedy groaned inwardly. He needed another planning story like a hole in the head. Still he feigned interest.

"See this area here, *Señor*." The man pointed to a section of the map bounded by a blue ink line. "It covers about ten square kilometres and at its heart is a beautiful undeveloped valley.

"Over the past 18 months all of the plots of land, the *fincas* and the few villas nearby, have been bought, bit by bit, by one company, Anglo Spanish Investors Ltd.

"In every case they have paid premium prices without complaint.

"And every contract has specified confidentiality for 12 months, a most unusual requirement in my experience.

"*Señor*, they plan a project that is more ambitious than any of its kind on the costa. Billions and billions of pesetas are involved. It is going to make Sotogrande look small by comparison. It will be like a... a mini-state... and it will have every facility the rich could want. They even plan to build an English-style horseracing track there."

He now had Sheedy's full attention. "Holy shit. You are right, Ramon, this could make a good story for the programme. How has it all been kept secret?"

"They have powerful friends, *Señor*. And they have been generous to the right people. But, I stress, apart from that... that generosity... and that's part and parcel of the way things work here... they have done nothing wrong. Just bought the land without fuss."

"They now own it all?"

"Ah, that's the point, *Señor*. All but this small plot here." He pointed to a small oddly-shaped area within the blue lines. "The owner will not sell."

"That must be extremely irritating for them."

"More than irritating, *Señor*. It's the ideal place for the main entrance to the whole area. While they can get round it, it won't be easy and it spoils their master plan. They want it... desperately. Its already costing them money, because, until they know whether they can get it, they can't go ahead with much else."

"Presumably," said Sheedy, "the owner is just holding back for a huge sum of money. This could make him a millionaire."

"No, *Señor*. Its more complicated than that. The owner wouldn't sell at any price. They tried to persuade us to compulsorily purchase the land and sell it to the project but that is not our way. So they have been greatly frustrated."

Sheedy's interest grew. "Bloody hell. Well, who is the owner?"

"That's the point, *Señor*.

"That's why I came to see you.

"The owner was the man about whom you spoke last night...

"...the owner was Pepe Rodriguez."

Canning drove down the highway to the turn-off to La Siesta beach club. Near to the club, on the edge of the beach, there is a *Conferencias Internacionales*, a small international telephone bureau from where holiday-makers can call their home countries. Canning called New York. For nearly 30 minutes he talked to Jordan. When they had finished he placed a call to Malaga. A Spanish voice answered the phone. *"Hola."*

"Hola. Señor Castillo?"

"Si."

"I am a friend of Mr Jordan's."

There was no reply.

"We need to talk."

Still there was no reply.

"There is a bar in Istan. On the street whereby you enter the town, at the front. Please meet me there at one o'clock tomorrow."

Only then did the other speak. *"Si, Señor.* I will be there."

Sheedy was pleased by the stunned silence around the table. A story teller by profession but also for pleasure, he had enjoyed building up to the climax and got his reward from the attention on the faces of those around him.

Miguel was first to speak. "A motive, Bill. We have a motive."

"You're telling me," Sheedy replied. "Billions of pesetas worth of motive "

"But why wouldn't he sell?" asked Kate.

"Aparicio said that the old man talked about keeping it in trust. 'I'm holding it in trust, *Señor*,' was all he said when he was asked."

"In trust for who?" Kate asked.

"Who knows? But presumably if he was keeping it in trust there must be a will. Miguel, you're positive there was no will in the papers?"

"No. But I think we must go back to the *cortijo* and look. We weren't that thorough because we didn't know we were looking for papers."

Sheedy, groaning at the idea of another painful journey to the *cortijo*, looked round the table. "So let's sum up what could have happened. And," he said warningly, "I stress *could* have happened.

"Now, the old man was in the way of these people, Anglo-Spanish Investors.

"A man goes to meet him in a bar in Ronda. He is made what was probably a last offer and says no.

"The man follows him out to the valley and kills him with a rock, throws him and the bridge to the bottom of the ravine, but also throws the empty matchbook down there.

"So we have two real mistakes: he was seen talking to the rabbit man, and he left the matchbook. I have a feeling if we investigate who's involved in the company we'll find a man who fits the Ronda barman's description and also goes to the Premier lap dance club."

He looked at his audience for questions but there were none.

"Right, there's work to do.

"Miguel, would you be prepared to get a detailed statement from the barman? And could you go back to *el cortijo* and search again? The old man would not have gone to all this trouble to protect the land for somebody without leaving a record or telling someone for whom it was intended.

"Manuel, I want you to find out all about Anglo Spanish Investors. Who and what they are.

"I'll follow up the matchbox. If he was killed, that matchbox was dropped by the killer?"

"What about me," said Kate. "I want in on this too ."

"I reckon we're going to need you. For a start I'd like to get the tv company to hire you to work on one or two other stories while Manuel and I concentrate on this. Would you mind?"

"So much for my holiday... but, sure. I'm surprised you're not afraid of the competition?"

He grinned. "Cheeky so and so."

Miguel interrupted. "We're still short of evidence, Bill. Even if we show motive and connect someone in the company to the old man, its too circumstantial."

"Maybe, but there's more than one reason to investigate it. If the land has been left to someone else, that person has to be found. For one thing they could be in danger. For another, if we can't prove the murder, we can at least avenge Pepe by stopping his killers getting the land or by making them pay a fortune for it.

"Also, its just possible that if we build up enough pressure we could cause them to attempt some other reckless act that would give the game away on the rabbit man's murder."

Some time later, after Manuel had gone back to Benahavis and Miguel had emptied the last bottle of Rioja and retired to bed in the spare room, Kate cleared away the remains of the langoustines, salad, and a glass of *sangria* Miguel had missed and went out onto the balcony to find Sheedy standing, tense, looking out at the lights of the *costa*.

"I remember you were always like this when onto something big in the old days, Bill. You change. You get all tense and single-minded. You're as much a hunter as the rabbit man was."

"Maybe we're imagining it all, Kate, but if that poor old bugger was killed so that some shit of a developer could make a few more bucks, then I'm going to get him."

"Ok, but in the meantime, remember me?" She put her arms round his waist and kissed his nose.

He smiled back. "Yes... yes... I think I do... just remind me where it was..."

"Swine!"

Cruickshank sat, glass in hand, in the garden of the villa and looked at the two men facing him. "What's your evaluation, Jim?" he asked.

"If someone really wants to dig, really wants to prove the old man was deliberately killed, he could find one or two bits of possible evidence... the position of the wood from the bridge, possibly a match thrown into the ravine by Canning, maybe a footprint or two. But none of it would be conclusive. Even if some fanatical policeman or the reporter Sheedy convinced himself it was a killing, none of it would be sufficient to incriminate us. I think you're OK."

"What about the barman?"

Miller looked puzzled. "What barman?"

"The one who saw Canning and the old man talking."

Miller looked at Canning with anger. "You never told me about that."

"You never asked me."

"Tell me now."

"I had a conversation with the peasant for a few minutes about a week before. How else do you think I established he wouldn't sell? It was in a bar outside Ronda. My guess is the barman won't remember."

"Well, my guess is that he will," said Miller, "especially if someone bothers to ask him when he last saw the rabbit man. Christ, Canning, its one thing to be a bloody criminal, but do you have to be a bloody incompetent one as well?"

Canning flushed with anger and began to respond but Cruickshank, who had been listening to this without expression, now surprised both men by interrupting calmly.

"Jim, I've given this some thought. There is no way we can avoid the link between the peasant and the project because we ourselves need to draw it to the attention of the authorities. Otherwise we can't move things forward. I propose, therefore, that Canning goes to the planning office today and tells them that he spoke to this man recently and was at last promised the right to purchase the land. Unfortunately, he can say, we discovered from the television programme that the man died before his promise could be confirmed."

"Will they believe that?"

"Maybe, maybe not. But Canning should make it clear that we're not expecting our word to be taken on this and we're happy to await the necessary enquiries into a possible will, or other family ownership. The more open and forthcoming and innocent we appear, the less it will look as if we have anything to hide. Its only if we hold back or deny any interest in the man that it will look suspicious."

Canning, pleased to be extracted from the cross examination by Miller, was eager to agree, but pointed out the peasant had already been contacted by the authorities and had told them he wouldn't sell.

"No problem," replied Cruickshank. "We'll just say we upped the offer to a point where he couldn't refuse. That would explain your contact with him in the bar. And its entirely credible. No-one is likely to believe that he didn't have a price. Everyone has a price - isn't that what you people say, Canning?"

Miller stayed after Canning had left, sitting still and thoughtful in his chair.

Cruickshank asked him "What is it, Jim, you don't look happy."

"Well, for a start, Sir Brian, I think you probably just saved that barman's life."

"What?" Cruickshank was shocked.

"You gave Canning an out. My guess is that without it the barman, too, would have suffered a nasty accident."

"Christ," the financier moaned. "I thought all this was over. I was assured they had learned their lesson." Then, looking sceptical, he asked "But what makes you say it?"

"I've met his type before. They're completely without scruples. And they don't take prisoners. They don't take them because they don't trust anybody. They don't trust anybody because they can't be trusted themselves. You once in a moment of anger called him a psychopath. My guess is that's exactly what he is. I have a feeling I'll have to spend most of my time watching him from now on."

Cruickshank began to walk around the room, agitated. "God, I hope you're over the top on this. But please do, Jim. Don't let him out of your sight."

"There's one other thing that worries me."

"What's that?"

"Sir Brian, what more do you know about the people behind Canning?"

Cruickshank frowned. "Not much more than I knew before all this happened. To be honest, Jim, I had assumed that this business with Canning would probably have a restraining effect on them. That from now on they would settle for the long-term financial benefits of the project and behave themselves. It never crossed my mind to have them investigated further." He paused and then apologetically added "I'm not even sure I want to know."

Miller shook his head. "I don't like it. I have a funny feeling about these people. I can't understand why they wanted to go for all-out ownership. They're supposed to be clever and discreet investors seeking a safe place for their money. They don't need the power as well. In the circumstances I would have expected them to keep in the background. Why have they taken control?"

"My guess is just greed, Jim. They like the project and its potential and just wanted more of it."

"But if they think like that they could have done the same with a lot of the American businesses they've taken shares in, and my impression is that they haven't, preferring a safe, respectable front and a safe return on their funds. Are you sure they don't want to use the land for any other purpose?"

Cruickshank laughed. "What? Do you think they've struck oil? No, Jim, they've supported all the plans for the project so far, and its this project and only this project that we've got planning permission for. Honestly, apart from acts of utter stupidity such as Canning's, I don't see what harm they can do. Obviously I dislike being involved with them but I'm satisfied once its rolling they'll see its best to leave well alone."

For a moment they sat in thoughtful silence then Miller said "Lets say the authorities find a will, or another member of the family. What happens if they won't cooperate?"

"I think they will. He was keeping it in trust for them to sell. Surely. What other value could it have? Anyway, I'm having the planning team work on a different way of establishing access. If there are any more problems we'll just go ahead without it. That's what we should have done anyway. Its a bloody nuisance, it will cost a lot of money, but its not the end of the world. Another murder would be."

He considered his own words for a moment. Then added: "And there won't be another murder. I've got Jordan's word for that."

Manuel had spent the day on the phone, often a frustrating business in Spain. More than once Rosa had blanched at his language as he had been cut off or picked up the phone and found it dead. When Sheedy arrived back from Gibraltar where he had been recording part of the following week's programme the younger man's usually tidy desk was covered in bits of paper and scrawlings.

"What have you got?"

"Anglo-Spanish Investors is a British company. Its chairman is a Sir Brian Cruickshank. He owns a villa down the *costa* and the company also has a yacht in the port. It looks highly respectable, Bill. Apparently Cruickshank was a British civil servant, very high up. He has a lot of his own money in this and I gather there's also American money but I haven't been able to get to the bottom of that yet.

"Apart from keeping the project under wraps in a way I would have believed impossible in Malaga province, they seem to have acted properly in every way."

"Is Cruickshank based in London?"

"Usually yes, but he's down here at the moment."

"Is he just? Maybe worth a visit. But first, Manuel, try to find out a bit more about the other investors. Whether there's any Spanish money involved. And who the Americans are. And we need to know who is working for them... and whether there's anyone who fits the description of the man in the bar."

Manuel nodded. "I thought I would wander down to the port and take a look at the yacht, see if any of the crew turn up in a bar."

"Ok, but take it easy. I don't want them to know we're digging - not yet."

Sheedy picked up the phone and made a number of calls to journalist friends in London. From each the story was the same. Cruickshank was highly respected, well connected, and, in the words of one city reporter on The Guardian, "about as straight as these people can be."

"Just one thing," the Guardian man added. "The word in the city is that Cruickshank has climbed into bed with an American outfit, the International Investors' Trust, headed by a man called Theodore Jordan."

"Yes?"

"Well, I was over in New York last year and there was a kind of rumour... not much of one and probably unfounded... that as well as a lot of respectable money the Trust was accepting a lot of cash from some rather shady sources."

"How shady?"

"Well, like I say, it was not a terribly reliable rumour, but the way I heard it, about as shady as you can get."

"Christ!"

"Don't act on it, Bill. You would need to know a helluva lot more than I've got. And even if there's truth in it, its probable that Cruickshank doesn't know."

"OK. Listen, thanks. I owe you one."

"Yeah, well, take care."

Sheedy put down the phone and sat thinking. Then he asked Rosa to get him an old friend, Teddy Gray on the New York Times.

Istan is a *pueblo* village so far largely untouched by the foreign invaders on the Costa del Sol. Perched on the top of a hill, it is approached by 16 kilometres of winding road between La Concha, the bare, grey mountain that dominates the view inland from the beach between Marbella and San Pedro, and the Rio Verde valley with its dam and reservoir.

Jason Canning had to abandon his car on entering the village because the streets were so narrow. He walked along the street at the front, oblivious of the magnificent view, until he came to a relatively modern bar. Outside it sat a man alone. Canning settled himself at the same table and called for a San Miguel beer. Only after he had it in front of him and had lazily lit a cigarette, did he speak. "*Señor* Castillo?"

"*Si.*"

"The time is approaching when we will need to activate our plans."

"I am ready, *señor.*"

"You have people in place?"

"In Morocco. And on the *costa*. Good people."

"OK. Jordan will be over in a few days. He'll want you to meet him in Tangier."

"No problem."

"Two other things. I need some phones tapped. And I need two or three good men available to me at any time."

"When?"

"The phones? Like yesterday. The men - from tomorrow. You have a place within, say, 30 minutes of the port where they can stay?"

"*Si*, in Fuengirola. We have a safe place there. Here's the telephone number."

"Good. I'll be in touch with it in two to three days. In the meantime, I want these two lines tapped *pronto.*"

Castillo rose, his drink only half-finished, picked up the piece of paper Canning had dropped on the table, and wandered down the road to a telephone box.

Canning leaned back, comfortable in the sun, and lit a cigarette. It was his last match.

Carelessly, he tossed the matchbook into the ashtray... on its front just four words: Premier – lap dancing club.

Soon the man from Malaga returned and the two strolled back up the street, climbed into their respective cars and left.

As they did so a man emerged from a doorway nearby. He walked slowly to the table where the two men had been and, picking up the matchbook, looked at it thoughtfully.

Then Jim Miller, too, went to his car and drove back to the Costa del Sol. Kate was dozing in front of the pool when the man from the phone company came. "Do not disturb yourself, *señorita*," he said. "There is a fault on the line. I know where to fix it."

It took him less than five minutes to place the bug.

When he came out of the villa she was asleep, the phone engineer already forgotten. Ignoring Sheedy's strictures she had slipped off her bikini top.

For a moment the man paused and looked at her half-naked form. "Holy mother of Christ," he muttered, "I would rather tap into you, *señorita*, than your telephone."

And he was gone.

Miller had only been back an hour when the phone rang.

"*Señor* Miller?"

"*Si*," he said. It was one of his only Spanish words. He hoped it would not lead, as it sometimes did, to a torrent of Spanish from the other end.

"I am a friend of a friend of yours in England. I have the gift you ordered."

"Good. Can you meet me tonight - at Puerto Banus?"

"*Si, Señor*. I will be in O'Grady's at l0 o'clock."

"How will I recognise you?"

"You have been described to me, *señor*. I will find you. But just to be on the safe side you can buy a copy of today's Times from the bookshop at the port and put it on the bar in front of you."

Miller poured himself a tiny gin... then added a tiny bit more... then filled it with ice and topped it up with mineral water. Lying down in his room, balancing the glass on his chest, he promised himself that when this business was over he would, for old times sake, have just one bender down at the port.

He could cope with that.

It had been hell but he was getting the drink problem under control.

And over the past few days he had, for the first time in years, begun to feel once more the thrill of the chase.

At six in the evening the yacht slipped out of the port. Cruickshank had decided to take Maria for dinner at sea. They relaxed side by side in comfortable armchairs near the edge of the deck, Cruickshank with his feet up on the railing. Both seemed content to sit without conversation in the late afternoon sun, drink champagne, and look back at the coastline and the hills beyond.

Finally she asked "Have you been busy today, Brian?"

For a moment, as the memory of his meetings with Miller and Canning returned, he frowned. Then, recovering himself, he smiled at her, pleased at her new-found ease with his Christian name. "A busy day, Maria. But now a beautiful one, made beautiful by you."

"Julio says you have some problems with a plot of land."

He frowned again. Julio talked too much. "Yes. We had difficulty finding the owner and now, sadly, we find he has suffered an accident and is dead. It may take time to sort it all out. But it is he we should feel sorry for, not ourselves. Our problems can be solved."

"I'm glad. I would not like any problem to get in the way of your villa on the hill."

His heart leapt. Was this a hint that she was she warming to the idea of the villa as her home too?

"My parents are coming for a brief visit soon, Brian. I hope you will meet them."

"I insist, Maria. Perhaps they could be persuaded to have lunch on the yacht."

She looked pleased. She stood and leaned over the side, her bottom almost within reach of her companion's fingers. She was wearing a pink blouse again, this time with black trousers matching the black hair cascading over her shoulders and down her back. Cruickshank felt a great desire building up within him.

As he looked at her he thought bitterly of the nights of arid hostility he had experienced in his marital bed. He remembered, too, the woman in Maida Vale. She had seemed to know by instinct, more even than he knew, what was necessary to relieve him of the tensions that had driven him there. Sometimes it had been a gentle massage and then equally gentle lovemaking, as if to meet a need for affection. Sometimes he had taken her, urgently, roughly, selfishly, as if his need was purely physical. Sometimes she would take charge, encourage him to do things beyond his own imagination or nerve. There was no act they had not at some time performed together. Cruickshank admitted to himself it was only possible because for some reason he trusted her. Yet every time he had left her flat he had felt degraded and swore to himself that it would be the last time.

And then a week, maybe a fortnight later, late at night or after a heavy day in the office, the need would come and back he would go.

He now knew, as he looked at this woman with her back to him, that while he had had physical experiences, he had never had physical love, never had the chance to pour his love into the depths of a woman who opened herself up to him because she wanted him, just him, and because she wanted to make him happy.

And only now, in his wanting, did he know what he had missed.

He wanted this young woman as he had never wanted before in his life.

He wanted her tenderly. He wanted to hold her and protect her and warm her.

But he also wanted her carnally, wanted to do terrible things to that beautiful woman leaning over the rails. He wanted to see her naked, hold her, enter her; he wanted her to draw him into her arms, to bury his face in her breasts, he wanted to sleep with her and wake with her and lie with her and love her.

He wanted deeply and desperately.

"If I can have this," he thought, "just this, I will never use the word want again."

Suddenly, as if feeling his intensity, she turned and looked at him. He went red. He knew his face had told her his thoughts. Yet she pursued them. "What were you thinking Brian?"

It was no good lying. "I was thinking that you look magnificent, that I want you."

She walked over and sat beside him, so close that he could hair her breathing, smell her scent. "Brian, what do you want of a woman, of a wife?"

"A companion. A lover. Someone to experience all the things of life with me. Someone to sit with in the evenings, to start the day with and end the day with. Someone who will end the loneliness I now realise I have been living with for too many years. Someone to give purpose to all that I am building and creating."

"Was none of this possible with your first wife?"

"No. We were companions for a while. We were poor lovers. And we ended up avoiding each other most of the day and all of the night. I felt sorry for her and she hated me, and I don't blame her. I didn't love her and I didn't know how to pretend that I did. It was my fault... by my ignorance I spoilt both our lives. Its only now I realise what I have missed. And what I caused her to miss."

"But why is it that you want me?"

"Because I believe if I spend every hour of every day with you for the rest of my life I will still be discovering new things, still be excited by you, still be proud of you. That you will enhance every moment of my life, whether I am with you at every moment or not."

She looked thoughtful. And serious. Then she said: "Yes, Brian, enhance... that is the word. Enhance. I believe you would enhance my life too. I never felt that about the young men I have met; I always felt that I would be their possession, that I would exist to enhance their lives. You are the first man I have met who I believe would enhance mine."

For one weak moment Cruickshank found himself fighting back tears. "Maria, does that mean you think it is possible..."

"Yes, Brian, it is possible. I have thought of little else for the past two days. And this morning... up in the hills... I knew I would be proud to have you as my husband, not because of what you showed me, your project, but because riding on horseback in the open air I saw your... your nobility. That and your kindness, they are rare qualities in a man."

In the distance, in the depths of the yacht, a phone rang.

Barely aware of it he took her gently in his arms, kissed her, and began to talk of all his hopes, his plans for them both.

"At this moment there is no man in the world I would rather be," he said. "And there is no woman in the world I would rather be with. At this moment I know what it is to be totally happy."

He was about to kiss her once more when, from the stairway, he heard the butler's voice.

"Sir Brian."

"Yes, Hobbs."

"There's a Mr Sheedy on the phone."

Cruickshank felt as if a small dagger had been plunged into the heart that a few seconds before had been so full.

"Take a message," he said. "I'll call him back."

CHAPTER SEVEN

Felipe Blanco stood naked in front of the mirror drying his black hair and narcissisticly admiring his own physique. Barely 18, he was only five and a half feet tall, slim and with the kind of Latin good looks that make the hearts of teenage girls throb... alas for them in vain, because since coming to the Costa del Sol from the *sierra pueblo* where he was born Felipe had found sexual, if not yet emotional fulfilment elsewhere.

He had been eagerly awaiting this evening off work ever since he spent nearly half his first month's pay on the pair of skin-tight white cotton pants he now pulled up over his otherwise bare backside. They were so close-fitting that he could only just fasten them. At the back they tucked revealingly into the crevasse between his buttocks; at the front they produced a bulge he now surveyed with pride before slipping on a navy-blue tee-shirt. After one last self-admiring glance, he left his tiny cabin and climbed the ladder-like stairs to the deck of the yacht.

Canning was sitting in a leather armchair in the open lounge area near the gangplank, a Martini in one hand, cigarette in the other, his feet carelessly resting on a drinks table. He leered at Felipe as he went by, his contempt only too clear.

The young crew member felt himself blushing. *"Bastardo,"* he muttered under his breath.

He hated Canning, all the more so because when he had first come to work on the yacht he had fallen hopelessly in love with the tall, blonde American. Spotting this, Canning had missed no opportunity to humiliate him.

But, Felipe decided as he proudly paraded down the jetty, not even Canning was going to spoil this night. Arrogantly dismissing admiring looks from young women and the occasional meaningful glance from a lone man, he walked silkily towards the lights of the bars and restaurants on the front.

In his self-absorption he didn't notice another dark-haired young Spaniard who had been sitting at an open-air bar just opposite the yacht, and who now quickly dropped some pesetas by an untouched drink before following him, unobtrusive amid the growing crowd of after-dinner strollers.

Felipe slipped down an alley-way between restaurants into the back street, Calle Ribera. From there he climbed a dimly-lit stairway and walked along a first floor landing until he came to one of the few doors without a neon sign, just a small brass plaque at its side. He pressed a buzzer. The door was opened just a fraction, he was inspected, and then allowed to enter.

A moment later the other Spaniard arrived at the door, pressed the buzzer, and was also admitted.

The Pink Coconut club had just one bar running the full length of a narrow, dimly-lit room, with a row of stools and just enough space to walk between them and the wall. At the end of the bar there was a small round dance floor, raised a few centimetres from the ground, and to its left a doorway into a pitch-dark back room. Every stool was occupied, and other customers leaned by the wall, their drinks resting on a high shelf, so that Felipe had to squeeze his way to the end of the bar. As he did so he felt exploratory hands touch his backside. He pretended he didn't notice but his heart thumped with anticipation.

In this bar Felipe was much-desired and he knew it and loved it.

At the end of the bar, from where they had been looking back up its full length, and from where they could see everyone else in the club, two men were abandoning their stools and heading for the back room. Felipe slipped onto one and ordered a cold San Miguel. The other, too, was quickly taken, this time by a man Felipe guessed was six or seven years older than he, also dark-haired and slim, with a warm, friendly smile that had the effect of engulfing Felipe as he turned and looked at him.

"*Hola*," the stranger said.

Felipe, who was determined not to succumb to the first approach of the evening, at least not too quickly, for he hadn't got himself looking so desirable to immediately disappear out of sight into the gloom of the back room, did not return the greeting but curtly nodded.

If the man was disconcerted, he didn't show it. Instead he casually ordered a San Miguel too and busied himself lighting a cigarette. Then he offered one to Felipe who, satisfied he had made his point, accepted, albeit with a rather ungracious shrug.

"I haven't seen you in this place before," Felipe eventually said, speaking Spanish.

The other repeated the warm smile that the boy found so extraordinarily difficult to resist. "No. First time."

"You're on holiday?"

"No. I live down the *costa*."

"Ah."

"And you?"

"I'm with a yacht in the port."

"Really? Which one?"

"La Gaviota."

The other looked surprised. "Really? You must be incredibly rich."

Felipe laughed. "No, I don't own it. I..." and he exaggerated..." I'm an officer on it."

His companion suppressed a sceptical grin. "Really? I bet that's a good life. I wish I was you."

Felipe was gratified. He looked around the bar. There were three or four men sitting nearby who he would usually have been happy to attract, men with more obvious *machismo* than his neighbour, and Felipe liked his men big and tough, but he felt a surprising affinity with this easy-going stranger.

The Pink Coconut meant a lot to Felipe. Because of the importance of *machismo* to the younger men in his sierra village and their contempt for *marica* (their word, full of distaste, for effeminate homosexuals), Felipe had been forced to suppress both his personality and his needs. Despite a rather pathetic attempt to appear even more *macho* than his peers, he had inevitably become a lonely and isolated boy. When he came to the port and another crew member on La Gaviota introduced him to the Pink Coconut, Felipe found himself for the first time able to relax and be himself in friendly, uncritical surroundings. He thrived on a sense of belonging, even more on the discovery that he was not only accepted but desired. Yet for all the easy companionship of the evenings he spent in this place, the boost to his ego from the men he picked up, the physical release, Felipe was still unsatisfied. He had never really met anyone with whom he could build a friendship, with whom he could sit drinking in the bars at the waters-edge, gossiping and making catty remarks about the passers-by, with whom he could go to parties or even for a day out in the country or swimming at the beach. Often on his way from the yacht to the club he would see two men dining together in one of the expensive restaurants, absorbed with their own company, and he would wish that he had a friend who could afford to take him there. So far it hadn't happened. The men who picked Felipe up in the Pink Coconut wanted him just as long as it took to satisfy their needs in the darkened back room, or at their hotel, or even on a remote patch of beach. And that was it. Just *"gracias* and *adios"*.

So when the young man offered to refill his glass and began to chat without any of the usual sexual come-on, treating Felipe as a friend, Felipe began to feel immensely happy. Sitting cross-legged on the stool, waving his cigarette in the air, and drinking too quickly, he laughed loudly at the other's jokes, and looked at the poker-faced men down the length of the bar as if to say 'Look at me; I've got a friend; I'm having a good time; not for me a night of solitary drinking and eye-contact assignations in the back room.' Felipe was showing off.

"I think I met someone else from your yacht the other evening," said his new friend.. "I was taken by a friend – a straight guy – to the Premier lap dancing club. There was a tall, blonde guy there, hair almost white. I don't think he was gay, though."

"Oh that would be Canning, he goes there a lot." Felipe said with distaste. "He's an *Americano*. He's not with the yacht. Not one of the crew. He's with the business that owns it." He looked at the other, surprised. "But what were you doing in Premier? Its not a gay bar."

The other took a leisurely sip of his drink and then, grinning, said "This friend of mine was playing a joke at my expense. Told me it was a gay bar. Its about as non-gay as you can get." He lit yet another cigarette and then picked up the earlier conversation. "Anyway I think that was the man, I think he said that was his name. Tony Canning."

"No, not Tony. Jason. Jason Canning."

"Right. *Si*. Of course. It was Jason. And he's not gay?"

"No. If you ask me he's not even human."

"Oh, why do you say that?"

Felipe happily launched himself into an attack on the character of his enemy. "Cold as ice. Thinks he's God. Doesn't like anyone and no-one likes him. The others on the yacht say he spends hours in that club, drinking alone, ignoring the girls, and watching people. He's always watching people."

"Is he the top man?"

"No. The Englishman is the top man. Cruickshank. Canning just works for him. There's been a lot of talk on the yacht that the Englishman hates him too, but he can't get rid of him."

"Why's that?"

"I don't know. And I don't care."

The other, not wishing to push the matter too fast, took his time lighting a cigarette, and then deliberately moved his stool closer until his arm and that of Felipe were touching.

The young Spaniard felt a hardening in his crotch and began to wish the new white pants were not quite so tight. He moved his hand to adjust himself and the other let his eyes slip down to the bulge then back up to Felippe's face. He smiled again, an intimate smile, a smile full of warmth and understanding. Felipe's heart lurched.

The stranger now re-opened the conversation, this time approaching similar territory but from a different direction.

"You must have a good life. How much time do you spend at sea?"

"Oh, we get out most weekends, especially when the Englishman is here. And sometimes for an evening. Occasionally we have a longer trip, across to Tangier or even as far as the Italian Riviera or the Greek islands."

"Do you have your own cabin?"

Felipe's smile faded. This was a familiar question, usually the opening gambit in the game of sexual proposition and counter-proposition that comprised the twilight life he led in this and the other gay bars. Maybe he was being illogical, but he was disappointed. "Yes, but we're not allowed to take friends on board," he replied coldly.

"Ah."

There was a moment's silence, then the other asked "So how big is the yacht? How many on board?"

"About seven crew members, some cooks and stewards, and then in the offices there are the Englishman, Canning, and some administrative people. The planners and architects operate from their own offices?

"What planners and architects?"

Felipe looked vague. "Oh, they're involved in some project the company is building in the hills. They say it will be *super grande*. Hotels and golf courses..."

He was getting bored with the subject and the other saw it. He put his hand on Felipe's thigh. The crew member's hand shook as he reached for his cigarette. The pressure within his now too-tight pants was becoming unbearable. He couldn't resist a glance towards the back room, yet it was not an eager glance. Felipe felt an ambivalence towards the back room; it was, of course, exciting, ideal for uncomplicated, raw sexual relief, but usually it meant that his search for love had once more ended in a soulless sexual encounter with a man whose face he couldn't even see. And he hated returning to the bar to the knowing look in the ever-watchful eyes of the others sitting in the gloom, and then to the yacht feeling abused and soiled and desperately alone.

But this was different. Felipe wanted this man, wanted to do things in the back room that even there would not be anonymous, then wanted to come out proudly, hand in hand, and leave with him, perhaps to go back to his place, more likely to make a date for another evening and the friendship and affection he craved.

So when the other turned and began to talk more quietly he was ready to acquiesce to anything. What he heard was the last thing he expected.

"Look, I have to go now."

Felipe's face must have revealed shock and indignation at the crushing of his hopes, for the other continued quickly. "But I really would like to meet you again when we can spend more time together."

Once more he rested a gentle, suggestive hand on Felipe's thigh and the younger man melted at the touch.

"When is your next night off?"

"Tomorrow. I have tomorrow off also."

"Tomorrow then? About nine?"

"*Si.*"

With that Sheedy's partner Manuel slipped off the stool and quickly left the bar.

Near the exit to the port he slipped into a telephone booth and rang Sheedy, catching him just after he had arrived at the villa.

"Bill, the man we're looking for: his name is Jason Canning. He works with Anglo-Spanish Investors, fits the description of the man who spoke to the Rabbit Man in the bar at Ronda and he drinks most nights at Premier."

"You did well. For when did you fix the next meeting?"

"Tomorrow night."

"Right. I'll talk to you about how we handle it in the morning."

Back in the bar Felipe was wrestling with conflicting emotions. He was elated that he had made a friend. Someone who had been happy to spend time with him despite knowing a sexual encounter wasn't possible that night. Someone who was anxious to see him as soon as possible. Tomorrow. Perhaps tomorrow after a drink they could go out and have dinner.

Felipe wondered if the other had money. Then it struck him: they hadn't even exchanged names. As usual, he had been too happy being the centre of attention to ask about his companion... to even ask his name.

Yet he trusted the other. He would come tomorrow. Felipe remembered the warm smile and knew he would.

In the meantime he was frustrated, and discomforted by the other's sudden departure. He felt he had lost face, especially after his, Felipe's, exhibitionist behaviour at the bar.

And he felt physically let down. He had waited a week for this night off the yacht and the encounter with the other man had excited him further.

Endeavouring to maintain as much dignity as he could, he rose from the stool and wandered to the edge of the dance floor, aware that his provocatively-exposed figure was under lascivious surveillance from the men lounging against the wall.

He paused at the door to the backroom and leaned against the doorway, cigarette dying in his hand.

A big, fair-haired man clad in blue jeans, denim shirt and black leather jacket came over to the doorway, turned and looked hard at Felipe and then disappeared into the gloom. Felipe, his heart thumping under his tee shirt, followed. As he too was enveloped in darkness he felt a hand guide him further into the room. As he obediently responded he bumped more than once into other men, and his protective hand felt naked arms and backs. He was now totally under the control of the other's guiding arm, his own will dissipated by the combination of physical need and the pull of a stronger personality. He felt himself being turned round to face the shadowy figure of the larger man. As rough, demanding hands reached down and began to fumble with the top button of his pants he closed his eyes and gave in to the forces of desire, egoism, loneliness that had brought him here to this uncaring darkness.

Later as, eyes downcast, he climbed the gangplank of the yacht he heard a sardonic chuckle. He looked up and saw Canning still sitting, smoking, in the leather chair, his face a picture of malevolent innuendo. Felipe flushed and half-tripped in his haste to escape the other's gaze.

Canning laughed.

The young Spaniard fled to his cabin, his heart full of hate. "*Bastardo*," he muttered. "I'll get you one day... one day I'll make you pay."

Only later, much later, after he had showered and climbed into his bunk, did he open himself to happier thoughts... about the nameless man with the warm smile who he would meet tomorrow.

Cruickshank could not have felt happier. Maria's guardians Juan and Cristina Garcia had come unexpectedly to the Costa del Sol and were now welcome last-minute guests of honour at a garden party and barbecue he had organised for influential local people.

It was all set up at the front of the villa, over-looking the beach.

To one side the chef from the yacht and two others were cooking over charcoal fires, filling the night air with an enticing aroma as giant Mediterranean prawns, lobsters and other fish sizzled at one end, whole chickens on skewers at the other, and steaks, chops and sausages between them.

A trio of guitarists were playing on the balcony overlooking the garden. At the candle-lit tables, decorated with displays of red roses and bowls overflowing with fresh fruit, guests were choosing from quality wines and the best Spanish champagne.

At one table in the centre of the lawn sat Cruickshank, the Garcias and Maria, Julio the architect and his wife, and the mayors of Estepona and Benahavis and their wives. Maria, as often in the evening, was dressed in white and looked sensational.

The Garcias were impressed by the enchanting scene and flattered by the special attention of their host.

Cruickshank had positioned Juan Garcia on his right and after dinner he took the Spaniard by the arm and under the watchful gaze of Cristina Garcia and the apprehensive one of Maria strolled down to the end of the garden. There he talked of the pleasure Maria's company had given everybody and how much inspiration she obviously drew from the Garcias.

As intended, Juan Garcia was charmed. Cruickshank, he insisted, must come as their guest to Seville. It was an invitation accepted with alacrity.

Later Maria said to Cruickshank "My adoptive mother has been watching us. I think she may guess. She asked me what I thought of you."

"What did you say?"

"That you are generous, that you have been kind to me, and that you are a man of honour."

"Oh God," he groaned. "Honour again."

Maria laughed, a gentle laugh that warmed his heart. "Well, it pleased her, even if it doesn't please you. Anyway, I changed the subject and she has not pressed further."

Cruickshank took her arm and drew her closer. "You look magnificent this evening, Maria. I wish I could order all these people away and have you alone to myself."

"I wouldn't do that, Brian. I do not think my guardians would be at all impressed."

Now it was his turn to laugh. "Very well. For that reason alone I will allow them to stay."

With that he began to expertly circulate, 'working the room' as his political masters used to say, ensuring that every guest left feeling they had been special to their host that night.

When at last they had all departed he strolled alone down onto the beach and looked out at the sea, black satin under moonlight diluted by light clouds. It was a warm night and the only sound was that of the small waves breaking on the stony shore.

I could be happy in this country, he thought. Happy with Maria.

He thought of London, the struggle to meetings through increasingly heavy traffic, the cold, damp winters, the hundred and one irritating problems that arose in his office every day, the same faces in the City and at the Club, the boredom of the 'games' that had once excited and enthralled him.

How could that compare with the colour, the warmth, the gentle pace of this place? Or with the life he could lead in his villa above the valley, the life he could lead there with Maria?

He resolved to progress the project with renewed vigour in the morning.

It was time he took it under even tighter control.

Nothing, but nothing, must upset his plans.

After he had spoken to Manuel, Sheedy checked his answer-phone. There were two messages.

The first said "*Señor* Bill. This is Miguel. I have found hidden in *El Conejero's cortijo* what I believe to be the answer to the mystery. Can you come to Ronda tomorrow? If you can, leave a message at *Guardia Civil* headquarters."

The other was from a secretary telephoning on behalf of Sir Brian Cruickshank. Sheedy was invited to conduct his interview over lunch on La Gaviota, the company's yacht, also the following day.

"Well, I can't be in both places," Sheedy said to Kate. "Miguel will have to wait."

"No need for that, Bill. Why can't I go and see him? I want to build up my portfolio on Ronda. And I want to photograph Gaucin. I can find out what he's turned up and you'll save a day."

Sheedy liked the idea. After leaving a message for Miguel he left Maria reading and drove down the hill.

The restaurant D'Herminia is positioned close to *Gran Paradisio campo de Golf.* Over a dinner of *gambas al pil pil* and suckling pig Sheedy asked Ramon Aparitico to tell him what was happening on the *costa.* "I'm seeing Cruickshank tomorrow and I'm a bit out of touch. Who's developing what? Is the pace slowing down?"

"Don't you believe it, *Señor*," said the Spaniard. "There's no stopping it. People from the north of Europe seem to have decided this is their equivalent of your California and the developers are queuing up to build for them."

Some land prices had doubled in just two years, he said, and that was an increase on what were already astronomic levels.

He began to describe the building boom on the costa.

Sotogrande now covered 4,400 acres. Over the past decade Fincasol had spent as much as 30,000 million pesetas developing two parts of Sotogrande including a hospital and a cricket stadium. The golf club and villa built at San Roque by a Japanese company had probably cost as much as 20,000 million pesetas, and Dutch company's marina at Benalmadena could eventually be even bigger than Puerto Banus, with more than 1000 yachts and 600 *apartamentos*.

Golf courses were ever - increasing and Cruickshank was not even alone with his idea for horse racing. A Spanish company had invested at least 35,000 million pesetas on a race track in the Mijas Costa area and it was already in operation."

Sheedy whistled. "All this activity must lend some urgency to the activities of Cruickshank and company. No wonder they're worried about the delay in getting the remaining piece of land. What do you think Anglo-Spanish Investors are spending on their project?"

"I don't know exactly, *señor*, but I believe it could be as much as 150,000 million pesetas including the land. I'm told that they are sparing no expense.

Sheedy sat quietly for a moment.

"That's a lot of money. I guess a man would do a lot to protect that sort of money."

It was a cold night and Miguel shivered and pulled his big leather jacket around him as he left the bar and began to climb the hill to the bridge over *El Tajo*, stumbling once or twice because, truth to tell, he had drunk a brandy too many.

The bars had been quiet and Miguel had lacked his usual company. Drinking alone had made him morose. Spotting two lovers whispering to each other on one of the stone steps by the bridge made him feel empty and sad. The civil war and then his duties as a civil guard had cut him off from community life when he was younger. He had missed out on the chance to court a *señorita*, to marry and have children. In this respect he knew life had passed him by. He would have liked, by now, to be a jolly grandfather, sitting in front of the fire on cold winter nights surrounded by grandchildren spellbound by his stories of the war. Now it could never be.

The Plaza de Espana was quiet and dark, the bars now closed, and he meandered up the main thoroughfare, the Calle Virgen de la Paz, past the Plaza de Toros and the Restaurante Pedro Romero. As he did so, as he did every night now, he thought of his oldest friend, *El Conejero*, and he felt sadder still. Often they had talked about Miguel retiring, about sharing their last years hunting together, drinking wine and dozing under the lemon trees at el *cortijo* during the hot summer evenings, and coming to town only for the *corridas*. Now that, too, could never be.

Now he was past the Alameda park, and walking up into the back streets until he came to a small alley between two rows of white-washed houses. At the end of the alley he paused. He wasn't ready to go home. He suddenly felt terribly alone. And tired. And old. He yearned for the noise and smoke and argument and laughter of the bar. But even if he had the energy to walk back into town those bars that were not closed were all but empty.

At that moment, standing at the entrance to the alley, Miguel took a decision. He would not go on like this. It was time to retire. He should have done so years back. He would tell them tomorrow that he would not wait for the fixed date. They wouldn't mind; they had already been indulging him, letting him stay on years after he should have gone.

The decision made him feel better. Now he was no longer reluctant to go to his bed.

His home was at the end of the alley. As he fumbled for the key he half-leaned on the door and to his surprise it gave way.

Miguel paused.

This was not right.

He had locked the door. He remembered doing it.

Struggling to sober up, he reached down, unbuttoned the leather holster, and slipped the old wood-handled revolver into his hand. He stepped into the dark and listened. There was no sound.

He took another step and the door slammed behind him. He swung round only to feel the sharp end of a knife at the back of his neck. A rough hand pushed him forward so that his face was pressed against the door.

"Drop the gun or you're dead," hissed a man's voice. Miguel let it drop with a clatter on the stone floor.

He was aware now of a man on each side, the one to his left holding the knife that was sticking uncomfortably into his neck.

He heard a third man moving on the other side of the room, heard him lighting the lamp on the table. "Turn him round."

As the lamp flickered into life Miguel saw that the men on either side of him were Spaniards, not, he thought, from Ronda. The man lounging back in Miguel's old armchair was tall, slim, blonde, almost white-haired. His accent was American. Miguel guessed this must be the man who had spoken to his old friend *El Conejero* in the bar... the man who had probably killed him. He looked at him in silent anger.

One of the Spaniards had picked up the gun and tossed it to the American who now sardonically waved it at Miguel almost as if it were a toy.

"Do these still work, *Señor* Policeman?" he asked. "Well, you believed it would save you so presumably it also has the capacity to kill you. Let's hope we don't have to find out."

Miguel found his voice. "What do you want? Why are you in my house?"

"Papers, my friend. Papers and photographs. You took them from the old man's farmhouse. "

"You mean *El Conejero*? His *cortijo*? I did not. They are still there. They were his. Why do you want them? What are they to you?"

The smile left the American's face.

"Don't lie policeman. You took the papers and photographs. You have them. We know that. I want them. And I want them now. We've searched this place and they're not here. Where are they?"

Miguel shook his head defiantly. "I think you killed him. Why? Because he wouldn't sell his land? Is that why? Do you need money so much that you must kill an old man for a bit more?"

The American's smile faded. Miguel felt a chill radiating from his grey eyes.

"Hold his arms."

He walked over and transferring the gun to his left hand, prodded it in Miguel's considerable stomach while reaching with his other for the knife. Once he had it in his hand he poked it between Miguel's legs.

"Now, *Señor* Policeman, I don't think you understand. I am a busy man and I want the papers now. I am going to count to ten and if you don't tell me where they are I am going to cut off your *cojones*. One... two... three..."

Miguel's stomach turned to water. There was a lack of humanity in this man's eyes, a madness. He didn't doubt the American would do exactly what he threatened. He tried desperately to think, wishing he had not drunk so much brandy. "Wait," he said. "I don't have them but I can tell you where they are."

The other smiled slowly. "That's better. Talk."

"I posted them."

"Posted them? To who?"

"To the reporter. To Bill Sheedy."

Miguel had decided there was no point in lying. The American undoubtedly knew of Sheedy's interest. If he also knew that Sheedy had the papers he would be discouraged from killing Miguel; there would be no point.

And if he, Miguel, could get out of this, there was plenty of time to warn Sheedy.

"When did you post them?"

"Today."

The American looked at Miguel suspiciously, but finally, to the Spaniard's relief, said "I think you're telling the truth, policeman."

"Then give me back my gun and go."

The American laughed humourlessly. "I'm afraid I can't do that policeman. You know that. You know too much. But what I can do is give you one of the bullets. Would that help?"

Miguel knew the time for talk was past. With a tremendous effort, and drawing on all of his weight, he threw the two men off him and lunged towards the American.

He nearly made it but one of the Spaniards grabbed his arm, pulling him off balance. This enabled the American to bring the gun barrel down onto the back of Miguel's head with great force. As he hit the ground he was struck a second time. And a third.

Telling the Spaniards to eliminate any signs of a struggle while they waited with the unconscious policeman, the American slipped out into the darkened street and round a corner to where his car was parked. He quietly drove it to the entrance of the alley and signalled to the two men to bring Miguel out. This proved easier said than done. Sweating and cursing they slowly dragged the enormous inert form of Miguel to the car and with enormous difficulty bundled him onto the back seat. The Spaniards then climbed uncomfortably into the single passenger front seat and the car slipped quietly away.

When it reached the Plaza de España it was driven under the archway with the big clock and into the empty car park alongside

El Tajo, a place where there is only a low stone wall between the Ronda plateau and the ravine.

There Miguel was taken out. The American poured brandy into the unconscious man's mouth and a little on his clothes.

Then the three dragged him to the edge and threw him over the wall.

Silently they watched him disappear into the black hole that was *El Tajo*.

Watched him begin his lonely, un-witnessed last journey... the fall onto the rocks 900 feet below.

And there, where many of his fellow countrymen had died before him, priests and revolutionaries and soldiers...

...there Miguel, who had himself survived the civil war and 50 years as an officer in the *Guardia Civil*...

...there Miguel, smiling, food-loving, fun-loving, wine-loving Miguel...

...there Miguel died too.

Sheedy had as a news editor always urged his reporters not to prejudge anyone. "Approach every story as open-mindedly as possible. The facts should dictate the story, not your prejudices." Despite these views he had formulated in his mind a picture of Cruickshank and he didn't expect to like him, not at all. As a result, he was taken by surprise.

For a start, he instantly recognised Cruickshank. He was the man who had been on the plane with he and Kate the other day. But the tall, thin, rather severe-looking man Sheedy had only half-noticed then greeted him now with a warm smile. The eyes looking at him over the half-moon glasses were intelligent but also full of good humour. This was a man, the reporter concluded, who it would not be difficult to like.

Cruickshank ushered him into the library, poured two glasses of champagne, and let Sheedy set the pace.

"I've heard rumours about your real estate purchases and how you plan to develop the land, Sir Brian. If they're correct its an unusual and impressive project. I would like to film a report on it for my programme."

Cruickshank looked - and was - surprised. He had assumed Sheedy had come to talk about the Rabbit Man. Could it be that the reporter had no idea of the connection? That this was a relatively innocent visit, just about the project itself?

Or was the reporter leading up to the real story slowly? If so, this approach could work to Cruickshank's advantage.

"You're well informed Mr Sheedy. Yes, we do plan a major project. To be frank with you, we've not publicised it till now because the land values would have been raised even higher than they already were. I don't blame the landowners for that. That's their right. But we equally have the right to protect ourselves from an excess of greed. However, we have the land we want now and we've been planning to announce our plans soon. When did you wish to do your programme?"

All journalists liked to be first with a story, Sheedy replied. He would like it before it was officially announced.

Cruickshank nodded. "I understand that, but you won't be surprised that the company would like to announce the details itself in its own way."

He refilled Sheedy's glass. "I wonder whether there is a compromise. If we can reach accord on the timing I could announce the project late in the afternoon of the day of your programme. Thus while it won't be a scoop - I think that's what you journalists call it - most people will hear it first from you. And, of course, we could assist you by recording an interview in advance."

Sheedy rose and held out his hand. "Its a deal." He walked over to the model. "Is this it?"

Cruickshank joined him. "It is... this is the *Valle de Maria*." He began to describe it in detail and, Sheedy noted, with infectious enthusiasm. This, the American decided, was no ordinary developer. This man was a dreamer.

Over lunch of fresh fish and salad Sheedy asked question after question and Cruickshank, open and friendly, answered them in a direct way that impressed the reporter. He commented upon it: "You're surprisingly helpful, Sir Brian. I'm accustomed to greater reticence from developers."

"I come from a career in public life, Mr Sheedy, I understand your profession. I'm also, you may have observed, proud of this project. And, to be frank, we will need a friendly response from people on the *costa*; fair and accurate publicity can only be helpful. So I have every reason to cooperate."

Sheedy laughed. "You make me feel I'm involved, Sir Brian. That's a rare talent. But I don't know that I want to be that involved. I don't know whether I approve. Tell me, what benefit is there to Spain in projects like this? I can't imagine many Spaniards will be able to afford to be members. And won't the profits go into the pockets of foreign investors?"

"There'll be work," Cruickshank replied, "both in building the project and in staffing it."

"You mean servants to the foreign rich? Is that such a good thing?"

"Look, Mr Sheedy, there are many aspects of the holiday and tourist explosion on the Costa del Sol that I don't like. I think the lack of planning control, the allowing of monstrosities to be build near the beach, the creation, at least for a time, of a safe haven for British criminals, the exploitation of many local workers in the catering and hotel industries, all this has been bad. But that's as much the fault of the Spanish authorities as it is of foreigners.

"For my part, I'm building a project of unprecedented quality.

"I'm building it on a piece of land that has not been good for agriculture.

"And I'm creating work. You may sneer about the Spanish being servants but Andalucia still has high unemployment and this will be reasonably well-paid and secure work. I suspect the Spanish won't be sneering."

Sheedy threw up his hands. "Ok, Sir Brian... let's not argue about it, at least not now. We can always do so on camera. Incidentally I wasn't sneering... just asking?"

Cruickshank was not, however, easily appeased. "Tell me, Mr Sheedy, where do you live? I expect in a villa that has been built by Spanish labourers on Spanish land. And I suspect your cleaning is done by a Spanish maid. And do you not eat in the Spanish restaurants and drink in the Spanish bars manned by the same allegedly underpaid workforce? Don't you think your questions would be more valid if you were not taking advantage as much as anyone else ?"

Sheedy laughed but didn't attempt to answer, preferring to ask where the money was coming from.

"Anglo-Spanish Investors is not a public company, Mr Sheedy. It is, in effect, a consortium of private investors, some in Spain, some in the UK, and some in the United States."

"Who in particular in the United States?"

Cruickshank hesitated. "I think it only fair that before I name them, I advise them I'll be doing so. I'll have to come back to you on that." Sheedy pressed. "Fair enough. But I imagine you have to be careful. I imagine this is just the kind of overseas project that would be attractive to people who have questionable funds to invest."

Cruickshank was more than up to the challenge. Smiling, he replied "Good heavens, Mr Sheedy, next you'll be suggesting our money comes from the mafia."

Then to change the subject, he rose and suggested they return to the library for coffee and a brandy. There the American asked Cruickshank for details about himself. The Englishman briefly described his career, missing, Sheedy observed, none of his achievements, yet covering them in a deprecating way that made the point without pressing it immodestly. It was impressive and, Sheedy thought, unless the man was a consummate actor, it was more than just a performance. The man's ego was well under control.

Cruickshank, too, had been sizing up Sheedy. He, too, had taken a liking to the man from the start. The reporter had an open face. Cruickshank felt there was a good chance the American was clever but not devious, sceptical but not prejudiced. He was the kind of man he liked to deal with.

On the other hand, he thought, if Sheedy did stumble onto evidence of the murder, there could be no question of his being persuaded to stay silent.

Offering the reporter a cigar, he asked Sheedy about his own career. The American briefly described it.

When he had done so Cruickshank, fascinated, said "The Costa del Sol seems a long way from Vietnam, or that matter the streets of New York. Don't you find it comparatively unexciting?"

"We all get older, Sir Brian. I've had more than enough gunfire for one life."

The Englishman laughed. "I know what you mean. I must admit I look forward to living in Spain myself. Are you married, Mr Sheedy?"

"My wife died."

Cruickshank looked genuinely compassionate. "I'm sorry."

"Thanks. Time heals. I have a friend."

"Then the two of you must spend a weekend at sea with me soon."

"That's kind. We'd love to."

Sheedy rose and walked across to the model.

Steeling himself to ask the key question, he turned towards the developer.

But to his surprise Cruickshank beat him to it. The Englishman had known it had to come and perceptively guessed when Sheedy rose that this was the moment. A master at getting an opponent off-balance, he spoke quickly, before the reporter could.

"By the way your programme the other night was of some relevance to my project."

Sheedy was taken aback. "Oh, why?"

"The man you spoke of. *Señor* Rodriguez. We had just negotiated with him to buy the last parcel of land we need. His unfortunate death makes things a bit more difficult, I'm afraid. We may have some delay and no doubt the beneficiaries of his will ask for even more, so it will also cost us money.

"By the way, do you really think he was deliberately killed?"

Sheedy thought quickly. Either Cruickshank was incredibly clever or the Rabbit Man's death was a coincidence. To his surprise the American found himself hoping it was the second. And he had to admit the story sounded entirely plausible.

If the Rabbit Man had reached a deal with Cruickshank's man, there was no incentive for Cruickshank to want him killed.

On the other hand there was the evidence - the stone that probably killed him, the position of the bridge planks, the matchbox. All explicable, of course, but not to be lightly discounted.

"It probably was an accident, Sir Brian. After all who would want to kill him? Obviously not you." He laughed to take the edge off the remark.

Cruickshank was equally light-hearted. "Obviously not. Apart from my sympathy for the man, its a damn nuisance."

"Still," Sheedy said, " its a coincidence. I take it you know nothing about the man that could explain it ?"

"No."

"How on earth did he come to own the land ?"

"I can't help you, I'm afraid. We discovered the name of the owner of the land and it took my staff months to find him. At first he didn't want to sell but eventually we made him an offer, far more than we should have paid, and he simply couldn't refuse."

Cruickshank looked at his watch and, explaining he was flying to London later that afternoon, guided the reporter to the gangplank.

Sheedy walked thoughtfully back to the car and drove to see Manuel at the office.

"Well?" the young Spaniard asked impatiently as he entered.

"Well, I don't know. He could not have been more open. He even raised the death of the Rabbit Man before I did. He said the old man's death is an inconvenience to them, will cause delays and cost them more money."

"Did you believe him?"

"Either that or he's a brilliant actor."

"So what are you going to do?"

"Wait until we hear what Kate brings back from Miguel and until we've had our little encounter with your boyfriend tonight."

"He's not my boyfriend." Manuel looked furious and Sheedy laughed.

"Ok, ok, no more jokes. Now lets see if we can get Teddy Gray on the phone and find out what we can about this man Canning."

While Sheedy had been with Cruickshank, Kate had driven up into the sierras en route for Ronda, calling first at Gaucin, a key stop-over point on the old smuggling trails. As her tiny hire car chugged up the hill and into the village, she could imagine shadowy figures of mule and man making their laborious way up during the night to disappear into the narrow streets and to shelter behind the big wooden doors, there to be fed, rested, and warmed in exchange for a carton of cigarettes or a bag of coffee.

She parked the car and walked up the narrow streets wondering what family dramas were being played out behind the silent, unrevealing white walls, the beaded curtains, the wooden doors.

In which of them was the peace being broken right now, at this moment, by the cries of babies, the laughter of children, the moans of lovers, the snores of slumbering old men, the prayers of black-clad widows?

In which of these houses had smugglers been made welcome, fed and rested?

Which of these old men chatting in the square or sitting on their steps had robbed, killed or even tortured in the civil war days... who were the heroes and who were the cowards?

Kate marvelled that this noisy people who lived so much of their lives in the bars and on the streets were yet also so enigmatic, sceptical, watchful, their secrets hidden behind layer after layer of caution and privacy.

She felt Gaucin was an ideal place to illustrate Lorca's poem "The Village":

Upon a barren mount,
a calvary.
Clear water
and century-old olive trees.
In the narrow streets,
men hidden under cloaks;
and on the towers,
weather vanes spinning.
Eternally
spinning.
Oh, lost village,
in the Andalucia of tears!

She drove on to Ronda, parking on the edge of *El Tajo*, in too much of a hurry to notice the two *Guardia Civil* officers who were, unusually, guarding part of the car park and keeping it free of vehicles. She soon located the headquarters of the *Guardia Civil*. The Spanish flag was draped over its doorway. On the tiles above it, on a yellow strip between two strips of red, were printed the words *"Guardia Civil... Todo por la Patria"*, All for the Fatherland.

She guessed that there was some kind of flap on; there were three cars outside the station, one bigger than the usual *Guardia Civil* vehicle, and several officers were standing in a group talking quietly, some obviously distressed.

She pushed past the group and, entering the office building, asked a sergeant at the desk for *Señor* Miguel. He looked at her questioningly for a moment, then asked her to wait.

Soon she heard a door open and turned with a smile to greet Miguel only to find herself facing another policeman, immaculately dressed in what she assumed to be the uniform of a senior officer.

Having established her identity he led her into a smaller room. Bare-looking and uncarpeted, it contained two tables, each with just a canvas chair. In front of one was an old leather armchair in bad need of upholstering. The officer indicated she should take it. She looked around. On a shelf beside her was a row of files that appeared to contain updates on *Guardia Civil* regulations. Hanging on a nail was a bunch of keys, beside it a black and white picture of King Juan Carlos. On the other desk was an old typewriter. Sitting behind it, oblivious to Kate and the other officer, an aged policeman was typing out a report, painfully slowly, and with occasional muttered curses as with a machine-gun-like ratatattat he put a series of crosses through a mistake.

For a moment the officer sat silently looked at her, then he asked "Why do you want to see Officer Ayala?"

"Who?"

"Officer Ayala... Miguel Ayala."

Kate realised she had never heard Miguel's last name before.

"I had arranged to call on him today. Just a social call. Is there a problem?"

"When did you arrange this, *Señorita*?"

"Yesterday afternoon. "Kate began to be alarmed. "What's the matter. Has something happened to Miguel? Why are you asking me these questions?"

"In a moment, *Señorita*. But first I must ask you some more. How long have you known Officer Ayala?"

"Only two or three weeks. But my friend Bill Sheedy has known him for much longer."

"When did you last see him?"

"Oh, about a week ago, when he came to our home near San Pedro."

"Where were you last night, *Señorita*? In Ronda?"

"No. At the villa in San Pedro. *Señor* Sheedy's villa. He was there too."

"I see." Again he looked at her silently, then, his voice softening, he told her Miguel was dead.

Kate felt tears spring to her eyes. "But where? How?"

"I'm afraid he was found at the foot of *El Tajo*, *Señorita*. This morning. It could have been an accident... but..."

"My God." Kate struggled to grasp what she was being told.

"He had been drinking, *Señorita*, so he could have accidentally fallen, but we can't think why he would have gone to that place. Unless it was suicide and no-one who knew him could believe that.

So we are for the moment treating it as a suspicious death. Do you know of any reason why this should have happened?"

Kate tried to think. What would Bill want her to do? Then, unable to see any point in not telling the truth, she said "I only know that he was investigating the death of the man they called *El Conejero*, the Rabbit Man. Oh God..." She was struck by the coincidence. "He also died by falling into a ravine. That, too, was made to look like an accident. Its all repeating itself."

She wiped her eyes, then added "Miguel had been collaborating with Bill Sheedy over that investigation. He is a television reporter."

The officer looked thoughtful. "I see. Had you come to talk to Officer Ayala about this matter?"

Kate was having difficulty associating the formal name with the friendly Miguel. "Not really. Except that he had some information for Mr Sheedy that I was to take back."

"What kind of information?"

Kate decided a small lie wouldn't matter. "I don't know. You will have to ask Mr Sheedy."

Satisfied, the officer made a note of her and Sheedy's address and telephone number and led her to the door. "Will you be alright, *Señorita* Callaghan, or should I have one of my men drive you back?"

She thanked him but declined the offer, and walked back into the *plaza* and into the Restaurante Meson del Puente on the cliff edge where she asked to use the telephone. From there she broke the news to Sheedy and arranged to meet him at the villa in the hour it would take her to drive back.

She found him sitting on the balcony looking out at the sea with unseeing eyes, whisky glass in hand. "I'm sorry Bill," she said, and sat at his feet, putting her head in his lap. For a while they sat like that wordlessly, he gently stroking her hair. When he spoke he sounded grim.

"Bloody hell, Kate, a couple of hours back I was ready to accept that it was all a coincidence, that Cruickshank and his bloody project had nothing to do with the Rabbit Man's death. But they've got to be, Kate. The two so-called accidents have got to be connected and they've got to be connected to Anglo-Spanish Investors and their bloody project. And they're going to pay for it. We're going to get these buggers. Don't doubt it."

"You think Cruickshank is personally involved?"

"I don't know. Possibly not. If what Teddy Gray in New York tells me is correct, one of the big investors in this project, a man called Jordan, is about as bad news as you can get. He could be looking after his interests independently of Cruickshank. On the other hand the project is Cruickshank's baby and he doesn't strike me as the kind of man to relinquish control to anyone. Anyway, whatever the level of Cruickshank's involvement, this man Canning is the executioner."

He stood up and restlessly paced about, going into the villa and then coming back out onto the balcony. "Listen, Manuel and I have some work to do tonight. We'll be through by about 10 o'clock. We'll come back for a planning session."

"Be careful."

"I will." Sheedy grabbed a jacket and the car keys and walked out of the room.

Kate looked after him, thinking it was strange how Sheedy the hunter took on a harder, younger physical look than when relaxed around the house or pool. She liked these two shades of the man, the "softie" as she called him when he was relaxing with her, and the restless tough guy when it came to work, yet as she heard the door slam and the car roar as his foot hit the accelerator, she thought she liked the relaxed Sheedy best. This one she felt she didn't really know.

Sheedy drove quickly down the hill, through San Pedro then left onto the main road to Marbella. Pulling up at his office, he carelessly left the car on a no-parking line and climbed the stairs two at a time. He found Rosa looking puzzled at a big pile of papers and photographs lying on his desk.

"What's this?"

"It came in the post, *señor*."

Sheedy picked up a few of the papers and recognised them immediately. They were the ones from *el cortijo*. With them was a brief note scrawled by Miguel on *Guardia Civil* letterhead: "*Bill, I tried to reach you or Señorita Kate at the villa to say that I was posting these after all. There is a chance I may be sent out into the country in the morning. I know that Kate will not have a wasted journey because she has her photographs to take. I went back to el cortijo and found a letter together with about 20,000 pesetas in notes in a old leader pouch stuffed up the chimenea. I'm sending it with the other stuff. Will ring you. Miguel.*"

Sheedy momentarily rested his head in his hands, the memory of the big policeman holding court in the corner of the Casino Club almost more than he could bear. Then he asked Rosa "What is a *chimenea* - is it the chimney?"

"*Si, señor.*"

Turning to the papers, he moved the pile to one side of the desk and began to transfer them, one at a time, to the centre, so that he could study them with care.

There were several notes clearly given to the Rabbit Man on his trips to Ronda on the lines of "Restaurante Pedro Romero orders 50 conejo soon as possible."

There were some old bullfight cuttings.

There were photographs, some old and faded, some more recent, some of bullfighters, some of the Ronda fair, including one with Miguel and the Rabbit Man taken by Sheedy himself, some of people Sheedy couldn't identify, and the one he remembered of the girl, the dark-haired child dressed in traditional Andalucian costume.

After careful inspection Sheedy set aside two items.

One was a photograph of the Rabbit Man with another man, taken on a bank overlooking a hill capped with a white town. Sheedy recognised it as Casares, a *pueblo* 13 kilometres in from the *costa* between Estepona and Gibraltar. The second man looked sufficiently like *El Conejero* for Sheedy to guess it could be his brother.

The second was an old yellow press clipping showing a group of young men on horseback, each holding a rifle. Sheedy guessed it probably dated back to the civil war. He couldn't, however, identify which of the men was the Rabbit Man.

He put the photographs on top of the pile of papers and put them all in a brief case, then asked Rosa if she would give top priority to transalating and typing out the letter Miguel had found. Then, looking at his watch, he bounded back down the stairs to the car and roared off in a cloud of dust towards Puerto Banus.

Felipe was just about to turn into the alley to the backstreet of Puerto Banus when he heard his name called and, turning round, saw his new-found friend from the Pink Coconut walking towards him.

"*Buenos noches,* my friend. Do you know, I did not ask your name?"

"Nor I your's," replied Felipe.

"Then I am Manuel."

"And I am Felipe."

"*Hola,* Felipe. I was thinking, let's not go to the Pink Coconut... Let's go to a happier place. What about one of the beach clubs?"

Felipe was pleased. This was how he had hoped it would be. Manuel's proposal that they should not go to the gay bar was reassurance that the other liked him for his company and conversation, was proud to be seen with him anywhere. That he didn't just want Felipe for sex.

"*Si,* Manuel," he said. "Let's do that."

"I have a car. We will drive there."

Felipe brightened up even more. So this man had a car, and that meant money, maybe enough for them to be able to go out for dinner and to the better clubs.

"*Bien,*" he said. "Lets go."

Manuel led him to a blue Seat, just a couple of years old. Winding down the windows and turning on the radio, he steered it out of Puerto Banus and onto the main road south. Soon they turned left and drove down towards the beach until they stopped by a wooden building on the edge of the sand. It was brightly lit and from it came the sound of loud music.

They walked into the bar.

"Manuel... Manuel.. come, have a drink. Bring your friend."

Felipe looked to the bar and saw a big, friendly-looking man waving to his companion. He frowned. Who was this? A rival? Perhaps an older lover?

Manuel introduced him as Bill. Felipe found him vaguely familiar. Perhaps he had seen him in the Pink Coconut. The big man insisted on buying a bottle of wine for the three of them and ushered them to an empty table. Despite his irritation that his intimacy with Manuel had been disturbed, and his fear of rivalry, Felipe soon relaxed. After all, had he not always pictured himself sitting in places like this with his own special friend, but also surrounded by others? And the big man was popular, judging by the number of people who waved to him or stopped briefly at their table. Anyway, he was difficult to dislike, he had gentle eyes and did not appear to be competing with Felipe for Manuel's affections, in fact he seemed pleased for Manuel that he had a new friend.

They had been chatting and drinking for nearly half an hour before the big man said "Hey, boys, I know you two would prefer to be on your own, but why not let me buy you dinner first. We could go to Toni Dalli's."

Felipe was thrilled.

Toni Dalli's!

He, Felipe, was being asked to go to Toni Dalli's.

Manuel looked doubtful. "I don't know..." he began, "maybe Felipe would prefer..."

Felipe, not to be denied, interrupted. "*Si*, Manuel, *si*, we can go. Lets go."

Manuel shrugged. "Ok. If it makes you happy, Felipe."

They decided they would all go in the car belonging to Bill, the big man having promised to drop them back afterwards.

Felipe was too excited to notice as they entered the elegant restaurant that their host seemed expected, and that a table for three had been reserved in the centre section.

It was not until they were on the main course that Manuel said "By the way, Bill, I think Felipe knows the man you have been enquiring about, what's his name... Canning... Tony Canning?"

"Jason," Felipe said without thinking. "Its Jason."

Sheedy looked amazed. "Is that right ? But how do you know him Felipe?"

"Felipe is an officer on La Gaviota," Manuel said, as if proud of his friend.

Felipe blushed with embarrassment; the lie that he was an officer may have had some plausibility in the unreal atmosphere of the Pink Coconut but it seemed only too transparent when repeated in this place. Fortunately the big man didn't appear to think so.

"An officer? Is that right? You have done well." The American looked at him admiringly. "But I'm sorry to hear Jason Canning is a friend of your's."

Felipe couldn't wait to reassure him. Over-excited by his new experiences, and already having had more wine than he was accustomed to, he unleashed his anger at the humiliations he had suffered at Canning's hands, pouring out his grievances. "He is a bully, *señor*. He is always sneering at me, making life difficult. If I could fight back I would. But I have always dreamed to work on a yacht. I daren't risk losing my job."

Bill looked at him sympathetically. "Well, this is an extraordinary bit of luck for both of us, Felipe. Because I don't like your Mr Canning either. I think we can help each other."

Just at that moment there was a stir in the restaurant. Felipe looked round. The owner, Toni Dalli, an Italian singer, once an international star, had come near to their table and, accompanied by a guitarist, was breaking into song. When he finished there was loud applause and then, to Felipe's amazement, Dalli came over to their table and greeted Manuel's friend Bill warmly. The big man then introduced Manuel and Felipe.

Well after the entertainer-restauranter had moved on, Felipe was still speechless. This was unbelievable. What would the others on the yacht, and the men he met in the Pink Coconut think of this?

"You know Toni Dalli well, señor?"

"For years," Sheedy replied casually.

"But you know him well ?"

Sheedy, struggling to hide a grin, shrugged and said "Well, what's well? I guess as well as anyone."

Manuel glanced at Sheedy who gave him a barely discernible nod. He turned to Felipe. "Bill is a celebrity himself. He has a television programme. You may have seen it. Bill Sheedy on the Costa del Sol."

Felipe, almost too excited to sit still, looked hard at the American. "Yes, yes, I knew I had seen you."

Sheedy leaned over the table. "Well, its the programme I think you can help."

Felipe was overwhelmed. This evening was exceeding his wildest dreams. "But, of course, señor, but how...?"

Sheedy began to talk about Canning, building on the young man's hatred of his American tormentor while flattering him by drawing him into the plot. "He's a bad man, Felipe. And we can deal with him. You could be rid of him forever. All you have to do is pick up what information you can. We need to know how many times he has been to Ronda and when. We particularly need to know where he was last night. We need to know who he talks to. And what he and Sir Brian Cruickshank say to one another. Whatever you hear will help. You can be our man on the yacht."

For a moment Felipe hesitated. Manuel leaned over and touched his arm gently, looking into his eyes. "Don't do it if you don't want to Felipe. Bill will understand. Won't you Bill?"

The big American nodded. "Of course. But I think it will help

Felipe too if we can get Canning off the yacht."

Manuel leaned even closer to the crew member. "*Si*, I guess it will. Why not have a go at it Felipe?"

Felipe was impressed by their consideration. "Have a go? *Si*, I will have a go."

"Great." Bill rose. "Let me give you a lift back." On the way he told Felipe where to telephone if he had any information. "Just leave a message that you rang and I or Manuel will meet you a O'Grady's in the port at nine o'clock the same night."

Felipe could hardly credit all that had happened.

The beach club. Toni Dalli's. Meeting the singer himself. His involvement with the friendly TV reporter. And Manuel... his new friend Manuel.

Such was his excitement that he was in his bunk before he realised that the two had dropped him off and gone away together, that he had not ended the night with Manuel as he had expected.

Still, so heady had the evening been that he didn't care too much. He was exhausted and anyway he knew his new friends were here to stay... as long as he had something to tell them about Canning.

He thought of the cruel, sarcastic American. Canning would pay for the way he had treated Felipe. He resolved to start his enquiries first thing in the morning."

CHAPTER EIGHT

Cruickshank was tired. He had taken the four o'clock plane from Malaga to Gatwick, flown to Battersea by helicopter, and been working in his office for over two hours. Now he pushed away the last of the stack of letters, memos and messages that had awaited him and, placing on top of them the dictaphone cassettes containing his comments and replies, he summoned his secretary. "I would like these typed by the overnight secretary and ready for me to check and sign at 7.30 in the morning. I shall be returning to Spain on the late morning flight."

She nodded. "Mr Jordan is downstairs."

Cruickshank looked at his watch. It was 9.30 p.m. "Show him up."

While he waited he looked out at the City lights and reviewed, not for the first time, his meeting with Sheedy on the yacht. It had gone well. He could not have handled it better. Provided they survived the next couple of weeks without further setbacks all would be well.

He had liked Sheedy and believed the feeling was mutual. And the reporter could be useful. He would cultivate his friendship.

His thoughts turned to the other American, Jordan, now on his way up to the office. He remembered how impressed he had been with the authority and elegance of the man when they had first met in New York. How was he to treat him - as ally or adversary?

Deciding it was vital to keep control of the moral high ground, he shook the American's hand unsmilingly and coolly bid him to sit down, relenting his severity only to offer him a drink.

The two sat in the window. Cruickshank liked to entertain foreign visitors in this way. The spectacle of the new tower blocks, competing with St Pauls Cathedral to dominate the skyline, was impressive in itself, and his position overlooking it conveyed a sense of power and influence that did no harm either.

Jordan wanted to talk about the race track proposal. Was it really practical?

"Of course. After all, planning permission was given for the one further east, near Mijas."

"Is that race course good news for us?"

"I think so. We only plan three or four meetings a year; the other will help develop the appetite for horse-racing. Provided we can make a deal with them on the timing of meetings, and that makes sense for them too, I think that each track will benefit from the existence of the other."

"But is the appetite there? For gambling?"

"Of that there's no doubt. Apart from your fellow countrymen and, I believe, the Filipinos, the Spanish spend more money on gambling than anyone else in the world."

"But on what do they gamble now ?"

"Nearly half of its spent on slot machines... one-arm bandits. And bingo is tremendously popular. I believe that in Andalucia alone nearly 10,000 million pesetas are spent every year on bingo. Then, of course, there are the lotteries. The Spanish are lottery-mad."

"If that's so," said Jordan. "why not add a casino to our plans?"

Cruickshank looked askance. "Apart from the fact that there's one at Nueva Andalucia, much more accessible than one on our land, I personally think it would lower the tone. The point about the race track is that we would be promoting the sport of kings in a setting and atmosphere appropriate to the project as a whole."

"A casino need not be a sordid place," Jordan replied. "It could be small, intimate, comfortable and very, very profitable."

Cruickshank's eyes narrowed further. Resort casinos conjured up unattractive images of Las Vegas and Atlantic City and the accompanying 'industries' of from prostitution and drugs, and this in turn resurrected memories of Canning's criminal behaviour and the way the Americans had taken financial control of the operation. He didn't like the sound of it, and he recalled Jim Miller's warning of a possible hidden agenda. Could this be it?

He rose and went to the drinks cabinet to refill Jordan's glass, but really in order to buy time to think. He was in no doubt that a casino had to be resisted. But it would be better not to have an argument with Jordan now, not until he had re-established his full authority over the project. There was a further point: if he handled the Spanish authorities well, it was possible he could get them to forbid a casino without it being necessary for him to make a stand at all.

As he handed the American his drink, he managed a relaxed smile. "I will explore the idea, Mr Jordan, but I would be surprised if you convinced me."

Jordan smiled in response, leaving Cruickshank unclear whether or not he had already succeeded in killing the idea.

The American asked about the remaining parcel of land. Cruickshank revived his severe look. "As I warned you, Canning's so-called solution has not been that helpful," he said. "For a start, questions have been raised about the old man's death. Canning was not as careful as he claimed. While there was, of course, no evidence to link the death with us, there apparently was evidence of foul play. And already the connection between he and our project has been exposed. I am, of course, taking the line that the... accident... was a considerable setback to us and that we have more cause than anyone to regret his passing. But it is vital we give no other grounds for suspicion. That is why I must ask you to keep Canning well under control."

Jordan moved to reply but Cruickshank was enjoying the opportunity to rub home the down side of Canning's homicidal behaviour. "It means we can't press it quite as hard as we would like," he continued. "If we're too anxious to get the problem solved it will look uncaring and that is contrary to the image I have been creating. At present it is the intention of the authorities to advertise for relatives of the peasant to come forward, informing them that there may be a small legacy. Once they do - if they do - we shall immediately make them an offer they cannot refuse... to use your jargon."

Cruickshank enjoyed that bit of sarcasm. If Jordan hadn't taken on board the unsuitability of his man's actions by now, Cruickshank would make damn certain he did before he left the room.

"If no-one comes forward," he said, " the land will be taken over by the authorities and sold to us. I have taken care of that. My plan therefore is to proceed at full pace on the assumption the land will become ours in six to nine months."

Jordan nodded appreciatively and, to Cruickshank's irritation, without any sign of anger at the Englishman's pointed remarks.

They turned to other matters, notably the availability of funds at appropriate times, and then the American rose to leave. For a moment they paused in front of the model. Cruickshank looked at it with his usual sense of pride. Jordan looked at it without expression, then shook the Englishman's hand. "It has, as always, been a pleasure, Sir Brian."

Cruickshank, feeling increasingly confident that all was back on course, did his best to maintain his severity and did not reply.

As he picked up his briefcase Jordan added "And we will look forward to hearing from you about the casino."

Then he was gone and Cruickshank was left alone feeling disconcerted.

Damn the man. Why was it that just when he felt he had the upper hand these people always succeeded in leaving him with uncertainty?

That last remark had not been a casual one.

Jordan had been telling him that the matter was not resolved. The question was still open.

Jordan wanted that casino.

And that "we" to Cruickshank spelt trouble.

Who in God's name was "we"?

He looked again at the model. The casino would be out of place.

He would be damned if he would let Jordan and company distort the project, cheapen it with their damn casino. What would they be suggesting next. A high class bordello?

He sat down in the window with another Scotch. That last thought had led to another... the woman in Maida Vale. Suddenly, for the first time for weeks, he felt an urge.

There was, he knew, no question of making love to Maria until they were married. He was sure she was a virgin and would want to be until after their wedding. And that's the way he wanted it too. His marriage to her must be perfect.

Just the same, proximity to her, the powerful desire she aroused, was frustrating. And now he had the woman in Maida Vale on his mind he couldn't forget her.

For nearly 30 minutes he wrestled with his conscience before making a call on his private line.

As always he left the taxi at the corner of the street and walked slowly up to the block of flats. He rang the bell and waited self-consciously while he was inspected via the small security camera above the door. Then, in response to the buzzer, he pushed the door open and, moving quickly now, climbed the two flights of stairs to her flat.

She was in her late 30's, shorter than Cruickshank, dark-haired and curvy, friendly and sexy. The flat looked just like he imagined the home of a single woman to be, and that he valued, because Cruickshank had come to terms with his visits by imagining her as a mistress rather than a whore, by thinking of the envelope he left on her dresser as a gift rather than a payment for services rendered, by closing his mind to the possibility, indeed the probability, in fact the reality of other men and other envelopes.

"Its been a long time," she said. She never used his name. He liked to think she didn't know who he was, shutting his mind to the probability that as she sat alone waiting for her clients she watched television and was only too aware of his identity and importance.

"Yes," he said, "its been a long time."

"A drink ?"

"Scotch."

She poured him one and, while he sat sipping it, she said "I'll be back in a moment. Why don't you undress?"

Usually this is what he would have done, but tonight he couldn't bring himself to move, just stayed in the chair, drinking the Scotch, looking round the room, until she returned, dressed now only in the black transparent nightdress he had always liked.

If she was surprised to find him sitting there, fully dressed, she didn't show it. Instead she sat on the arm of the chair and looked at him. He was acutely aware of her scent, her eyes smiling at his, her white breasts stretching the negligee. He reached out a hand and cradled one, succumbing to her proximity and to the scent as if injected with a drug.

Yet still all he could think of was Maria, her big brown eyes looking, it felt, deep into his soul, her soft voice talking of honour and trust.

Suddenly he knew he shouldn't have come. He stood up abruptly and began to reach for his coat, apologising clumsily. But she rose, too, slipping the negligee over her shoulders so that it fell to the floor. Naked, she walked up to him so that her dark, firm nipples were touching his chest. "You're troubled," she said. "Can't I help you relax." She put her arm round his neck and gently kissed him on the lips.

But all he felt now was foolish. He picked up his coat and, reaching into the pocket, took out an envelope. "This was going to be my last visit. I won't be returning. I would like you to accept this gift. I have been grateful for your kindness and... your... discretion."

She rose and taking the envelope, slid her finger under the top and opened it, gasping at the wad of banknotes inside. "But there must be..."

"Yes, but I owe you much. Ours may have been a business arrangement but I've not felt uncomfortable with it. You have been a friend. And I have trusted you. Please accept it."

Still naked she came back up to him and gave him a hug. Then she kissed him on the cheek. "Thank you."

As he began to walk to the door she said: "You are going to marry, are you not?"

"What makes you say that?"

"I don't believe that you're changing to another business girl. And an unmarried man of your age, your kind, doesn't just have an affair. You're going to marry."

He smiled, said goodbye, and left, pausing in the darkened doorway for a moment before walking quickly down the street and round the corner into St Johns Wood Road where he called a taxi to travel the short distance to his town house near Regents Park.

She had been a good friend. He would miss her. Yet he was pleased it had ended this way... that he had not succumbed to the drive that took him there. He would always know that from the moment he met Maria there had been no-one else.

Still, he was grateful to the woman. He didn't begrudge the £3000 he had given her. With it he had, he felt, paid a debt and at the same time earned her further discretion.

After he had gone the woman tossed the negligee onto the bed and pulled on a dressing gown. She put the money in her handbag. Behind her a door opened and a man's voice said "Well done."

She looked at him and shrugged. "I'm sorry. you didn't get much. But what could I do? The man's fallen in love."

Jordan grinned. "Don't worry. The scene was explicit enough. I'm just glad I made it in time. He must have come directly after his call."

He handed her an envelope, her second of the night. "My clients will be pleased." Then, slipping a small cannister of film into his overcoat, he walked to the door. There he paused and looked back.

"They never learn, do they?" he said. "That there is no such thing as a whore with a heart of gold."

"Just for that," she replied, "next time you'll pay double."

"Just for that," he said, "there won't be a next time."

She went to the window and watched him walk down the street.

Actually, he was wrong, she thought.

Well, a bit wrong.

She did feel sorry for Cruickshank.

Well, a bit sorry.

Once home, Cruickshank telephoned Julio in Marbella and asked to speak to Maria. He sat delighted as she told him with enthusiasm what she had been doing during the day.

As he listened it struck him that this was the first such telephone conversation he had shared with her. He sensed that she had been looking forward to him ringing, storing up the things she wanted to say. He rejoiced in the sound of her voice. How marvellous it would be to be able to ring her every time he was away, from wherever he was on business, and talk in this way.

After he put the phone down it struck him that she, too, was lonely.

He felt his heart fill with love for her, with joy at what lay ahead, of what they would share together.

Thank God it was all coming right once more.

The woman in Maida Vale was in the past.

The project was back on course.

The reporter was no threat. It was obvious from their meeting that Sheedy had no evidence to link he or the project with the murder. Nor would there be any.

He had Jordan's word there would be no more 'indiscretions' and, while Jordan's word wouldn't ordinarily count for much, he believed the American now realised that strong-arm tactics just couldn't work in Spain.

So all he had to left to do was squash this casino idea, fast and firm. That would be no problem.

There was now nothing on the horizon likely to spoil his happiness with Maria.

And nothing was going to be allowed to.

Nothing.

Full of new confidence he went to bed and for the first time in over a week he slept well.

It was a relatively chilly night and Kate had built a fire. She, Bill and Manuel settled in front of it with a bottle of Rioja.

Kate reminded Sheedy that he should expect a visit from the police. "What will you tell them?"

Sheedy thought for a moment. "Well, obviously that Miguel believed the Rabbit Man had been murdered and was making enquiries and that there is a possibility, in fact a probability, that whoever committed the first murder has also committed the second because Miguel knew too much."

"And the link with Anglo-Spanish Investors?"

"I don't know about that. At the moment they don't necessarily think they're in the frame. I held back with Cruickshank. If he is personally involved its better that he is allowed to become complacent. If the police descend on them they'll be on the defensive. I reckon I can get more out of them at this point than the police can."

Manuel looked concerned. "Wouldn't that be withholding evidence?"

"Maybe for a few days. But if the police move in, Cruickshank and company will close up. I just have a feeling that will make it harder to prove the link."

"What was in the papers, Bill?" Kate asked.

"That I don't know either. I left the new letter with Rose. I hope to get the translation tomorrow."

Manuel picked up the two photographs Sheedy had set aside and looked them. "And these?"

"I think one is the Rabbit Man's brother. It was taken at Casares. We'll have to go up there and talk to him. And this other picture, the old one of the group of men, I don't know... probably means nothing. But I just wondered whether Miguel had seen anything in it that could have been a motive from the past, nothing to do with the Cruickshank project at all. Miguel was holding something back the other day, something I suspect from the deep past, perhaps involving them both."

"Kate said: "So how close are we to proving that Anglo-Spanish Investors were involved, that this man Canning killed them both ?"

"Its all so bloody circumstantial. If, as we believe, the Rabbit Man was murdered, it's too much of a coincidence to suggest that Miguel's death is unconnected. We know Cruickshank's outfit had a motive - a fortune's worth of motive. We know Canning goes to the Premier club and that a matchbox from it was found near the Rabbit Man's body. Yet we still have the problem that no-one seems to have seen either killing. My guess is that the police will find it all a bit weak."

Kate asked "Do you not think that to turn the police onto it will mean that more people will be looking into it, there'll be more publicity, and a much better chance of getting at the truth?"

"Its possible. But we have to consider Felipe. He's one of our best prospects of getting more information and once the police get involved my guess is he'll be frightened off. We need to give him some time."

Manuel had been listening carefully. "Look, Bill, I don't like it. I don't like holding back from the police. I don't like what we're doing to the kid on the yacht. He's harmless and we've been conning him. Doesn't it strike you that his life's at risk? And maybe yours and mine too?"

Sheedy poured another glass of wine. "Manuel, these bastards have killed two harmless old men to save themselves a bit of inconvenience or a bit of money. They're getting away with it. And if they do, why shouldn't they just keep doing it? I know we can get them. I know it. Let's at least give it a few more days."

Kate was troubled. "I feel the same as Manuel. Its one thing for you not to go to the police voluntarily and another to hold back when they come to you. After all, you're only responsible for a television programme. Their job is enforcing the law."

Sheedy looked at her sharply. "Its not just the bloody programme. If it hadn't been for me the Rabbit Man probably would not have been found. And Miguel would still be alive. I have a responsibility too."

"And what will you say if the boy on the yacht is killed? Or even Manuel? That you're even more responsible? That you have even more reason to go it alone? For Christ's sake, Bill, stop acting like the lone avenger."

Sheedy rose to his feet, flushed with anger. "I don't need this shit, Kate. These men were my friends and I believe I can prove who killed them. Doesn't that matter?"

Kate stood too, her temper flaring. "And Felipe? You don't give a damn about him. You're just using him. Why? Because he's gay. Do you think because he's gay he doesn't matter so much, that he's expendable. You're just exploiting his vulnerability. What happened to Sheedy, crusader for the little man?"

Sheedy put his glass down and, ignoring her, turned to Manuel. "Let's call it a day. I'll talk to you tomorrow." And he walked out of the room onto the balcony.

Kate and Manuel looked at each other. The Spaniard shrugged. "Forget it for tonight, Kate. He's upset about Miguel. Maybe he'll see it differently tomorrow."

When Manuel was gone Kate threw another log on the fire and calling Sheedy in, pulled him down to where she was sitting on the carpet with her back resting on the sofa. Gently she massaged the back of his neck as he sat leaning back on her. "Sorry, Bill, I didn't want to argue with you. Its just that I think you're in danger of losing your perspective on this. You're too involved. And I'm frightened... for you... and for us."

When he didn't reply she added "I know you. You're capable of making a deal with the police and working with them. You always did in New York. Why can't you do it now?"

Still he was silent. Kate moved her hands over his back, then put her arms round him, pulling him back to her, hugging him. "You're getting too tense, Bill," she whispered. "Time to relax..."

At last he turned and looked at her, then said "I'm sorry I shouted at you. I guess its because you suddenly reminded me of... of Jan... telling me what to do. For a moment I resented someone else doing that. But I don't really." He kissed her warmly. "I'd forgotten what it was like to have someone who cared enough about me to argue. I'm grateful." And they rolled over on the carpet and in the warmth of the fire they made love, first gently, then with mounting passion, until as the blaze gathered force in the grate they reached a climax together and lay in each other's arms becoming increasingly drowsy until he rose and picked her up and carried her off to bed.

Julio and Isabella had a long-standing engagement and the Garcias and Maria had chosen to spend a quiet evening together at the architect's home, one interrupted only by the call from London.

Cristina looked at Maria, resting back in her chair by the log fire, lost in thought, her beautiful face illuminated by the flames. She had never seen the young woman look happier.

"Doesn't our child look beautiful, Juan?" she said.

Maria sat forward and blushed.

"And happy," said Juan. "You've had a good time on the *costa*. You should come more often."

Cristina looked at her husband and then at Maria. "I don't think the *costa* is the reason, Juan," she said. "I think our child is in love."

Juan Garcia looked up sharply. "In love. In love with whom?"

Maria looked at Cristina, half annoyed, half embarrassed, and then at her impatient-looking guardian.

"I did not say I was in love. Mama did."

"But are you?"

She sighed. Then, standing, she poured a coffee and walked to the fire, her back to them. "Sir Brian has honoured me with a proposal of marriage."

Both man and woman gasped. It was Juan who responded first. Rising and walking over, he turned her to look at him. "And you?"

"I want to, Papa. He is the kindest, most intelligent man I have ever met... except for you. And a man I could trust."

"But he's so much older than you ?"

"That is no matter. I don't want to marry a man of my own age. They don't please me."

"Juan." It was Cristina. "Sir Brian is a distinguished man and would give our Maria a good life. And he seemed a kind and considerate man. If Maria loves him..."

"But she hardly knows him... I am not opposing this, but I would wish Maria to know him better, and I would like to know him better."

Maria stepped between her guardians. "Please don't worry. Sir Brian will not wish me to hurry and is anxious to get to know you both better. But, mama and papa, I do care about this man."

Cristina gave her a hug. "Don't you worry, our dear Maria. We will rejoice if he is the man who can make you happy."

Juan sat looking thoughtful. "I'm surprised Sir Brian did not say a word to me about it when we talked at his villa."

"Sir Brian is not Spanish," Maria gently reminded him. "I think in England men assume that women can speak for themselves. He is too much of a gentleman to raise it with you until I have spoken to you."

"And when were you going to do that?" Juan asked.

"When I was brave enough," she replied.

"Do you need courage to speak to me," Juan said, looking hurt.

"No, papa," she replied. "Just to overcome my shyness."

He looked at her and smiled. "And yet you are not shy with this important Englishman?"

"No," she said. "No. Does that not say a lot about him?"

The sociologists would have had real difficulty with Jason Canning. He didn't fit the usual pattern. There was no chapter in their textbook that applied to him.

He didn't take drugs, so didn't need extra money to satisfy a dependency.

He didn't come from a criminal background, so wasn't born into law-breaking like many of those who operate in the middle-management of organised crime.

He hadn't been raised in poverty or in slums, hadn't had to fight his way out of them, so wasn't rebelling against an unjust society.

On the contrary, he was the only son of an affluent businessman, had apparently been content at home, had emerged from college with academic honours, and was just beginning to make a career for himself on Wall Street when he took a conscious decision to make a career in crime.

That's what the sociologists would not have been able to fathom.

Most people drift into crime, or are bullied or dared or talked into it, or are driven into it by desperation, by need of money, or to protect themselves from some threat.

But Canning's was an intellectual decision. He simply decided he wanted to work in crime... just as his peers intellectually decided they wanted to go in for commodity-broking or some other form of money-making.

No doubt if they could dissect his brain, the scientists could one day come up with an answer to the conundrum but, until it was found, there was only one word to describe Jason Canning.

Ammoral.

He believed rules were there to keep others in check, to create an ordered society in which a rule-breaker could thrive.

In a society in which everyone patiently queued, he reasoned to himself, a skilful queue-jumper couldn't fail, provided he didn't mind being disliked. And Canning didn't.

He kept his distance from other people, shared his thoughts with no-one, lived alone.

Not without physical needs, he satisfied them with whores. He figured you made your deal with them, you took what you wanted, you paid them and they were gone. There was not a whore girl in Puerto Banus he hadn't had once; there was no-one he had slept with twice. He wouldn't give even them the chance to get too close. Not that they wanted to; the same compulsion to concede nothing meant he was in his sexual relations with them cold, hard, even brutal.

People had meaning for Canning only if they could help him, in which case they were used for that purpose and then dropped, or if they were in the way, in which case they were removed.

Or they were there to be toyed with.

Canning liked to play with people as you would play with poker chips, pick them up, turn them over, juggle them, drop them, bet with them, and then cash them in - you win some, you lose some.

He had first been attracted to the Premier lap dancing club because men tended to make fools of themselves at Premier and Canning liked to watch them do it and record it in his memory in case he could make use of it at a later date.

Canning liked to watch. For all his indifference to them, he understood what made most people tick. He liked to think he could work out what everyone in the bar at a particular time wanted... what they wanted that night, what they wanted from life. Canning reckoned if you knew what people wanted you had them.

This night, however, things were quiet. The Premier was not yet open and he had been drinking in Navy. He tossed a handful of 100 peseta coins at the barman, and left, wandering up Calle Ribera. From there he planned to make his way to the car park. Canning didn't live on the yacht preferring as always to keep his distance; he lived in an apartment on the Nueva Andalucia complex nearby.

Now, as he neared the end of the Calle Ribera he saw a familiar figure, the little fag from the yacht, the one he liked to toy with and to bully. Felipe. On an impulse he followed, reaching the top just in time to see Felipe pushing open the door of O'Grady's.

Not his usual territory, thought Canning.

He paused for a moment, then with a few quick steps was himself in the bar. At first he couldn't see the slight Spaniard but then spotted him with his back to the bar, sitting on a small round stool talking to two men who were listening intently. Canning recognised Sheedy immediately.

He ducked onto a low stool at the far end of the bar where he could just see the three but was side-on to them and out of their line of vision. From there he settled down to his favourite game - watching.

Felipe was doing most of the talking. Every now and then Sheedy would speak, apparently asking questions.

Canning waited until they were engrossed and then slipped out. He quickly climbed the steps of the block of the flats above and, lighting a cigarette, stood in the dark, waiting.

It was some 30 minutes before the big man left. Felipe was still inside with the other. Canning continued to wait.

Another 15 minutes passed and the two younger men come out. They stood close, talking quietly. Canning could see Felipe was upset, clearly trying to encourage the other to go somewhere with him. The other was seeking to reassure him. He heard the other say "Next time.... we will... I promise..."

Then he watched Felipe begin to walk disconsolately down the backstreet, then up the alley in the direction of the yacht.

Canning stayed for a few more minutes finishing his cigarette. Then thoughtfully he strolled back to his car and drove home. Once there he put in a call to the Spaniards in Fuengirola.

Maria was out, dining with Cruickshank, and Juan took the opportunity to tell Julio and Isabella of Cruickshank's proposal to his ward.

The architect responded enthusiastically. Cruickshank was a man of distinction and integrity, rich and generous. Yes, he was older than Maria, but fit. If the young woman loved him it would be, said Julio, a good marriage.

Juan said he wished it could have been a younger man. But Cristina gently suggested that the choice of an older man could be partly Juan's fault. "You have been such a kind and sensitive guardian to her, Juan, that she has looked for a similar man. She is proud of your sense of honour and that is why she sets such store by it in Cruickshank."

"You mean she wants a father figure?" he asked.

"No, I don't mean that. Maria has great inner strength. She does not need someone to look up to, but she does need someone she respects as she respects herself. You have set a standard and the young men she's met have not been able to match it. Sir Brian has."

"One good thing about that, Juan," said Julio, "if Maria marries Sir Brian you will have no worries about her future. He is a man of great integrity. He would never be mixed up in anything she would have cause to be ashamed of."

Juan looked reassured. "*Si*, that is so. That is one thing we don't have to fear."

Pleased with that thought he suggested they opened a bottle of champagne to toast the absent couple - his dear ward Maria and her Knight.

Jim Miller was not happy. Things had been slipping out of his control and it was partly his own fault.

When he had gone to pick up the gun on Tuesday night he had lost Canning. He had checked at the yacht, looked into Linekers and then the lap dancing club above it, and eventually parked his car in the dark near Canning's apartment and waited for him to return. It had been nearly 3 a.m. when Canning got back. Miller had a feeling he had been in the wrong place at the wrong time.

Then there had been tonight. He had nearly missed Canning leaving Premier from his own vantage point in the window of the bar on the corner of the alley. Then he had nearly been seen by Canning when the American had stopped up the alley to stand in the dark watching O'Grady's bar.

Miller had not felt any happier to see Sheedy come out of the bar. Was that who Canning was watching? If so it could be for no good reason.

He had followed Canning home and only when happy that the American was settled in his apartment did he return to the villa, picking up a copy of *El Pais* on his way. Miller made a practice of struggling through the Spanish newspaper each day to improve his Spanish.

Once home, he bathed and, climbing into bed, switched on the bedside light and flicked through its pages and began to slowly read the stories that captured his interest. It was on page six that he saw it. Just three paragraphs.

'An officer in the *Guardia Civil*, a Civil War veteran, Miguel Ayala, was found dead last night at the foot of *El Tajo*, the ravine dividing the town of Ronda.

'Police say they have no reason to believe it is a case of suicide. Ayala had been drinking and an accident was not ruled out. But for the moment it is being treated as a suspicious death.

'Ayala, believed to be in his early seventies, had been given special dispensation to continue his career in the *Guardia Civil* but was due to retire in a few weeks time. He had become a popular local character. His most recent investigation had been into the death, believed to be by accident, of his close friend of many years, Pepe Rodriguez, known as the Rabbit Man of Ronda.'

Miller sat up in shock. This was too much of a coincidence. 'Last night'... that was the night before last, Tuesday night, the night he had lost Canning's trail, the night the American had not got back till 3 a.m.

Miller threw the newspaper to the ground. "Shit!" He said. Then repeated it. "Shit."

He got out of bed, put on a dressing gown and lit a cigarette, looking out of the window across the swimming pool to the sea shining in the distance. "Shit," he said for a third time. "The man's mad."

He looked at the clock. It was 1.30 a.m. Cruickshank would be back in the morning. What would he tell him

It was bad enough that he had let Canning loose for a night, but another murder?

Of course there was a chance it was a coincidence but Miller didn't believe in coincidences.

Why had Canning done it?

Had the policeman been in touch with him?

Surely the American wasn't just cleaning up... eliminating anyone with an interest in the affair.

If so, who was safe? The Ronda barman? The TV reporter, Sheedy?

Miller suddenly recalled that Canning had that night been watching Sheedy.

"Christ," he thought. "I'm right. He's cleaning up. He's starting to eliminate them one by one. This is crazy. Its got to be stopped."

He lay back on the bed but the headache had returned, worse than ever. He felt on the edge of panic. Somewhere in the deepest recesses of his brain he felt a stirring of memories, things he didn't want to remember, things to do with his experiences in Belfast, things to do with fear and pain, and even more fear.

He got out of bed and paced up and down. Then, deciding that keeping his nerve was paramount, he went downstairs to where the drinks were kept. There, gleaming seductively amid the other bottles, was an unopened quart of Beefeaters.

He picked up a glass, half-filled it, and drank it.

Without ice.

Without tonic.

Neat.

Neat gin.

He felt it work its way into his blood stream, into his brain.

The memories faded. The panic was stilled.

He felt better.

It had been the right thing to do.

He had just one more...

Sheedy slipped quietly into the villa so as not to wake Kate, poured himself a Scotch, and sat down to think.

Felipe had come up trumps.

Canning, the boy had reported, visited Ronda at least twice. He hadn't been able to get an exact date but at least one of the trips was after he had been seen with the Ronda barman. So there was a real possibility of a second meeting with the Rabbit Man... at the *cortijo*.

But there was more. Felipe said the talk was that Canning had been involved in a row, some kind of showdown with Cruickshank, and that since then Cruickshank and Canning had hardly been talking. The Englishman had a new aide, a man called Miller.

Sheedy reckoned there was a real chance that the row had been over the murder of the Rabbit Man. There was no way Cruickshank would have authorised that. On the other hand, if that was the cause of the row, it meant Cruickshank had been lying when he met Sheedy. He may not have been part of the murder but he was most definitely part of the cover-up.

Felipe's most interesting revelation was that of the seven crew on the boat, only he, Felipe, the youngest, and one other, a relatively new sailor, had not been employed by Canning; the rest were, according to

Felipe, involved in some kind of secret bonus scheme he had been unable to get to the bottom of.

Anglo-Spanish Investors, Sheedy concluded, was up to its eyes in shit.

Only two problems remained: how to get proof that Canning was the killer. And how to discover whether Cruickshank approved the murder or was just covering it up.

He decided the time had come to force the issue into the open. He would please Kate by mobilising the Ronda police and the *Guardia Civil*.

And in the day or so that it took the police to get their act together to approach Cruickshank he would put together a programme linking the project with the killings and raising questions that would force it all into the open.

Cruickshank had organised a party on the yacht as part of the build-up to the official public relations launch of the project, an event that Sheedy's inquiries had now made inevitable. He had invited the editors of local Spanish newspapers and also the editorial staff of English magazines based on the *costa*. His aim was to soften them up for the launch by establishing friendly relations.

The decks of the yacht were brightly lit and a small string quartet was playing on the upper deck. On the jetty a small crowd of evening promenaders gathered to gaze at the scene and to speculate about the guests as they arrived.

Cruickshank's executive team and others in the know, including the architect Julio, and Maria, were briefed to be discreet about the project itself. They could hint there was a big story coming up, but that was all.

Cruickshank himself was delayed at a finance meeting in Malaga and only just beat his guests to the yacht, hurrying to his cabin to change. Hobbs told him that Miller wanted to see him urgently but Cruickshank said it would have to wait. "Tell him I'll have a word later, after the party and after *Señorita* Garcia has gone home."

The party was in full swing when Sheedy and Kate came up the gangway. Cruickshank, who had been standing by the railing on the top deck chatting with the celebrity bookseller James Ross, excused himself and quickly descended the steps to welcome the American couple. After a few smiling words to Kate he took Sheedy's arm and drew him aside. "Just one word, Mr Sheedy. If I'm to help you achieve your exclusive I take it you will assist me by not sharing the news of the project with your colleagues tonight. I would appreciate your discretion."

Sheedy looked at him grimly. "I'm afraid things have changed since we met, Sir Brian. In view of the second death I have no choice but to bring my story forward. I intend to cover it in tomorrow's programme."

Cruickshank stared at him, uncomprehending, and then with growing concern.

"Death... second death?"

Sheedy observed him closely. Either the man was an unbelievably good actor or he didn't know what Sheedy was talking about. The American believed it was the latter and was surprised at the strength of his sense of relief.

Before Cruickshank, clearly stunned, could press him further, some new guests arrived, effusive in their greetings. Their host did his best to make them welcome, his eyes apprehensively following Sheedy as the American, aware of an advantage, deliberately climbed to the upper deck and with Kate joined a group of other journalists who were sitting in a circle of deck chairs gossiping and laughing at the stories of one of their number, Perrott Phillips, a travel journalist and contributor to Lookout who was on a research trip from London.

Phillips was celebrating being allowed to donate a bottle of wine to Madrid's famous Bottle Museum. Of the 22,000 bottles in the museum, he claimed, his bottle of Konjagi from Tanzania was the most undrinkable... almost as bad as Mick's Red Rotten, sold at a journalists' pub in London. The label said it was "an unusual rough-guts red wine that has the distinctive bouquet of old and ill-cured animals. It is best drunk with the teeth clenched to prevent the ingestion of seeds or skins. Avoid contact with eyes or open cuts. Keep away from naked flames."

As the group broke into gales of laughter, Sheedy noticed out of the corner of his eye Cruickshank looking desperately at him while half-heartedly conversing with other guests. For a while he avoided the Englishman's eye but eventually he took pity on him and chose a moment to leave the group when Cruickshank was hovering nearby. As he strolled over to a waiter to collect another drink, the Englishman moved quickly to his side.

"Mr Sheedy, you referred to another murder. What did you mean?"

"Did I say murder?"

"Sorry." Cruickshank bit his lip. It had been a careless remark. "I meant death." He groaned inwardly; the correction sounded even worse.

Sheedy told him "The Rabbit Man had a close friend, an officer with the *Guardia Civil* called Miguel. On Wednesday morning he was found dead in Ronda. Also at the foot of a ravine, this time *El Tajo*. Too much of a coincidence, don't you think?"

Cruickshank was shocked, but responded decisively.

"Mr Sheedy, I don't see why your programme on the project should be related to your concern about these accidents. I hope you're not suggesting that I have any connection with either death. That would be outrageous. As I have told you, the death of the man you called the Rabbit Man and his connection with my project are purely coincidence, one, as I explained to you, that causes us considerable inconvenience.

"As for this other man, the policeman, if there is a link between the two deaths and they weren't accidents, this would suggest some other affair entirely, as we had no interest in him or dealings with him at all."

"Except that he was investigating the old man's death," said Sheedy.

"Well, I for one did not know that. Come, Mr Sheedy, be reasonable. Do you really believe I'm the kind of man to have people assassinated all over Andalucia?"

"Frankly, Sir Brian, no. But there is a link, albeit coincidental, between your project and at least one of the deaths and that is a story and I'm afraid I have no choice but to tell it. I'm a journalist and that's my job."

"And will you make it clear that I am not the kind of man to be associated with violence of any kind?"

"Sir Brian, I will, if you like, quote you as saying that. But it is not for me to make the judgement. 'Associated with' is a vague phrase. My experience is that the best people sometimes find themselves 'associated with' the worst kind of behaviour, not by design but because a drift starts and at the key moment, when it can be checked, they hesitate and end up betraying their own standards."

"I'm beginning to wonder whether you're a journalist or a novelist," Cruickshank snapped. "Assuming the former, I must a least assume you're educated in the laws of libel and slander."

"Indeed."

"When does your programme appear next? Tomorrow you say?"

"Tomorrow night"

"Then you must not be surprised if I also do what I feel I must, Mr Sheedy. You say our arrangement is outdated by events. I will, therefore, announce the project in my own time, probably tomorrow morning."

"That is your right, Sir Brian, but you may wish to consider one thing. If I am reporting on both the project and the coincidence of the two deaths then there will be a better balance on the programme than if the project is already old news and the only story I have is the coincidence of the deaths."

Cruickshank struggled to keep his temper. "I hope you're not blackmailing me, Mr Sheedy."

"Not at all. I'm telling you what any journalist would have to do in the circumstances you describe."

The Englishman sighed. "Whoever is responsible for these deaths, presuming they're not an accident, has a lot to answer for, Mr Sheedy."

"Yes, Sir Brian, but not just inconvenience to you. Also two lost lives."

Cruickshank looked chastened. "That is a fair point, but you must appreciate I didn't know these men, whereas the project has dominated my life for over 18 months. And I'm not accustomed to being accused of complicity in murder."

Before Sheedy could reply Kate was at his elbow, anxious to introduce him to Cruickshank's fiancee.

Sheedy turned to find himself facing a woman of exceptional beauty, dark, wearing a simple white dress and smiling warmly at his host.

Cruickshank, looking pale and annoyed, smiled half- heartedly as the introductions took place. Then almost immediately he excused himself. For a fleeting moment Sheedy saw the young woman's smile fade. She was clearly not accustomed to Cruickshank being preoccupied in her company. Sheedy guessed she was taking his abrupt departure personally, that she was unaware of the pressures he was under.

Cruickshank had gone looking for Hobbs. "Where's Canning?"

"He said he had to make some calls to the United States, Sir Brian."

"Get hold of him and tell him and Miller to go to the library at the end of the evening and wait for me."

Then with a superhuman effort he concentrated on his guests for the remaining hour or so until the majority, including Sheedy and Kate, had drifted away. Urging the rest to stay as long as they wished, he bid them goodnight. Taking Maria's arm, he told her he had some urgent business that would preoccupy him for some time. "I think it best if the chauffeur takes you home, my dear. I am sorry. I had so much looked forward to chatting with you. Lets have a long lunch together tomorrow."

Taking her in his arms, he warmly embraced her, begging a last smile before she left. Then he watched her disappear into the night before going quickly to where Miller and Canning were waiting, drinks in hand, eyeing each other with hostility.

"Alright," Cruickshank said without ceremony. "Sheedy tells me there's been another murder. This time a policeman. What do you have to say about it?"

Canning spoke first. "I can tell you nothing, Sir Brian, except from what Miller tells me it was probably either an accident or suicide."

"Accident?" Cruickshank looked at him with fury. "That's what you said about the old man."

"No, with respect Sir Brian, I told you exactly what happened to the old man. I said his death would *look* like an accident, not that it was one. Now I am telling you that I have no knowledge of this policeman or what happened to him."

"Jim?" He looked at his minder who, Cruickshank noted with irritation, was pouring himself another drink, a substantial gin.

He sounded sober enough however. "Here's the newspaper story, Sir Brian. As far as I can see there's no evidence of murder. Sheedy was wrong to use the word. On the other hand he probably thinks its too much of a coincidence and I don't blame him. May I question Canning?"

"Please."

"Canning, where were you the night before last - until you returned home at about 3 a.m.?"

The American turned white with anger. "Have you been following me Miller? How dare..."

Cruickshank interrupted. "Answer the question."

"Well, if you insist, Sir Brian, I was with a companion. A young woman."

"Where ?"

"For a while at the Premier club and then at her flat."

"Will she confirm this story?"

"Of course. But it shouldn't be necessary."

"Who was the man I saw you meeting the other day at Istan?" Miller asked.

Canning looked at him with hatred. "So you have been following me. This is the personal service you perform for Sir Brian."

Cruickshank interrupted again. "Canning, you're trying my patience. Answer the question."

"I don't know. I went up there for a drive and he just happened to sit at the table where I was having a drink. I've no idea who he was."

Miller scoffed. "You never go anywhere just for a drive Canning. You went there to meet him."

"Prove it."

Cruickshank replied "Miller doesn't have to prove it. This is not a court of law. I'm happy to accept the balance of probability and that is that you went to meet this man. Did you instruct him to kill the policeman?"

Canning rose. "For Christ's sake, I've had enough of this. If you wish to discuss this matter properly, I will. But I'm not going to be cross-examined by you two. The police report says the man had been drinking. He probably just fell over the edge. It happens."

"Unfortunately it usually happens when you're around Jason."

Before the American could reply, Cruickshank turned to Miller. "The reporter Sheedy is going to do an item on this. What is the most he can say?"

"He can only point to the coincidence. He's got no evidence to link the deaths and even less evidence to link us to them. The worst he can produce is innuendo."

Cruickshank nodded. "At least we're forewarned. We must have a statement ready to release after the programme. It can frankly acknowledge the coincidence but point out that we're the big losers by the old man's death. We can offer a reward for anyone who can produce information. That way, we go on the offensive."

Miller warned Cruickshank that the police were bound to call. "If you're going on the offensive, you may wish to do so with them too. You could call them before they call you. Then you can state publicly that you've been in touch with the police and are doing all you can to help. The offer of a reward is a good idea. And you could say that you're hoping to identify relatives of the old man in order to buy the land; this would show that you're ready to pay its market value and that there was no profit for you in his death."

Cruickshank looked at Miller appreciatively. "That's helpful Jim." Miller, pleased, struggled to resist the temptation to celebrate his employer's goodwill with another gin.

Both men now looked at Canning. Cruickshank was the first to speak. "Jason, I have no reason to believe you. You killed the old man. The policeman was investigating the murder and now he's dead. I don't know how to get through to you but I just cannot accept this. You've got to understand that if the project has to be abandoned that will have to be the price we pay to stop this."

"I didn't do it."

"I wish I could believe you." He stood and walked to add ice to his drink while thinking furiously. How could he get to this man, make him understand the insanity of his behaviour?

Sitting once more he looked at the hostile American and with a change of tone, authoritative, but friendlier, made an attempt to appeal to the intelligence he knew was there: "Look, Jason. Can you not see that we are on course? The project will happen. There will be no problems. Unless we make them for ourselves. I've compromised far more than I would wish by not uncovering what happened to the old man, because whatever I did would not bring him back, and because I believed I could do more for the people of the area, perhaps make amends, by continuing. But it was clearly understood that there would be no repeat of this behaviour - that it would put me in an impossible position and jeopardise the project. Now, I know you say you were not involved in the death of the policeman, and maybe... maybe... you're telling the truth, but it is indicative of the position we're in that you can hardly blame us for our scepticism. Now this is the last time... the very last time... I'm going to say this: one more step out of line, one more act outside the strict letter of the law, one that we even suspect, let alone can prove, and I am going to cut my losses and get out. And, believe me, I'll take everybody else with me. Will you... can you... understand that - and cooperate?"

The American looked at him coolly. "I understood your position when you spoke to me after the death of the Rabbit Man. You have no reason to believe that I have done other than respect it since."

Cruickshank sighed. He was tired and he felt weighed down by it all, by his feeling of impotence in the face of Canning's obstinacy. Eventually he told the American to go but keep the yacht informed of his movements. He asked Miller to stay.

"Look, Jim, did he do it? Is he out of control?"

"I'm sorry, Sir Brian, that I lost him the other night. But I have to say that I have no doubt."

"Jim, don't leave his side. Even if you have to sleep with him. I'll speak to Jordan and I'll see the police when they come and then we'll have to think hard about what we do." He began to pace around the library.

Miller felt sorry for, even affectionate towards the financier. "Sir Brian, assuming Canning killed them both, there's one thing that has to be said for him, not that its a lot of consolation to you. He's not given a lot away. The police can't even prove the deaths were deliberately caused, or that they were connected, let alone identify a possible killer. All they have are two unrelated deaths, possibly accidents, possibly suicides, possibly… but it can't be proved… murders by a person or persons unknown. You can afford to act as if that is the case."

As he left Cruickshank smiled at him weakly, not apparently willing to be uplifted by such a pragmatic message. He walked slowly out onto the deck, lighting a cigar. It was a clear night and the stars twinkled brightly from the sky.

He felt deeply despondent. No matter what he did, this psychopath got in the way.

He remembered his hopes as he had stood on the balcony of the villa only a few days back, and his optimism in London.

He had, he thought, been extraordinarily naive.

He was being dragged down into a mire of amorality.

Even half of his conversations tonight had been concerned with cover-up rather than helping justice take its course.

His failure to act after the first murder made it more difficult to act after the second.

But if he didn't speak out now, what would his position be when a third occurred?

And Maria? He had so looked forward to being with her tonight and now she was gone. He had had hardly a minute alone with her. He had not even had a chance to ask about her parent's reaction to the news of their engagement. No wonder she had looked sad when she left.

His hands gripped the ship's railings till they were white.

Damn, damn, damn.

Felipe lay on his bunk in the cabin covered only by a towel. He felt like crying. He couldn't understand his new friend Manuel. Why did he appear so affectionate yet keep Felipe at arms length?

He leapt up, dropped the towel, and inspected himself in the mirror. Manuel would not find a more beautiful boy in Puerto Banus. What was the matter with him? Was there someone else? Was it his other friend Bill? Were they lovers after all?

He picked up a magazine and flicked over a few pages before throwing it petulantly into a corner of the cabin. He turned his small bedside radio on and off. He lit a cigarette and, pulling the curtain aside, looked out of the cabin at the bright lights of Puerto Banus.

To hell with it. If Manuel didn't want him, there were plenty of others who would.

He tossed the towel onto the bunk and wriggled into his tight white pants. Stuffing a 1000 pesetas note in his top pocket he switched off the light, climbed the ladder to the deck and, pleased not to have to endure Canning jeering at him, left the yacht and began to walk round to the Pink Coconut.

As he did so he became aware of another man walking alongside him. He turned and found himself staring into the face of a dark-haired Spaniard of just above medium height, but powerfully built, muscles rippling under a sleeveless tee shirt. The stranger smiled at him. Felipe looked sharply away but, a few yards on, couldn't resist another darting glance. The man was still there. Another smile, and this time he spoke.

"Buenos noches pretty child," he said.

"I'm not a child," Felipe said indignantly. "And I would be happy to prove it."

"Want to come for a drive then?"

"Sure."

He followed the other round to the car park and was impressed to find himself being helped into the passenger seat of a powerful-looking low-slung sports car.

This, he thought, would teach Manuel to treat him with indifference. Why, he, Felipe, could get anyone he wanted. And he was going to.

Defiant at life in general and Manuel in particular, he wound down the window, switched on the radio and lit a cigarette as the driver guided the car out of Puerto Banus and east towards Estepona.

After a few kilometres they turned right and headed towards the hills. "Where are we going?"

"Just a place where we can be on our own," said the other, reaching out a hand to touch the young man's thigh.

The road wound up a hill and down into a valley out of sight of the costa and got rougher and then all but disappeared. Felipe realised they were driving across open ground to the ruins of an old *cortijo*. For the first time he felt slightly apprehensive. "Where is this?"

"Just a place where we won't be disturbed... where you can show me you're not a child," smiled the other.

He pulled the car to a halt and they both climbed out and entered the open door of the deserted farmhouse.

It was dark inside except where the moonlight, coming through the windows, created spotlights on the dirt floor. The man gently steered Felipe, now trembling with anticipation, into an unlit corner and stood him facing the wall, his hands moving round to touch the front of the white pants.

Felipe felt himself hardening. The hands came from behind, moving slowly up to his chest. One of them appeared to be clutching a hard object... like the handle of a...

Felipe tried to cry out but it was too late. With one sharp movement the knife was pulled across his throat. For a moment he was held as life faded from his body, then he was allowed to slip to the ground.

Moving quickly now the other went outside and began to gather wood. This he took into the *cortijo*, building a bonfire around the body.

Then he went to the car and took out two drums of gasoline. One was tipped over the body and the bonfire, the other over all the wooden parts of the building. Standing well back, he set fire to a bit of brush and tossed it through the window. Within seconds the *cortijo* was an inferno.

He quickly climbed into his car and drove back to the rough road and down towards the costa.

A kilometre away a woman looked out the window of her bedroom and called to her husband. "There's a fire. The old *cortijo* is on fire."

Grumbling, he climbed out of bed and walked to the window to look at the blaze. "It was no use to anyone," he said. "Forget it."

He got back into bed. "It will be just ashes in the morning," he said. "You won't be able to tell what was there."

Then I realised I had been murdered
They looked for me in cafes, cemeteries and churches....
but they did not find me.
They never found me?
No. They never found me.

CHAPTER NINE

At the heart of old Marbella is the 16th century *Plaza de los Naranjos*, the square of the oranges, named for the small orchard in its courtyard, a square within a square. The orange trees shade nearly half a million people a year who come for coffee or wine and *tapas* served by waiters from the bars and restaurants that surround them.

Kate had spent a pleasant hour there, drinking coffee and writing letters, and now began to meander into a maze of Moorish alleys, past more bars and restaurants and bazaar-like shops, until she came to the main Marbella produce market.

Once inside the two-tier building she wandered past the imaginatively-displayed, cleaned and polished fruit and vegetables and headed for the *pescaderia y mariscos*, the fish market, passing by a row of lottery sellers and fishermen selling from wooden boxes their overnight catch of tiny anchovies, silvery-blue sardines and small rosy-red mullet. Turning hurriedly away from the stare of an evil-looking, one-eyed octopus, she went inside to photograph the proprietors of the 20 or more stalls as they gutted, scaled and sliced or filleted the disconsolate-looking fish on marble counters, using big sharp knives with wooden handles. There were big swordfish and tuna, their wide tails creating the appearance of grounded airplanes. There were wide, flat sole, huge lobsters with their claws still wriggling frantically in complaint at their fate, red and orange jumbo prawns and grey and brown langoustinos, whole bags of live, moving tiny crabs, blue and yellow amberjacks, pink-gold *dorada*, olive-grey flounders, good-looking silver sea bass and hake, ugly bright-red furnard, black, sinister-looking mussels with seaweed still clinging to their shells, squid and octopus, menacing with their bulbous heads and tentacles... all shining clean in their beds of ice.

After the fish market she paused at stalls devoted to herbs and spices, saffron, rosemary, sage, basil, estragon, oregano, thyme, coriander, pure bee honey, burghol, tahine, aniseed, basmati rice, nuts and raisins of every kind. So absorbed was she by the aromas and atmosphere that she almost didn't respond a young woman greeted her. Then she recognised Maria, Cruickshank's fiancee.

The young Spanish woman seemed pleased to see her and Kate suggested they walk back to the Plaza de los Naranjos for a drink. They were soon chatting happily in the sun, Kate talking about photography, about working with Sheedy in the States and her first few days in Spain, Maria content to encourage the talkative American, fascinated by stories of New York, full of questions.

"You should go there, Maria. In the Spring, that's the best time."

"But its also the best time in Seville."

"Then go in the Autumn, when the trees in Central Park are all gold and red and brown and the squirrels are out collecting nuts, when everybody is just back from summer vacation and in good spirits."

"I would like to... maybe I should go to New York in Autumn and you should repay the visit by coming to Seville in Spring, for la Semana Santa, holy week, and for the fair that follows."

"Its a deal," Kate promised.

She suggested lunch. Maria hesitated, and then, deciding. smiled and nodded.

They wandered back into the old shopping area and up the Calle Virgen de los Dolores to El Cortijo, a restaurant with decor like that of a Spanish kitchen. Once they had ordered, Kate a salad and a plate of grilled fresh fish, Maria a simple lettuce and tomato salad, the food to be accompanied by a bottle of rose, Kate said, "Now, Maria, tell me about this fiancee of your's. When are you going to marry?"

Maria looked shyly down at her lap for a moment, then answered. "I don't know exactly. It's all happened rather suddenly. There are details..."

Kate interrupted to encourage her. "You know, we're in the same boat..."

"The same boat... what boat...?"

"Sorry, just an expression. I mean't that you and I are in a similar position. Bill is also older than me, 20 years older. We've only really come together recently. So you can see, you and I are probably both experiencing many of the same feelings."

"Feelings?" enquired Maria cautiously.

"Happy, and content, apart from just a little regret it didn't happen earlier."

"Do you plan to marry, Kate?"

Kate laughed. "Sheedy? I doubt whether the idea has entered his head. I think he's just getting used to the idea that he can be happy with someone other than his wife. She died some years back. I guess we'll make it. Its just that he's one of those people who's too busy living each day to actually stop and think where he's going and what he should do about it. Maybe one day I'll suggest it to him. But not yet."

Maria was amazed. "You would suggest it to him?"

Kate laughed. "I guess that's not on in Spain. But surely men don't still rule in this country in the way they once did?"

"Kate, its no coincidence that *machismo* is a Spanish word. While the status of women has dramatically improved over the past 20 years or so, its still largely a man's country, especially away from the cities or tourist areas. The woman is only really equal in the role of home-maker and mother. But with that privilege goes all of the work. And there's a lot of hypocrisy. For instance, while a man who sleeps with a single woman or even another man's wife is often respected for it by other men, the woman is just as likely to be written off as a whore."

"No wonder you prefer an Englishman," Kate said dryly.

"Oh the Spanish are not that bad. And things are much better than they were." She changed the subject. "Anyway, your Bill seems a friendly man."

"But I liked your man too, a real gentleman," Kate replied.

"He is." Once more she looked shy.

Kate smiled at her. "Maria, I hope we can become friends."

Maria looked pleased. "I would like that. I would like that very much. Let's hope your Bill and my Brian become friends too."

For a moment a shadow passed over Kate's face. "Yes," she said thoughtfully. "Yes, I hope so too."

The red light came on and Sheedy began talking.

"Hi, this is Bill Sheedy.

"Tonight two stories that may be connected.

"First, I have news of a remarkable project being planned for the Estepona-San Pedro area and when I tell you that it will even put Sotogrande into the shade you'll have some idea just how ambitious it is.

"And then more news of *El Conejero*, the Rabbit Man, whose death I reported a couple of weeks ago."

Sheedy then described the proposed Cruickshank project, showed a map of the area, and, using still pictures of Cruickshank because an interview had in the circumstances been frostily refused, spoke of the personalities behind it.

This segment was followed by interviews with the mayors of Esteponas and Benahavis, both affected municipalities, and also with a local resident who objected to the project and argued there should be controls on further construction on the Costa del Sol.

Then there was a filmed discussion between Sheedy and two local personalities about whether it was right that gambling on horseracing should be encouraged in the area.

Then the report was concluded:

"Undoubtedly this project will go ahead... but it has been made easier by what its sympathisers hope is just a bizarre coincidence, or series of coincidences.

"Remember my item about the Rabbit Man of Ronda, *El Conejero*? I asked whether his death in a ravine near his lonely *cortijo* was an accident, or whether there could be some other explanation.

"It now emerges that *El Conejero*, Pepe Rodriguez, was the owner of a piece of land that was crucial to the new project. And he was refusing to sell. You can imagine how frustrating that was for Sir Brian Cruickshank and Anglo Investors Ltd.

"Now his untimely death has opened up the way for the project to proceed - provided, that is, that *El Conejero*'s heirs will sell it, or - if there are no heirs - provided the authorities will allow it, as seems likely.

"There will be those who say this is almost too remarkable a coincidence, but - and I stress this - there is no evidence to suggest a connection.

"However the possibility that Pepe's death was an accident has been lessened in the eyes of some by the death of his closest friend Ronda policeman Miguel Ayala just a few days later - a death that also appears, on the surface, to be the result of an accident.

"Were they the victims of coincidental accidents? Its possible of course. But likely?

"Did Miguel commit suicide as a result of distress at the death of his friend? That's possible too, although, knowing him, I have to say, its extremely unlikely.

"The police have much to think about, and this reporter will be turning his files on the case over to them immediately after this programme.

"If you can help, contact me, or the Ronda police.

"That's all for now. This is Bill Sheedy. Good night."

Cruickshank, Canning and Miller had watched the programme together and, as he switched the television set off, Cruickshank turned to the American and, his voice heavy with sarcasm, said "Whatever the truth about the policeman, Jason, I hope you're proud of your handiwork. What should have been a big moment, the launch of the project, is totally ruined. Instead of positive publicity about what we're planning to do, we begin on the defensive, not merely answering the usual questions about developers but also having to deny we killed a harmless old peasant. Congratulations."

Canning looked uncomfortable. "I understood we were not going to continue with these recriminations," he snapped back. "It's clear no-one can prove we were involved in the man's death and if you act decisively we should kill the story stone dead. For a start you could informally warn the rest of the media that you're considering legal action should anyone suggest a connection between the deaths and the project."He produced a sheet of paper. "I've prepared our comment as you requested."

"Let's hear it."

Cruickshank had to concede that it was cleverly worded:

"Anglo-Spanish Investors confirms the report on a Gibraltar television programme that it is about to announce plans for a major project in the municipalities of Benahavis and Estepona that will create employment and in other ways benefit the economy of the area and of Spain generally.

"However, with respect to the tragic death of one of the land-owners with whom it has been negotiating, Anglo-Spanish resents the programme's suggestion that it has in any way benefited from this tragic accident... rather than benefiting from his accidental death, the company is greatly inconvenienced by it. Not only will it cause expensive delays but it is likely to lead to an increased price for the parcel of land involved."

Miller wondered whether it was an over-reaction but Cruickshank argued that the programme couldn't be ignored. "If we couple its release with a private warning to the media that we'll take legal action if there is any further innuendo we should be alright." He turned to Canning: "Fax it now to the daily papers, local radio and television. That should stop the story being repeated tomorrow morning."

"I notice the release doesn't refer to the policeman," Miller said to him after Canning had left.

"No. Canning's right there. Our position is that the policeman was unknown to us, as in fact he was - except, perhaps, for Canning, and we'll come to that in a minute. As far as we're concerned he's a stranger who was involved in an accident far away from where we're operating. We shouldn't risk acknowledging by denials that there are grounds for even considering a possible connection between the two deaths, let alone any possibility of our involvement."

"But you surely don't believe Canning?"

"I don't know what to believe. I know what I want to believe... I want to believe that its just a coincidence. Or the old policeman just drank too much and wandered over the edge. I gather from the newspaper reports that this is possible." He looked at Miller hopefully but the latter looked sceptical.

"Look, I'm sorry, Sir Brian, "I know that's what you want to believe but you're overlooking the other coincidence. That Canning came back at three o'clock in the morning and his only alibi is a whore he claims to have picked up in Puerto Banus and has no doubt paid to back up his story. And Canning's meeting with the Spaniard in Istan... what was that about if it was not to set up the killing of the policeman?"

Cruickshank paced around the room. "Christ, Jim, I don't know. I don't know what's going on. And, frankly, you haven't been a lot of help."

Miller looked embarrassed. His head was beginning to ache and he was in desperate need of a drink. "I'm sorry, Sir Brian. It was incredibly bad luck. But from now on he won't change his underwear without me knowing about it, that I guarantee."

Left alone, the Englishman called for a whisky with ice and sat out on the balcony. It was a warm night, the sea was still and in the distance he could see fishing boats, their lights bobbing up and down.

He began his methodical review of the position. Two men dead now. Probably both killed by Canning or someone sent by Canning. By not going to the police after the first one he had made it extremely difficult to go to them now, especially as he had no proof whatsoever about the second one. He imagined the scene:

"What evidence do you have that Canning killed the policeman, Sir Brian?"

"None."

"Do you know whether he was in Ronda that night? Can you disprove his alibi? Do you know whether Canning had even heard of the policeman?"

"No."

"Then why are you making this charge?"

"Because he did admit killing the first man."

"But that was weeks ago. Why did you not report it then?"

"I... I... decided not to."

Great. That would sound just great. He remembered what he had told Miller, that one small lie always led to another. He had allowed himself to be trapped in a web of deceit, one murder had led to another, and he no longer knew how to extricate himself. It was even possible - he felt a deep sense of shock at the idea - that he could too be charged, if not with murder, at least with conspiracy to murder, or obstructing the course of justice. That would be the end - not just of the project but his whole career.

He thought about Jordan. Jordan was the only hope. The man wasn't a fool. Surely he could see this had to stop. Surely he would recall Canning now, leave Cruickshank in charge.

He called to Hobbs to telephone the American at his home number in New York State. Convinced now that Jordan held the answer, he paced up and down waiting on the reply. Eventually Hobbs returned. "They say he's not there, sir. That he's out of the country. That he's in Europe."

Cruickshank looked at him sharply. "Where in Europe?"

"They said they didn't know, sir. Just that he didn't return from your meeting in London but was intending to go on from there to somewhere in Europe."

Cruickshank felt alarm bells ringing. Europe? Where in Europe except Spain did Jordan have an interest? Was he on his way? Was he already on the Costa del Sol somewhere? If so, why? And why hadn't he told Cruickshank he was coming?

His eye caught the picture of Maria he had placed beside his bed. Oh God, he thought, Maria. Would she have seen the programme? Then he remembered the reason they were not together that evening was that she was attending a dinner party in Malaga with Julio and Isabella. She wouldn't have seen any television. Thank God for that.

Thinking of her made him want her, want the feeling of confidence he felt when in her company, want the way she reminded him of who and what he was.

Maria was on a different plane from these other people, Jordan, Canning, even Miller, all people Cruickshank should never have to deal with.

Maria. He compared the sordid nature of the problems that engulfed him with the purity his love and imagination had invested in her. It seemed to him that, whereas before the murder of the peasant all had seemed possible, now a chasm was building up between the hideous reality of his position and the dream he had nurtured - a chasm that was widening every hour.

After the programme Kate and Sheedy drove back into Spain with Brian Hunter, the company's director of news and documentaries, for dinner at a small, back-street restaurant Sheedy had discovered in Estepona. After feasting themselves on spare ribs and fresh vegetables, and homemade apple crumble, all cooked in a cave-like baker's oven, they were having coffee with the proprietor when a telephone call came from the television station for Hunter. After jotting down a lengthy message he handed it to Sheedy. "They didn't waste any time."

"Hell no," said Sheedy after reading it. " Look at this, Kate." It was Cruickshank's press release.

Hunter lit a St Julian cigar and, leaning back in his chair, looked at Sheedy thoughtfully. "You know we don't have a lot to go on Bill. We'd better be careful with this one."

"You don't have to tell me," the American replied. "I know the evidence is circumstantial. But I'm convinced that Miguel and the Rabbit Man died because of Cruickshank's project. The problem is to prove it." His listeners looked at each other, both amused at the way his eyes lit up at the challenge. Sheedy continued "I'm hoping tonight's programme may lead to someone coming forward with fresh information, as Ramon Aparicio did."

"Ok," said Hunter, "but just the same they're threatening legal action if there's even the slightest suggestion they've been guilty of murder and I don't blame them. If they're innocent they've every reason to be furious. You've ruined their launch for no reason. And if they're guilty they've every reason to be furious too. Bill, you know we'll back you up as far as we can, but one libel action could close the station and we're a Gibraltar station, not Spanish, so a libel action would be easy to bring."

Kate asked "Apart from that, you don't think Bill is in danger too, do you Brian?"

Hunter looked taken aback. "Christ, I hope not. I hadn't even thought of that." He pondered for a minute. "I guess if they've killed two people they wouldn't stop at more. But it would be so obvious. Everyone would know who was behind it."

"Actually that's what puzzles me about the whole business," Sheedy said. "It *is* obvious. And its hard to believe they gain that much by it all. Which is why I can't believe that Cruickshank is so stupid as to allow it."

"And I don't think he's so immoral, Bill," Kate added. "He strikes me as being someone of real stature. I just don't think he's that kind of man to let all this happen."

"Well that only leaves two possibilities," said Hunter. "Either the deaths of the two men have nothing to do with Anglo-Spanish Investors, or Cruickshank is not in control of what's happening. And if he isn't, who is?"

"Ah ha," said Sheedy, "that was going to be my next story. Brian. Do you think we could invest some additional money in research for a few weeks. I want to pay someone in the States, a friend of mine called Teddy Gray, to look into the American investors. Its possible there's money going into this project from organised crime, maybe even Mafia money."

"Christ, Bill," said Hunter, "don't even think of broadcasting that till all the angles are covered and that includes protecting the station. In every way. Listen," he added half laughing, "I tell you, I'm trying to run a quiet profitable little TV station, I don't want the whole station blown up, let alone bankrupted by a huge libel suit."

"Don't worry," said Sheedy, "I take your point. Anyway, there's a long way to go yet. We may get some inside information from the yacht"... he waved a dismissive hand to the curious Hunter to indicate there was no point in questioning him about the source..."and Kate has become friendly with Cruickshank's fiancee. She may pick up some a few facts too."

"Look Bill," said Kate, "forget it. I'll be damned if I'm going to involve Maria. Jesus," she looked at him, exasperated, "there's no stopping you."

"Ok, ok," he said, in too good a humour, as he always was after the programme, to take offence, "but maybe a question or two. She may even be able to help clear Cruickshank if he is not involved himself."

"Listen Bill," said Hunter, "have you thought what Cruickshank must be feeling and thinking. Let's imagine he was not involved... that this man Canning killed both men without authority from Cruickshank. The Englishman is, as you say, no fool. He knows of the deaths, he knows you're linking them with the project. Surely he would be furious and would be investigating Canning's behaviour and pressing for information too."

"That's what I'm hoping - that there'll be a row between Cruickshank and Canning, or whoever is behind him, maybe on the yacht, and that we'll get to hear of it."

"But wouldn't Cruickshank go to the police if he got any evidence?"

Sheedy sat silent. "Well now, that's the question, isn't it? That's when we find out just how much a man of honour Cruickshank actually is."

The two officers from the *Guardia Civil* came to the villa at about ten o'clock. The senior, the one who had spoken to Kate in Ronda, introduced himself as Colonel Rivas.

Kate, who had arranged to go swimming with Maria, made some coffee and orange juice and left them to talk.

Sheedy told Rivas of his friendship with the two old men of the sierras, of the Rabbit Man's death, of his and Miguel's suspicions, of the project and the possible motive for the Rabbit Man's murder, about Cruickshank and what little he knew about Canning and the man in New York, Jordan.

"Its a pity you did not come to share this with us before, *Señor* Sheedy."

"It wasn't for me to do so," Sheedy replied. "After all, Miguel was one of your officers. Naturally I assumed that if he believed there was evidence justifying official action he would have told you. In any case, had you begun investigating the project, the company would have shut up like a clam, whereas there was a chance my unofficial investigations would provoke them to make a mistake." Observing the policeman frown, he hastily added "Of course, once Miguel was killed I realised that you had to be fully involved. I intended to make contact... today. In fact I said as much on my programme last night."

Rivas was unimpressed. "Unfortunately we do not see your programme in Ronda, *Señor* Sheedy. In any case coming to the police after you have taken half a million people into your confidence hardly suggests you're taking us too seriously. What evidence have you discovered that the two men were murdered because of the project you describe?"

"That's the point. None that you can act on. There was the evidence around the body of the Rabbit Man suggesting that it may not have been an accident and there was the observed meeting between this man Canning and the Rabbit Man. But, to be fair, Anglo Spanish admit that link."

Rivas rose, saying that it was his intention to see Cruickshank and Canning later in the day. "Can we hope *Señor* Sheedy you will cease your freelance policing of the area and leave it to us?"

"I'm afraid I can't promise that, Inspector. I'm a reporter. I have a duty to follow this story now I've started. And I am also under a personal obligation to two friends."

"And we have a greater public duty, *Señor* Sheedy. It would be unfortunate if you were to get in the way."

"With respect, not only have I not done so but what little you know is entirely due to my work."

"Had we been acting as a police force, *Señor* Sheedy, it is possible that Miguel Ayala would still be alive."

"That was his decision."

The inspector looked at him coldly. "May I ask what you plan to do next ?"

"We have a connection within the company. I can go no further, because he must be protected. I hope he may come up with some new evidence. But I give you my word I will share it with you. My only wish is to see that whoever killed my friends comes to justice."

Sheedy watched the police car go down the hill and then rang Manuel in Benahavis. "Any news from Felipe?"

"Not a word. I've looked out for him for two nights now and there's been so sign of him, either on the yacht or on land."

Sheedy felt apprehensive. "Look, they don't know you. Why not go and say you're a friend and ask to see him "

"Bill, I can't do that. Felipe would panic. It would be betraying him. We don't have the right."

"I know there's a risk but I don't like the sound of this. We had him excited. Why should he have cooled off? I think enquiring after him is the best of two unattractive options."

Manuel reluctantly said he would have another look for Felipe that evening and, if he didn't show up, he would go to the yacht.

West of Marbella there are a string of beach bars and clubs of varying degrees of luxury. Some are built round swimming pools and have their own entrance to the beach so that customers can either swim in the pool or in the sea. Others, usually made of wood, are on the beach itself, and sell cold drinks and a lunch of grilled fish or paella.

Kate and Maria chose the beach just west of Puerto Banus, in front of the extraordinary Arabian Palace-like *Gray d'Albion* complex with its roof gardens and ceramic domes. Maria had suggested one or two more exclusive clubs but Kate said she wanted to be around people who were not sweating money out of every pore and by noon the two of them were propping up the wooden counter of one of the noisier bars drinking ice-cold San Miguels.

Kate felt a bit guilty about questioning Maria but the memory of Miguel's round, smiling face stiffened her backbone, so she began to gently probe.

"Tell me, Maria, why is Sir Brian down on the costa so much? I would have expected him to leave the details to others while he's wheeler-dealing in London."

"I don't know," Maria said, puzzling, "except that this project means a lot to him. Its not like the other business deals he's involved in. Its a kind of dream. He plans to live in the valley some of the time. That's why he has to be close to it now."

"Maybe its you he wants to be close too, Maria."

The Spanish girl blushed. "I would like to think so. But I think he is too practical a man for that to be the only reason. Anyway, I think he's had one or two problems with it, that's why he's been on the *costa* so much."

Kate sipped her drink for a moment, not wishing to appear too interested, then, as if remembering, said "Oh yes, Bill said that one of the landowners was killed."

"Yes, an accident in the mountains. It has caused a delay I think."

"Sir Brian must be upset."

"Upset? I don't think so. He didn't know the man. I think just, how do you say... irritated? Yes, irritated."

Kate decided to press one more time.

"Bill met someone else from the company. Canning? Would it be a Mr Canning?"

"Maybe. I haven't met him. Why?" Maria looked at Kate questioningly, and the latter decided it was time to drop it.

"No reason. Bill just mentioned it." She felt sorry for the Spanish girl, in love and blissfully unaware of the dark clouds assembling around her fiancee's head.

The two young women walked back down to the water's edge, dropping their shoulder bags on the beach and hopping about as they abandoned their sandals and felt the heat of the sand. Maria asked a young Spanish woman lying nearby to guard their belongings and, clad only in the briefest of bikini bottoms, their breasts proudly displayed, they both waded into the water.

All over the beach men sat up, pretending to stretch, look out to sea, put on sun lotion... all actions to explain to their wives and girlfriends why suddenly their paperbacks had lost their appeal.

"You know what this reminds me of, Jim," Cruickshank said as the two of them and Canning gathered in the library of the yacht before lunch. "It reminds me of Watergate. How Nixon got involved in a cover-up of a relatively petty and totally unnecessary break-in and the whole business grew and grew as a result of journalistic investigation until he spent most of his time in pathetic plotting meetings with Haldemann and Erlichman. Remember the Watergate tapes and the level it all sunk to?"

With mounting anger he said "I let myself cover-up for you Jason, for your totally unnecessary violence, and now I'm spending all my time in these bloody meetings. I feel as if a net is closing in and I'm powerless to act. Damn it, will your criminal interference with what should be a relatively straight-forward business operation never end?"

Taken aback by the anger on his face, the others didn't speak immediately. Miller looked contemptuously at Canning and the American looked equally contemptuously at Cruickshank. "Perhaps if you stopped panicking we could all get on with other things. There wasn't a word in the papers this morning about the deaths, only details about the project. It was all presented positively. Our strategy is working. They'll never prove our connection with the old man's death. And we have no connection with the policeman, so why don't we just get on with our work?"

Cruickshank snapped back. "Because the police are on their way here now, Jason, that's why? I am about to be reduced to answering questions from some half-illiterate Ronda policeman because you've been running round the countryside like a Spanish version of Baby Face Nelson."

Then, remembering, he said "By the way, where is Jordan?"

Canning looked shifty. "What do you mean where's Jordan? In New York, I presume."

"No, Jason, he's not in New York. He's in Europe, probably on his way to Spain or in Spain. I want to talk to him and I want to do it now. So where is he?"

Canning stood up and walked to the port-hole, looked out for a moment, and then turned to the Englishman. "I'm sorry, Sir Brian, I'm not authorised to say."

"Not authorised! " Cruickshank was on his feet, furious, almost out of control. "What the hell do you mean, not authorised? This is a business we're running. Jordan is part of it. I want to speak to him. You find him and get him on the phone or I will turn you over to the police before the day is out. Now get out."

Canning, rose and abruptly walked to the door.

Turning, he looked coolly at Cruickshank.

"Bullshit," he said.

Then he left.

Cruickshank sank into his chair, too angry and unhappy to speak.

That last word had been a blow.

He had convinced himself he was back in charge.

But he wasn't; that was made only too clear by his impotence when confronted by the arrogant young American.

It was Miller who broke the silence.

"I'm sorry, Sir Brian, I can't help you on this. I tapped his phone but he's been making his calls from bars and call boxes. He's clever."

Cruickshank looked amazed. "Tapped his phone. You tapped his phone? My God, it gets worse and worse."

Miller, startled at his employer's discomposure, gently drew his attention back to the forthcoming meeting.

"Sir Brian, if I may suggest from my experience as a former policeman, you should not be too charming in dealing with the police. Your position is that you have been libelled and slandered by the very suggestion of a connection with these deaths. As an innocent man, you are an aggrieved party and have a big interest in the matter being cleared up. You must demand that they establish whether the deaths were accidents or not, and if they were not, they must arrest the killers. Your whole approach must be anger at the inconvenience caused by all this and by the challenge to your integrity. And you should hold the police responsible for not moving faster. Don't be insulting… remember the strong Spanish pride… but do be impatient and demanding. That way they'll be on the defensive rather than you."

Cruickshank reached for the coffee on the side board and poured himself a cup. He looked at Miller gratefully. Perhaps he had misjudged him. Maybe his minder drank too much but he was thinking more clearly than Cruickshank. "That's good advice, Jim."

As Miller was leaving the villa a few minutes later, fortified from a bottle of Beefeater gin now kept in his room, he heard Cruickshank's voice from the library. He was evidently talking to Colonel Rivas of the *Guardia Civil* in Ronda. "Now I hope you're going to get this business cleared up, Colonel. Frankly, I'm shocked that these irresponsible journalists could link my good name and that of my company with these tragic accidents and I'm counting on you..."

Miller was pleased. Cruickshank was acting on his advice. He still had his employer's confidence. As he went in pursuit of Canning he resolved to do all in his power to get Cruickshank out of the mess he was in. He liked the man.

And for himself he saw the possibility of a bright future.

The project would need a security service, and the security service would need a chief...

Sheedy had a leisurely swim and then, alone in the garden, settled into a deckchair in front of the pool, and began to review the story. He recognised the distinctive sound of Manuel's motor bike as it came up the hill. It was deafening.

"For Christ's sake, Manuel," he greeted his colleague, "can't you get a silencer on that thing. Its a public menace. How can I run a campaign about the noise caused by motor bikes when you're running around on that?"

For once the young Spaniard did not respond to the bandiage.

"Bill, Felipe's gone."

"Gone?" Sheedy sat up.

"When I asked at the yacht they said he had left. Gone home."

"When?"

"They said a couple of days back. They said he just left a note that he was homesick and left without even picking up his back pay. But took all his belongings."

"Did anyone see him go?"

"Well, I couldn't question them too closely... but no-one mentioned seeing him."

"Who did you talk to?"

"A couple of guys guarding the gang plank."

"Did they ask who you were?"

"I just said I was a friend from the Pink Coconut and that we had arranged to meet. They seemed to accept it. There was no big deal about it."

Sheedy was worried. He asked where Felipe came from.

"North, somewhere near Cordoba."

"Ok, I think the best thing is to get the *Guardia Civil* to check out whether he got home. I'll talk to Colonel Riva later. I want an excuse to ring him anyway, to ask how he got on with Cruickshank."

He walked in and got a couple of bottles of San Miguel beer from the fridge. He opened the bottles and carried them without glasses back to the pool. The two sat drinking silently for a few moments. Then Sheedy looked at the young man.

"I'm sorry Manuel. I don't think I've handled this well. Its becoming a terrible mess. Its just that nothing adds up. I never thought Miguel was under threat and I thought we could keep Felipe safe and I was wrong on both counts. And I still don't know what to make of Cruickshank, I find it hard to believe he's involved. Yet its equally hard, logically, to believe he's not. I accept we've got to work with the police now but my fear is that the police stumbling around will cause them all to tighten up their operation and it'll be even more difficult to get at the truth."

"Well, maybe this will help." Manuel handed him an envelope. "Its from Rosa. Its the letter. She had a helluva job translating it."

With that the Spaniard left with another deafening roar that caused Sheedy to wince and look apologetically at the windows of the surrounding villas. Then, putting his feet up on the other chair, he opened the envelope .

On top of the typescript there was a note from Rose:

TO: SEÑOR SHEEDY

I have done my best to translate the letter. It was not easy. Some of it is indecipherable. For some reason the handwriting of the opening and closing is particularly bad, I think because the old man wrote these few words himself, so I cannot make out who the letter is addressed to or the signature at the end.

ROSA

Sheedy put the note aside and began to read...

CHAPTER TEN

"My... (indecipherable)...

At writing I am not good. To help me tell my story an old friend will write for me. I hope one day soon to discover where you are and will then send this to you.

My dear niece, I am your father's brother. We had another brother, Francisco; I have not seen him for many years but I think he has a cortijo near Casares where like me he hunts the rabbit. He and I were the only family left to care for you when your dear parents died when you were small.

It was not because we didn't love you that we asked old friends, a good gypsy family, to look after you as one of their own. It was simply that our lives were hard and we wanted more for you than we could make possible. It was not right for you, a little girl, to share the lonely life of a hunter in the mountains without other children to play with, with no woman to understand your needs, with no chance to go to school.

I was at first deeply upset and angry to hear that our friends had experienced bad times and abandoned you, but, just as I was setting out to find you, I learned from the gypsies that you had been adopted by a good man and woman who had many pesetas. Do not fear, my niece, I will not embarrass you by coming to see you. This letter will tell you all you need to know... about the life of your family and about me, your uncle.

Did you know that the Rodriguez family has lived for over 200 years in the sierras west of Ronda, for nearly a century in the pueblo of Grazalema where your father and I were born? You may even have been there. If so, you will know that it is said to be the wettest place in Spain. This is because it is nearly 3000 feet above sea-level and is built under a mountain that stops the momentum of the clouds swept by the winds from the oceans. As they cannot pass, they fall as rain.

Your great grandfather, Pepe, and his son, my father Antonio, worked at the beginning of the century in a wool mill making blankets and ponchos. Many in the village did this. The ponchos were sold to shepherds and also to other men, middle men, who sold them in faraway countries, even one called Argentina in South America. As a boy I would help my father take stacks of ponchos by mule all the way to the port in Cadiz, over 110 kilometres on rough tracks, sometimes no tracks at all, over high hills and across hostile country. We did this no matter what the heat of the summer day or the cold of the winter night.

Sometimes my father would return with his mule loaded with contraband smuggled in from Africa via Gibraltar or unloaded late at night on the beaches of the costa, usually coffee or tobacco. This he would buy from the contrabandistas or carry for them. Everyone who helped us on the journey, with water for the mule or food or shelter, would be paid with a carton or two of cigarettes or some coffee. Near the village the goods would be transferred to other men with a truck and we too would be paid. Please do not think harshly of this, dear niece, for in those days smugglers were not seen as bad or dishonest but as heroes, people who outwitted the wealthy merchants on the coast and the Guardia Civil and gave to the people not just goods they would never otherwise have had but also their dignity in the face of these scoundrels and oppressors.

Then in the 1920's, when I was still a small boy, people began to buy fewer woollen ponchos. They could more easily buy clothing made of cotton. The mills in the village began to close. The family was forced to do other work. Some became shepherds, protected from the cold in the hills by the same ponchos they used to make. The sheep they guarded provided the wool for those who still tried to survive by blanket or poncho-making and the sheep's milk was used for cheese.

But these were hard years, especially in the winter when it was cold and wet in our pueblo, and especially for the older members of the family.

Of course it was not so hard for me. I was a child. I think maybe all childhoods in Spain are happy, for children have no reason to know life can be better, nor that their loving mother and father are going hungry so they can eat and lying cold at night so they can be warm. I played bandido games in the hills around the pueblo with other children. We played late into the evening, oblivious at the time to the activities of the adults around us, the mothers and grandmothers sitting in the doorways, the courting couples talking to each other through the grills over the windows, the men arguing and philosophising loudly inside and outside the bars.

Once when I was nine I was taken with the men of the family all the way to Ronda to sell ponchos, go to the fair, and then see a corrida. I will never forget how excited I was. The journey by mule took three days but I was so proud to be one of the men that I hardly noticed. We slept in the gardens near the plaza de toros and while the men drank in the bars I walked the streets, looking into the windows of shops and staring in wonder at beautiful señoritas promenading in the evening air. We sat in the cheapest rows at the top of the plaza de toros. It was hotter than I had ever experienced for we could not afford seats in the shade. But I will always remember that first corrida and how we shouted for the bravest of the matadors to be awarded two ears and a tail that day, my cries louder than anyone's. And he was. On the way back I was too tired to hurt from the riding. My father said I slept for three days on the mule's back.

The best day of the year in our pueblo was at the time of the Fiesta del Carmen in July. At about seven o'clock in the morning we would line up to run from the bull that would be let loose at the top of the hill and allowed to charge down the narrow, winding lanes of the pueblo. All the previous night and throughout the day the young men would drink to build up their courage, for the bull was let loose twice more, once at noon and once at eight o'clock in the evening. By then the village was full of people, many of the men fairly drunk, and there was much noise and excitement. I am told the bull is still let loose at the Fiesta to this day.

Alas, my dear niece, such happy times were few. I remember the cold damp winter in Grazalema that killed your grandmother. We decided then to move east away from the rain. Your father, my brother Mario, was to learn be a charcoal-burner. It was decided I should learn to make CAL - whitewash. I was put into the charge of the man we knew as old Fernando, the elder brother of your mother, who took me with him high into the hills to collect bits of wood from olive or pine trees to bring down by mule. He lived in a lonely cortijo on the side of a bare hill and into the side of that hill we built a calera, a furnace, taking two weeks to do it. It was a small cave with a hole only big enough to enable us to throw in more wood to maintain the heat. The walls we strengthened by stone and mud and inside we stacked the cal stones we had collected and loaded on the mule and carried for many kilometres. For three days we would stay there, building and rebuilding the fire until it was white-hot, then we would take turns to guard it for another few days until it was cool enough to break open so that we could extract the cal stones and break them down into white, crumbly stones or powder, ready to be sold for the making of whitewash. It was hard back-breaking work.

Then, my dear niece, came the civil war. How can I explain to you why we fought, Spaniard killing Spaniard, Andaluz killing Andaluz, why such horrors were committed, except to tell you what life had become like. Hundreds of thousands of peasants in Andalucia were living at the mercy of the caciques, the autocratic landowners who took advantage of the poverty to hire labourers a day at a time for little money. Somehow my family became in debt to them so that all we earned from them with our labour had to be used to pay the interest on their loans. Your father Mario, when only 10 years old, was working 24 hours a day as a shepherd, sleeping with the sheep, having to eat only bread, maybe a little soup, and stewed chickpeas. When the politicians in Madrid decided we could share ownership of the land and we tried to possess it we were badly beaten and denied further work. I knew little about politics except that the Republican politicians in Madrid had at least tried to help, to give us some land, and that the nationalists were the supporters of the landowners who refused to implement the policy and met our legitimate demands with violence.

One day the pueblo near where I was struggling to survive with my parents was taken over by an extreme group of Republican guerilleros and they killed those Nationalists they could find. A day later the Nationalist forces arrived and exacted their revenge, killing nearly 60 of the villagers. I fled to the hills and joined a band of guerilleros fighting for the Republican cause. I will not attempt to tell you of what I saw in those years, of the cruelty and the horror of the civil war, or of my confusion at the wars within wars, for even those who professed to be Republicans were divided. I only know that there seemed no choice but to be what I was and that not a night went by without my praying that I and my parents and my brothers would survive. For three years I never slept easily at night, always we were in danger of being captured or killed. That we were not was a miracle for it is said that more than half a million people died in the three years of the war.

One day a group of us were ambushed in a small valley from where there was no retreat. Soldiers blocked off the entrance and came riding in and shot and killed everyone but me. I had slipped into some bushes only a moment earlier to relieve myself. I lay there, under a thick bush, shocked and terrified and, thank God, they missed me. Our numbers in that part of the sierras had been getting fewer and I now spent many weeks alone, hiding in a tiny cave in the hills, living on a few berries and on my skill in trapping rabbits or the occasional goat that had wandered from a herd. Even then I had to cook it quickly away from my cave so that the smoke would not give me away and scurry back there like a wild animal with its captured prey. Often I caught nothing.

In the winter it became unbearably cold. Twice at night I woke just in time to avoid being attacked by hungry wolves. I finally decided to try to creep into Ronda and find some food, perhaps somewhere I could stay. I knew the chance of capture was high but I believed I would die if I stayed out.

I had walked for three days across the hills, twice narrowly evading soldiers on horseback, when I found a small clutch of trees in a valley and tearing off some branches made a kind of tent to sleep in overnight. I woke to find a light in my face. Standing over me were two Nationalist soldiers. My blood froze. One was thin, with a sharp nose and hard eyes. He pushed me down and held me there with his boot at my throat. The other was different. A big man, fat, he had a kinder face, one that gave me hope. He was, I suspected, no older than I.

I was so weak by now and so shocked that when the older man, the thin one, said "What are you doing in this place, you bandido, are you a Republican?" I blurted out "si" before I realised what I was doing.

"Let's not waste our time dragging him back to be tried and executed," said the thin man. "Let's shoot him on the spot."

I was terrified. I thought I was about to die. I began to pray for my mother and for my family. But, thank God, the big man would have none of it. The two argued and then reluctantly the thin man roughly tied my hands behind me and tied a rope around my neck. They climbed on their horses and the thin man made me walk in front. For hours I stumbled across rocks and shrubs with him jerking the rope.

Eventually he pulled me to the ground and told me to lie there. They got off their horses and sat under a tree, unwrapping some food and drinking from a bota of wine. The thin man ignored me but the fat man walked over and gave me a piece of bread and a swig from the bota. I looked at him gratefully but the older man just laughed and called him a weak young fool.

Then they tied the rope to a tree and lay down to rest. I must have fallen asleep because next I knew the thin man was leaning over me cutting the rope and telling me to run. "Run, bandolero, run," he kept saying. I could not *understand why he had changed towards me but I began to run. I had got only about 10 metres when I heard the click of a trigger and realised I had been trapped. He had helped me to escape in order to have an excuse to shoot me. There was a bang and I felt a terrible pain in my side. I fell, twisting round as I did so. He was raising his gun and aiming it at my head. There was another bang and then to my amazement the gun toppled from his hand. A terrible look of pain mixed with surprise came onto his face, and then he fell forward on the ground. The other soldier had shot him.*

I do not remember much about the next few days except that we were in a cave and the soldier who should have been my enemy helped me to recover, bathing what was apparently not a serious wound, and feeding me with meat obtained by shooting wild goats and rabbit. Then he told me that I was to go, taking both horses. He would walk back and tell his superiors that they had been attacked by Republican guerillas, that his colleague had been killed and that he had escaped and been forced to return on foot. He even gave me his gun.

I asked him why he did this. He simply smiled and said "we are all Spaniards. The difference is that you and I are not of the past. We still have our lives to live, we can still do good. He was a man who never would. The war is nearly over. You and your friends have lost. I see no reason why you should die now. So go and be safe." With that he was gone.

Three weeks later I met some other Republicans in the hills. The war was over. Some were going home. A few were planning to keep fighting, to become guerilleros, living in the mountains. They said there would be no pardon. That we would all be punished, maybe killed. I did not know what to do so I chose the guerilleros. And I did hear of many killings of those who went home, of much retribution. For many more years I lived in the mountains armed with a shotgun, but never a full member of one of the Communist guerilla bands.

Our enemy now was the Guardia Civil. There were attacks on Guardia Civil headquarters and kidnappings by guerillas and, I know, some killings, but I saw little of this. Then one day I was riding with a comrade in the hills when we saw some Guardia Civil officers coming down the valley. We hid above the pass and watched them go by. One of them was told to remain and guard the entrance to the valley. My comrade drew a knife and signalled to me that he was going to jump down upon him from a rock above his head; he made a gesture with the knife across his throat to indicate what he had in mind. Then the policeman turned his head and I saw his face; it was the man who in the Civil War had saved my life. In the split second that it took my comrade to jump I called out a warning. The big policeman turned, his horse moving, so that my comrade hit the ground. As he did so the policeman hit the back of his head with the butt of his revolver. He then looked up and our eyes met. For a moment he said not a word then he slowly smiled. "I knew that one day you would do good, my friend," he said. I dragged my comrade to our horses while the policeman rode on as if it had never happened.

I'm told more than 2000 guerilleros were killed and 25,000 guerilleros or so-called accomplices were arrested in those years. But once more I survived.

Years went by and I became part of the land itself. By the time a full amnesty was announced in 1959, about the time you were born, I had been living, half-human, half-animal in the sierras for more than 25 years, most of it an outlaw, yet not known to the Guardia Civil for I had always evaded capture and not been with any one band enough to become well-known or be betrayed.

Yes, I had survived, but my younger years had gone.

In the years after the war, while I was still an outlaw, things had been no better for our family. Andalucia was desperately poor. Whole families left for the big cities to live in poverty in shacks on the outskirts. Many smallholders abandoned their cortijos and left them to decay. Your father Mario, who had returned to charcoal-burning and cal-making after the Civil War, suffered much illness probably caused by getting the dust and smoke in lungs already damaged by the cold and damp of his childhood. Mario, who was born in the mid 1920's, six or seven years after me, was nearly 35 when he married your mother and you were born two years later, about 1960. Tragically your mother died giving birth to you.

My dear niece, your father was a good man, a good brother, and though he was poor in those years he always gave generously to me when, putting him at risk in my desperation, I crept late at night from the hills looking for food or warmth. He never recovered from the loss of your mother and I believe died as much from a broken heart as from the effects of years of struggle.

My dear niece, you must forgive these ramblings of an old man, but I have never before had cause or desire to remember or recount all these things. It is right you should know what has gone before in your family. And also you need to know some things that I pray will make your life an even better one.

Your mother's uncle who lived in Malaga came to Mario's funeral and *talked to me. He said that he owned some land near the costa. It was not worth much because it was unfit for growing things. But he wanted it kept for you, his only niece. It was decided it should be registered in my name and that it would one day be given to you. Now things have changed; there is much building of grand houses on the costa. I'm told its possible that the land is now worth many pesetas. If you go to your other uncle near Casares you will find he has the details and the written authorities transferring its ownership to you.*

My dear niece, you come from a family that was always loyal to each other, that lived in hard times but was as honest as it was possible to be and survive.. For my part, I know only one life now, the life of the sierras. I can read or write only a few words, I have never known the warmth of a woman in my bed, and for me the inventions of my lifetime, radios and television, even electricity itself, are things I see when I pass other people's houses or when I am invited in for food. But I do not want you to think I write in complaint for I love this magnificent country, these hills and mountains, the flowers in the valleys, the peace I share with the eagles and the conejo and my faithful old mule. I am, too, at peace with myself. I have only one duty and that is to fulfil my obligation to your father and to you, so that you will live a better life, for in your good fortune lies the hope that our family will never know hardship again.

So, my dear niece, take care and live a good life. Think kind thoughts of your old uncle. I write with love on behalf of your mother and father,

your loving uncle,
(name indecipherable).

P.S.
If you ever need help from the police see my good friend Miguel. He is a captain in the Guardia Civil in Ronda. You may guess from the above story that we share many memories.

CHAPTER ELEVEN

Sheedy let the letter drop from his fingers and fall to the ground beside the deckchair and, closing his eyes, pictured the two old men, Miguel and the Rabbit Man, sitting in their customary corner of the Casino bar in Ronda, Miguel full of life, expansive, talkative, the other sitting completely still, listening, watching. He remembered them differently in the *plaza de toros*, Miguel leaning back, relaxed, cold beer in hand, the Rabbit Man tensed forward, his face alert, his eyes on fire.

What lives the two men had shared. What loyalties. What secrets. Now he knew why Miguel had been so restrained about the Rabbit Man's past. Each of had betrayed his allegiances by saving the life of the other; at one point both must have been at risk, if these acts of mercy were exposed, of being executed by their own comrades. To the end the Rabbit Man, his suspicion engrained by years of living outside the law, had felt it necessary to keep his past from the police; to the end Miguel must have feared he would face a court martial if ever his killing of a fellow officer became known.

How sad that having fought and survived in the civil war, fought poverty, fought injustice, fought the severity of life in the sierras, and survived to draw solidarity and strength from each other, that they should be killed by a casual foreigner for so trivial a reason.

With a sigh, the American picked up his drink and the pages at his feet and walked back into the villa. He showered and changed and made himself a coffee. With this he sat at the table on the balcony and, picking up a ruler, placed it vertically on the last page of the old man's letter. Using a formula that had served him well in the past, he began to slowly move the ruler across the signature, trying to isolate each letter of each word.

He got it down to two words, one with four letters and one more difficult to work out, but probably 9 or 10.

Now he moved the ruler back to the left and moved it slowly from letter to letter, endeavouring to work out what each was.

He was, of course, helped by the fact that he knew already the two words should be Pepe Rodriguez, so he looked first for the letter P then the letter E and so on. It wasn't difficult. If you knew the letter was probably a P it was easier to decide it was in fact a P. And there was no doubt about it; the signature was Pepe Rodriguez.

Now he turned his attention to the greeting at the top. This was more difficult because he didn't know what he was looking for.

Once more by moving the ruler slowly along he was able to work out that there were three words, one with just two letters, one with six or seven, and the last and most difficult possibly four, five or six letters.

The first he distinguished as Mi, my, and the second as *quehido*. *Quehido?* He reached for his Spanish dictionary and it wasn't there. He checked other possible words. Then he saw it. *Querido* - dear, beloved. "My dear..."

But the most difficult word was the last. It was written in a scrawl as if his hand had lost energy at the end of the line and it was made even more indistinct by time and damp. He knew the best he could do was guess.

The first letter was completely indecipherable. The second was either an a or an o. The third was either an r or and h. The fourth was once more either an e or an i. The final one was either an o or an a. Five letters. Ario? Was the first letter an M - M for Mario?

He looked for an m in the letter. There it was in Miguel in the postscript. He compared them. It was possible. But Mario was surely a boy's name.

Beginning at the front of the alphabet, he tried changeing the last letter to an A.

Maria. Maria? Could that be it? It was the most likely possibility.

Yes, that must be it. Maria.

Deciding he had done as much as he could with the letter he returned to the other papers, this time concentrating on the photographs. The old faded ones - were they of his family? Were the two men pictured with the Rabbit Man his brothers, one of them the girl's late father? Was the other one of Pepe with his brother, the one who lived near Casares? Sheedy put it aside to take with him when he went to search.

Finally he moved to the top of the pile the colour picture of the smiling dark-haired girl in Andalucian costume, pictured with a *feria* in the background. The more he looked at the picture the more the background looked familiar. He realised that it was a corner of the huge fairground at Seville.

Behind him he heard a car pull up in the drive. Leaving the papers he walked through to give Kate a hug as she came in. "Hi, lover," she said, "had a good day?"

"So so."

"I'm dying for a drink. Shall I open a bottle of wine?"

"Sure. I put some dry white in the chiller. Bring it out on the balcony."

Sheedy returned to his chair and, picking up the picture of the girl, looked at it thoughtfully.

Behind him Kate came out onto the balcony, put two glasses of wine on the table, and standing behind him threw her arms round his neck and kissed the top of his head. "What are you up to?"

She reached out and took the photograph from his hand. "Hey, where did you get this picture of Maria?"

Sheedy looked at her in surprise. "What did you say?"

"I said where did you get this picture of Maria?"

"How did you know her name was Maria?"

"Well for Christ's sake, Sheedy, its obvious. It is Maria."

"Maria who?"

"Maria - the Maria we've met. The Maria I've just spent the day with. Cruickshank's Maria. "

Sheedy slumped back in his chair. "Well, for Christ's sake. How did I miss it? I must be going blind. You're right. Its her. And it ties in with the name on the letter."

He stood up and paced up and down. "I wonder if Cruickshank knows. Heavens, Kate, what's going on?"

Kate looked bewildered. "Bill, what on earth are you talking about?"

"Sorry - read this." He tossed the letter to her and went in. "While you're reading it I'll get some food together. Fancy *gambas a la plancha* and salad?"

"Sure." She sat and began to read. By the time he called her to eat she had been sitting silently for some time on the balcony.

"Bill, are you thinking what I'm thinking?"

"What's that ?"

"That Cruickshank and company could have had the Rabbit Man killed so that Maria inherited the land... that Cruickshank is only interested in her for the land."

"I was trying not to think that."

"But if it isn't so, its a fantastic coincidence."

Sheedy relied that coincidences did happen. "I've been increasingly coming round to your point of view. I find it bloody difficult to believe Cruickshank is the instigator of murder. I've been giving him the benefit of the doubt and assuming that he's probably been dragged down by having to participate in a cover-up.

"Look, Kate," he continued, "I don't know what to think any more. But we're getting closer. Let's consider the options.

"If neither Cruickshank or Maria know the old man was her uncle, then when Maria does discover she owns the land she will naturally be happy to let Cruickshank have it. Happy end to story. Apart from two dead."

"Maybe three," interrupted Kate, thinking of the missing Felipe.

"Ok, maybe three," Sheedy acknowledged. "Inspector Rivas tells me Felipe hasn't returned home. He's just vanished. Not that we need assume he's dead; boys like Felipe can spend their lives moving from place to place seeking... well, maybe only they know what they're seeking." He continued with his theorising.

"Option two: Cruickshank knows about the land and Maria doesn't. If Maria finds out that Cruickshank knew about the Rabbit Man and kept it from her, that he stands to profit from their marriage, bang will go her belief in him as a man of honour. She'll break the engagement off. Then what? She probabably won't want them to have the land, so they have two choices... they either get by without it, or they eliminate her as well."

Kate looked shocked. "Surely not. They couldn't go on like that... killing anyone who gets in their way. God knows they're on a tightrope now."

"True. Except if Cruickshank doesn't know about the connection but Canning does, then we have real problems.

Canning and whoever is behind him clearly have a ball game of their own going, and the stakes seem high enough for them to do whatever they think is necessary."

"So what do we do?" asked Kate.

"We have to get to Maria and tell her the position. If she's involved we'll soon know. If she isn't we can put her on her guard."

"Bill," Kate said decisively, remembering their conversation on the beach, the idealism in Maria's eyes. "Its inconceivable that she's involved. She's in love with Cruickshank; in fact I think she idolises him. She keeps talking about a man of honour. She hasn't got it in her to get into such a thing."

Sheedy nodded. "So is it all a coincidence or has Cruickshank deliberately set about wooing her to guarantee he gets the land?"

But Kate's mind had moved on. "Here's another question? How did he or Canning find out that the Rabbit Man was preserving the land for Maria if we only just did?"

"I don't know. Except that Canning has seen this picture too. And he must have seen the girl. So he could have been cleverer than I and made the connection and told Cruickshank. Maybe Canning made contact with the brother in Casares. Hell, we should have tried to find him before now."

Kate was restlessly pacing up and down the balcony. "Bill, there's another possibility. Maybe Canning didn't recognise her. You didn't. If he and his associates don't know and if Maria's involvement with Cruickshank is just a coincidence, then they will have no idea what an opportunity they have." She thought on. "We must be careful that whatever we do doesn't get her into any more danger than she's in already."

Sheedy thought for a moment. "She's staying with the architect Julio Aparico isn't she? Look, he lives in a villa between San Pedro and Estepona. Why don't you ring her and suggest she could come to Casares with us tomorrow. We could kill two birds with one stone. Talk to her over lunch and then see if we can find and talk to the brother."

Kate went to the phone book and found the architect's number. After a couple of false attempts to get through she did so. Maria was due back from dinner with Cruickshank. Julio thought she would love to go to Casares but would get her to ring back when she got home.

The two then spent some time examining the pictures, reducing them to the two containing a man who was most likely to be Maria's other uncle. By then Maria had telephoned to confirm arrangements for the next day.

Tired, Kate went to the bedroom, slipped off her tee shirt and jeans and her underwear and, naked, walked back into the lounge and past him on her way to the bathroom. "I'm going to take a shower."

Sheedy watched her thoughtfully. He was still surprised at how quickly he could be aroused by seeing her undressed. He heard the water running in the shower. He couldn't rid himself of the memory of what he had just fleetingly seen, the straight back and athletic legs, brown from the sun, the firm, round bottom, milky white. Getting up, he walked towards the bathroom, shedding clothes as he went, and pulling back the shower curtain, he stepped in, taking her in his arms.

"Sheedy..."she chuckled deep in her throat. "What are you doing here?"

"In Spain," he said, taking the soap and beginning to lather her breasts, "we save water where we can."

"Saving time more like it." The chuckle came from deep in her throat..."Hmmmm..."

Troubled as he had been all day by the death of the policeman and the possibility of Canning's involvement, Cruickshank had, as always in Maria's company, been able to relax and forget. Now, as he walked her to the car, the front gates to the villa opened and Canning's Porsche rolled in and up to the front steps. The American got out looking, Cruickshank noted with irritation, as cool and immaculate as ever.

The Englishman did not disdain to introduce his young fiancee but also noticed, with even greater irritation, that Canning was taking a close look at her. "Perhaps you would wait in the house, Jason," he said coldly.

The American began to walk to the front door, then stopped and turned, and took another long look at Maria. Cruickshank was just about to rebuke him when, with a final glance at both of them, he turned on his heel and walked into the villa.

"I'm sorry about that, Maria," he said. "The man has no manners." He leaned into the car and kissed her on the cheek. "I look forward to seeing you tomorrow."

Inside the house he found Canning looking uncharacteristically agitated. "Sir Brian, before the meeting, I wonder whether we could have a private word."

"If you insist."

He took the American into a small sitting room off the main lounge and snapped "Well, what is it?"

"Forgive me for asking, Sir Brian, but the young lady..."

Cruickshank flushed, furious at this intolerable intrusion into his private affairs, and virtually shouted "What about the young lady. What business is it..."

Canning doggedly interrupted: "Sir Brian, I believe I have seen her before. Or at least a picture of her."

"Well man, that's not unlikely. She comes from a well-known family. Her picture will have appeared often in magazines."

Canning deliberately kept his voice low in contrast with Cruickshank's, trying to calm the Englishman down. "I told you that when I was in the old man's hut, the man they called *El Conejero*, there were some old papers and some old photographs. One was of a young girl. Sir Brian, I would swear it was the same... the same lady. Only much younger of course."

Cruickshank looked at him uncomprehendingly. "The same? Don't be ridiculous, man. How could it be?"

"Forgive me for asking Sir Brian, but what do you know of her background?"

Cruickshank rose. "Damn you, man. This is too much. How dare you pry into my affairs in this way. *Señorita* Garcia comes from a respectable family in Seville. The suggestion of a connection with this... this peasant... is ludicrous."

He stood over the younger man. "Canning you despoil everything you get near. I tell you now if you go anywhere near Miss Garcia or even mention her to me or anyone else I will show you there are others who can act as violently as you. Now get out."

Canning shrugged. "Very well. But I have said nothing to her discredit. I just wondered whether she could be related to the old man. And think about the possibilities if she was, Sir Brian. It would mean..."

"Get out you idiot." Cruickshank was almost incandescent with rage. It was bad enough that Canning was endangering his project but he was damned if he was going to allow him to intrude into the one untarnished part of his life - the part that he shared with Maria.

Canning shrugged again. "Very well, Sir Brian."

He walked from the house, climbed into his Porsche, and drove quickly to the nearest telephone booth. From there he rang a number in Tangier, and afterwards a number in Fuengirola.

Cruickshank, in his rage only half aware that he was allowing the project to take second place to his personal feelings, gave instructions to cancel the meeting he and Canning had been due to have with Julio Aparitico and others, went upstairs, stripped and showered, and then in a dressing gown lay on his bed listening to the sounds of the night. All the troubles of the day returned to plague his thoughts, but now compounded by what Canning had said. He tried to push the conversation out of his mind but he couldn't. On the contrary the more he considered Canning's words the more worried he got.

He struggled to recall what Maria had told him that night over dinner at La Cote.

She had been raised by a gypsy family because her uncle or uncles hadn't been able to take care of her.

And she had been abandoned in Seville when she was 12. The girl Canning claimed to have seen in a picture at the peasant's house had been, he said, 11 or 12.

What if it were the same girl? Could it be possible? Was the old man her uncle?

It would be an incredible coincidence but then Cruickshank was beginning to wonder what in this whole business could surprise him any longer.

One thing he knew; Maria had no idea of the connection between the peasant, the land, her and the project. If she even knew the name of her uncle, she didn't know he was the one who had been killed. And she didn't know there had been innuendo that his death had not been an accident.

Not yet.

But she would soon. The way the reporter Sheedy was pursuing it, the problem would not go away. Someone was bound to talk to her about it.

What would she think of him when it was alleged that her uncle had been deliberately killed.... not by him, but in his name?

He sat up. He must get to her first. Must tell her the whole story. Yes, that was it. He would tell her the truth, and even ask her what he should do. Perhaps with her support he could still go to the police and reveal all.

After all, with her by his side, what did it matter if he had to answer criticism for not revealing Canning's behaviour earlier? What would it matter if the project itself had to be abandoned. He could live without it. What he couldn't do was live without Maria.

He thought of going to her immediately. But, no, he had already her arranged for them to have dinner the following evening. Nothing would happen in the meantime. He would tell her then.

Miller was taken unawares by Canning's abrupt departure. He had assumed the American would be involved with Cruickshank and other project executives for two or three hours and had been relaxing in his room, smoking a small cigar and persuading himself that the gin he was drinking was definitely the last he would have that night. When the American left the villa driveway you could almost hear his irritation in the roar of the car's engine. Miller had to race downstairs, grabbing his jacket as he went, and only avoided losing the Porsche because of the time it took Canning to slip into the heavy traffic on the main road. Even so, Miller had to make an almost suicidal entry into the stream of fast-moving vehicles in order to keep the Porsche in view.

He knew that following someone in a car and remaining unobserved appeared ridiculously easy in films but, unless the driver of the car in front was navigating with a white stick, it was damn-near impossible in practice. Even more so when the driver was someone as streetwise as Canning. It had proved a nightmare from the start of this assignment. Despite employing every bit of his experience and skill, Miller had an uncomfortable feeling that Canning always knew he was there and that he either didn't care or was confident that if he wanted to slip the net he could do so with ease, not least because in a race the American's Porsche had a considerable advantage over Miller's characteristically modest choice of a medium-sized Seat.

This time they didn't go far - just to the Andalucia Plaza hotel. Miller, following the other at a discreet distance, saw him disappear into the casino on the ground floor. He waited for five minutes to allow

Canning to get to a roulette table and then attempted to enter himself, only to be stopped by a burly man in evening dress demanding to see his passport. Miller who, not surprisingly, didn't have it with him, was told in that case he couldn't enter. In an unenthusiastic attempt to bribe the man he waved a 5,000 pesetas note at him but that elicited such a look of contempt that he hastily retreated, embarrassed and annoyed.

"Why didn't these things ever happen to James Bond?" he muttered to himself as he got into his car and drove quickly back to the villa, fortunately only a few minutes away. Snatching up his passport and available cash he returned to the casino.

Canning was still at the roulette table, one of a number in a huge cavernous room half-full of people, more of them spectators than players. Miller took an empty place at a blackjack table. It was ideal because while he could see Canning, the American had his back to Miller.

Absent-mindedly he let the dealer change the whole pile of notes he had dropped on the table. There must have been 50,000 pesetas worth. He was disconcerted by the pile of chips that appeared. Miller, interrupted while drinking his 'last gin of the evening', felt deprived and edgy. His headache returned. He looked at the pile of chips with distaste. He didn't like gambling. Still, he figured, there was no problem. He could change the chips back.

He put down a 500 pesetas chip and found himself with a Jack and a four facing the dealer's Queen. Fourteen. He took another card. Another Jack. He was over 21. The chip disappeared. He felt mildly irritated.

He replaced it with a 1,000 peseta chip and drew a King and Queen - 20. He rested, confident that the dealer with only a six would go over the top. In fact the dealer drew a 7 and then an eight and finished with 21. The chip disappeared but the headache now returned with a vengeance.

And so it went on.

Miller cut back his bets, but still lost, his concentration not helped by his need to keep an eye on Canning.

He totted up his chips; he had lost nearly 25,000 pesetas worth. He was just considering moving to a less expensive vantage point (he had just observed a bar at the other end of the room) when he saw Canning move away from the roulette table and out of his line of sight. He cautiously turned to his left and saw the American heading for the door. He turned back to pick up his money and to his horror saw that in his haste he had accidentally elbowed the whole pile of chips onto the square. The first card was already in front of him... a six, and there was 25,000 pesetas at stake.

Miller, desperate to chase Canning but also concerned about his money, groaned inwardly but tried to look calm as the dealer produced an ace for himself and a 7 for the Englishman. With only 13 and the dealer with a good chance of getting a blackjack, Miller had no choice but to draw. It was 10. "Over," said the dealer and the 25,000 pesetas disappeared.

Miller, humiliated by the amused gaze of the other players and in a hurry to find Canning, fled the table and the casino.

Canning was turning from the car park up the calle that led to his apartment. Miller waited a moment and then drove up the same way. By the time he got there Canning's car was parked outside the building.

Miller waited a couple of hours, hungry now, thirsty, head aching and cursing his misfortune at the blackjack table. Finally, half an hour after the lights went out in the American's window, he decided it was safe to call it a night.

As he drove back to the villa he reflected that the trip to the Casino, the race back to get the passport, the loss of 50,000 pesetas, and the wait outside Canning's apartment had all proved unnecessary.

His headache was now horrendous.

Miller was beginning to hate Canning.

After making love with Kate and seeing her fall asleep Sheedy had driven down to Puerto Banus to make a few of his own enquiries about Felipe. It was one in the morning by the time he drove the car up the San Pedro-Ronda road towards the villa. His mood of near euphoria after the discoveries of the day and his love-making with Kate had turned to unease. No matter how he rationalised his behaviour, he felt guilty about Felipe. He simply hadn't considered the danger the boy was in.

He turned up the approach road to the villa and swung the car into the small parking lot. As he walked past the swimming pool he began to sense that something was wrong. There were more lights on in the villa than usual and he could almost feel the tension in the air. He walked quickly but quietly up the steps and then just as he was reaching the door heard a woman's voice, Kate's voice, cry out "No."

He took the last two or three steps in one leap and flung the door open, taking in the scene at a glance. Kate was spread-eagled, naked, across the back of the sofa, face down. Around her, grinning with malicious pleasure, stood three men, one tall, Arabic-looking, the other two shorter, Spanish. The Arab was standing behind her and Sheedy was in no doubt what he was planning to do. The usually mild even-tempered American became in an instant a man possessed. Not thinking or caring that he was outnumbered and roaring like a bull he moved like lightning across the room, kicking the Arab so hard in the backside that he fell forward over Kate. Sheedy pulled him off, turned him round, and hit him so hard in the face that blood spurted onto the floor. The Arab reeled back, falling to the ground. One of the other Spaniards moved towards him but Sheedy couldn't have been stopped by an army. He grabbed the smaller man by both arms and hurled him against the wall. The third took once look at Sheedy's face and raced out of the open door. By then the Arab was staggering back to his feet. Sheedy picked up a chair and raised it to strike him. As he did so the other Spaniard hit him with an empty wine bottle from the table. He was swung off balance and fell dazed. By the time he was back up the other two were gone and Kate was kneeling over him, sobbing and laughing hysterically and thanking him all at the same time.

He pulled her up and held her tight, his face in her hair, his hands gently rubbing her back, his voice softly whispering in her ear until she quietened and then he picked her up and carried her to the shower, tearing off his own clothes, so they could stand under the hot water together, being soothed, cleansed of the experience.

When they lay together in each other's arms on the bed, she said they had claimed that Miguel told them Sheedy had the Rabbit Man's papers. They were trying to force her to give them up. "I was just going to do it, Bill, give them the papers. Then you got back."

"You should have. Of course you should have." Sheedy could hardly contain his anger. "Well, that settles it. I'm going to end this business once and for all. I'm going to get it out in the open with Cruickshank."

He rose from the bed and went to the phone. He rang the Englishman's number but was told he was not to be disturbed. Sheedy would have to call in the morning. He put down the phone frustrated. Then he telephoned Inspector Rivas. He was away too. He left a message for him to ring.

Among the hesitant
branches
went a maiden
who was life.

Among the hesitant
branches.

With a tiny mirror
she reflected the day,
which was the sparkle
of her clear brow.

Among the hesitant
branches.

Upon the dark of night
she walked about lost,
weeping dewdrops
of this captive time.

Among the hesitant
branches.

I'm sorry, Kate, Sheedy thought as he lay awake. I'm sorry. I'll never let anyone give you cause to weep again.

They slept late the following morning and Sheedy decided to leave his calls to Cruickshank and Inspector Rivas until they had been to Casares. In any case, there was a chance they would know more by then. They picked up Maria who noticed immediately that Kate was looking pale and had a bruise on her forehead. This they had anticipated; they told her that Kate had slipped in the shower.

To get to Casares they drove about six kilometres south of Estepona on the N340 and then turned inland for a further 13 kilometres. It was not the first time that it seemed to Kate that within a few minutes of leaving the *costa* they entered a magic door from one world to another. They seemed almost immediately to be in an earlier century, the hills of scrubs and rock dotted with peaceful white-washed *cortijo*. They passed a herd of sheep and goats grazing on the roadside, the shepherd, a short man with flat cap and a wooden crook as tall as himself, bright, alert eyes gazing out of a sun-darkened, wizened face. They traversed a valley shaped like a saucer, with a green, tree-covered base and rocky hills around the edges, and then the road began to climb and wind up into the hills and the countryside to become greyer and rockier. Many of the trees had been stripped of their bark as high as a man could reach. About 10 kilometres from the coast they turned a corner the road wound round the edge of a magnificent valley and then climbed steeply away and up another hill. A short drive, a sharp turn to the right, and there was the extraordinary spectacle of Casares, a dramatic-looking white town perched on top of another hill, more of a huge rock than a hill, and on top of it the ruins of an old church.

They lunched in El Meson Los Claveles near the town square, its walls packed with wooden farm implements and paintings of the sierras, its little tables covered with the familiar red and white cloth. Sheedy, who was known to take this 45 minute detour frequently to sample the restaurante's specialities, notably its whole rabbit cooked in garlic, urged Maria and Kate to join him in having the rabbit with crisp chips and a juicy salad of fresh tomatoes and lettuce.

He waited until the food was ordered and they had a glass of wine before, at his most low-key and gentle, saying "Maria, by a coincidence we have come across some information that concerns you."

The girl's eyes widened. "Coincidence, *Señor* Bill?"

"Yes. I have... had... a friend who lived in the hills near Ronda, in fact two friends, one an officer in the *Guardia Civil*. Recently they both were killed in what appeared to be accidents and in one of the old men's effects we found a photograph." He handed it to Maria. "It is you, isn't it?"

"*Si.*" She was astonished. "*Si.* I remember when this was taken, at the fair in Seville, just before I was left at the orphanage. But why did your friend have it?"

"Maria, what do you remember of the uncle in whose charge you were briefly after your parents died?"

"Not a lot. I was only tiny and so much has happened since."

"Have you never wanted to find him?"

"No, *señor.* I suppose, deep down, I always felt rejected by him, that he didn't want me, that he just passed me on to a gypsy family to rid himself of me. They were good to me but I've often wondered whether he cared one way or the other. Anyway, I've come to see the Garcias as my family. But why do you ask?"

Sheedy told her the old man had cared more than she knew. He gave her the letter and she silently read it, by the end with tears in her eyes.

"But how did you know it was addressed to me?" she asked. By way of reply Sheedy pointed to the photograph.

For a while they sat quietly. The food arrived and they began to eat, though none now with the enthusiasm the rabbit could usually be expected to engender.

Then she said. "You say he is dead, *señor?*"

"Yes. This is where it gets difficult, Maria. You see it appears the land you now own is the piece of land Sir Brian has been trying to buy. The peasant he had been negotiating with was your uncle."

Maria looked at him wide-eyed. "That is a coincidence as you say."

"Yes." Sheedy looked at her sympathetically. "The question Maria is how far does the coincidence go?"

"I don't understand."

"Let me put it to you bluntly. Sir Brian needs that land desperately. Your uncle owned it and wouldn't sell. Then your uncle had an accident. And Sir Brian begun to court you, the new owner. It could, of course, be a coincidence, but..."

Maria reacted with anger. "*Señor* Sheedy, Sir Brian is a man of honour. What you are implying is unthinkable. He loves me. And would do so irrespective of all this."

"You think he has no idea you were related to the old man? That he doesn't know you own the land?"

"I am certain of it. You say my uncle probably died accidentally. That is what Brian thinks. He told me of it. That it was an accident. He said it made life more difficult for him. It is as you say a coincidence."

She looked at him, coldly now. "I am angry you should suggest otherwise."

Kate interrupted. "But there is also Miguel, Maria."

"Miguel?"

"Miguel, the policeman. He was your uncle's oldest friend, obviously the man who saved his life during the civil war. He was investigating your uncle's death and he had an accident too. That is another coincidence. Bill and I are journalists; we have learnt to distrust one coincidence, but two...?"

Maria rose and stamped her foot, her brown eyes flashing with anger. "No. No. I will not believe this. Brian is not a criminal... a... a murderer. This is not possible. You are horrible to suggest it."

She began to leave the restaurant. Sheedy told Kate to go after her and called to the restaurant owner. "Do you know the man in this photograph?"

"*Si, señor*. He is Diego Rodriguez. He has a smallholding and also hunts. He is the source of many of my *conejo*. Look, I can show you where he is." He took Sheedy by the arm and led him round the back of the restaurant and up some steps and then a winding path to the top of the hill. From near the old church and the small, flower-decked cemetery on the hilltop he pointed out the man's small *cortijo*. It was at the end of a huge valley, towards the coast, perched on one of a number of smaller hills in the valley, almost directly under one of a row of big electricity pylons. Pepe Jose pointed out it could be reached by driving from Casares towards the Gaucin-Ronda road, and then turning south towards the coast.

Sheedy found Kate consoling Maria. They were both sitting on a low white wall by the car, looking over the valley.

"Maria," said Sheedy, "Please understand, I also want to believe what you believe. But we have to find out. You are also in danger. And maybe your uncle Diego. In an case, the police are also going to investigate and if we can find an answer that does not involve Sir Brian that will help him too."

The Spanish woman looked at him with hostility but didn't reply.

Sheedy told her they were going to call on her uncle on the way back. He showed her the faded photograph of the two men, the Rabbit Man and the other who Pepe Jose had identified as Diego Rodriguez. "At least come and see what he has to say."

It took less than 10 minutes to drive there. From the main road they drove between the electricity pylons up a rough lane. At the end was a small white *cortijo* with a brown-red tiled roof, next to it to a small corral made of wood, and there were two other small huts. Scattered about, scratching in the dirt, were a number of goats and chickens and a small black pig.

They parked the car 50 yards away and walked quietly over, not wishing to disturb the livestock. Sheedy called out "Hola."

There was no answer. Maria began to step forward but Sheedy, an uncomfortable feeling in the pit of his stomach, took her arm. "Wait," he said. "Wait here."

He walked up to the curtain of beads that acted as a door, its threads moving slightly in the breeze. "Is there anyone there?" he called out in Spanish. There was no answer. Gently he pulled the curtains aside.

At first the *cortijo* looked much like that of the Rabbit Man, bare, stone floor, a few pieces of furniture. There was even the same smell o f rabbit skins. But there was another smell too and Sheedy, veteran of the holocaust that was Vietnam, recognised it with a sinking heart. You never forgot the smell of death.

The old man's body was lying half-covered by a pile of old skins in the corner of the *cortijo*. It was naked from the waist up and covered in cigarette burns. Whether he had provided the information his assailants wanted Sheedy could not tell, but even if he had, his reward had been the same as if he had refused. There was a single bullet hole in his forehead.

Sheedy began to back away, then heard a gasp of horror behind him. Standing in the doorway was Maria, her eyes wide, her face losing its colour.

The American moved quickly, took her by the shoulders, wheeled her round, and pushed her outside. She half ran, half stumbled to a nearby tree where she stood shaking, then being sick, and then weeping loudly.

Kate tried to put an arm round her but it was shrugged away. Sheedy spoke to her sympathetically but urgently. "Maria, I want you to go home and pack and drive straight back to the Garcias in Seville."

The young woman didn't or couldn't speak.

"This was not an accident Maria. And three deaths in a row are no longer coincidence. They're all connected and they're all to do with the project and the land. This business has taken a turn for the worse."

"What do you mean?" Kate asked.

"So far they have made some attempt to make the deaths look like an accident. Now they don't seem to care. That's the difference."

"But Brian...?" Maria cried out, still weeping.

Sheedy held her arms and looked her in the eyes. "Maria, I find it hard to believe Sir Brian would sanction murder. But you must believe that at the very least he's covering up."

"What are you going to do?"

"About your uncle? I'll have to get the police. But don't forget there is no evidence that the project or Cruickshank or his American friends are connected with any of these deaths. That's where they've been so clever. So no-one is going to be arrested or taken into custody... unless someone comes up with more than we've got at the moment. That's why you're not safe. Until the killing stops you've got to get away from all this."

Maria sadly nodded and Kate led her gently back to the car. Sheedy went back to the *cortijo* to see if he could find any papers but if they had been there before, they were not now. He looked around for any evidence as to who had been there, but as before there was nothing.

His mind whirling with all the implications, he got in the car and took Maria back to Julio's place and then, asking Kate to take a taxi back to the villa, went to his office, rang Inspector Rivas and told him about Diego Rodriguez. Lastly he rang Hunter in Gibraltar and told him to cancel all the items planned for the next programme.

"We don't have to enter into innuendo. All we need do is spell out the facts, in detail, point by point. We can offer Anglo-Spanish Investors an advance look at the contents and a full opportunity to reply. I'm convinced if we simply tell the story the whole of Spain will be demanding a full inquiry," he said. "Even if we can't pin the murders on them we'll make it almost impossible for the municipalities to continue to give them planning permission to develop."

After his detour on the Gaucin road, Canning had returned to the N340 and driven down to Gibraltar to catch a plane for Tangier. On arrival he took a taxi to the El Minzah hotel and asked for Mr Theodore Jordan.

The tall, bald American came down from his room immediately and, limping more noticeably than Canning remembered him doing before, led the younger man onto the terrace for lunch.

Canning quickly updated him... on the girl in the photograph and Cruickshank's involvement with her, and on the hunt for the old man's letter and the ownership papers. He showed them to Jordan. "We'll have to get our Spanish lawyer to look at the documents. I had hoped they would be incomplete but in so much as I can understand them it looks as if she is already the legal owner of the land. We're back with the same problem we had with the old man. Only this time I'm positive there's no other member of the family to worry about. She's the only obstacle left."

"Do you think Cruickshank can persuade her to sell him the land?"

"I doubt it." Canning looked uncomfortable. "Look, Mr Jordan, its just been bad luck, but in retrospect killing the old man was a mistake. I'm afraid the reporter Sheedy will convince the girl that Cruickshank had her uncle killed. To sell him the land then would be to vindicate the murder. From what I'm told, I don't think she'll do that. She has been raised by a highly conservative, respectable family and appears to be instilled with a belief, almost an obsession with what she calls honour. This is what attracts her to Cruickshank. Once she becomes disillusioned with him we won't stand a chance."

Jordan looked at him, expressionless except for the chill in the eyes, one that sent a corresponding chill down Canning's back. "Look," the younger man said, uncharacteristically rattled, "there was just no way I could have known that the old man was friends with a reporter on the *costa*, no way I could have known about the girl. We've been the victims of bad luck and coincidence."

Jordan still looked at him coldly. Then: "Will she sell it to us... not directly, of course, but to one of our American companies, if we choose one that has not been involved so far? She could even be persuaded that it is a way of avenging her uncle by punishing Cruickshank."

"My guess is that she'll now be careful who she sells it to, and if Sheedy keeps in touch with her he'll check on any potential buyer. Its possible your plan would work but I don't give much for our chances."

Jordan turned his thoughts to Sheedy. "The reporter is a menace. Still, Cruickshank rang me, desperately anxious that we should not attempt to lean on Sheedy in any way. He says that everybody will come down on the case like a ton of bricks if Sheedy is harmed... and I'm inclined to think he's right."

Canning reluctantly concurred.

Jordan asked: "Is it still your view we must have this piece of land?"

"If we don't get it, the access to the site will be via Estepona. If we want to bring the drugs in from North Africa in considerable quantities it will be extremely dangerous to transport it through the town. Its fairly efficiently policed. But if we get this piece of land and with it a private access road to the valley, we would have full control over the point of entry. And we would have our own security guards. Thus, provided we present the right face to the authorities, they won't bother to police the area at all, figuring that we've got it covered. It will be just like Sotogrande; It too has its own security guards at its own entrance and I doubt if the *Guardia Civil* or the other police ever go near it.

"It will also be a more convenient and discreet entry-point for people going to the casino's or looking for the girls. A lot of our customers will come on impulse; we don't want to put too much time between the impulse and the action, or make it easier for people to see who comes and goes and when. If they have to enter via Estepona they will have to drive a further 10 kilometres south and then through the town; its bound to have a negative effect on business.

"Also a change of plan will involve considerable redesign and delay and additional cost. "Also, there's a considerable aesthetic consideration; the land is not in a neat square, its a valley that winds into the heart of the project.

"All and all," he concluded, "while we can get by without the land it will create all sorts of problems we don't need."

"So what do you propose?"

Canning suggested there were three options... at least in theory.

"One, we change the plan and face the problems I've just outlined.

"Two, we make an offer to the girl she can't refuse.

"Three, we remove the girl."

Jordan looked at him expressionlessly. "And?"

"The first is possible but, as I've said, expensive and brings real disadvantages. The second would in my view be impossible. The third is possible, need not be too risky, but, while it would not be traceable to the project, would be bound to cause an outcry and investigation and would not make getting the land easy."

"Would it make it impossible?"

"No. Difficult. We'll need all the respectability Cruickshank's involvement brings and maybe a bit of expensive bribery as well. But if Cruickshank believes we are responsible for any harm to the girl we lose his input."

Jordan frowned. "Cruickshank is a problem. Of course we have him in some trouble. I have a slightly doctored version of the tape he made with you on the yacht. Its proof that he was involved in a cover-up of the old man's murder... in fact it makes it appear he was implicated. Also I have a little film from London that he would not be happy to have widely circulated. Just the same, if the man's besotted with the girl then he's not going to forgive any harm coming to her."

For a moment the two men didn't speak, each eating and engrossed in their thoughts. Then it was Jordan who broke the silence.

"Clearly we can't just stage an accident. There's been one too many. He wouldn't believe it. I think we'll have to arrange a freak killing. I have given this some thought. She'll have to be one of a number of victims of a maniac, a massacre - on an aircraft, or in a crowd." He thought for a moment. "I'm told that there's a lot of fervour, sometimes almost uncontrollable passion, around the Semana Santa processions in Seville and that the Garcia family would normally be in a prominent position there... an easy target. Imagine if she were one of a number killed by a madman there... why would Cruickshank link it with him or his business

He then spelled out in chilling detail how it could be done. Almost anyone else would have been appalled but Canning listened with admiration.

When he had finished, Jordan called for coffee, then added "We'll have to bring someone in. You must be seen to be well out of it and I don't want to trust it to someone local who we don't know."

Canning nodded. "Good thinking."

The flippancy of the remark irritated Jordan. He looked at the younger man even more coldly. Really, Canning was becoming a bit of a liability in Spain. After the girl was dealt with the younger man would have to be removed.

In the meantime, however, business was business, and Jordan spelt out what he would arrange and what Canning should do.

Then he asked Canning for details of the project. The younger man put two plans in front of his boss. One was the plan as approved by Cruickshank and currently being proceeded with. The other was a variation to be enforced upon the Englishman after the land was fully-owned and various political and other problems taken care of.

On these matters Jordan was more impressed with the younger man. There was no doubt Canning had it well set up.

A pity Canning was also a psychopath.

Jordan couldn't care less that the younger man was a killer, but a compulsive one, an undisciplined one, was a walking time bomb over any operation.

Yes, after this was sorted out, he would have to go.

It was 4 o'clock by the time she got home. Maria was relieved to find the villa empty apart from a maid. She quickly wrote two short notes, one to Julio and Isabella, and one to Cruickshank. Then she packed her two cases in a hurry and, leaving the notes on the table inside the front door, she tossed the cases into the back of her small sports car and, backing with a roar out of the garage, set off for the main road, choosing to drive west to near Gibraltar and then take the Jerez-Seville road rather than take the cross country route via Ronda.

As she drove tears rolled down her cheeks. She couldn't bring herself to believe that Brian had caused her uncle to be killed, and also his friend Miguel... that he had been wooing her for the land.

But she also couldn't believe he didn't at least know about the murders. He had to be covering them up. Bill Sheedy was right about that.

Whatever the truth was, Brian was involved. He had acted dishonourably. Yet she still believed it wasn't in his nature. Was he being blackmailed for some reason? What kind of pressure was he under? If he was in some trouble, why hadn't he been straight with her? Why hadn't he come and told her? She would have been proud to support him.

Had she put too much value on his honour? She didn't think so. It was what she had respected, and without trust and respect, what else could there be with him?

She drove past the town of San Roque on the hillside on her right and past the turn-off to La Linea and Gibraltar and only when reaching the outskirts of Algeciras did she turn west, off the N430, and begin to climb the foothills to the ruta del toro - the route of the bulls.

This time Miller dreamt he was in a war. And when he woke that's what it felt like. Little soldiers in big boots were running round in his head tossing hand-grenades at each other. They were exploding in his temple. His eyes had become the barrels of guns; every few seconds one would be fired, causing a blinding flash. His whole head felt as if it was aflame.

As he fell off the bed and hit the floor he knocked the empty gin bottle and the alarm clock off the dresser. With a tremendous effort he focused on it. Four o'clock.

Four o'clock! Please God, not four o'clock in the afternoon. He crawled to the window and blinked out. The sun hit him between the eyes. The pain was unbearable. He felt as if he had been struck in the head by a cruise missile.

Canning! He had intended to be back in position by 6.30 in order to tail the American. There was no way he would still be at his apartment at four o'clock.

He crawled to the shower and soaked his head until a few of the flames were dowsed. Still feeling dreadful he climbed into his car and drove to Nueva Andalucia where he looked at the empty parking spot in dismay. He walked across the road to a telephone booth and rang the yacht and then the villa to check whether Canning was there. He was not.

Miller recalled that the last time he had let Canning out of his sight had been the night the old policeman had been killed. Bloody hell, he thought, what's he up to now?

Deeply disturbed, he settled down to wait, every now and then walking to the phone booth to check back with the yacht and villa. It was hot and the war was erupting in his head again. He desperately wanted a coffee, even more desperately a gin. But he dare not move. He wanted to keep this assignment, wanted to keep Cruickshank's confidence, and to do that he had to keep tabs on Canning.

He fell asleep. When he woke Canning's car was back in its place. He looked at his watch. It was five o'clock. He felt so bad he even considered going and asking Canning for a coffee and an aspirin. There was little doubt that the American had see him sleeping at his wheel so he would not be breaking his cover. But he couldn't do that; apart from the humiliation involved, for some reason he couldn't in his present state understand, it suited them both not to acknowledge the obvious.

So awash was he in misery and self-pity he almost missed Canning leaving the building and walking quickly to his car, a small case in each hand. Within a few minutes he found himself pursuing the American on the Ronda road. Miller wished he had a faster car. He also wished he had some idea how far they were going. He also wished that he was better prepared. Canning's cases had not suggested a short trip. He wished he could get the chance to ring Cruickshank. He wished for food, for coffee. Above all he wished he could have a gin. Just one gin. A large, cold, neat gin.

For over an hour they climbed until they reached the plateau and Miller saw Canning's car heading towards the lights of Ronda. The American did not stop in the town, however, but drove quickly up the main street to near the gates of the Hotel Reina Victoria and turned right and then left onto the Seville road. Miller guessed that this was the destination. He looked at the petrol guage. It was half empty. God, he thought, what's wrong with me? Elementary training had taught him to keep the tank filled. To have funds with him (because of his losses at the casino he was running low), and to be ready for a long journey at short notice.

He reached down and felt the pistol in his inside jacket pocket. At least he had that.

Maria had been on the road for 70 minutes when she reached the extraordinary rock, shaped like *matador*'s hat. This she knew was known as the *Montera del Torero*, the hill of the *matador*, the beginning of the *ruta del toro*, so named because it runs across some of Andalucia's best bull country, the place where the fighting bulls destined to appear in bullrings are bred.

She drove on, passing forests of cork trees, bark stripped off the trunks, leaving them bare, a tawny brown colour. Then she was back amidst rolling hill country, looking at the fighting bulls, big and black with wide horns, and puzzling at how these fierce animals could live so harmoniously with the little white storks who seemed always to accompany them, pecking at the ground at their feet.

She passed the proud and private bull town of Medina Sidonia, then the El Maccohoro ranch, and whole hills of yellow sunflowers, and after crossing the Rio Guadalete she diverted into the town of Jerez de la Frontera (so named because it was one of the frontlines of the battle between Christians and Moors), passing the beautiful old railway station, its name in ceramic tiles, and driving down pleasing cobbled streets and shaded lanes past the old and well-preserved buildings, rows of orange trees, then via the Calle Seville, to a wide avenue passing the Royal Sherry Park Hotel and the Andalucian School of Equestrianism. She approached the huge fairground, where the horse fair takes place, and recalled her own appearances there riding beside Juan Garcia, both of them looking aristocratic and handsome on their big black horses.

Past the fairground she turned east onto the main highway to Seville, paying the 600 pesetas toll to drive on the motorway past the fields of grapes that would eventually become the world famous sherries made in Jerez.

Less than an hour later she was turning off the main road and driving up to the hacienda that was home.

Cruickshank looked at his watch. He had sent the car for her in plenty of time. Where on earth were they? He walked out onto the balcony and looked at the beach. He remembered seeing her for the first time, remembered how striking she had been, and clenched his fists with frustration at the way the joy her friendship gave him was being marred by the problems over the project.

He thought again of what he would say to her, of how he would tell her the truth, ask for her understanding, make himself open to what she wanted him to do.

He heard the car in the drive and picking up his jacket walked impatiently down only to meet the new chauffeur on the steps coming into the house.

"Sir Brian, the *señorita*, she was not there."

"Not there? What do you mean. not there?"

"She has gone."

"Gone!" He went cold . What had happened. Surely Canning... no, it couldn't be possible.

"She left a letter, *señor.*"

Cruickshank was relieved. If she had left a letter then she had not been taken. There had to be a straightforward explanation. He snatched it from the chauffeur's hand and walking into the sitting room tore the envelope open and read the letter with mounting shock.

"Dear Brian,
I am sorry to inconvenience you this evening. I have returned to Seville. I have decided that it would be better if we do not see each other any more. Please do not pursue me. My decision is final. Thank you for your kindnesses. Maria."

It didn't make sense. Something had happened. Damn it... Canning. It had to be Canning. Everything that had gone wrong so far had been Canning's fault... why should this be different.

He snatched up the phone and rang the yacht. Canning wasn't there.

He rang Julio and asked him what he knew.

"I don't know Sir Brian. She left us a note too. To be honest, I assumed you and she had had a... misunderstanding... and that she had gone back for that reason."

Cruickshank asked for her address and phone number in Seville.

The architect sounded ill at ease. "Well, I don't know..."

"Damn it, Julio, do it. I can find it without much trouble. But you will cost me time. Do it!"

The architect disappeared for a moment and came back with the details.

Cruickshank rang off abruptly and then called the Seville number. A Spanish maid answered the phone. In near-fluent Spanish Cruickshank asked for Maria and was told she was not there but was expected shortly.

Then a man came on the line. "Sir Brian?... this is Juan Garcia. My daughter has called and told us she is coming home and that you would probably call. She has requested that you do not seek to speak to her for the moment and I would be grateful if you would respect her wishes. I hope that whatever the misunderstanding is can be sorted out but until she wishes to speak to you I must request you honour her wishes."

Cruickshank gripped the phone tightly in his hand. "Of course I respect your request... I must ask you, however, to assure Maria of my devotion to her and to tell her that whatever is upsetting her will be put right. Will you do that much for me."

"Of course, Sir Brian. If explanation is due to you I assure you that you will receive it."

Cruickshank poured himself a Scotch and went out onto the balcony.

"Maria," he thought. "I will do whatever I have to do. But please, please don't leave me."

For two more hours they drove until they reached Seville. Miller had made a half-hearted attempt to avoid being spotted as he drove behind the American but once more it had proved extremely difficult and he still had the uneasy feeling that his presence was noted and considered of no consequence. Why did Canning not care?

It was after midnight but the city streets were alive with people. Canning drove into the centre, passing the magnificient Plaza de España and making his way via the Glorieta de Don Diego and the Avenida del Cid to the Calle San Fernando. He then turned the Porsche into the grounds of the palatial Alfonso Xlll, a magnificient old hotel within sight of the Cathedral and the Giralda.

Christ, thought Miller, only the most expensive hotel in town. He would have to get Cruickshank to send up some money in the morning.

He followed Canning into the big car park and, stopping some distance away, watched in the rear view mirror as the American took his cases and went into the hotel. He allowed 10 minutes for him to get his room and then walked in and enquired whether there was a room available. Only one, a double at 50,000 pesetas. Miller groaned inwardly but smiled outwardly and accepted.

Unfortunately it wasn't as simple as that .The clerk looked suspiciously at his unshaven, gaunt face and the rumpled suit and enquired whether Miller had luggage. Told that he didn't, the clerk then insisted he be paid in advance. Miller had to struggle even harder to appear unperturbed. This wuld completely clean him out. Still what could he do?

As he paid with the crumpled notes from his pocket he said "By the way, I hope to meet a friend of mine here, a Mr Canning. Has he checked in?."

"*Si, señor*, just a few moments ago."

"Good. I'll look him up. What room is he in?"

"Just a moment... room 503, *señor*."

Miller was pleased to see his first floor room overlooked the car park. He could see Canning's car and reckoned he could get out to his own within two minutes in time to follow the other if necessary. He sat in the window and waited.

Canning left his room about 30 minutes later. As he walked past the reception desk towards the restaurant the clerk called out to him: "Your friend has arrived, Mr Canning?"

Canning paused. "Friend?"

"Yes, Mr Miller. He's in room 347."

"Ah... yes, of course, thank you."

Canning smiled to himself, paused to thing, then re-traced his steps, ordered food in his room, and settled down for the night.

Miller, he guessed, would have little choice but to stay awake watching for him. All night. And that Canning found amusing.

Miller was a frustrated and unhappy man. A prisoner in his expensive room, without money and unable to contact Cruickshank, he had sat in the window for three hours watching both the front entrance and Canning's Porsche without reward.

Morosely he picked up the phone to try once more to contact Cruickshank to tell him his fiancee, the love of his life, was in danger of being attacked by a psychopath and that he, Miller, had no idea where or when the move was likely to come.

But Cruickshank still wasn't reachable. He had been due after having dinner with Maria to take the last plane from Malaga to Madrid to see the headquarters of the project's bankers in the morning and wouldn't be back till at least mid-afternoon tomorrow. Usually there would be a hotel number but, because the meetings had been fixed at the last minute, Cruickshank had said he would organise accommodation himself when he arrived in Madrid. He had not been in touch since. He could, therefore, not be contacted till the morning. Miller left instructions that he was to be telephoned urgently at the hotel.

He would, he decided, ring Maria in the morning - if he had not heard from Cruickshank by 10 a.m.

He decided Canning was holed up for the night and turned on the television set and disinterestedly tried all the channels and then switched it off. He had a shower and lay down on the bed but his head was aching and he still felt restless. Then he noticed for the first time   a brown safe-like box in a corner of the room. A refrigerator. He tried to open it but it was locked. He checked the keys provided by the hotel. One of them fitted. He opened it and there he discovered shelf after shelf of bottles. Little bottles. Shiny bottles. Wickedly enticing bottles of alcohol.

Miller hesitated. He could recall no hour in his life when he wanted... no, needed... a gin as much as he wanted and needed it now. Yet he also knew that he had reached a moment of truth. The assignment of Cruickshank's he had accepted so lightly in London had turned out to be fully justified, possibly vital to the safety of not just his client, but the girl too. He hadn't blown it yet. He was on the scene, on Canning's trail. He had to stay on the alert, mobilise all of his skill and experience, call on every reserve of energy.

What he didn't need was gin.

Yet what he desperately did need was gin.

For several minutes he stood looking at the refrigerator. Then he was struck by a thought. All the bottles were different. There was only one bottle of gin. One tiny bottle. There was, therefore, no way that one could lead to another.

One gin. It would reduce the pain of the headache. It would help him to think more clearly.

He quickly removed the bottle, unscrewed the lid, and drained it neat.

CHAPTER TWELVE

This time he dreamt he was in a quarry and when he woke up he was. They were breaking rocks in his head, pounding at them with sledgehammers, just behind the eyes, and the pain was all but unbearable. The dust had accumulated in his mouth and throat so that he couldn't breath properly. And he was lying on a lot of rocks, small rocks that were sticking into him. He rolled over and slowly, painfully, lifted his head from the floor and stared around him. He could see the rocks now. Small, round shiny rocks. Like bottles.

Hang on. They were bottles. Small bottles. With a tremendous effort he picked one up and squinted at it. The label said gin. He picked up another. Whisky. A third. Brandy. He looked around him. Vodka. Dubonnet. Sherry. All bottles. All empty. Miller groaned. The bottles in the refrigerator. He must have drunk the lot.

He crawled to the bathroom and was violently sick. He grabbed some aspirins and stuffed them down his throat in an attempt to combat the splitting headache. He put his head under the cold water tap. And he vowed that if he survived this he would never touch a drink again.

Somehow he succeeded in making himself a cup of coffee in the room, and then tried to contact Cruickshank. The yacht was unresponsive (probably, he decided, on instructions from Canning) and Hobbs at the villa couldn't help either. So he telephoned the hacienda only to be told that the Garcia's were out for the day, visiting their horse ranch north of the city. He asked the man-servant who took his call to pass on a message to the ranch for Maria to ring him urgently.

He slowly, painfully dressed and pulled the curtains just in time to see Canning, one of his small cases in each hand, striding towards his car. Grabbing his own car keys, he raced unsteadily down the stairs and round the front of the hotel to the car park. Canning's Porsche was already disappearing onto the road. As his own car approached the exit to the car park he realised there was a pay booth and, blocking his way, a wooden barrier. Miller had only a few pesetas left and no time to negotiate with a Spanish attendant in a language he was nowhere near mastering. Deciding, therefore, that he had no other option, he accelerated towards the barrier, lowering his head just as he reached it, and reducing it to splinters.

Fortunately it had taken time for the American to negotiate his way into the heavy traffic in the Calle San Fernando and Miller was able to catch up, getting too close to the Porsche for comfort. Not that he cared too much about that. Miller still had the feeling that Canning knew he was there and didn't care. He even wondered whether Canning had slowed outside the hotel to let him catch up. But why would he do that? What was his game?

They turned almost immediately left and appeared to circle the hotel before driving past the back of the Universidad to the big roundabout at the Glorieta de Don Diego. From there the Porsche accelerated up a series of wide avenues following the signs to Cordoba.

Miller couldn't understand it. Cordoba? If Canning had wanted to go to Cordoba, why come to Seville? It made no sense.

They were almost on the outskirts of the city when he realised that there were another series of signs on the route. *Aeropuerto*. The airport. They were going to the airport.

And soon they were there, turning into the car park, Canning carelessly swinging into a vacant space, taking his cases from the car and locking up. Miller parked nearby and discreetly followed, still half convinced, feeling foolish, that Canning couldn't care less that he was there, was laughing at him while pretending not to notice.

From a telephone booth he watched the American go up to the Iberia Airline desk. He appeared to be buying a ticket with a credit card. The purchase made, Canning now went across to the bar and, buying a drink, settled down to light a cigarette, always looking straight ahead of him, making surveillance easy. Too easy, Miller thought, its as if he wants me to see him leaving.

He looked at the departure board. The only Iberia flight was one to New York in an hour's time. That at least made sense. Canning must be flying out for instructions.

He wandered over to the newspaper stand and purchased a copy of *El Pais*, both to pass the time and to make it easier for him to stay out of view just in case Canning was not aware he was there.

Canning, who had managed to get a fix on Miller in the mirror high above the bar, seized the few seconds he needed to look round the bar and catch the eye of a thin-faced, dark-haired man with piercing eyes sitting alone at the other end of the bar. There was the briefest exchange of glances. Contact made, the other man rose and walked away in the direction of the toilets.

Canning waited until Miller had returned with his newspaper and then stayed on for a further three or four minutes before, after casually standing up and stretching, he strolled slowly to the toilets himself.

Miller watched him go. It was pointless to follow. He knew where Canning was and in any case if he followed he would be seen - assuming, as always, that he hadn't been spotted already.

Had he followed Canning he would have seen the American slip into one of the booths, next to the only one that was already occupied. He would have heard the click of Canning's small case and seen a package, an object wrapped in black canvas material, slipped under the partition between the two booths. He would have heard the toilet flush, would have seen Canning emerge and look around, then leave with a satisfied smile. And some two minutes later he would have seen the other man emerge and go to the taxi rank and from there depart for the centre of Seville.

But Miller saw none of this because there was no way he could follow Canning into the toilets without a confrontation. Instead he took the chance to spend his last pesetas on a drink at the bar, gin being fully justified for medicinal purposes, and waited until the American came back to the bar, until his flight was called, until he actually climbed the steps to the plane, until his plane took off.

He then drove back into the city centre. Not far from the *Palacio de Justicia* his car ran out of petrol. As he had no money left, he was forced to abandon it and walk back to the hotel, his head aching badly once more, sweat pouring down his back, his legs so weak he could hardly stand up. He found a back pedestrian entrance to the hotel and slipped in, thus avoiding the mini-crowd of hotel staff, police and passers-by, who were standing around the car park, speculating about its demolished barrier.

High in the hills north of Seville, Maria and her foster-parents arrived to have coffee before riding out to inspect their horses. This day they would select the one's they would ride at the Seville Fair after Easter and the Jerez Horse Fair some weeks later.

Maria was handed a message to ring Miller in Seville.

"Oh Brian," she thought, "you could at least have come to plead for yourself."

Petulantly, she screwed up the note and threw it away.

Sheedy sat trying to put together a thousand thoughts.

The days after Kate had come to Spain had been happier than any he had spent since before he went to Vietnam, since before Jan became ill, since, he now realised, nearly 10 years back. And now it was all such a mess. How much of it was his own fault?

Perhaps he should have taken her advice and pressed the police to act after the Rabbit Man's death. Undoubtedly he should have been more cooperative after Miguel's death.

Then there was Felipe. What had happened to him? Sheedy found it hard to believe the boy had run away. Maybe he had been scared away. But if he had been threatened, would he not have come to he, Sheedy, or to Manuel? Manuel had been right; they shouldn't have conned the kid?

His thoughts moved to Maria's second uncle. Diego. Why hadn't Sheedy considered the threat to him earlier?

And Kate. Even she had been harmed. He remembered the scene last night, her trembling body in his arms as they lay awake together, and he felt his anger return.

Well, he would sort it out now. He would have a talk with Inspector Rivas, see if police pressure could now be applied on Cruickshank and his cohorts.

But what could they discover? It had all been so damn neat. There was no evidence the so-called accidents were murders, let alone any evidence as to who committed them. There was no evidence that Felipe's disappearance was the result of foul play either. At least Diego had clearly been murdered - and tortured. But still there was no evidence to link anyone to that crime. In summary, the killers were currently in the clear.

What had been the connection between the deaths of the Rabbit Man, Migel and Diego, and the attack on Kate?

It had to be the papers from the *cortijo*, the evidence of ownership. They had not found it on the Rabbit Man, had traced it to Miguel, then to Sheedy, hence their visit to the villa, and then to Diego. Somehow they had been a step ahead of him all the way.

But how had they known Miguel had found papers of importance? What had led them to kill the policeman in Ronda?

He thought back. Miguel's note to the office. It had only been seen by Rosa, he and Kate. But Kate had telephoned Miguel from the villa. And also telephoned Maria about going to Casares. And on each occasion the killer or killers had got there a few hours before.

He thought about the telephone calls. Surely the place hadn't been bugged. He hadn't even considered to it. Yet why not? It was not difficult to do. He went to the phone and unscrewed the base.

Damn it. There it was.

Christ, he thought, I've been careless.

He would never have acted like this in the United States.

He groaned at his arrogance. He had revealed a contempt for the Spanish he didn't know he had. He just hadn't considered anyone here competent or fast-moving enough to beat him. That's why they had found his home easy to bug, why they had beaten him to one place after another. He had just assumed that in Spain there was no reason to hurry.

Still there were questions. Always questions. Why was the land so damn important? Why had they changed their approach, come out in the open with their attack on Kate, their murder of Diego? And could Cruickshank really be behind this, sanctioning it. It just didn't seem possible. It wasn't consistent with the man's history, his personality.

As he sat trying to put the bits of the jigsaw together Kate came in, dressed only in a soft dressing gown of white towel material, her red hair flowing around her pale, tired face. His heart went out to her and he rose and took her in his arms. She kissed his neck and said "Its ok, Sheedy, I'm ok."

She handed him a telegram that had been lying on the mat. He opened it quickly. It was from Teddy Gray. "Am coming today, will arrive about noon. Please be available. Important. Ted."

What the hell did it mean? Sheedy told Kate the key to the mystery must be on its way, in the form of the American reporter. He wasn't coming all this way for a holiday and he wasn't one for amateur dramatics. If he said it was important, it was important.

Kate took his hands and looked into his face.

"Bill," she said. "Will you do something for me. For yourself. And for Maria? Will you go and see Cruickshank. I don't think he knows about any of this, I don't believe he would sanction what happened last night. The project must be out of his control and if you can help rescue him you should."

"I don't know, Kate. He and his kind are the root cause of this, the reason this country is being invaded by people like Canning."

"Come on, Bill, for Christ's sake. This country has been invaded for centuries , from the Moors to the Romans to the Turks, God knows by you and I for that matter. Cruickshank is a businessman and his project is no different, apart from being better, than thousands of others in every tourist area of the world. But this behaviour is different. The thing is being attacked by a cancer and we can help to dig it out now."

Sheedy looked doubtful.

"You want me to go?" Kate said defiantly.

He laughed and drew her to him. "You know better. Ok, you're right. I'll ring Cruickshank."

He rang the yacht. Cruickshank was in Madrid. Unreachable. No-one knew when he would be back.

Sheedy looked thoughtful. "I don't like it. Cruickshank is always reachable."

He rang Manuel. "Get down to Puerto Banus quickly and wait till you see Cruickshank arriving. Get a message to him to ring me immediately. Tell him he must ring from somewhere off the yacht."

Jim Miller was not a happy man. He had booked in for a second night and still didn't have the money to pay for it. (Fortunately keeping the room had been easier than getting it in the first place.) God knows what was happening to his car. He had to sneak round the hotel to avoid being seen by any of the car park attendants and asked to explain their demolished barrier. He was terrified of the refrigerator, now re-stocked, and sitting invitingly in the corner. He still hadn't been able to speak to either his employer or the young Spanish woman, Maria. And, after the initial sense of relief, Canning's departure from the country had not ended his feeling of unease.

He couldn't imagine why the American had left, and in particular why he had chosen to fly from Seville?

His every instinct told him that Maria was in danger. But from who? From what direction would any attack come?

Despite Canning's departure, he decided he would wait in Seville until he had spoken to Cruickshank.

He wandered down to the beautiful inner courtyard of the old hotel and ordered a black coffee. As he casually stirred it he looked around at the others relaxing in the big leather armchairs. He was just about to return his eyes to the coffee when they rested on a man sitting alone in the far corner of the courtyard. There was something vaguely familiar about him... especially the piercing eyes, staring out of a distinctively thin face. Miller looked at him closely. But it didn't help. He couldn't place him.

He returned to his room and tried Maria's number once more.

The Garcias had been relaxing over lunch under the verandah of their ranch. Juan, never happier than on horseback in this rugged country and in no hurry to leave, suggested they could have more time at the ranch and avoid crossing the city if they went directly to their Seville flat and changed there for the Holy Week processions.

A servant came out of the house with a message for Maria. Miller had phoned the hacienda near Seville several times, still pressing her to call him at his hotel.

The message only made her feel even more depressed and sad. Why couldn't Cruickshank try to make contact himself? This was not the behaviour of a gentleman, not at all what she had expected from the man she loved.

"I'm going to have a *siesta*," she said. And went to her room where, the note torn up and left on the floor by the bed, she wept in her desolation.

The false hope of dawn
and of kisses,
vanish.
The desert
alone remains.
An undulating
desert.

Trapped in his room by lack of money, by the need to wait for phone calls from Cruickshank and Maria, and by fear of the security guards, Miller had been dozing and trying to ignore the pounding in his head. Until he remembered. The man downstairs with the piercing eyes; he *had* seen him before. He had noted him in the bar at the airport when Canning was there. Now Canning was gone but the man was staying in the same hotel where Canning had stayed. Of course it could be a coincidence but there had been too many coincidences in this whole business already. And why had the man been at the airport bar? If he were leaving he would now be on a plane. If he were arriving it was unlikely he would have gone to the bar; he would have done what all travellers do and get out of the airport as quickly as possible to head for the city. Unless he had been there to meet someone. Canning, for instance.

Miller began to think back. What had happened in the bar? He remember Canning going to the toilet. And he remembered noticing that at that time there was no-one at the bar at all. That meant the other man must have left before Canning. Had he gone to the toilet too? Was it possible that when they were alone Canning had given the man instructions?

Then Miller remembered the small case? Had Canning given the man a gun? Had they sent in a new killer - a new Canning? if so, who was next on the list?

It had to be Maria.

With a new sense of urgency Miller got on the phone. But he still couldn't get a reply from Maria and he couldn't track down Cruickshank.

Then he remembered the television reporter, Sheedy. He got on to directory enquiries and 10 minutes later was talking to the friendly American.

Francisco Benegas could hardly contain himself. It had been three months since the priest and one of the *Confraternity,* the brotherhood, had come to his family's casa in the crowded Triana district of Seville and told him that he had been chosen to be one of the penitents in the *Semana Santa* procession. He would carry the great gold cross from behind the alter of the church and walk in front of the paso, the float containing the church's statue of the Madonna. Francisco at 17 would be the youngest penitent.

It was the fulfilment of a dream. The last of eight children, he had been born some six years after the others, and had always been his mother's special one. Lithe, with jet-black hair and brown eyes, he had been the only one of the younger children not clothed in pass-me-downs, had been unashamedly favoured, and for as long as he could remember had gone night after night in Holy Week to watch the great processions, holding his mother's hand, and hearing her whisper "One day Francisco you will carry the Cross."

On Sundays, long after the other children had mastered the art of evading mass, he had still gone to church with his mother and his sisters and sat gazing in awe at the great gold cross and dreaming that his mother's promise would be kept and that, clad in penitent's garb, he would carry it across the bridge and into the heart of the city, past the dignitaries in the big plaza, and into the great Cathedral itself.

It had become an obsession, shared between mother and boy, and, once Francisco reached an age and developed a strength that made it possible, his mother had applied ceaseless pressure on the priest, inviting him to dinner, feeding him his favourite robo de toro even when she could ill-afford it, assisting with the flowers in the church, helping decorate the float for the procession, and raising it with him so often that in the end he had given in and begged the *Confraternity* to give Francisco preference and get the woman off his back.

For days the excited Francisco had talked of little else. His mother had made for him the dark-brown cloak that stretched from head to feet and his father added the pointed black hood with slits for his eyes and mouth. He had scorned shoes. If he was going to be a penitent he was going to play the part to the full and walk barefoot the whole way.

Now the moment had come and he proudly joined the others as they assembled at the church at four o'clock in the afternoon. The senior brothers briefed them once more on the programme. They would take about an hour to parade down the narrow, crowded streets of Triana and cross the bridge, the Puente de Isabel ll. They would continue up the Calle de los Reyes Catolicos into Calle de San Pablo and past the big church, the Santa Maria Magdalena. From there they would begin to veer to their right up the Calle de Rioja until they got to the famous traffic-less street, the Calle Sierpes. They would make their way down between the bars and bazaar-like shops until they came to the Plaza San Francisco where they would parade before the city fathers and dignitaries and the huge crowds that would be sitting in stands on either side of the specially-created amphitheatre. After leaving the *plaza* they would proceed down the Avenida de la Constitucion to the cathedral, entering by a side door and making their way through the cathedral and out beside the Giralda into the Plaza de la Virgen de los Reyes where they would be greeted by another huge crowd. From there they would begin on a shorter, more direct route back to Triana. All this would take about six and a half hours. Francisco would share his cross-carrying duties with another as the cross, gold and be-jewelled, was too heavy for him to carry all the way.

At last they were on their way. In front were the priests and church elders, in golden and red robes, some with containers of perfumes and incense, several carrying great crooks embellished with jewels, silver and gold. Behind them came the penitents, carrying crosses or big white wax candles ready to be lit at dusk. Behind came the *paso*, the float carrying the Madonna as Our Lady of Sorrows. Under the float, bearing its weight, hidden by a purple curtain, were some 20 shuffling *costaleros*, porters, their backs bent, unable to see a thing, gasping for breath, and having to rest every few yards and be supplied frequently with drinking water and occasionally be exchanged with someone else to share the burden. The Madonna, beautifully carved from wood, was seated on a throne, surrounded by flowers and sheltered by a velvet canopy, and was bedecked with jewels and lit by candles on silver sticks. Behind the float came a small band of trumpeters and drummers, the latter setting the tempo with a sombre, steady beat.

It was a proud procession that set off from Triana, no-one prouder than Francisco himself.

It was 5 p.m.

It felt to Cruickshank as if the day had already gone on forever. He had tried to pay attention at the two Madrid meetings, one financial and one legal, but his thoughts kept straying to Maria. What was she doing? What was she thinking? What should he do? Eventually he couldn't stand it any longer and, cutting the second meeting short, he took an earlier plane back to Malaga, arriving back at Puerto Banus in his chauffeur-driven Rolls at about about 5.15 p.m. Manuel met the car at the entry-point outside of the marina itself and, after knocking on the window to attract his attention, asked him to ring Sheedy before he went to the yacht.

"What? Nonsense."

"Sir Brian, I am a colleague of Mr Sheedy. He has information that suggests if you return to the yacht you will be in danger. He has also asked me to tell you that Miss Garcia is in danger. Can you please telephone him now."

Cruickshank hesitated. Then asked the chauffeur to steer the car round the round-about and back over the main road to near the Nueva Andalucia bullring.

"What's the number?"

Manuel told him and he telephoned. For nearly a minute he listened, then told Manuel to direct the chauffeur to Sheedy's villa.

On arrival he found Sheedy with a short, over-weight, balding American, his feet up on the balcony rail, what appeared to be a third or fourth beer in his hand judging by the bottles at his feet.

Sheedy introduced him as Ted Gray, a crime reporter on the New York Times, an old friend and rival, and suggested the Englishman listen carefully to what Gray had to say.

The American accepted another bottle of San Miguel, and then, leaning forward in his chair, began to describe a two-year investigation into the way organised crime syndicates had in the US invested their income in legitimate businesses.

Billions of dollars were involved. Whole industries were under-pinned by criminally-raised finance... money from drugs, prostitution, protection rackets, illicit gambling. Yet it was almost impossible to prove. Jordan was at the centre of the story, the acknowledged genius at laundering dirty money - transferring the profits of crime into legal and respectable businesses. So brilliantly was it done, so superficially sound was the facade around Jordan and his range of finance and other companies, that Gray after two years had little credible evidence to sustain the major story, the book, he hoped to write.

But now the journalist's investigation was coming together, thanks to Jordan's activities overseas. The financier had begun to look for new opportunities to invest his "client's" money and outside his usual territory was more visible and more vulnerable. Gray had established that the financier had opted for the Costa del Sol, not only for the laundering of criminal cash but as a place where additional money could be made. Jordan, it appeared, was no longer content to be the banker, the investor, the middle man. Ten per cent was not enough. He had his own dream... centred on drugs and gambling.

Its proximity to North Africa, its wide open coastlines, its broad boundaries with France and the port of Marseille and also Portugal meant that it was relatively easy to smuggle in drugs. Marijuana trafficking was already rife, and the profits considerable. A kilo of resin purchased in Morocco for 50,000 pesetas was worth 150,000 pesetas a few miles across the Mediterranean in Marbella (600,000 pesetas if smuggled into the UK). Spain also had special links with Latin America; there were considerable imports of Peruvian and Bolivian cocaine. And the youth population was believed to be more vulnerable than most to the appeal of crack, the cocaine derivative, there was already evidence that Spanish youth were taking to drugs, especially because of the high unemployment factor. There had been an increase in police activity (last year they picked up half a ton of Moroccan hashish in one haul) but it was hardly adequate or sophisticated enough for what was planned. The big tourist industry offered opportunities for an expansion of gambling. And the big numbers of men with plenty of ready money over on golfing holidays etc provided the base for a prostitution and possible blackmail racket. On top of which land and real estate were ideal vehicles for moving the money into legitimate investments. There was, too, no shortage of experienced imported villains employable locally; there were believed to be around 100 Britons living on the *costa* who were wanted in their own country.

Gray held Cruickshank's increasingly concerned attention as he turned to the project. "They need a base for their operations. Your project has a lot of the ideal ingredients. For investment. For gambling. For drugs and prostitution. What you see as an up-market oasis, Jordan sees as a Spanish Las Vegas. Just imagine it - a European Las Vegas. Provided the authorities could be squared the potential is unlimited. And I´m sorry to tell you Sir Brian you were the ideal front, respectable in the extreme, diplomatic and good at handling the Spanish, beyond suspicion, and vulnerable ."

"How do you mean vulnerable," Cruickshank asked, his face flushing.

Gray looked at him without sympathy. "Ambitious and vain...

fascinated by money and power. Somebody whose obsession with a dream would make him blind to what was happening. Someone who could be persuaded that ends justified means until he was in too deep to extract himself. These men are clever. Show them a fraction of vulnerability and they'll have you."

Cruickshank, to his credit, made no attempt to defend himself. "Maybe so, but I can't understand why the killing. It wasn't necessary."

"I suspect Canning is their Achilles heel. As you will have discovered he is a brilliant operator but he's a psychopath. Probably the killing of the old man was an accident in the sense that it was unplanned. The opportunity arose, too good an opportunity to miss, and Canning just took it. And with a bit of luck he would have got away with it. But as for the policeman and Miss Garcia's other uncle, that's been Canning getting out of hand. And not realising the difference between the US and the Costa del Sol. Over there you can wipe out a few people and it virtually goes un-noticed. In Spain its not so."

Cruickshank looked at the end of his tether. He looked to Sheedy. "What can we do to put it right?"

"You have to expose it now."

Cruickshank thought for a moment, then nodded disconsolately. "I'll do what has to be done."

But, first, he wanted to get to Maria. To ensure her safety. To discuss with her what he had to do. He gratefully accepted Sheedy's offer to go with him to Seville, it being explained that it would only take about two and a half hours.

It was 6 p.m.

Sheedy persuaded Cruickshank that his two-seater would cover the winding roads and the traffic in Seville more quickly. They took less than an hour to climb to Ronda and then drove up past the Hotel where Sheedy remembered, with a sudden softness, he had first held Kate's naked body in his arms, and out on the Seville Road. Within a few kilometres they entered a dramatic mountain pass between steep, rock and shrub covered hills and past a *cortijo* Cruickshank assumed was abandoned until he saw a peasant piling wood around it. Once over the pass they were in the midst of rich farming country, fields full of corn, and hills covered with sun flowers. On their left they spotted in the distance Grazalema, clinging to a mountainside, and near it the famous pine trees to be found nowhere else - except, it was said, in parts of North Africa. Sheedy pointed it out to Cruickshank as the place where the Rabbit Man had been born.

He looked at the grim-faced financier and felt sorry for him. "Look, Sir Brian, do you not think you should tell me all you know?"

Cruickshank looked almost gratefully at the American. Then, with evident relief, began to talk - about the call from Canning telling him of the death of the old man, about his plans to expose the killing, about Jordan's intervention, about his decision to cover up and why he took it, about his belief that all the problems had been overcome... until the death of Miguel.

"There is no point in denying it, Mr Sheedy. I should have gone to the police about the Rabbit Man and I didn't. But I genuinely believed it would achieve little and that by staying in control I could help the project into being in a way satisfactory to everyone."

"Would you have done the same thing if it had been in the UK?"

"What do you mean?"

"I mean that when people move onto foreign soil, places like the Costa del Sol, they play by different rules. A dead worker in the UK and you would have been talking to Scotland Yard within minutes. A dead Spanish peasant, who cares?"

Cruickshank thought. "No, I don't necessarily accept that. My actions were not influenced by the fact he was Spanish or a peasant. But that one acts differently out of one's own setting, yes, that's possible. Perhaps I don't belong here."

"You don't strike me as the usual kind of Mediterranean developer."

"But that's the point, I didn't want to be. I wanted the project to be special. The Costa del Sol was just the place chosen; it could have been anywhere where the climate and the land was suitable."

"Exactly. Don't you think developing Spain should be in the hands of people concerned about Spain rather than just another project and another buck?"

"Well, that's the role of the planning authorities and the politicians. If they thought it was inappropriate they should say so."

"Yes? Were there no incentives?"

"Maybe a few. But that's their way of doing business, not mine.

Simply following local practice. Business has to do that all over the world."

Sheedy smiled wryly. "Has to?"

Francisco was tiring already. He had been walking now for over two hours. Twice he had stubbed his unprotected toes and one was bleeding. He was sweating under the heavy costume and the prickly material was scratching his skin. Also the cross had been heavier than he imagined.

But still he would not have changed places with anyone. The sidewalks had been crowded in the Triana district as the locals had come out from homes and shops to applaud their own procession, one they wanted to be more splendid than any other. The crowds had become thinner once they crossed the bridge and entered the wide Calle de Los Reyes Catolicos, but were now beginning to build up as they approached the big church, Santa Maria Magdalena, halfway up the Calle San Pablo.

As people pointed to the ornate, gold cross, Francisco had raised his head proudly, sorry that the pointed, sinister-looking Ku Klux Klan-style hood meant they could not see his face and know that it was he, Francisco Benegas, the youngest of the brotherhood, who was carrying it.

In particular he looked out for his family. They had promised that before they went to the Plaza San Francisco they would wait on the church steps to see him pass. And there they were, his mother looking as if she would burst with pent-up pride, his father looking ill-at-ease in a suit but breaking into a broad near-toothless grin as he recognised the slim figure of his son near the front of the procession. Francisco gravely bowed his head in their direction and was rewarded by his mother breaking into tears. For a few moments he forgot his aches and pains; he could have been floating on a cloud for all he was aware of the concrete under his feet.

It was 6.30 p.m.

For a while they drove in silence. The smart motorway outside Ronda had given way to a much rougher country road with potholes and multiple repairs. Soon they reached the Province of Cadiz, crossing the boundary river, the Arroyo Montecordo, and passing the turn to El Gastor before approaching the dramatic mountain village of

Zahara. They could see its cemetery cut into the rock, and an abandoned castle or fort on top.

They were now on a better-paved road and Sheedy increased his speed. He asked "What will you do now. Will you abandon the project?"

Cruickshank replied "That will depend."

"On what?"

"On Maria Garcia."

"Why?"

"Because I could not live in Spain without her. She and the project are now merged in my mind. If she does not want to marry me after all this, I will withdraw and dismantle the project or sell my interest in it."

"You really love her?"

"Yes, Mr Sheedy, for the first time in my life I know what it is to really love and be loved. In some ways I wish I had not found out, but now I have and I cannot live without it. At least not in Spain."

Sheedy smiled at the Englishman. "I understand."

"Do you?"

"Yes, funnily enough we are both within a few years of each other and both newly involved with a younger woman. I understand exactly. Of course I had loved before... my wife. I never thought I could be that happy with anyone else, but I am."

"Ah yes, Miss Callaghan?"

"Yes."

They drove through a low flat town, El Coronil, with its extraordinary pointed blue church tower, watched as they passed by rows of men chatting on corners or sitting outside bars, chatting, and then within half a minute were back into rolling farming country with fields of sunflowers as far as the eye could see. At one point they passed a lone peasant, bent over a white mule; Sheedy thought it could easily have been the Rabbit Man cutting across country. Even beside the cattle he looked antiquated, as stick in hand, he picked out a route between the bulls and guided the mule to safety.

Sheedy looked at the pale face of the man beside him. He looked desperatete. "Look, Sir Brian, I know this is no consolation but I feel as responsible for all this as you. If I had left the question of the old man's death its possible Miguel would still be alive. And Diego. And possibly someone else." He thought sadly of the vanished Felipe."And my friend Kate would not have been assaulted. I thought I could play

God and its caused havoc. We both thought we could play God. You over part of the Costa del Sol. Me as self-appointed policeman. We'll both have a lot to think about when this is over."

They passed by Utrera, a functional town rather than a *pueblo*.

Cruiskhank began to think aloud. He would, he said, give Jordan two options: to withdraw immediately or to be publicly exposed."

"You will admit you covered up the death of the rabbit man."

Cruickshank looked at him. "I suppose I have no choice,"

"No," said Sheedy, "none at all."

"I see. Yes, I suppose it always was inevitable." He shook his head sadly. "That makes my continued involvement in the project equally improbable. Probably the whole project. It won't do me much good in the UK either."

"All because your people could not adapt to the priorities of one old Spanish peasant."

"Ah well, Mr Sheedy, I have always said that its not big things and big people who bring big people down, its little problems and little people who are underestimated or taken for granted."

It was taking longer than planned. The youths carrying the float were finding it hard going and having to rest frequently, and the traffic chaos caused by the assembling crowds led to further unscheduled stops. Processions from a number of districts were converging on the centre, causing their own traffic congestion. The heart of Seville was rapidly becoming a huge slow-moving mass of people. The police were having to create uniformed human barriers at the junctions between streets, stopping and starting the spectators as they walked to the centre just as if they were cars being controlled by traffic lights.

Francisco was hungry and glad his mother had insisted on putting a chunk of bread with *serrano jambon* in a pocket sewn on the inside of his cloak. But there was another problem. He was desperate to relieve himself. And it wasn't going to be easy. He was in the middle of a procession in the middle of a crowd and there was a long way to go. He could, of course, just do it under the cloak as he walked, but someone could notice and call out, and Franscisco would die rather than suffer that humiliation. He would just have to struggle on.

This was all proving a greater penitence than Francisco had expected. It was 8 p.m.

The clear sky was replaced by smog. Seville lay ahead. They passed huge blocks of commuter workers' flats. The regional command centre of the *Guardia Civil* was about five kilometres from the centre, on the junction with the N4. The road to Malaga and Cordoba was on the right, the one to Cadiz on the left, and Seville in front of them.

Sheedy swung the car off the road and drove up to the police headquarters. There the two men impatiently waited three or four minutes until directed to a senior officer. Sheedy briefly told him the story. The officer listened impassively until the Garcia's were mentioned. Clearly it was one thing to be indifferent to the appeals of a couple of manic foreigners, another to overlook a warning that one of Seville's most distinguished families was in danger. His problem was that many of his men were on duty on the streets of Seville coping with the crowds gathered there for the processions. Others were taking part. Never-the-less he put together a group of half a dozen men, telling Sheedy and Cruickshank that the Garcia's hacienda was only a few kilometres away on the Jerez road.

It was 8.40 p.m.

The Garcias had stopped for drinks with friends who lived in the centre of Seville within sight of the Cathedral, and there they changed ready to take their place with the Mayor and other city dignitaries on the platform of the Plaza San Francisco.

It was Maria who proposed they should ring the hacienda and remind the servants they were going directly to the plaza and it was her guardian who asked permission to use the phone and dialled the number. But it was unobtainable. The telephone appeared to be cut off. No matter. As he said, the servants would guess what was happening.

With their friends they shared a bottle of sherry from the Garcia's own small *bodega* in Jerez.

It was 9 p.m.

The procession had been at a standstill for nearly 20 minutes. Another from a church to the west of the city had reached the Calle Sierpes just before the Triana one and they were having to wait until it made its way past and then allow a gap of 20 minutes or so between processions. Francisco couldn't wait any longer. He whispered to the penitent nearest to him. "I'm desperate. I'm afraid I'll wet myself."

"Its no problem," he was reassured. "We won't be moving for several minutes. Give me the cross and just slip down that alley there. Maybe somebody will let you into their house."

Grateful for the minimal encouragement he needed, the youngster slipped past the thin line of spectators in the narrow street and into a deserted alley. There were plenty of doors to old houses, their upper storeys over-hanging the alley, but they were all closed. No doubt all their owners were in the Calle Sierpes or the Plaza San Francisco watching the procession.

Francisco saw that one house was little more than a shell, apparently being modernised, and was in the meantime only protected by carelessly-erected boarding. He found a gap and edged himself into the derelict building. Moving quickly to a dark corner he obeyed with unbounded relief the call of nature.

He had just zipped himself up and checked his costume was in order when he heard a sound behind him.

He turned, peering through the slits in his mask, just in time to see a face in the dark, a face briefly illuminated by the light from a lamppost in the alley, a thin face with piercing eyes.

In the second that was left of his life he was aware of a flashing object coming at his chest.

Then... oblivion.

Francisco, his sins confessed, his last mass attended, dressed in penitent's clothes and with bare and bleeding feet, had gone to join his maker.

Dead he was left in the street,
with a dagger in the chest.
Nobody knew who he was.
How the lamppost was shaking!
Mother.
How that little lamppost shook
in the street!
In the dead of night. Nobody
was able to glance wide-eyed
out into the harsh night air.
And he was left dead in the street,
and with a dagger in his chest,
and nobody knew who he was.

It took but a few minutes for the thin-faced killer to slip on the costume, to take the compact repeater rifle Canning had given him out of its black canvass wrapping and hide it under the robes, and to pick up the big candle and join the group who were just ready to move off, down the Calle Sierpes and into the Plaza San Francisco where the Mayor and the other dignitaries were waiting.

It was getting dark and the candles were now burning brightly. The Madonna glittered in the flickering light, the reflections from its eyes making it appear to come to life, and as it passed the crowds became silent, looking up in awe, the women's lips moving in silent prayer, and even the most *macho* of men crossing themselves, briefly humbled by the pageantry and affected by the surge of emotion around them. In front of the float the penitents with their tall wax candles found new energy, new pride from the cries and the applause of the crowd, and behind it, as it neared the square, the trumpets blared into new life. The centre of Seville had become a great living theatre, the night full of unforgettable, magnificent spectacle, as one procession left for the Cathedral and the procession from the Triana district entered.

In the stand at the Calle Sierpes end of the plaza Francisco's mother, who with the family had cut across the city centre for another view, rose from her chair, eager to see her son. Her eyes ranged the row of penitents, her smile fading as she failed to spot him. She looked more closely, inspecting first one shrouded figure, then another. But he was nowhere to be seen. "Something's gone wrong," she cried to her husband, "our Francisco isn't there."

"Something's wrong," she called wildly at the crowd. "My boy is not there."

Those around her shrugged their shoulders and looked away. In the emotional atmosphere of *Semana Santa* people sometimes did strange things. No-one was going to take any notice of the cries of one hysterical woman.

It was 9.30 p.m.

"Down a road travels
Death, crowned with
withered orange blossoms.
Death sings and sings
a song

with her ancient white guitar,
and sings and sings and sings."

The plane was an hour out of New York. Jason Canning, who had been dozing for a couple of hours, woke and looked at his watch.

It was 9.35 p.m. Spanish time. The deed would be done soon. And he had the best of all alibis – he was not even in the country and had Cruickshank's man Miller as witness to his departure.

He smiled to himself and, summoning the First Class steward, ordered a glass of champagne.

It was time to go. The Garcias walked from their friends' flat down the narrow Calle Granada and behind the grandstand in front of the *Ayuntamiento*. They climbed up the carpeted steps and, after stopping to shake hands and chat to others on the platform, took their places not far from the Mayor.

To the right a procession was just leaving the plaza on its way to the Cathedral. They were just in time to see the Madonna swaying in the candle-light and then disappearing round the corner into the Avenida de la Constitucion.

To the left, from the Calle Sierpes another procession had half-emerged and stopped, presumably so that the porters could rest. They recognised it as the one from Triana.

It was 9.45 p.m.

Sheedy and Cruickshank were lost in the crowds heading for the cathedral.

The last half hour had been a nightmare, beginning with a wasted trip to the hacienda where a servant explained the Garcias were going directly to the Semana Santa festivities in Seville.

Sheedy groaned. "We'll never find them there. There'll be hundreds of thousands of people on the streets."

"No, *señor*," said the servant, "you can't miss them. They'll be on the main platform outside the *Ayuntamiento* in the Plaza San Francisco. You can't miss them."

Sheedy had looked at Cruickshank and said grimly "An assassin couldn't miss them either."

It had been a relatively short drive because the traffic likely to go to Seville this busy night was already there. They drove past the factories and the worker flats on the outskirts following the signs *Centro Ciudad* until they reached the city's wide tree-lined avenues, competing for space now with black and yellow taxis and orange buses decorated with Expo 92 posters. Ahead they could see the illuminated Giralda tower. But the traffic soon became slower and eventually came to a halt, engulfed in the crowds surging towards the pageantry around the Cathedral. Sheedy and Cruickshank decided they could get no closer by car and abandoned it, seeking to make their way by foot, pushing past the spectators, young couples, whole families, old folk, and tearing at their ties as they began to sweat in the warm evening air.

Taking the Giralda as their focal point they made their way to the cathedral, two middle-aged foreigners lost in a fervent Spanish crowd.

In other circumstances Cruickshank would have been enraptured by it. *"Let us build a church so great that those who see it completed will say we were mad"* the authorities said in 1401 when they decided to build the Cathedral in Seville. They laboured on it for 100 years and the result is the third biggest cathedral in the world after St Peters and St Paul's. Even in his panic Cruickshank marvelled at its size and spectacular beauty, the dark interior brilliantly illuminated by street lights penetrating the stained glass windows and by the multitude of softly-lit chapels. It was a colossal man-made cavern of antiquity, of treasure, unanswerable evidence of the power and wealth the Catholic church had wielded in Spain.

And it was packed with people and full of spectacle as one by one the processions of the Semana Santa entered by one huge wooden door and trekked between its huge pillars to resurface from the Giralda exit into the triangular Plaza de la Virgen de los Reyes, its beautiful fountain and its orange trees lost in a sea of faces. The two men headed for the far corner dominated by La Giralda Meson restaurante and made their way slowly past the crowds up a narrow one-way street where Sheedy, lost, suggested they cut through the Barrio de Santa Cruz, a maze of alleys with whitewashed houses and bars, flower plots and plants on the window sills, walls covered in posters for bullfights or the theatre.

But they were becoming even more hopelessly lost. Finally Sheedy established from a policeman that they were on the opposite side of the Cathedral to their destination, the Plaza San Francisco. They forced their way back, twice halted and literally pinned down by the density of the crowd as another procession made its way by. Eventually they were at the back of the cathedral and Sheedy spotted the Calle Colon. He called to Cruickshank that this was the one they wanted. They battled up it to the Calle Hernando and from it Sheedy at last spotted the green canopy of the Bar Laredo. Many times he had sat at its pavement tables, or behind it, in the old Calle de Manteros, at the tables of the tapas bar El Porton. He knew the Bar Laredo was on the edge of the plaza. They had found it. Their struggle with the Seville crowds was nearly over.

It was exactly 10 p.m.

Miller, his face white with fury and frustration, was locked in the manager's office of the Hotel Alfonso Vlll, awaiting the arrival of the police. He had been captured earlier by the security guards while following the man with the piercing eyes out of the back door.

His protests that he could pay his bill and for the damage to the car park barrier if he could only contact a Sir Brian Cruickshank had impressed no-one, especially as Cruickshank was unreachable.

As for his claim that another of the hotel guests was a hit man and that he, Miller, should be freed to pursue him, it was the most pathetic story the manager had heard invented in 30 years in the business.

There were, said the manager, too many con men attempting to defraud hotels. Miller was going nowhere - except eventually to prison.

Miller, defeated, then asked if he could have a gin.

What else could he do?

The procession from the Triana, now four hours from its starting point and at last free of the Calle Sierpes, was crossing the plaza, making its way down a lane between spectators packed into the space between the two grandstands. Sheedy and Cruickshank, having climbed some steps at the back, now emerged on top of the stand looking directly across to the platform and the three gold-carved chairs occupied by the mayor and two other dignitaries. Around about, behind trestle tables with white table clothes, sipping wine and chatting, were other well known Seville families and officials. Near the centre were the Garcias.

Cruickshank found the scene both impressive and frightening. The nearer he got to Maria the more he sensed the danger. Anyone could get at her and both the sound of a shot and the gunman himself would go unnoticed in the tumult. He tried to call out but it was hopeless. The brassy trumpets, the pounding drums, and the applause and cries of the crowd were deafening. He and Sheedy were face to face with the Garcias now but for all the chance they had of catching their attention from across the plaza they could have been a million miles away. There were no aisles so they began to tried to fight their way down the rows of chairs, climbing over each one, drawing complaints and being obstructed by annoyed spectators as they progressed towards the front.

Eventually they were there, climbing over the front row of chairs and trying to push into the ranks of the procession itself. A *Guardia Civil* officer intervened, ordering them to go back. Sheedy shouted that they had an urgent message but the policeman, convinced they were just two tourists seeking a better view, restrained them. Sheedy, desperate now, pushed him back and was immediately pinioned by two more officers. Cruickshank took the chance to break clear and, pushing his way between the priests in their heavily-ornate gowns, got to the other side and began to climb towards the platform.

In her place near the Mayor, Maria, pale and sad, had been looking into the plaza with unseeing eyes but now even she was becoming moved by the magic of the night, the fervour of the crowds and the special enthusiasm of the Triana procession. As she began to look intently for the first time she saw at her feet two columns of penitents in dark pointed cone-like hoods, their faces covered except for slips for mouth and eyes. Her eyes on the glittering procession, she did not see Cruickshank climbing the stairs to her left and running down the row towards her, impatiently stumbling over the feet of the other dignitaries on the dais.

One penitent she noticed was different from the others. Instead of looking straight ahead, he was staring at the platform. Directly, she felt, at her.

In the flickering light of his candle she could see his eyes staring through the slits in the hood. Glinting, piercing eyes.

He was, *he definitely was looking at her.* She saw his cloak rustle. It was as if he was pointing towards her.

Then she heard a familiar voice. Brian's! It was Brian's. She looked up, her heart leaping with hope and joy. He had come. To explain. To reassure. It was going to be alright.

Then he was in front of her. He was speaking but his words were drowned by a loud banging noise. Fireworks perhaps.

She heard a woman screaming and became aware of people falling over the trestle table in front of her.

There was pandemonium. People were climbing over the seats and shouting. Others were lying across the tables and on the ground. She saw some were covered in blood.

It all happened so quickly she could not get a grasp on it... then there was Brian, standing over her, between her and the procession, his face full of love... and then shock, as with a shudder he began to fall, to fall towards her as she opened her arms to embrace him.

Then she became aware of more blood, blood on Cruickshank's shirt, blood on his hands.

He saw her white dress, the shape, the beautiful shape of her breasts, the place where he so desperately wanted to bury his head. He reached for her. There were red marks on the dress now. He heard her call his name. He felt her hands, pulling his head down, and then he was there, home, falling into the softness of her, he could hear her heart beating even as his own slowed to a stop.

"I've come home Maria... just in time... its the last, Maria... the last of the 10,000 deaths..."

From the upstairs window of a building overlooking the plaza, a tall, bald, distinguished-looking American watched the scene impassively.

Then he limped over to a telephone in the corner of the room and made two calls.

The first was to book a taxi to take him to the airport.

The second was to a number in New York.

"Canning," he said.

Just the one word.

But the man he was calling understood.

In the world of Theodore Jordan, failure was unforgivable and absolute failure was punished absolutely.

EPILOGUE

It was spring of the following year and with spring came flowers, every day adding fresh colour to the hidden valley until it was ablaze with blue and purple, crimson and scarlet, yellow and gold. The orange and lemon trees around the abandoned *cortijo* were heavily pregnant with fruit, the now plentiful rabbits plump in the long grass.

The two riders, man and woman, paused at the top of the hill and looked down at the peaceful scene below. Then, holding tightly to the reins, they carefully guided their horses down the rocky track to the foot of the valley and round the ravine to the *cortijo*. On reaching it they dismounted, the woman choosing to rest under the trees while the man went inside alone.

Little had changed, except there were a few missing items, including the old rifles, no doubt taken by passing hunters who heard on the sierra grapevine that their owner would never return. He tore down the curtain from over the door to let in the air and pulled down the decaying rabbit skins from the rafters and tossed them out of the back window ready for burning together with the old bedding and bits of clothing. Then he took an aerosol from a bag on the back of his horse and, re-entering the *cortijo*, he energetically dowsed it in an air-cleansing spray.

He left it to recover from this initial assault and the two sat on the grass and ate fresh bread, *serrano* ham and a salad of lettuce and fresh Andalusian tomatoes. They drank from a *bota* of dry white wine. Then they lay in the grass under a lemon tree and dozed for an hour or so.

Later, escaping the afternoon sun, they both went back into the *cortijo* and swept and dusted and cleaned. While the man collectedcones and pieces of wood from under the pines near one wall of the valley, and water from a spring near the ravine, the woman laid out blankets and sleeping bags on the floor and prepared the food they would cook that night under the stars.

In the early evening the man took from his saddle bag two small urns. On one was etched the name Miguel, on the other Pepe... *El Conejero.* Taking one each, they walked slowly and silently across the grass until they stood in the centre of the valley. There they let the breeze catch and sprinkle the two Spaniards' ashes across the land they had loved.

Later, much later, sated with barbecued chicken and hot garlic bread and wine, they lit a fire and, naked and shiny in its glow, they made love on top of the soft bedding, rolling over and over as first one, then the other, set the pace and rekindled the passion of an act that in its intensity seemed to transcend their own desires, as if they were determined to inject human warmth back into the bare walls, the stony floor, and the tiled roof of the itself.

When, eventually, they lay in their separate sleeping bags, the woman spoke.

"I'm glad we came."

"So am I. You know, I once felt sorry for the Rabbit Man, because he lived alone in these mountains. But he wasn't alone at all. There was life all about him. And beauty. And peace. Thank God there's not much chance we'll do to this l place what we've done to the Costa del Sol."

"Its funny," she said, "to think it all began in this valley. If Canning had not thrown that stone the company would probably have got that land in the end, the Rabbit Man would still be alive... and Miguel... and Felipe... and Diego. And Cruickshank would be married to Maria.

"Do you think he acted on impulse, that in a way it did all happen by accident, or did he come to the valley intending to kill the old man?"

"Who knows? But I keep remembering what Cruickshank said... that its not big men who bring other big men down, its the little men they under-estimate, who they take for granted, who they arrogantly assume to be of no consequence."

"Maybe Canning, and possibly Cruickshank too, assumed the Rabbit Man had no friends, no one who would care."

"Well," he said, "maybe there were only two who really missed him... but two were enough."

She leaned over and kissed him. He buried his face in her hair and, with the fire still crackling and flickering in the hearth, they began to fall asleep.

The valley was silent now. And still.

And then, out in the moonlight, by the ravine, there was a movement.

It was a rabbit, resting on its hind-legs, its nose twitching with curiosity at the horses grazing near the old building.

A contented rabbit.

Well fed.

Safe.

Or was it?

Back indoors, Bill, reaching out to touch her hair, now aflame with gold in the firelight, said to Kate: "Tomorrow I'll catch you a rabbit for supper."

"Oh God," she giggled sleepily, "Its the return of the Rabbit Man. Poor little *conejo*. *El Conejero* is back."

Out by the ravine, acting as if it had heard and understood, the rabbit became tense, sprang onto all four legs, and disappeared into the night.